9788845903105

1

SIERRA

"Three months since your last period?" Dr. White says, looking at the questionnaire I filled out.

"Yeah, but I'm irregular," I say, lying on the examination table. I wish we'd talked about all this before I got on the table, my butt bare and lady parts exposed, but Dr. White likes to talk throughout appointments and go over anything that bothers her about my condition—or my answers on the questionnaire I filled out when I arrived in her office.

"You've never gone beyond six weeks." She's been my doctor since forever and doesn't need to consult anything to know. She taps something on her phone. "I ordered a pregnancy test, just to be sure."

"I can't possibly be pregnant," I say with a laugh to cover up a surge of mild are-you-kidding-me annoyance.

"You've been celibate since the divorce?" She is aware of the pathetically unceremonious end of my marriage to Todd.

"No, there's a new guy in my life." But my getting pregnant is as probable as my giving birth to Bullet and G-Spot's baby. Bullet and G-Spot being my hamsters.

Dr. White should know this. She's the one who told me I couldn't get pregnant due to blocked fallopian tubes. How can she remember my cycles but not this critical point? "Let's do your pap

I

and I'll do the sonogram, just to be sure. That'll be quicker than the test anyway."

"Okay." I'm already half-naked. When she finds nothing, I'm going to say, "I told you so."

I stare at the ceiling as she does her thing to gather cells from my cervix. Then she takes a thin tube.

"What's that?" I ask.

"For transvaginal ultrasound. Since it's your first time, I want to make sure everything looks good."

"Aren't you supposed to do that over my belly?" I remember seeing that on TV.

"It's too early for that. Don't worry, it won't hurt. You won't even notice."

Contrary to her reassurance, I most definitely notice. But it isn't super unpleasant.

"Look at that screen." She gestures at one of the monitors.

I tilt my head. All I see are black-and-white dots. Nothing that could pass for a baby. "Looks like I'm not pregnant," I say with a triumphant grin.

She gives me a look. "Actually, you are. You are most definitely pregnant."

I jerk my head up off the table. *Wait, wait, wait—I'm what?* Is she messing with me? It could be some sort of morbid medical humor.

"Congratulations. I know you wanted to have children for a long time." She beams, her pale gray eyes crinkling. *She sucker-punches me, and now she's smiling like she just won the Nobel Prize in Medicine?*

This awful bedside manner isn't like Dr. White. She gave me the news about my blocked fallopian tubes with sympathy and kindness, allowing me plenty of time to regroup, think and ask questions. This woman has to be the good doc's evil twin, out to ruin her life. Give patients a broad grin after telling them they're pregnant—or they have cervical cancer.

"Could you, uh, look again?"

"Why don't we both look?" She points at the monitor.

What's on the screen is as meaningful as tea leaves. "I have no idea what I'm seeing."

"Well, this is your womb." She moves the wand around. It's

unpleasant, but I ignore it because maybe from a different angle, we won't see the baby that she apparently can see.

"I'd say you're about ten weeks and three days pregnant."

My brain quits. It takes at least a full minute before I can speak. "But that's impossible! You said my fallopian tubes were blocked. So no sperm"—I raise my left index finger—"can meet my egg there"—I raise my right index finger—"for fertilization!" I bring my fingers together and squish and rub them against each other in a biology demonstration.

Dr. White blinks. "No," she says slowly. "I said your tubes are *partially* blocked, which makes it *very difficult* for you to get pregnant. But it isn't impossible. Sometimes the sperm and egg can still get through."

"Oh my God." I cover my mouth with a shaking hand.

Dr. White pats my other hand gently, apparently having mistaken my reaction for stunned joy. "Thankfully, everything looks great. No ectopic pregnancy for any of your babies."

Okay, so at least that part is good. Ectopic pregnancies can become life-threatening if not treated properly. Even rupture your fallopian—

Wait a minute. "Did you just say *babies?*"

She nods and gives me that smile again. And I know that whatever comes out of her mouth next is going to upend my life. Permanently.

"You're having triplets."

2

SIERRA

–ten weeks and three days earlier

Do you know what happens when you get rid of a deadweight husband who thinks you're an embarrassment?

You *soar*.

And I'm ready to soar until I hit the sun!

The engine of my cherry-red Ferrari roars like a lion as I hit the gas hard. Today is the first day of my reclaimed singlehood, and I plan to make it *awesome*.

As I take the final curve into the company parking lot, something catches my peripheral vision. *Todd.* My ex would look presentable if he lost the twenty-five pounds of blubber he started gaining the moment our wedding vows were exchanged, all of which went to his waist. He looks like he's wearing a saggy, partially inflated swimming tube underneath his blue and yellow Rams T-shirt, which is his go-to when he wants to appear down to earth. If he'd spent the last two years doing something other than eating a metric ton of potato chips every evening while complaining about my job—which *paid* for those potato chips—he might be having an easier time squeezing past the two security guards who are doing their best to block him from getting to the building.

My Grumpy Billionaire

Todd sees my car—it's impossible to miss a flaming-hot Ferrari—and shouts, waving his arms like he's lost at sea and just spotted a friendly vessel. Thankfully Freddie Mercury belting out one of my all-time favorite songs, "Don't Stop Me Now," is drowning out whatever garbage is spewing from Todd's mouth.

My shoulders moving to the upbeat tune, I ignore Todd and slide smoothly into my parking space. I turn to the passenger side, where I've seatbelted in a large hamster cage.

My sandy-colored Roborovski hamsters, Bullet and G-Spot, are hopping and running in their wheel. Even hamsters know amazing music when they hear it. But not Todd. He actually told me he found Queen "crass" several months into our marriage, which resulted in a huge argument.

I should've known we were doomed. What kind of heartless jerk hates Queen? And really, an adult man should have at least as good taste as a hamster.

And yet I stayed, out of a desperate hope that died a sad, lonely death six months ago. I grieved. Todd raged.

Stop thinking about it.

I kill the engine, swing my tote bag and purse onto my shoulder, then unstrap the cage and carry it in my other hand as I climb out of the Ferrari. Without the car door and Freddie Mercury, Todd's shouting becomes clearer.

"Sierra! We need to talk! You can't end it like this!"

I roll my eyes. He's probably distraught that he can't access my funds anymore. Fortunately, he didn't get a penny, thanks to the prenup he signed.

Or maybe he's worried about his job as an adjunct professor of English Literature. My family has strong ties to Wollstonecraft College and has a building named after us. He probably assumes I'm going to get him fired. But just because *he's* petty doesn't mean I'm going to stoop to his level. I want him out of my life, not professionally and financially ruined. People with nothing to lose are impossible to reason with.

He tried to change my mind after I filed for divorce by sending me hand-written copies of John Keats's poems. But that just shows how little Todd knows me. He would've done better to serenade me with a Queen song.

Then again, a butthole like him doesn't deserve to sing the great song.

"Sierra!" he screams, channeling Brando from *A Streetcar Named Desire*. "We aren't finished!"

Oh, yes we are. If he keeps this up and continues to stalk me, maybe I will be forced to use my influence at Wollstonecraft. I'm sure the head of the English department can think of something to keep Todd occupied.

I walk into Silicone Dream's gorgeous lobby, which gleams with glass and polished stone. In the center is the huge lavender statue—a monolith, really—of the company's first product. We put a clock on it to make it more functional, since the firm is all about fun functionality.

"Good morning, Sierra. Looking fabulous today," says Dan, the head of security. He's a tall man in his late forties, thick with bulging muscles that intimidate anybody who thinks they can screw around here just because we make sex toys. The light reflects off his shiny bald head, and tats flex on his arms as he waves and gestures. He talks more with his hands than his mouth.

"Good morning, Dan." I smile. "Your team's doing a good job out there."

"Thanks. I'll let 'em know." He squints, gazing out through the glass walls. "That your ex they're wrestling?"

I sigh. "Yes." Todd didn't want a divorce. He wanted the respectability that came with being a college professor, and the lavish lifestyle of being my husband, even if my job embarrassed him to the core of his being.

"Shoulda treated you better." Dan's never liked Todd, probably because my ex viewed him as a barely literate moron—a fact I didn't know until very recently.

"He should've treated everyone better."

"Can't argue with you there." A corner of his mouth twitches up as he looks at the cage. "Cute little things. What are they, hamsters?"

I nod. "My babies." Which I adore to death. Todd doesn't care for them. Told me he finds "tailless rats" gross and suggested I might as well have cockroaches for pets. As if!

Dan shakes his head. "Barely the size of two of my fingers." He holds out a couple of fingers, each of which is as thick as a D battery.

"They're the smallest breed. I got custody." Todd claimed he wanted them, but it was just to spite me. All I had to do to thwart him was act like that was exactly what I wanted to see happen.

"Good for you." Dan beams and puts a finger up to the cage, which G-Spot comes over to sniff. "These little critters need love." His tone says, *Your ex isn't capable.*

I can't argue. The only reason I didn't see through Todd immediately was that I met him soon after the devastating loss of Grandma three years ago. I wasn't myself. But now my judgment is one hundred percent again. And I know that, no matter how hard I try, he's never going to be the kind of family I long for.

The elevator takes me up toward the twentieth—and top—floor. The mirrored doors show my reflection, and I use the ride to make sure I look as powerful and free as I feel. My hair in a perfect French twist—check. Makeup—check. A sleeveless magenta dress—check. The employee badge proudly proclaiming me as the CEO of Silicone Dream—check. Power stilettos in nude—check. My favorite pearl earrings and necklace from my late mother—check.

I smile. Damn, I look good.

When the elevator reaches my floor, I walk out, a spring in my step. Even the corporate air feels freer.

Of course, Silicone Dream isn't your typical company. You can't take yourself too seriously if you make sex toys. Not that we think our work is frivolous or silly. But we believe in fun because that's what our products are about—*fun*. There are no joysticks more joyous than our dildos and vibrators. But because we are in the industry we're in, we also emphasize respect. Because "fun" without respect is no fun. And respect is what makes trust possible.

That's why our dress code is "wear what you want within reason," we work flexibly, and everything's geared toward achieving our objectives rather than people putting in a requisite nine-to-five. According to HR's employee satisfaction surveys and metrics, Silicone Dream is one of the best companies to work for in the state, if not the entire country. And I'm proud of that.

I stride through the hall. Most desks sit empty, but that's to be expected. There's a surprise donut and coffee social today, sponsored by the R&D department. I'm skipping it, mainly because I'm not a huge donut fan. I prefer chips and salsa, but it's too early in the morning for Mexican.

Our head of accounting, Barbara, is in her cubicle, though. She limits junk food because everyone on her mother's side keeled over from heart attacks before they hit fifty. She runs every morning for an hour—and has the wiry gym-bod to show for it—and eats healthy. Says she plans to live to see her grandkids. I admire her grit because it can't be easy to overcome temptation, but she's never asked her coworkers to give up their snacks for her.

So whenever we have a company party or event, I make sure to have a delicious healthy option for her. But R&D can sometimes be forgetful.

"Good morning, Sierra." Barbara smiles.

"Morning! How did Michelle's auditions go?"

"Pretty good. She got a callback from one of the acting schools." She beams with maternal pride, reaching for a small Ziploc bag of baby carrots.

"Good for her." I make a mental note to follow up later on where Michelle decides to go and see if she qualifies for any of the scholarships Silicone Dream offers.

The moment I enter my office and set my bags and cage down, Heather comes over. My assistant's silver bob is neat, her pale gray eyes sharp and observant. She's carrying her tablet, although I don't know why she bothers because everything's in her head. Every time I ask a question, she can answer without consulting anything.

She's wearing a white boat-neck top and dark brown slacks. Both look fabulous on her slender figure. Her feet are in dark beige walking shoes that are designed more for comfort than style. She has the energy of a teenager, but prefers comfortable shoes for her late-fifties joints.

She's been with the company for ages. I inherited her from Grandma, and depend on her for everything. I told her she could never, ever retire or quit. And I make sure she knows how much I appreciate her in every way, including a generous compensation package.

"Good morning," Heather says, handing me a cup of coffee. She knows I always have a mug before I leave the house, but she still insists. Says I function better with an extra dose of caffeine.

To be honest, I think she's right. I feel better on the days I get Heather's coffee. "Thank you," I say, sitting down.

"Would you like me to take the cage?"

"Just leave it for now. I'll introduce you to Bullet and G-Spot later, so you know which is which and they can smell and get to know you."

Heather's going to take care of my babies while I have my divorce-cation in New Orleans—starting later today! My best friend Ellie, who is taking some well-earned R&R with her family in St. Louis, is going to join me, and we'll hit a masquerade party to kick off my newly revived singlehood. I won't be back until late Sunday, and don't feel comfortable leaving Bullet and G-Spot at home alone, even though they're low-maintenance pets.

"G-Spot, huh?" Heather says.

"Todd could never find her." I waggle an eyebrow.

Heather laughs. "By the way, Saori said everything for the display in New Orleans has been confirmed and shipped, if you want to check that out."

"You know I do." I'll be at the party where the display is going to be set up. "Tell her I'll take a few pictures for our social media profiles."

"Splendid." Heather taps her tablet. "You have the taste meeting for the strawberry-flavored lube options in five minutes."

That's one flavor we haven't been able to perfect yet, unlike the chocolate that's going to be featured in New Orleans. "Weren't we supposed to do that after lunch? What happened to the new product line meeting?" That was scheduled for the morning, and I refuse to delay it. Silicone Dream hasn't had a major new product launch since my grandmother's death three years ago. Creating a new product line successfully is going to prove to everyone, especially my father and his wife, that I deserve the mantle of CEO.

"Product development wants to combine it with the market survey meeting."

I drum my fingers on my desk. "How long is the taste meeting going to last? I don't want to rush the market survey discussion." I need all the data points I can get for the next new product line.

"Not long. They only have two samples for you to look at."

"Just two? They must be confident." *Impressive.* Strawberry isn't an easy flavor to replicate, especially in lube. There's always an aftertaste like cough syrup.

"That seems to be the case. Are you ready to go?"

"Yes. Let's."

3

GRIFFIN

I don't have time for this.

But my mother's drama doesn't happen according to my convenience and schedule. If I ignore her summons, she'll have an episode and check herself into a hospital for chest pain or some other catastrophe that will drag on for at least a week. Afterward, she'll not only make sure I hear about it, but start contacting reporters to tell them who her son is and why he is cruelly abandoning her in her time of need.

So here I am in New Orleans when I should be in my office, working on the new research I'm doing with Keith Lenin from Stanford. He reached out after I won the John Bates Clark Medal last year, which is a prestigious award given to American economists under the age of forty.

"This is simply...simply heartbreaking."

Mom's words flow out slowly, like ice in a river about to freeze over. Her voice cracks a bit for maximum effect.

And she's prepped for the scene. She's wearing a diaphanous white dress, the kind appropriate for a young virgin about to be sacrificed to a dragon. Her makeup is perfect, but doesn't look too obvious. Just enough to render her skin flawless, her azure eyes impossibly wide and her mouth full and vulnerable. Her glossy golden hair is brushed out and tumbles over her shoulders like a waterfall. If she could, she would've set up a fan to blow it gently, but of course she knows you won't get the desired effect if your spectators can see the equipment.

I swallow an impatient growl that wants to push its way out of my chest, since it would only add fuel to her *scene*. Now that she's said the opening line, the tears will come.

With great difficulty, I arrange my face into an appropriate I-care-deeply-about-your-terrible-situation façade and sit back on the white leather sofa in her swanky suite. I count slowly to three, all the while wondering what the hell I did to deserve this punishment.

Exactly on three, she starts sobbing into her hands. Actually, not her hands. Rachel Griffin does not cry into her hands like a common woman. She sobs into a white silk handkerchief with her initials embroidered in pale lavender.

Ethereal elegance and beauty are her signature. That's what gave her fame and fortune in her youth as a supermodel. Every man wanted to sleep with her and every woman wanted to emulate her.

It's too bad she slept with Ted Lasker during his Vasectomy Fail and ended up pregnant. *With me.* He named me after her last name, saying that it was an homage to her beauty, but really so that he wouldn't forget what to call me. At least I didn't become Ted Junior —*shudder*—but that's a very minor consolation.

If I had a choice, I would've picked a normal, everyday American couple from some staid and boring Midwest town for parents. And if I absolutely *had* to have famous parents, I'd have chosen Adriana Mitchell and her husband Don Kasher. They're the most wholesome couple in Hollywood, doing charity work and promoting family values for various brands.

But instead, I got a degenerate Hollywood movie producer and overly dramatic former supermodel who's trying desperately to cling to her youth and influence.

I grunt to show I'm paying attention. But mentally, I'm going over the statistics I've been talking about with Keith during the last few weeks. I just got tenured a couple of years ago, and I'm not about to lose it by slowing down on research, especially when I poured all my energy into my career and recognize how fortunate I've been. Most newly minted PhDs are hired as lecturers and adjunct professors without any possibility of tenure, much less decent pay and benefits.

Not that money is an issue. My bank account has more than enough zeros to set any self-respecting gold digger's heart aflutter.

Still, being tenured doesn't guarantee permanent employment, despite what people think. It can be revoked if the college finds my behavior inappropriate—ha!—or if I fail to publish because I'm too distracted, participating in my mother's latest drama. But I'll be damned if I don't get to keep my sign of recognition and respect. It's one thing that can't be bought. And I earned it through hard work.

Mom sheds more tears. The woman can calibrate the rate at which her eyes excrete fluid—it feels wrong to call it *tears*, as most of the time she isn't really crying—more precisely than Dad's pastry chef can add sugar to a vat of buttercream.

Since I'm expected to do more than grunt, I make myself listen for a moment to catch the gist of her current issue.

"...and then he left and went to *Europe*! And now I don't have a date for the masquerade party tonight!"

"I'm sure Fabio will see the error of his ways." I say the words with more hope than truthfulness, while praying I don't sound as annoyed as I feel.

Mom's latest boy toy is probably incapable of seeing anything other than his next meal ticket or a movie role that could break him out despite his mediocre talent. Mom doesn't choose her beaus for their intellect or fascinating conversation. She prefers them young and flashily handsome—in other words, Instagrammable.

For his part, Fabio has been dating Mom because he knows she's still friendly with my father, the movie mogul Ted Lasker, who hasn't produced a single flop in his decades-long career. My parents get along fabulously, since they never had any real feelings for each other to begin with. It's difficult to be bitter about unmet expectations and broken dreams when there *were* no expectations and you care about the other person about as much as a dog does salad.

Regardless, my calmness will hopefully help lessen her theatrics.

But the scene is simply too perfect, and she's too opportunistic to let it go to waste. An elegant white suite with white leather sofas. Fresh pale cream orchids and a pitcher of lemon water with two crystal glasses on the coffee table. I can see the bed behind her through the open door. The sheets are pristine white, with subtly threaded gold and silver stripes to add to the air of delicate opulence. The suite smells exactly like the kind of expensive perfume Mom loves, and the heartrending strains of a violin solo come from the music system to accompany her tragedy.

"But what if he *doesn't*?" She raises her face and looks straight at me. Tragic tears spike her lashes. They're so long and thick that people assume they're fake.

But they're not. I have them too.

"He will. The man can't *not* see how wonderful you are." I want to be back home. Go over my research notes. Think of some evil ways to torment the lazy and unmotivated students in my class who should've never attempted econometrics in the first place. They're bound to fail—or do badly enough that they won't be able to major in economics without retaking the course. The issue is that many of them are terrible at math—they can't do high school algebra, much less the statistical analysis necessary to understand the economic data that is the heart of econometrics.

Teaching students who don't care is utterly unrewarding and a gross waste of my time. I could be gathering data on interesting fields like sports gambling or semiconductor production or predicting children's future outcomes based on a multitude of factors. But I don't say any of that. Mom doesn't need another reason to throw herself into this tragic heroine role she's created for herself over the latest breakup.

"But..." She sniffles delicately.

"And if he takes too long, you'll simply get yourself another man. It'll break Fabio's heart, but then, he should've known better." *I need a drink.*

"It's so hard to find a man who respects you." She sighs and gently brushes a tear away.

I don't think Fabio ever respected you. He respected your bank account and your connections.

Mom confuses need with respect, and doesn't understand that respect can't be bought. It has to be given because you did something worthy. Because you're a person of accomplishment.

I keep that to myself, since saying it would only up the ante in her drama. I made that mistake once, and will never do it again, especially since I want to be able to leave in the next twenty-four hours. My head hurts and I don't have much tolerance left for her scenes. She used up most of her annual quota in January over an ex-boyfriend "cheating" on her at an orgy they attended together.

"Will you take me to the masquerade party tonight?" she asks.

"Me?" My patience is fraying rapidly, like a stray thread being pulled from a sweater. "You want me to be your date?"

"I intended for Fabio to, to…" She swallows, and her breath hitches. "I can't *possibly* go alone. It would make me look silly. Trivial, even. And you're almost the right age."

I don't bother to point out that I'm her son, not a boy toy of *almost the right age*. She's beyond listening, too lost in her role.

She should've been an actress.

"I don't have a mask." This will hopefully let her know I'm not interested in attending the ridiculous event. Ideally, she'll find some easily influenced fool to accompany her, and I can fly back home to California and sleep in my own bed tonight.

"Don't you worry about that." Her tone is a dulcet now-I-have-you that never fails to make my stomach clench. "I have the mask Fabio was going to wear."

"Is it new?" I'm not wearing a used mask, especially when it belonged to my mother's two-decades-younger ex-boyfriend. He might have worn it while they were fooling around, and I'd rather eat roadkill sushi than ask my mother about the specifics of her sex life.

"Of course! You know I don't believe in wearing the same thing twice. Now, please?" She bats her eyelashes. "Pretty please?"

Rolling naked in a field of broken glass would be preferable to attending this idiotic masquerade. But she'll go into hysterics if I turn her down.

For once, I wish I'd taken after Quasimodo. Then Mom would never ask me to be her plus-one to parties, since she has "an image to maintain." But no. I got Mom's features—just more masculine and refined, according to my brother Huxley. Of course, he said that mainly because he wanted me to model for an overpriced mid-tier scotch his ad agency was peddling.

"There'll be lots of great drinks," Mom says with a smile, like I'm a broke college kid who can be bought with free booze. I'm a college *professor*, damn it.

"Fine." I'm smiling, but my teeth are clenched.

She claps her hands once, like a teenager excited before her prom, and the tears vanish. "Perfect! Let me just go get ready!"

This damn trip can't end soon enough.

4

GRIFFIN

The masquerade is at an old mansion with red walls and trellises. Balconies overlook the crowd in the French Quarter. It's probably owned by some friend Mom made during her years as a model.

The inside is also full of ornate wrought-iron railings and chandeliers that seem more fitting to a seventeenth-century Aquitaine castle. It's dimly lit for ambiance—or maybe they're trying to conserve electricity. Who the hell knows with Mom's eccentric friends? They've all got too much money and very little sense.

Scantily dressed women and men mill around like stoned zombies. Despite the scarcity of fabric on their bodies, their outfits likely cost some ovaries and left nuts. Mom doesn't go to parties that just anybody can attend. The events she selects are exclusive, with lots of money and gloss. Even the air inside the mansion smells expensive.

Compared to them, I'm overdressed in my suit. But I don't own any man-skank outfits.

My hand at my mother's elbow, I escort her farther inside. Everyone is wearing masks, of course. One must play to the stereotype. But that doesn't stop them from taking selfies to record this nonsense on social media. That way, everyone in the world can see what they're up to and express outward admiration while inwardly seething with sickening jealousy.

Personally, I'm thanking God I'm in a mask. I don't want my students or anybody at Wollstonecraft College recognizing me. Frat boys would stare in envy, while sorority girls would size me up like a piece of the calorie-free "chocolate" they devour. And the other professors wouldn't even know what to make of the fact that I—a rather morose econometrics specialist—got invited to this swanky, hedonistic party in the first place.

"Isn't this simply *maaaaarvelous*?" Mom says, leaning in so I can hear her over the music.

"Yes." Telling her I hate everything about this damned party would earn me nothing but another dramatic scene from her and opprobrium from everyone else here.

"Xander said he was going to be here."

She talks like I should know who this is, but I have no clue. Nor do I care to. He's probably another pretty face two or three decades her junior with a flashy smile and bleached teeth.

But if he is here, that would be fantastic. He can cater to her dramatics and I'll be able to make my exit.

A tall guy in a black cat mask comes over. He has the lithe, defined body of a model or a dancer—probably the former. He doesn't have the kind of innate grace dancers have, but does strut like he's on a runway in Milan. He's carrying two glasses of champagne and offers one to Mom.

"Hello, Aphrodite," he purrs, like an intellectually challenged cat. "Don't you look beautiful? The goddess of beauty, fresh off the half shell, a-hahaha."

Is he stupid or blind or both? My mother is wearing a skintight black Versace maxi dress. Aphrodite came out of sea foam, not an oil spill.

But I don't get a chance to voice my objections and rebuff his ridiculous pickup attempt because...

Mom makes a sound that's more giggle than a laugh. "Well, aren't *you* the perceptive one?" she says with a coy tilt of her head.

No. Just *no*. I don't need to see this.

"When I'm around a beautiful woman..."

I look away before I can hear more garbage coming out of his mouth. Mom's already leaning toward him, placing a hand over the arm he extends with a theatrical flourish. She then presses her breasts against him...

My eyes! I'd rather gag on a dick.

From the way she's smiling and gazing at this man, I can tell he's just replaced Fabio. Now she won't take her old beau back even if he comes crawling, bearing offerings fit for a deity. I don't feel sorry for him, though. It's his fault I'm being inconvenienced on Saturday.

Since I've done my filial duty, I turn and move off toward the exit. I'm going to catch the first flight back to LAX. The weekend might still be salvageable if I can just get away…

My phone buzzes. I take it out, praying it's not Mom being hysterical because Mr. Cat is uglier underneath the mask than she expected.

–Dad: I know what I want for my birthday. I want a baby.

Although the text is coming from Dad's number, it isn't really from him. It's Joey, his assistant, who should know better than to ask for an infant. The FBI needs to toss him in jail without a phone or Internet access for soliciting baby trafficking.

–Me: Buying a baby to hand out as a gift is illegal. Didn't you consult Dad's lawyers about that?

Or maybe the lawyers said they could fix anything as long as Dad can pay their billing rate. Who knows with the kind of people who circle around Dad? I don't have the time or patience to deal with Joey—or Dad—when they're this drunk or high.

–Dad: I'm not saying BUY a baby. I'm saying MAKE a baby.

Make—? Somebody definitely snorted something they shouldn't have. I don't even have a girlfriend. Actually, I haven't had sex since I broke up with my last girlfriend, which was…half a year ago? Something like that. I lost all appetite for any more association with her when I found out she only wanted to date me because she knew about my connection to my father—a connection I do my best to hide, since I don't need the embarrassing publicity of Dad's women and scandals weighing me down.

It's the kind of baggage that causes nothing but a lifetime of public humiliation and lost relationships. I'll never forget what my first girlfriend said: "I just can't respect people who think behaving like that is acceptable." And she gave me a look that clearly indicated I was one of *those people*.

But wanting to avoid baggage isn't the only thing that's kept me celibate for the last several months. I've had to deal with a fresh batch of overeager coeds who seem convinced that having my dick inside their vaginas is a life goal. Unfortunately, the semiannual let's-seduce-Professor-Lasker-athon is probably going to continue for the foreseeable future. Getting plastic surgery to turn me into a sewer troll sounds *really* tempting right about now.

–Dad: Grandkids are special.

Right. Special*ly* embarrassed by their grandparents. Putting a young child through what I had to go through around my parents should earn you jail time.

I put the phone away and resume my exit, pushing my way through the crowd before I lose my temper and sanity. Restless energy roils inside me like thunder, ominous and vicious. A dangerous mood to be in, since it's times like these I do things I shouldn't.

And the last thing I need is piling more shit on my already fucked-up night.

5

SIERRA

"Holy shit," I breathe as I step into the masquerade party. I've never been to one that didn't take place on Halloween, but apparently in New Orleans it's an everyday thing.

I look around, taking in the vibrant scene. I've been to expensive homes before, but this one is...

Well, it's something.

Most mansions in SoCal are fairly new, slick and shiny monuments showcasing modern sensibilities and wealth. Every inch drips with the money their owners are dying to flaunt, so everyone can see that somebody *very* important, *very* successful and *very* rich lives there.

Not this place.

It's oddly understated, with a décor that reminds me of old European palaces. Sedate, but no less expensive and important. It's the kind of place kings and queens from the Renaissance might've felt at home. What it lacks in modern gloss, it makes up for with class.

I love it.

I wish Ellie were here, because she'd get a kick out of the place. But that darn airline! How can they be so unreliable?

Since there's nothing I can do about the fact that she's stuck in

St. Louis right now, I take several pictures to send her. I also snap a selfie next to a huge suit of armor in an alcove. It's super cool.

I preview the picture to make sure it's good. The armor really adds to the photo. I look mysterious in my pearlescent white mask, with its tiny feathers and cubic zirconia around the edges. In the left-hand corner are the small embossed letters *SF*—my initials. The dress I picked for the masquerade is pink, with spaghetti straps and a skirt that stops at mid-thigh, showing off my legs. My wig is long, wavy and purple. I seriously adore how the colors go together for me.

I send the photos to Ellie, then take a look around. The lube display should be here somewhere. Saori told me over a month ago that the organizers of the party requested Silicone Dream send them some of our lubes to give away. Marketing sent an entire display for them with samples of our chocolate-flavored lube in penis-shaped bottles.

Which was smart.

Silicone Dream makes the best adult products. The kind that are more reliable than your significant other, and I do speak from experience. I'm confident that if people try our catalogue even once, they'll become fanatical customers for life.

But even after weaving through the crowd in several rooms, I don't see our samples anywhere. *Darn it.* The organizers better not have hoarded them for themselves! It's a problem when your products are too good, and we do have a blacklist of hoarders.

Finally, I spot a bar and march toward it. People thirsting for alcohol mill around. There are three bartenders; I wait until the one closest to me gets a moment, then slip her a ten.

"Have you seen the lube display?" She might've noticed it earlier when the staff came to set things up. It's disappointing that the organizers didn't put our stuff next to a bar. Once you have the right packaging and hook, getting as many eyeballs as possible is the name of the game.

She looks confused for a moment. "Oh, you mean the little chocolate dicks? Over there." She lifts an arm covered with a thorny rose and points at a room behind me.

"Great, thanks. Love the tat."

"Thanks." She smiles. "Something to drink? It's on the house."

Right. The eccentric billionaire—or his minions—who organized this party made everything free and plentiful. Most of the complimentary stuff is probably provided by companies like Silicone Dream.

I think for a second. Shedding Todd from my life definitely deserves a flute of Dom, but I should save that particular toast for later with Ellie. "How about a dirty martini?"

"Not a problem." The bartender goes into action, mixing the drink and then handing it to me.

I give her another ten and take the glass. As I sip the martini, vodka with a tinge of sweetness from vermouth burns a fiery trail from my mouth to my gut. The drink leaves a refreshing aftertaste. Strong and reinvigorating. It's probably the best martini I've ever had.

Must be the city. People in New Orleans drink like bosses and party like bosses. Just look at this place. Upbeat music's in the air, and the masked guests are dancing and laughing. A couple I pass by starts kissing, somehow moving toward a wall without hitting anybody in the process, even though their eyes are closed.

Like bosses.

It makes me think. Maybe if I hang around long enough, I might get some inspiration for the new product line. The morning meeting was a bust. The ideas weren't *bad*...but they didn't make me jump with excitement, either.

I need an idea that puts fire in my blood. Something that will keep me up at night with feverish enthusiasm. Because if *I'm* not excited by a product, I can't sell it. Silicone Dream's customers deserve the very best the company has to give.

But first, I'm going to do what Saori wanted. I walk into the room the bartender indicated and immediately see the display to my left. A giant board with our lube is set up on a table next to the buffet. The dick-shaped mini-bottles are stacked delicately like a tower of happy time.

Excellent. Close to food is a great location. Even the health-conscious folks in this crowd will come by because there are carrot sticks, cucumber slices and celery.

And there's no way anybody's going to miss our samples.

Maybe we can work with whoever put this party together again. Some events are awful about displaying our product samples correctly. I've seen ones where they forgot to put out the boards or brochures we sent, which meant that nobody would have the QR codes that make it easy to grab more information about us.

The people in charge of this masquerade seem to get it: nothing we sent is optional. More boss-worthy behavior.

I make my way through the crowd to the display table. A few samples are tipped over and lying there like unwanted trash on a sidewalk. *That won't do.* Silicone Dream has a certain image to maintain—excellent, classy products for the sexually discerning among us.

I right the mini-penises so they're nice and tidy again. Then I step back and look at them with maternal pride. Silicone Dream does the best work, helping people achieve better orgasms every day.

The flavoring we use for our lube is the best in the industry. The liquid in the bottle tastes like real chocolate syrup. We've done blind tasting with multiple test groups to make sure. I personally tasted enough of them during development that my tongue became numb. But if the CEO doesn't put in maximal effort, who will?

I take a picture, then upload it to all of Silicone Dream's social media accounts with the proper hashtags. That done, I put my phone away and finish my martini in a couple of big swallows. It's giving me a good buzz, but then, I've already had two drinks—thanks to Ellie, who arranged to have them delivered to our hotel room upon my arrival.

There's a table for placing empty glasses and plates to be bussed. I put the martini glass on it and start to walk away.

Somebody lays a hand on my shoulder. "Finally!" comes a familiar growl.

What the...? I turn to look, then expel an impatient sigh.

It's Todd, with the world's most annoying *gotcha* sneer on his face.

6

SIERRA

I immediately shake Todd's hand off my shoulder like it's a snake.

He's in a peacock mask that covers his face except for the mouth and jaw. It has large feathers sticking out like unkempt morning hair in front of him. The mask glows various shades of gaudy neon in the dark—and it's blinding in the dimly lit interior of the mansion. There are weird colors, and I realize the mask has letters: Byron.

"Your mask has the wrong name," I point out, too stunned to think of anything else.

"What?"

"It says Byron."

He huffs. "It's a reference to *Lord* Byron, not that I'd expect you to recognize the name."

I roll my eyes. I know about Lord Byron—some British poet who I remember mainly for his womanizing ways. He was probably dashing and sexy, though, not paunchy and annoying. But then, Todd always was absurd in his sense of the grandiose.

He's sporting an untucked and unbuttoned white dress shirt and tight leather pants, like a model for an old-style historical romance novel—the ones that featured barely dressed hotties. Except who would feature *him* on a romance novel cover, unless the publisher wanted to repel readers?

"How did you know I was going to be here? Are you stalking

me?" I demand. Being confronted by your ex-husband should never happen on a divorce-cation!

"Of course not." He snorts, like I'm stupid. "I would never do that."

Uh-huh. Apparently, he's forgotten about the scene he made this morning at Silicone Dream.

"I simply asked around," he says. "There are people who feel terrible about our divorce, you know."

My mood sours faster than a tub of yogurt left out in the sun. Heather and Ellie would never let anything slip, but my stepmom or stepsister might have, since Todd is Linda's nephew and Felicia's cousin. I don't make a habit of sharing my activities with either of them, but my divorce-cation isn't exactly a secret.

"And the rest was easy," he says. "I just had to sneak in here and hang around, waiting for you."

"You knew who I was when you saw me?" No way. He's too oblivious. He didn't notice when I dyed my hair pink during our first year of marriage.

Which should've been another flashing neon sign that he couldn't be the kind of husband I wanted. And I should've paid more attention, instead of telling myself that things would change—that Todd just needed some time to adjust.

I was so stupid back then. Some people are beyond help.

"Yeah, it was hard to find you in this crowd, but I knew you'd come by to check the sample table." He shoots me a smug grin. "All I had to do was leave a few bottles out of place and then reel you in."

Ugh. He got me. But even if I knew he'd be watching, it wouldn't have mattered. My work is important, and I'm not letting an irritating ex-husband stop me from doing what needs to be done.

I cross my arms and give him a hard glare, the kind Dan will level before he eviscerates trespassers and troublemakers. "What do you want, Todd?"

"To talk to you, of course. Since you won't see me back home." Todd speaks like it's all my fault. But he loves to blame me for everything, including the fact that he won't get tenured. He probably still refuses to accept that I can't get him tenured when he was hired for a non-tenure position!

"Talk to Samantha if you have something to say."

"She is the enemy." His tone says, *Don't you get it?*

"She's my lawyer! I have nothing to say to you." Uncrossing my arms, I turn around and start to leave.

He grabs my wrist and yanks me back. "I never said you had to talk. But you *will* listen to me."

I don't think so. "Get your hands off me!"

"No! This is important! You're going to hear me out!"

"You mean you didn't say enough before?" He would *not* shut his mouth when we were going through the divorce proceedings. Mainly to complain about how unfair I was for not recognizing his need for self-respect, love and support—all of which could be fulfilled by the handsome sum of ten million dollars in a settlement if I couldn't stay married to him.

"I did, *but you weren't listening.* You never do!" He shakes the hand wrapped around my wrist so hard that my whole body rocks back and forth. "Do you know how terrible this divorce is for my career?"

I wish I weren't in strappy sandals. Otherwise, I'd kick him. *Hard.*

"Let *go!*" I try wrenching my arm away, but his hold is too tight. I don't have to be able to see into his eyes to know they've got that stubborn you'll-listen-like-a-good-little-girl gleam in them.

He doesn't care that we're surrounded by partygoers. In fact, the general noise and hubbub is giving him cover. He also doesn't care about hurting me, not from the way he's clenching my wrist.

Cold goosebumps rise on the back of my neck. He's been meticulous about maintaining a scholarly image. To the point that he's almost a caricature—he actually started wearing non-prescription glasses to "lend gravitas" to his recitations of English romantic poems.

Holy crap, Sierra. How could you have missed that he hasn't talked anything like a pompous, self-important professor since he ran into you?

Okay... Is this how Todd acts when he knows people won't recognize him? The only thing that renders civility to my ex is that he cares about his image. Without that, he's just a bully who likes to make himself feel smart and important by putting others down. Although he's never gotten physically violent with me before, he's bigger and stronger and will use whatever means at his disposal to make me do what he wants. It won't be easy to shake him off.

I look around for something I can use as a weapon. Unfortunately, none of these sample tubes of lube are large enough to do any damage.

"Nobody's coming to your rescue," Todd sneers.

"Nobody would need to if you'd just—*let*—*go!*" I grind out, trying to pull away. Todd doesn't budge. Damn it. When I get home, I'm hitting the company gym! "I *said, let go!*"

"You heard the lady. Let her go," comes a voice behind me.

Despite the coldness of the tone, there's a dark edge to it that put my lady parts on full alert. In a very good but slightly inappropriate way, given the circumstances.

Who cares? He's here to save you. Chivalry isn't dead! my internal voice squeals with delight.

I twist around to look at my savior. He's at least a head taller than me, his broad shoulders impossibly wide. Unlike the other men at the party, he's wearing a black suit, cut to show off his trim waist. A black satin mask blends in well with his dark hair, making him look like some kind of god of midnight. There's an air of languid menace about him, and his powerful presence commands respect. He's focused on Todd, his mouth set in a flat line of disapproval.

My ex takes in the Midnight God, seeing the same things I'm seeing. I can almost hear the gears turning in his head as he tries to figure out a way to look and sound superior. Finally he steps forward, his mouth twisting into a sneer. "Get lost, you overdressed lunk." He tries for superior disdain but then ruins the delivery by licking his lips nervously.

I can't believe Todd is making fun of the Midnight God because of the suit. Okay, it's a bit too formal, but at least he doesn't look like a doughy romance cover model reject.

Besides, I think a man who looks fabulous in a suit is hot as hell. And the hotness triples if he's coming to my rescue.

"Don't be an idiot," I tell Todd, who's demonstrated the manners and sense of a boar on psychedelics.

"Idiot? I'll wager I'm the one with the higher IQ here." Todd snickers, likely encouraged by the fact that my savior hasn't done anything about the initial insult. "Isn't that right, lunk?"

"Are you going to let her go?" the Midnight God says.

"I'm thinkin'...nah." Todd puffs his torso up like a bird about to fight for territory—or an ex-mate. The quivering, glowing feathers on his mask only enhance the ridiculous effect. "You gonna do something about it?" He actually bumps chests with the Midnight God, jabbing a finger hard into his shoulder.

My savior gives a fractional shake of his head. The movement says, *Some people just need to be taught a lesson*, and he's done playing nice.

Todd probably fights dirty. Although my money's on the Midnight God, Todd might land a punch or two.

If my savior gets injured fighting my idiot ex, I'm going to comp him a lifetime supply of anything he wants from our men's pleasure line. Plus, I'll personally nurse him back to health. Oh, and hire a lawyer to sue Todd on top of it.

The Midnight God places a hand on my shoulder, the gesture reassuring and oddly protective. I feel the pressure change slightly, and there's a thud that sounds like someone hit a tree stump with the blunt side of an ax.

Simultaneously, Todd suddenly yanks on my arm, pulling me sharply forward. "Ack!" I jerk back hard, so I don't land on my knees.

His grip on my wrist slips away. Todd tries to grab my dress instead—*asshole!*—but his hand can't seem to get any purchase on the slick material.

Then he's lying on the floor. It's hard to see in the dimness, but it looks like something wet is oozing from his mouth. I think he's moaning a little, too, but it's hard to tell because the music hits a climax, the singer belting out high notes.

Or maybe it's just my heartbeats that are loud. Because *oh my God, oh my God* the Midnight God just took Todd down, and I didn't even see him *move*! It was like magic. Like he has superpowers—my very own superhero.

The thought is making me melt.

"What did you just do?" I ask.

"Kicked him in the head."

"You did? I didn't see anything."

"In this light? If you could have seen it, I'd have been way too slow." He lowers his gaze a little, then exhales. "Do you really want to go around like that? We are in New Orleans, but..."

"Like what?" I look down at myself, wondering if I have Todd's disgusting drool or blood on me.

Then I choke back a scream and quickly put an arm up to cover my bare breast. My face flames, and I start to fan it before I catch myself. *When did my dress decide to malfunction?*

No wonder my torso felt oddly cool. I thought it was just a delayed reaction to being harassed by Todd. But he must've broken one of the straps when he fell and tried to grab my dress. Jerk! This dress is *brand new*!

Now I wish he'd get back up, so the Midnight God could kick him again.

"I didn't mean to flash you," I say, desperately trying to pull the fabric back up over my boob. "I didn't even realize…"

I can't read the Midnight God's expression behind his mask. But his mouth is no longer so tight. He steps back and shrugs out of his jacket. "Here."

He drapes it over my shoulders and does up one of the buttons so I'm modestly covered. The jacket's warm and smells amazing—soap, wood, spices and something else that's uniquely male. Delicious enough to make my insides flutter.

"Thank you," I say, doing my best to sound calm.

"No problem."

I glance down and note Todd isn't moving. I worry my lower lip. "Did you, um, kill him?"

If the police show up asking for a statement, I don't want to lie. But I also don't want to tell them that the Midnight God kicked Todd's head so hard he died. Maybe I can provide him with a great legal team. Todd's head being full of self-important tofu has to be a legitimate legal defense, if you get the right lawyer.

"Just knocked out," the Midnight God says. "His jaw might be dislocated, but he'll live."

Holy cow. I'm not usually a violent person, but something about the way this man came to my rescue and protected me is *hot*, especially when the heroic act is combined with lethal skills. He's as casual as if he just ate a sandwich.

It's the utter confidence and control he's displaying. Plus he risked himself to save me.

Now I understand why Ellie auto-buys romance novels with bodyguards and protectors in them. I'm never teasing her about it again.

"Would you like me to take you to your friends?" His dark, deep voice brushes over me like the most luxurious silk.

I shiver as my nerves prickle with awareness. "I'm, uh, actually here alone."

"Oh." The single syllable carries some surprise. But no judgment.

"Yeah, my friend was supposed to show up but her flight got canceled. So I'm here by myself to enjoy the party. I've never been to a masquerade before, you know?"

"I see." He looks around. "Well, if you're going to stay here—"

He's about to leave! And I don't want him to. I don't know exactly what I want with him yet, but it's been so long since I felt something for a man. Not to mention I don't want to stay here with Todd, even if he is currently lying on the floor like a speed bump. Who knows when he'll wake up? And if he was annoying and aggressive before, now he's going to have a heck of a headache on top of it.

Without realizing what I'm doing, I put a hand over the Midnight God's arm. His muscles leap and flex, and my fingertips tingle. The sensation doesn't stop there, though. It races up my arms and wraps around my shoulders and down my torso, stopping briefly over my nipples until my toes curl, then ends in my clit. The intense sexual awareness is so sudden and shocking that I just stare at him, my mind empty of all but one thought: *He's yummy.*

His mouth purses briefly, and he glances down at my hand on his arm.

And the sexual trance is broken. Ack! I've been staring at him! Hopefully I'm not drooling as well. But I probably look like a starving raccoon eyeing a slab of steak.

"Actually, I'm not sure if I want to stay." My words tumble out fast. "I don't feel super safe after what happened."

He raises his eyes back to my face.

"And my dress is ruined. Would it be okay if we left together?"

His lips purse again. *Crap! He's going to say no!*

The notion rips into me like a knife. I don't know why the possibility of rejection from a stranger—and one who will never recognize me again at that—hurts. But it does.

Then I realize it isn't even eleven. He probably doesn't want to leave this early.

My shoulders sag a little. I'm being selfish about the situation. *This man has done plenty already. He doesn't owe me anything. It's just...*

"Sure," he says. "We can leave together."

I jerk my head up, gazing at him. I can't help but smile, warmth filling me from head to toe. "Thank you."

He extends a hand, palm up.

He probably means for me to hold it, but I ignore all the conventions. I'm a newly minted re-singled woman who's starting a brand-new chapter in her life. And I want to feel this divine man.

Feeling exceptionally bold—or maybe more drunk than I should be—I loop my arm around his. But as I shift my weight, a sharp sensation stabs into my right ankle. "Ow!"

"Are you okay?" he asks.

"Ugh. I think I twisted my ankle a little when this jerk"—I point at Todd—"yanked me downward."

The Midnight God goes down smoothly onto one knee. His fingers brush my ankle, the touch methodical and brisk. And yet hot shivers rush up my body anyway.

Oh my God. You have it bad, Sierra. Stop before drool starts dripping down your chin.

Shut your mouth, self. I haven't had sex in over a year, so I'm entitled to a little panting. Besides...

I look down at the man. Those broad shoulders...and the power that not even his current hunched posture can hide.

When God created him, He did it so I could appreciate him. Why else would He have created such a fine specimen? Not ogling —sorry, *admiring*—the man would be get-burned-at-the-stake-level blasphemy. So I'm going to do the right thing.

He stands back up, towering over me again. "Can you walk at all?"

I put my hand on his arm and check. "It hurts a bit when I put my weight on it, but I should be okay with a little help."

"Where are you staying?"

"At the Aylster." In case he doesn't know where that is, I add, "It isn't that far. Only three or four blocks away."

He shakes his head. "That's going to take forever."

"I'm a fast walker." I try not to laugh at the way he makes managing a few blocks out to be like climbing Mt. Everest.

"No doubt, but you're also injured."

My heart does a funky cartwheel. Todd would've shrugged and told me not to make such a big deal about such a "minor inconvenience." How is it that a stranger I just met can show so much concern?

Maybe the Midnight God is the universe's way of saying, "Sorry we paired you with that butthole. Here's a premium male to help you forget him."

The Midnight God puts one arm behind my back and the other under my knees and lifts me up. With a small yelp, I wrap my arms around his neck. This close, I can smell him—a mesmerizing scent that makes every nerve in my body quiver. And feel his delicious heat seeping into my bones.

Most importantly, the way he's holding me like a princess makes me feel cared for. I can't remember the last time a man aroused such a sensation in me.

"You okay?" he asks.

I nod, not trusting myself to speak in my normal voice. Squeaking would ruin the moment.

"Then let's go."

7

GRIFFIN

Even as I carry Purple Girl out of the mansion, I have no clue what's prompted me to do so. She said she wasn't hurt that much. Her ankle didn't seem too badly injured, either. Slightly swollen, but nothing a little rest and icing won't cure.

I should call her an Uber to take her to the Aylster.

Yet here I am, carrying her like she's Cinderella.

It's exactly the kind of dramatic scene Mom would love to star in. And the kind I'd give up a kidney to avoid.

But with this woman, my distaste for theatrics never got a chance to rear its head. All I'm really registering is shock that she isn't acting like we're in the middle of an apocalypse because her dress is torn and her ankle is a little achy.

Mom certainly would've done that.

You had your chance to put Purple Girl down.

That's true enough. When she yelped, I could've just said, "Sorry," and put her down.

Except I didn't want to let her go. She felt too soft and sweet against me. Like cotton candy to a child.

Plus, I'm also staying at the Aylster, and it really isn't that far. I'd love to hold her the entire time.

It's been too long since you got laid.

So what?

But there's an image in my head of her bare breast—pert and rounded, tipped with a tight pink nipple. It begged to be pulled into my mouth and sucked until she plunged her fingers into my hair and whimpered with bliss.

I can feel myself stiffening, and it's not with resolve. *Stop*, I order my dick. I'm not embarrassing myself by walking around with an erection, especially when it could easily poke her as I carry her.

What if she knew who you were and set up a scene with the thuggish moron? It isn't completely out of the question. It's happened before, remember?

True. Not to me, but to my brother Grant.

But how would she know who I am—that I'm Ted Lasker's son? I've done an excellent job of hiding that fact, and it requires a lot of legwork and effort to dig up the connection. On top of that, even if she figured it out, stalking me from LAX is too much work. Given the spontaneous nature of this trip, she would've had to be watching me for a while. It'd make more sense for her to stage something like this in California.

You know how far some will go for fame and fortune.

My analytical mind says it's foolish to pursue them to this degree. You might as well spend all your savings buying lottery tickets and hoping for the best. You'll at least get the fortune, if you're lucky.

However, just because something isn't logical, it doesn't mean people don't do it. There's even a new discipline within the department called behavioral economics, which studies the many ways people behave irrationally, contrary to their best interests.

Perhaps I should play dumb about the introduction to my dad she probably wants and see what she does. It's a startling thing to consider. When I suspect women are after me to get to my dad, I drop them faster than they can swat cockroaches falling into their hair.

For some bizarre reason, I don't want to dump Purple Girl. She's resting her head on my shoulder and smells divine. Like an apple orchard, but better. My violaceous vixen.

My dick perks up again.

No, you're going to stay down. Think of something else. Like Dad wanting a baby.

The horrific thought settles my hormones. Still, my blood

simmers. Purple Girl is so beguilingly soft—the smooth warmth of her bare skin when I examined her ankle still lingers on my hands. I spent a bit more time examining the injury than was strictly necessary. But she caught my attention like a flame in the darkness as I waded through the crowd to leave. She probably isn't the I'm-into-you-so-you-can-introduce-me-to-your-daddy type, I decide. Doesn't have that desperate edge to her. What she does have is the confidence and assurance of a woman who is already working toward her goal. It's evident in the straight-backed, self-possessed way she holds herself. She wasn't hunting for someone to take her where she wants to go.

I carry her to the hotel, our masks on. Nobody looks at us funny, but that's New Orleans for you.

I walk at my regular pace—actually a little slower—to prolong our time together. Her fingers flex and unflex against the back of my neck. A sharp prickling sensation spreads over me.

"If you want, I can probably walk now," she offers after a couple of blocks.

"Has your ankle magically healed?"

"No, but… Aren't I getting heavy?" Her voice goes small at the end, as though she expects the answer to be a yes. "I'm sure I can manage," she adds when I don't respond immediately.

I scoff. "I don't think so. Just to let you know, if anybody ever complained you were too heavy, it's because he's a wimp." I have blunter words—something my former kickboxing trainer might say, but this nice woman shouldn't be subject to that sort of vocabulary.

She laughs a little. A weird tickling sensation starts in my heart, like something as light and soft as a baby bird's feather is twirling in the center of it. I can't decide if I like it or not, so I push it aside.

"Did *you* go to the party with friends?" she asks after another beat. "I just realized you might've left them behind to help me."

If she's fishing to see if I went with another woman… Well, she doesn't do subtle very well.

"No. I went by myself." Mom found herself a new boy toy to grace her arm. She won't even realize I left until next week, if then, as long as he doesn't pull a Fabio on her.

Purple Girl's plump pink lips curve gorgeously. The sight does something odd to me—something I've never experienced before and is a bit unsettling. I can see a glimpse of her eyes—sparkling and pretty behind the mask, and I wish she weren't wearing it so I could see them better.

But if I ask her to take it off, I'll have to reciprocate. I don't want to do that and ruin the charged anonymity of the moment. Even if she knows who I am, as long as we have masks on, we can pretend.

It's an odd thing to think for an economist. Imperfect information is never good, but here I am, trying to remain ignorant.

When we reach the Aylster, a startled doorman hurries over to hold the door open. I carry Purple Girl into the opulent lobby. The spotless marble floor is set in a complex geometric pattern consisting of triangles of different sizes. Above, a giant rectangular chandelier shines golden light over the guests and their murmured conversations. The crisply dressed concierge smiles in greeting as he passes by.

"Can you send a bucket of ice and several plastic bags to twenty-six-oh-four?" I ask.

He nods. "Certainly, sir. I'll take care of that right now."

I thank him. A cool jazz melody swirls from a bar to our left, floating in the air like a lover's whisper. I walk past it to the elevator bank. There's a car waiting, and I step right in.

"Reach into my jacket pocket and take out the key card, would you?" I ask. The upper floors of the hotel aren't accessible without it.

"Sure." She rummages in my jacket and pulls out the plastic, then pushes it into the slot and hits twenty-six.

I move back, so she can't reach the buttons anymore.

"Wait, what about my floor?" she says.

I should let her return to her room, but I don't want to let her go. Not yet.

"Why don't I ice your ankle first? You said your friend isn't here yet, and it'll be awkward to try to do it yourself."

"Oh... So that's why you asked that man to send up some ice."

"Yes."

"I think it'll be okay if I just elevate it for a few hours."

"I doubt it. Trust me." But she's probably correct. It's just that icing will make it feel better faster, and also gives me an excuse to spend more time with her.

"Trust you, huh?"

"Yes. And let me take care of you."

8

SIERRA

I almost forget to breathe.

Let me take care of you.

I can't remember the last time Todd said something like that to me. The Midnight God knows exactly what to say to slice right past my defenses and slide into my heart.

A tiny internal voice blares a warning. *That isn't all he wants to slide into. And Todd was smooth like this, too, when you first met him. You were dazzled, remember?*

I brush aside the little voice of reason. It's useful to listen to when I'm running Silicone Dream, but it's being annoyingly negative right now. It isn't like I'm trying to marry the Midnight God. I just want to see where this chemistry between us goes. We both have masks on. We haven't exchanged names. And I'm in another city that might as well be a galaxy far, far away.

I can play a night of make-believe. Live a fairytale dream for a few hours. I deserve that after two years of crappy marriage that left me with an ex who refuses to accept it's over.

The Midnight God carries me to his suite. It's spacious and has an open archway that connects the living room to the bedroom. No door for partitioning, but it makes the suite appear bigger and airier. A minibar, a couch, an armchair, an ottoman and a coffee table occupy the living room side. A vase full of freshly cut white lilies fills the air with a heady perfume.

This suite is almost identical to mine on the floor below, except his is much more sedate—more ivory and cream than bold teals and pink. Somehow the pale colors suit him, making him appear more stark and powerful.

Another wave of awareness shoots through me. I lick my dry lips as he places me gently on the couch and puts my right foot on the ottoman in front of it.

There's a knock on the door. He vanishes for a moment and then returns with a silver bucket filled with ice and a few Ziplock bags with the hotel logo on them.

Without saying anything, he makes an ice pack and wraps it in a towel. His movements are graceful and precise, a finely tuned marvel of male anatomy and human evolution. If civilization ended tomorrow and we all had to go back to hunting bison to survive, he'd be the leader of the hunting party. The alpha male.

He places the pack on my ankle, adjusting it just so. I let out a soft sigh. The cooling sensation feels heavenly.

"Thank you," I say.

"You're welcome." He gives me a small smile, then goes to the minibar. "Something to drink?"

"Do you have whiskey or scotch?" I want another martini, but I don't want to ask him to make me a cocktail after having done so much already.

He nods. "Scotch. Ice?"

"Please."

He puts some ice into a glass and splashes the amber liquid into it. He pours one for himself, too. Two fingers, straight. He brings both over to the couch and sits next to me.

"Here." He hands me mine.

"Thanks." I sip it. The liquor is stronger than I generally prefer, but it has such a lovely oak note, with hints of smoke and caramel, that I can't complain. "I feel like I should've bought *you* a drink. You know, to thank you for rescuing me and all that."

"It's nothing. All in a night's work."

"Is that so? Make a habit of recuing damsels in distress? Well, that still doesn't mean I'm not going to show you some gratitude." I smile, the alcohol making me mellower. The drinks I had earlier are still coursing through my veins.

He takes another swallow of scotch, and I can feel the weight of his gaze. He's sizing me up in that male way, top to bottom. It would be threatening if I didn't feel comfortable with him. Or if there were no sizzling heat zinging through my system.

My mind is already stripping him. He wasn't even winded after carrying me those four blocks. I felt the solid muscles against me when he had his arms under my knees and back, and had to bite my lip to contain a sigh of longing. My imagination is already conjuring an image of us tumbling on the couch—*or the bed, I'm flexible*—arms wrapped around each other and our mouths greedy.

"What are you doing in New Orleans?" he asks.

"It's for a celebration."

"For what?"

"For..." I stop, suddenly not wanting to talk about Todd or the divorce. It's embarrassing that I was such a poor judge of character, and that my decision not only had consequences personally but professionally. Not because he got a piece of Silicone Dream—he didn't—but because he became a distraction that made me less effective at my job.

On the other hand, I don't want to lie to the Midnight God either. So after a moment, I say, "A breakup."

"A trip to New Orleans seems a little disproportionate for a simple breakup."

I let out a self-conscious laugh. "Yeah, well... It was a particularly long and ugly one. We were together for entirely too long. But I'm free now." I smile and lift my arms in the air. "Yay me."

He doesn't have to pull down his mask for me to feel his scrutiny. It sends a frisson of electricity racing along my spine, leaving my body tingling.

I finish the rest of my drink to gather my thoughts. My heart is racing, excitement fizzing like champagne bubbles. I've never fallen into a bed with a guy I just met, but then, I've never met a guy who made me feel like this.

And right now, there's no way I can leave without tasting his lips.

Seize the moment.

I lean over and kiss him. He stiffens for a second, but I don't let that stop me. My mouth moves over his. There's scotch and something else I've never tasted before. Something that sends fire blazing in my veins until I'm digging my fingers into his shoulders with naked greed.

He parts his lips, and his tongue slides into my mouth in one smooth stroke. Need thrums hard, beats through me, matching the erratic rhythm of my eager heart. Liquid heat has already slickened me, and I whimper over how aroused I am by a simple kiss. It's like he's created entirely out of aphrodisiac.

The world tilts as I fall back on the sofa with him leaning over me, caging me between his arms and body. Instead of feeling trapped, anticipation pulses through my system. I want to be dazzled…lost in him.

He moves carefully to avoid bumping my injury, adjusting my leg so it isn't sticking out on the ottoman awkwardly, and claims my mouth in a carnal kiss that makes my head spin. Incandescent bliss starts in my belly and spirals through me until the tips of my fingers and toes tingle. I wrap my hands around his warm, strong neck and shoulders, like I'm scared he's a dream that's about to vanish.

Our mouths still fused, he puts one of his arms under my shoulders and the other under my butt. I have a vague sense of being lifted again and realize he's carrying me into the bedroom.

Yes, please.

The light here is dimmer. As he lowers me, I slide down his hard, lean body and groan at the shivery, erotic friction.

"I want you," I whisper, my mouth only a hairsbreadth away from his as I balance carefully, putting my weight on my left foot.

Our breaths mingle as he stares at me, his eyes dark and glittering behind the mask. "I want you too." His voice is gravelly and low now, nothing like the controlled tone he was using earlier.

Knowing that I did that to him is hot. I wish I hadn't hurt my ankle so I could squirm to ease the aching emptiness between my legs.

I shrug out of his jacket and let it drop on the floor. Half my dress falls from my torso, revealing my breast. I stand there, completely unashamed and honest in my need for him.

He reaches around my back for the zipper, then finds and lowers it. He pushes the ruined dress down, and I let it slip down my legs, leaving me in nothing but a tiny red thong.

He hisses, then pushes me back gently until I'm sitting on the soft, bouncy mattress. He hooks his fingers on the tiny waist string on my thong and pulls it down. Once I'm stripped of everything except my mask and heels, his warm, large hands on my knees keep me spread wantonly.

"You're dripping," he grates out.

"Looks like you might be, too." I try to say it playfully, but it's difficult to act carefree when you're so turned on you feel like you're going to die without him on you.

At least I'm not the only one going crazy with need. His erection's pushing hard against his pants. I eye it with greed, but I don't get to stare for long because he's licking and nibbling on my neck, sending hot shivers along my spine. His palms cup my breasts. God, that feels so divine. I moan as the pads of his thumbs circle over my nipples. The pleasure is so intense, I can only think, *Yes, yes, oh yes!*

When his head starts to migrate downward, I swallow with anticipation at having his mouth close around my nipples. But instead, he presses hot kisses between them and moves lower until he's kissing the soft flesh of my belly, like he can't love me enough there. It's surprising, because most guys I've been with avoided my belly, like it wasn't the main attraction.

But not the Midnight God. He's kissing me like every inch of me is worthy of his worship.

His breath fans over my folds, and I quiver, then twist around a little. I'm pretty comfortable with almost all types of sex, except oral. It's hard for me to experience an orgasm from it, and when I don't really feel much from the act, the performing guy tends to get offended—like it's a personal criticism of his sexual prowess—and it ruins the rest of the evening.

I don't want the rest of our evening ruined, and I don't want to fake it, either. Not faking it—in every way—is a promise I made to myself when I decided to divorce Todd.

"Wait," I say quickly, lifting my head from the bed to see the Midnight God better. He looks so hot with his face between my legs...

I continue to stare. "Wait what?" he finally says.

Oh, right. "You don't have to go down on me."

His gaze drops back to my lady parts. "Why not?" He sounds mildly irritated.

"Um." I don't want to tell him I'm frigid with oral sex, but... "There are other options...?"

"And we'll explore them later." He dips his head, closing his mouth over me.

The vague discomfiture, awkwardness and embarrassment don't come. Instead, my back arches as electrifying pleasure strikes me like a bolt of lightning. My vision turns hazy as my eyes lose focus. Every cell in my body tightens, then quivers as he devours me down there—licking and sucking like I'm the best damn feast he's ever had.

Then I feel his finger slipping into my pussy. I clench around it, silently demanding more. He adds another, and I rock my pelvis, lost in the moment.

Oh my God. Oh my God. *How can this feel so good?*

My whole being is buoyant, like a balloon flying in the air. Then it comes, an orgasm that sweeps through me like a storm. I scream, digging my fingers into his hair. Holy shit. I didn't know it could be this good.

The Midnight God stands over me, his mouth curved with masculine satisfaction.

He's still in his dress shirt and slacks, all neat and tidy. The only thing that betrays that he's been wicked is the mussed-up hair and the glistening lips. And that enormous erection.

I want him as naked as me—bared to my view.

"Take off your clothes," I whisper over the rapid hammering of my heart.

His eyes on mine, he unbuttons his shirt and strips out of it, then removes the rest of his clothes. The mask stays on. His body is stunning—a powerfully proportioned frame layered with muscle that ripples every time he moves. Watching him is like watching a work of art come to life.

And his cock...

Oh my. We could use it as a dildo model.

It's so long, so thick. Tipped with the most perfectly shaped head.

I want it. And I want him. "Come here."

He leans over, and our lips meet. I crave everything this man has to offer. I wrap my legs around his waist. His chest brushes against mine, creating blissful friction, before he moves down and takes one breast in his mouth.

I hear myself say something, but I have no idea what. This is an undiscovered level of sex; it almost feels like I'm going to come again just from getting my nipples sucked.

Desperate, I hold on to his shoulders and shiver uncontrollably when another orgasm—different from the last one, but no less amazing—rips through me.

He laughs, his mouth still around my nipple, almost making me shriek at the way a sudden streak of ecstasy blazes up.

"I didn't think anybody could be this responsive." It's the first time he's actually sounded happy about something this evening, and that makes me happy in return. I reach down and wrap my hand around that cock, still thinking *prototype*. It's thick, heavy and hot, pulsing in my grip like a separate organism. I move my hand, and he inhales, his cock growing harder and thicker. I swipe my thumb over the tip.

"*Fuck.*"

He reaches down for his pants and grabs a condom. I hear the foil tear, and he covers himself in the rubber before taking my mouth again.

Oh yes.

I spread my legs, eager and lusty. I want him inside me. I'm already so wet, so ready.

He drives his cock into me in one stroke, hard and fast. I cry out, my body arching. The invasion feels so good, so *large* inside me. While we're so intimately connected, I can feel every pulse of his shaft.

"Good?" His soft, dark voice ripples over me.

I shiver. "Yes." I wrap my legs around him, like I'm never letting go.

He laughs, the sound wicked and devilish. Then he's moving, driving in and out of me with a power and control that leaves me breathless and shaking. He places his mouth on my neck, his lips and tongue dancing over the sensitive skin.

Another orgasm is cresting, bigger and even more relentless. All I can do is hang on, my nails digging into his taut skin, and submit to an electric pleasure that brings every nerve ending to life.

I sob out my climax, my vision going white. His hands grip my ass tighter and his cock starts hitting a new spot inside me—

"Oh my *God*," I scream as another orgasm wrecks me.

He lets out a low rumble and then goes absolutely rigid as his own climax hits.

He collapses on me, but then props himself up on his elbows so he doesn't crush me. I cup his masked face between my palms and take a moment to settle my breathing. My heart is going a thousand beats a minute.

We share a leisurely afterglow kiss and then he rolls off, landing heavily next to me. He's puffing too, but doesn't struggle the way I do. He gets up and goes to the bathroom. There's a loud curse, and he returns to the bed within a second, looking at me with his mouth absolutely flat.

"What's wrong?"

"The condom broke." His voice is calm, but there is a hint of oh-shit and please-don't-panic-and-scream in his tone.

"Oh. Uh... Well, are you clean?"

He opens and closes his mouth. "Yes," he says after a moment. "Are you?"

"Yes. So we have nothing to worry about."

"We don't have *one* thing to worry about. Preventing STDs isn't the only thing condoms do."

"I can't have kids," I say in my most nonchalant voice, then shrug to hide the awkwardness of having to share a little too much information. Which is weird because we just had sex, but...

He shuts his mouth so fast his teeth click. "Oh. I..." He clears his throat. "I'm sorry."

I laugh at how uncomfortable he is about my revelation. "I don't generally think about it. I'm only telling you so you don't worry about a surprise baby."

He nods. "Okay. Well...thank you."

I start to get up, but he catches my arm. "What are you doing?"

I should tell him I'm leaving. We're done having sex, which was great. But it'll be awkward in the morning, when we'll have to unmask and there won't be the cover of night to lend a dreamy atmosphere to what we've done.

At the same time, I'm loath to leave his bed. He's... Well, he gave me the best damn orgasms I've ever in my life. And it's a shame to end our time so soon.

When I don't respond, he murmurs, "Stay a little longer." It's like he knows exactly what's going through my mind.

And I can't say no.

"Okay," I say, and lie back down, only to have him take me into his arms and cuddle, giving me the kind of warm comfort I've never experienced with a man before.

9

SIERRA

"You made it!" I say as Ellie walks into my suite a little before nine a.m. I'm in the bathrobe I put on after sneaking out of the Midnight God's suite on the floor above. My hair's still damp from a quick shower, but I'm feeling too lazy to blow dry it. Given the humidity in New Orleans, my curls won't stay tamed anyway.

"I know! Finally!" Ellie huffs dramatically, bending over like she's just hiked a tall hill. Then she straightens up and adjusts her glasses. Today, she's wearing black plastic ones. They don't have a prescription—her vision is perfect. But she claims they make her face look slimmer and sexier.

I personally think men who don't approach her because of the glasses—or lack thereof—don't deserve her. Ellie is gorgeous, with her dark brown hair curling effortlessly around her shoulders. Her eyes match the color of her hair perfectly, and the bright fire-engine-red lipstick she loves to wear does magical things to her mouth, drawing your attention to it like nothing else.

Since she values comfort above all else, she's in a stretchy blue shirt, purple yoga pants and sneakers. She leans in and hugs me tightly.

"Sorry I missed your big celebration night," she says.

"Hey, it wasn't your fault." I hug her back.

"I'm *so* mad I missed the party." She pulls back. "It must've been wild. How late did you stay? You still have a mask outline on your face."

I touch my face and feel the indentation from the edge of the mask I fell asleep in. "I actually didn't stay that late. It's just that I kept the mask on all night."

"How come?"

My cheeks heat. "It's...a long and exciting story."

"Argh! I missed all the fun. I want to sue that damn airline!"

"If you do, let me know and I'll join the suit."

"I'm adding it to my to-do list." She makes an exaggerated show of tapping her phone. "Now, you need to tell me everything."

Laughing, I pick up the hotel phone. "I will. But let's order breakfast first. I'm starving."

We order scrambled eggs, bagels and coffee and sit down on the couch. The ottoman in front of me reminds me of how the Midnight God took care of me last night. And protected me from Todd.

I already miss my oh-so-hot savior. Would it be weird if I went upstairs and knocked on his door? Asked him for his name and number? Or would it look clingy and desperate?

"So," Ellie says, pulling me out of my impulsive thoughts, "what happened?"

"Well, first of all, *Todd* happened."

She gasps. "*What?*"

I give her a blow-by-blow of the confrontation, with all the details I can recall.

"Oh my God..." Ellie's eyes are huge as her fingers cover her mouth. "I didn't know he could get physical like that."

"Me either. I was totally shocked that he grabbed me and wouldn't let go. He's never done that before."

"Guess he's super desperate to have you undo the divorce." She does an as-if eye roll. "Why didn't he put in the effort to make you feel special before? It would've been easier."

"Ha. Who knows?"

"So how did you get him to respect your boundaries?" Ellie looks at me. "I'm not saying you aren't a strong woman, but Todd's not a small guy."

"Well—"

The doorbell cuts me off. I stand up and have the bellboy set up breakfast for us on the coffee table. I sign the slip and shut the door firmly behind him.

Ellie is pouring two cups of coffee. "Caffeine will help you tell it better." She winks.

Laughing, I take the proffered mug and sip the hot brew. "Oh, this is good. Okay, so anyway…" A small sigh escapes my parted lips. The Midnight God's just so perfect. "This guy came to my rescue."

The heroic gesture of saving me—a damsel in distress—and carrying me here in his arms. A gorgeously sculpted physique. And the most amazing orgasms of my life. I know Silicone Dream makes the best toys in the world, guaranteed to give you awesome Os, but— loath though I am to say it—he is superior.

The only man I've ever met who could make that claim.

"Oooohh…" Her eyes sparkle. "You're blushing."

I clear my throat. "Okay, fine, so you caught me mooning over him. He's hot. What am I supposed to do except blush?"

Grinning, she does a come-on motion with her fingers. "Give it to me. You know I want to hear every delicious morsel of detail."

Laughing, I go over everything, except for the sex part. She doesn't need details on that, except that it was amazing. Just freakin' fantastic. My lady parts tingle from just talking about the night.

"Wait, so Todd never gave you a good orgasm?" Ellie says.

"I mean, he gave me some orgasms, but they weren't anything to brag about. Our vibrators do better. A *lot* better."

She makes a what-a-loser face. "Then why does he act like he's some hotshot sex machine?"

"Delusion? He thinks he's God's gift to English poetry as well."

She scoffs. "Instead of hiring him to teach poetry, Wollstonecraft College should've hired him as a subject for a study on delusional narcissists." She bites into her bagel, generously smeared with cream cheese. "So do you have a picture of this hottie?"

"No," I say. "We kept things anonymous. That's why I still have the mask marks on my face, because I kept it on all night. So did he. I had to take it off when I woke up because my skin was so irritated and itchy."

Ellie doesn't seem too thrilled with my explanation, but nods anyway. "Name?"

I shrug.

"Okay, hold on. At least tell me you exchanged numbers."

"Uh..."

She looks at me like I've lobotomized myself with a steak knife. "*What?* Why? How are you going to get in touch with him for more orgasms?"

"Because. It's obvious he isn't from SoCal."

"How can you tell?"

"Ellie, he wore a suit to the party. Nobody from SoCal would've come to a masquerade in a suit."

"Hmm." She taps her chin thoughtfully. "Okay, that's a good point. Still, you could do weekend dates, especially if his penis is that magical."

"That'd be taking us into relationship territory. I'm not looking for a long-distance we-only-meet-on-weekends thing. I want somebody I can see every evening and share moments with."

"God invented video chat for a reason, Sierra."

"It's not the same. You can't cuddle with your phone."

"Ah, but you *can* have phone *sex*," Ellie says.

I pause for a second. Yes, that'd be hot, but I'm not letting sexual attraction derail me from what I want, even when it comes with incredibly good sexual chemistry. "That's not the same thing either. I'm looking for somebody to share my life with, not just have sex on weekends when our schedules work out."

Ellie doesn't look convinced. "If you're sure. But I still think you should've gotten his name and number. Just in case."

10

GRIFFIN

–two weeks later

"It really hurts when my dad just over*looks* me like that," says a young woman on a podcast one of my brothers Noah recommended. She's almost sobbing.

Lady, thank your lucky stars! I think as I drive to Wollstonecraft College, where I teach econometrics with a great deal of annoyance and resignation.

"It's like he doesn't even know I exist," the woman adds.

Oh, cry me a river. I pull out champagne and make toasts when my father forgets my existence. If I could, I'd make him think I was dead. Which might be possible if he were on his own, but he has a pesky assistant who reminds him of the fact that all seven of his sons are still alive.

Which is why I'm getting another bullshit text, which Siri dutifully reads out.

–Dad: So we all agree that this year's birthday gift will be a baby, correct?

Siri's delivery is flat and monotone, but there's nothing flat and monotonous about Joey, the pesky assistant. He has an unnatural fervor to please my father and is also the one who sends texts on my dad's behalf. The oh-so-important Theodore Preston Lasker would never deign to actually compose his own messages, even to his sons.

I ignore the message because it isn't worth any time or energy. Dad apparently sent hookers to my brothers over the weekend, but somehow forgot about me. Hopefully he'll continue to forget. I can find my own bed partners, thank you very much.

Like Purple Girl?

I frown a little. It's been two weeks, but the memory of that night still has my blood boiling. It wasn't just the sex, as amazing as that was. It was everything else about her—the way she let things roll off her shoulders. The way she focused on *us*, rather than what I could do for her career. The unabashed way she clung to me.

Why did she have to sneak out while I was asleep? Women don't usually pull disappearing acts on me.

What would you have done if you'd known, though? Handcuffed her to the bed?

The image that follows is hot—her hands pulled up and her lush body open for my pleasure and hers. But before the notion can harden my dick further, I kill it.

It was just a one-night stand. So what if it was the best damn sex I've ever had?

She left, and I left. I kept our masks as souvenirs from our encounter, but I shouldn't relive the night so often. I'm not going to see Purple Girl again. She could be anywhere by now. Even if my octogenarian next-door neighbor, Mrs. Kuznetsova, passes away and Purple Girl buys the house and moves in, I wouldn't know, since we didn't bother to exchange names.

You exchanged plenty of bodily fluids...

Ah, geez. I have things to do today, and none of them involves Purple Girl. Or this inopportune erection.

Besides, it isn't like me to waste mental energy on something that can't be. People overcoming enormous odds to find each other only happens in fairytales. And even then, the stories are ludicrous.

Just look at Cinderella. Prince Charming didn't get her name despite the fact that they danced at a *non-mask* ball. The only thing he had was that slipper. The man was so stupid he couldn't recognize her without her fancy makeup or dress. And yet, even though she was the last woman to try on the slipper, he got the right girl.

Statistically speaking, either the kingdom had fewer than fifty women or Cinderella had very peculiarly shaped and sized feet—which wouldn't bode well for their future offspring. And given Prince Charming's obsession with that slipper, I suspect he had a foot fetish.

Then again, of course she would have been the last woman to try it on. Because Charming would have stopped looking when he found her.

My logical econometrics perspective can be a killjoy at times.

The second I park my midnight-blue Prius in the faculty lot, a tall, dark-haired kid rushes toward me. A few sheets of paper flap as he pumps his arms. "Professor Lasker!" he bellows.

I don't think he realizes how loud he is. He's one of my most oblivious students.

"I want to talk to you about the midterm!"

Ah, of course. Students bristling with outrage over their grades are undoubtedly crawling around in front of my office like angry ants. It's a semiannual ritual—the office hours immediately following posting midterm grades is when I get the most visits from students. If they'd spend half that zeal on actually studying the material, we could skip the unpleasant discussion.

This kid is trying to cut the line and ambush me in the parking lot. *I don't think so.*

"Your grade stands," I say in my most professorial tone, then start walking.

He follows, torso twisted awkwardly so he can face me better. "What? You don't even know what I'm about to say!"

"You want to contest your grade."

"Yeah, but you don't understand. I worked so hard!"

"We all do, Mr. Tanner." The name fits—this kid had to have dedicated most of his semester to getting that golden-copper tan. Too bad he didn't apply the same vigor to his coursework.

"Yeah, but see, I need this to major in economics!"

By *this*, he means a decent grade in econometrics. You need at least a B- for the course to have it count toward your major.

"My dad's counting on me getting this degree," he adds, like that will make a difference.

"There's always the final," I point out blandly.

"But the midterm's worth thirty percent of the grade." His incessant whining makes me briefly fantasize about gagging him with the midterm he's clutching.

"And the final is worth seventy. Your time will be better spent on mastering the fundamentals of statistics, because those are your weak points. Breaking your habit of napping during class would also help."

His face turns red. It's likely that I have the dubious honor of being the first person in his life to drop a fact bomb on him.

I know his type. SoCal golden boy from a rich family who can do no wrong. Get into trouble? No worries. Mommy and Daddy's money will fix it for you.

I give him a thin smile. "If you don't have anything to say except how much you need me to give you a better grade you didn't earn, you should probably go now."

"But—"

"Every word out of you will cost you a point on the final." I know for a fact he can't afford that.

His fist tightens around his test, the bright red C- catching my eyes as he does so. Huffing, he walks away stiffly. I'd bet my entire investment portfolio that he's going to waste the next two weeks complaining about me and my class to anyone who'll listen.

It won't help. He can't switch to another class, since I'm the only one teaching econometrics. Most professors at Wollstonecraft hate teaching the course because of how frequently this sort of encounter with students happens. I don't like it either, but I don't have the seniority to avoid it.

I reach Fullilove Hall, which houses the econ department, and take the stairs up to my office on the second floor. There's a long line snaking down the hall. At least eighty percent of the class is here. The other twenty received a B- or better, and they're probably too relieved and scared to argue their grades, in case I change my mind.

Without making eye contact with any of them—their pitiable, pleading gazes already feel smothering, and I want to Hulk-smash the lot before they say a word—I march straight to my office door and unlock it. I open the door and turn around.

"Who's first?" I say.

"Me!"

I frown at the young woman to my left. She's somewhat short, her long red hair curled artfully and flowing over her shoulders. She wearing a trench coat, which is a bit odd, but then, college kids get desperate when they forget to do their laundry. And it is windy today.

The problem isn't just her outfit, though. I don't remember seeing her before. I know every student in my class, but nobody with a button nose like hers or a mouth that looks like it's just gotten an injection. It might be the makeup. She's wearing tons of it, including fake lashes so long they look like dead butterfly antennae. Maybe she's considering switching her major to drama.

"All right, come in," I say, jerking my chin.

Shooting me a saucy grin, she saunters inside, her hips swishing left and right in what's no doubt supposed to be a sexy walk.

I leave the door open and sit down at my desk.

"You sure you don't want to close that?" the girl says without taking the empty seat in front of the desk.

"No. It's my policy not to close it." I gesture for her to sit down.

She blinks, as though an open door is an unexpected obstacle. She's definitely not cut out for my class. "Why?" She pouts.

"It discourages some students from doing imprudent things." Such as coming on to me at the beginning of the semester. It's the face. Huxley swears I can do better with modeling if I ever get fed up with teaching, and my five other brothers agree.

No, thank you. I don't want fame or fortune. Fame comes with notoriety, and fortune… Well, I have plenty.

The redhead purses her mouth, then shrugs. "Suit yourself."

"So what's your name? I don't remember seeing you in class, and it's too late to sign up for the course."

"Sandy." She smiles.

"Why don't you sit down?" I'm getting tired of looking up at her.

"Not yet." Her smile grows wider. "But I will soon, Professor Lasker."

The overt sexual purr in her voice makes the hair on the back of my neck bristle. My brothers' furious ranting over the weekend flashes through my mind…

Oh, shit! Dad sent me a fucking hooker!

I jump to my feet, but it's too late. She's already undone the belt and tossed the coat on the floor. Now it's just her in her heels. Her body is exactly Dad's type—skinny, with huge boobs, and not a strand of hair anywhere. Although I can't see from this angle, her ass must be exceptional, too.

A collective gasp and a few baritone *holy shit*s come from the students outside who are close enough to see what's going on. My first instinct is to slam the damned door shut, but that would only fuel speculation and gossip. Besides, it's too late; they're already pulling out their phones. This incident will hit social media before I can get this crazy woman out of my office!

The redhead—Sandy—comes around the desk. It's surprising how fast she can move in those heels. I jump back before she can wrap her tentacles—I mean, *arms*—around me.

"Out! Out before I call the police!" I say, pointing at the door. I'm going to *murder* Dad! I swear I will.

"The *police*? Why? Don't you want to be a star?"

"No!" *I'd rather commit patricide!*

She keeps coming for me. I weave around her—she's nowhere near as quick as my sparring partners—and grab the trench coat. Quickly, I wrap it around her, back of the coat against her chest, and tie the sleeves behind her in a makeshift straitjacket as she struggles and complains. Finally, she's secured. I don't care if my students can see parts of her bare ass as long as she's restrained.

I look at a pizza-faced frat boy who's recording the entire incident. His tongue is sticking out between his lips. "You! Call 911!"

His eyes glued to his phone, he doesn't hear me.

"Mr. Porter, if you want to discuss your grade with me, you'd better call 911 *now*."

His eyes shift as he finally registers that I'm talking to him. The desire to continue to film her ass and the need to plead his case with me rage a furious battle, every blow reflected on his ridiculously transparent face.

"*What* is going on here?"

I squeeze my eyes shut. That's Charles Phillips's stentorian voice.

This day can't get any worse.

11

GRIFFIN

"I don't even know what to say." Charles has traded *stentorian* in for *ponderously important*.

After all, he's the head of the econ department.

Right now, he's seated at the desk in his office, which is four times the size of mine, his thick, Vienna-wiener fingers steepled. His over-gelled wig stays rigidly on his skull to cover the huge bald spot on his bowling-ball head, and his cheap charcoal-gray suit sits slightly crooked on his body, saggy from decades of parking his ass in a chair. Behind the rimless glasses he loves so much—they make him appear "intellectual"—his beady brown eyes are judging.

Not that it isn't undeserved. It's just that *I* didn't earn that judgment.

The price you pay for being Ted Lasker's son.

Having a Hollywood movie producer dad isn't as cool as people assume. I'd rather be the son of an occupant of some premium real estate under a bridge or pier.

"She probably made a mistake," I explain in my calmest voice. "Most likely got lost or confused."

I'm going to murder Joey. If he was going to send me a hooker, he should've done so at *my place*, just like he did with all my other brothers. This is blatant discrimination.

That bastard knows how important it is to maintain a certain image, especially in my profession. Being seen as a disreputable hooker-banger would be a death sentence.

I wager he's still holding a grudge over that time I told him—actually Dad—to fuck off. But that was deserved.

"A mistake, you say. Mmm." Charles gazes up at the ceiling for a moment. "According to some of the students, the woman referred to you as 'Professor Lasker.' That does sound rather specific."

"I didn't hire her, if that's what you're implying." There is a ball of pure acid lodged in my throat. Sexual misconduct can be viewed as just cause for loss of tenure—and termination. If I become unemployed, I'm going to run Dad over with a car. Not my Tesla, but my Prius. Dad isn't worth banging a Tesla up for. "If I had, I wouldn't have asked her to come by during my office hours. And most especially not right after the midterm grades were handed out."

Charles nods ponderously. "Of course. That does make sense. Still, it would be difficult to let this go without some...stipulations."

"Such as?" I ask.

"We could call a departmental meeting about the incident, but as you say...perhaps you weren't entirely to blame. So a less, ah, publicly visible act of atonement might be fitting... Not that you would be admitting that you had anything to actually atone for, of course. But something I could hold up in the event that someone decided to make an issue out of this little peccadillo. Some small service, say, that you could perform to restore the dignity of the economics department."

Dread knots my gut. When Charles says "service," what he really means is indentured servitude. "Such as...?"

"As it happens, the Fullilove family would like one of the professors here to bring their students over and do a case study for the company."

You have to be kidding. "This is an econ department, not undergraduate business. We don't generally do case studies."

"You're correct, of course. But finance and marketing students shouldn't be the only ones learning about how real life works. *Our* students deserve the same opportunity. Besides, we can't overlook the importance of the Fullilove family to the college." Charles gives me an I'm-sure-you-take-my-meaning smile.

How could I forget? Every time I teach my class, it's inside Fullilove Hall. It's nauseating how Charles—and everyone else—acts like simply because the family gave some money to the college, we should all kowtow and kiss their billionaire feet. Screw that.

The Fullilove family *bought* respect and their name on the building, just like Dad did at a film and acting school by donating a tiny fraction of his bank account. It's a shortcut cop-out, a cheap way to hide how corrupt and disgusting they really are. They're beneath my notice.

"Don't you think the case would be better handled by a professor teaching law and economics or financial economics? Or maybe behavioral economics? The economics of marketing?"

"Perhaps, but they already have their semesters planned out."

It's all I can do to rein in a scream. "And I don't?"

"Not that you don't, but you can probably be more flexible. Those professors are set in their ways."

Right. They've all been at the college for over a decade as tenured professors. So let's mess with the newly tenured lackey.

"Also, of course, none of them have recently suffered the embarrassment of having a professional, ah, escort in their office."

I sigh. "How about Benson? The micro-econ guy we hired last year?"

"He's too junior. It would offend the family."

I get it now. Charles wants somebody who's senior enough to satisfy the Fulliloves, but not so senior that they'll put up a fight.

"Actually, I would've mentioned this sooner if there hadn't been a mix-up," he adds in a just-between-you-and-me tone, leaning forward a little. "The Fulliloves' request apparently went to Chuck in the English department, who had no clue what it was about."

Chuck Phillips is the new head of that department, replacing Dr. Monroe, who retired last year. Chuck and Charles sometimes get mistaken for each other by new admins and support staff, given that they both have the same last name. If you meet them once, though, you'll never make the mistake again. Chuck is a nice, unassuming man who is rail thin from an inability to sit still. He practically vibrates with nervous energy, while Charles likes to appear as ponderous as a sloth the size of a mammoth.

"But what company needs an opinion from an English major?"

Charles laughs. He believes economics is superior to all the other departments we have at the college—excepting only the hard sciences.

"No one, obviously," I respond. "Unless the company wants to publish a collection of public domain poems."

Charles laughs again. "Just so. I'm sure the family's letter looked like Greek to Chuck. But be that as it may, it's a great opportunity for your students. And for us as well."

I wait for him to explain. I don't see how it's an opportunity for "us," and I can't fathom who this "us" is.

"They might be persuaded to fund a brand-new center for economics research."

Oh, for God's sake. He's been seething with envy over the sparkling new economics research lab at Orville College, where his archrival is the head of the department. He'd give up both balls to get the same for Wollstonecraft, not that that would be much of a sacrifice.

Charles sighs, the sound full of hope. "The Fulliloves never forget our kindness. They're a charming family, and the business they want your help with is as well."

I rub my forehead. Essentially, I have no choice. If I turn him down, he'll call a meeting to discuss the hooker incident. And nothing good will come of that. "What is this company?"

"Silicone Dream."

Silicone? "What sort of business is it?"

"Something high tech," he says vaguely. "But they're very socially conscious." He smiles, showing teeth like a hungry shark.

If Charles meant to reassure me, he's failed. All I can think is how much I'm going to hate acting like I care about a shitty tech company that isn't even named right—*silicone, really?*—or couldn't make it in *Silicon* Valley.

"Is that all?" I ask with the bland smile I've perfected over the years.

"Yes, I believe so. I have high hopes."

And they'll remain hopes, because I'm not going to toady to the Fulliloves to get funding for a research center. Charles can do the kowtowing himself if he's that desperate.

He nods, and I get up and leave.

I do my best to control my temper as I make my way back to my office. *Must. Not. Storm. Back.* Instead, I walk like a civilized human being who hasn't just been ambushed by a hooker *and* the head of his department.

My students apparently dispersed while I was talking with Charles. Not surprising. They correctly assumed there won't be any discussion of grades today.

I stalk into my office and shut the door firmly but quietly. There are other professors on the floor, and they probably heard what happened. I don't want to give them anything else to gossip about over afternoon coffee.

God damn it. This is not how I wanted the day to go, getting roped into some bullshit I am not interested in.

Once I'm ensconced in the privacy of my office, I start to pace, furious. Somebody needs to pay. Ideally with blood...although punching Dad out would create headlines, and I don't need any more behavioral issues to get me into trouble.

Physical violence against a famous Hollywood movie producer and getting arrested and having that splashed all over the national media? Definitely grounds for the college to revoke my tenure and fire me.

So instead, I go for the second-best option. I call Dad.

"Hello?" comes Joey's annoyingly smug, I'm-really-important-because-my-boss-is voice.

"Joey," I growl. The bastard knows who's calling—and why.

"Oh, Griffin. Hi! How are you?" he asks perkily.

"*How am I?* Is that supposed to be a joke?"

"Just being polite. You don't have to be such a stick-in-the-mud."

He's baiting me. He thinks he's safe because he isn't within physical reach.

"If politeness matters so much to you, you shouldn't have sent that hooker," I spit out between clenched teeth.

"She's not a *hooker*," he says with asperity. "She's an *aspiring actress*. You would've known that if you'd tried to be open-minded and talked to her like a civilized person."

"Are you saying it's my fault that I mistook her for a hooker, despite the fact that she got buck naked in front of me and my class?" *What's the probability of getting caught if I hire a hit man to throw Joey over his own balcony?* I wonder if there's an average market price.

A pause. "Is it?"

"*No!*" I immediately clamp my mouth shut—no need for people to hear me screaming in my office. I'm already on everyone's radar because of what happened today. So instead, I fantasize about pulverizing Joey's already not-so-pretty face into putty with Muay Thai knee-strikes. Permanently downgrade him from a *four* to a *one*.

"I told you your father wanted a baby for his birthday. You're the one who was being difficult. I was simply trying to help you provide him with the gift he wants." The slimeball is talking to me in the same tone I use on particularly lazy and dim-witted students who nonetheless believe they deserve an A in my class.

"I—am—not—giving—him—a—baby!"

Joey sighs. "You see? Unnecessarily difficult."

God save me from the drama king and his idiot assistant. "It's called being normal and respectable."

"Look. Your behavior with your father has been extraordinarily contrary. You won't do anything he'd like you to do. You won't give him a baby, you won't sing for him, what am I supposed to do?"

"I am not singing like a child in a school play for his birthday party." I had enough of being paraded around like that when I was younger to gratify Mom's narcissism. Finally, one day I refused to hit a single note, and I haven't sung since. "I'm not some *thing* he can use to score points against his rivals, especially Josh." Dad has this weird fetish with Josh Singer. When Noah made the mistake of asking about it, Dad went into a long and nonsensical story about how Josh is vile, but then he contradicted the narrative at least twenty times. Basically, Dad hates Josh just because, not for any good reason. I refuse to be a pawn in his weird competition that only he—and Joey—understand.

"It isn't about Josh Singer," Joey says stiffly.

"'Josh has a son who sounds like Sinatra.' Your words, not mine."

Joey huffs. It's a sign he's upset that I pointed out his lie.

My satisfaction is short-lived. A muscle under my left eye starts twitching. I put my hand over it and press.

"You're being impossible," Joey says, "but I guess there's nothing to be done. You're just too uptight to make your father happy one day out of the year."

Oh, Joey, personal attacks are too predictable. Dad has no right to feel this way since he couldn't make himself available one day out of our lifetimes, when we graduated from college.

Joey starts to say something else, but I hang up. I'm not listening to any more of his garbage. And I have some statistics to look up about getting away with commissioning a murder.

12

SIERRA

I guide my Ferrari along the driveway leading to Ted Lasker's enormous mansion, where a Hollywood birthday party is taking place. Grandma was friends with him, and she introduced me some years ago.

He's an interesting man. Successful. Has a great sense of how to tell a good story that gets people talking and coming back for another viewing in theaters. He invited me to a few movie premieres, and I went when I could with Grandma.

After she passed away, I started to receive invitations to his birthday parties as well. Apparently, Ted thinks of me as his own daughter. Sweet of him to do so, although I don't see how sincere or deep that "feeling" can be, since we haven't spent much time together while Grandma was alive.

Although he sent me birthday party invitations for the past three years, I've never attended. The first time I received one, I was getting married, and the subsequent two years were occupied with wedding anniversaries.

But this year I'm divorced! So why not enjoy the day by going to a fancy Hollywood birthday party?

Ted Lasker's ivory home is opulent, with lots of turrets and terraces. It would remind me of the New Orleans masquerade party venue if it weren't for the fact that this place is a bit too shiny and slick.

Wonder if the Midnight God will be here...

I shake my head and snort. What are the odds?

The straw hat I'm wearing has a wide brim. I push it down so the breeze doesn't rip it off my head and turn my attention back to the mansion. The windows are arched and spotless. The lawns are cut evenly, bushes trimmed just so. Contemporary statues of people in sexually suggestive poses dot the garden. Tastefully done, since they aren't overtly displaying any genitalia or breasts. Their faces are sort of weird—not because the artists did a terrible job but because I'm not a fan of statue expressions. All those blank eyes above expressive mouths. Whatever they're supposed to emote always appears fake.

The eyes are the window to the soul for a reason.

I walk into the foyer. Black and white squares stretch out like a chessboard. An orange-haired man is at the entrance with a tablet. His huge forehead reminds me of Tweety, if you bleached him and made him less cute. Guess he isn't joining the party, since he's in a teal shirt and jeans. The invitation specifically said we should wear bathing suits, and I have a bikini on underneath a pink kimono.

He looks me up and down, then pins me with a haughty green gaze. "You are...?"

"Sierra Fullilove." I smile.

"I'm Joey, Ted Lasker's *primary and chief* assistant." He introduces himself likes he's announcing the Queen of England. "Give me a moment." He checks something on his tablet. "There you are." He lifts his head and shoots me a perfunctory smile. "Presents go there."

"Okay." I put a wrapped box on the huge pile he indicated.

"Enjoy." He waggles short fingers, dismissing me.

What an odd man. But maybe he's tired from having to check everyone in by himself.

I walk down the air-conditioned hall and note suits of armor and heads of horses. Another reminder of the mansion in New Orleans.

And the Midnight God. Actually, the only thing I'm really thinking about is the Midnight God. *Why didn't I listen to Ellie?* I could've gone back upstairs and gotten his name and number instead of sitting on my butt and telling myself it wasn't meant to be.

Even if he isn't local... I don't know. Maybe we could've texted. Or something. Or maybe I could've opened a satellite office in his town. Anything is possible.

What I did was akin to passing up a fifty-percent-off sale on the most amazing chocolate in the world.

Wait, that's not right. The most amazing *vibrator*.

Although he's more like a dildo...

When I reach the pool outside, a blonde in a bikini rushes over. "Hey, want a balloon?" She waves a vagina-shaped red balloon in front of me. "We're about to have a game, and Team V needs another player."

"Um. No?" I want to find Ted and wish him happy birthday before getting roped into playing some game.

"You sure?"

"Maybe later. I need to say hello to Ted first."

Her eyes widen. "You're friends with *Ted*?"

"Yeah. Aren't you?" Why else would she be here?

"Well, yeah, sort of. But could you introduce me?" She steps forward, invading my personal space.

I take half a step back. "Um. Yeah." A rabid determination fills her gaze. I don't think Ted would appreciate an introduction. "But later, okay? I need to grab a drink first."

"Okay. Don't forget. I'm Madelaine."

"Madelaine. Absolutely. Got it." I make a mental note to avoid this area and the crowd, then step onto the small path to my right to avoid talking to any of her vag-balloon friends.

The walkway is shaded. Splashes and laughing shrieks come from the pool. I wonder how I'm supposed to find Ted in the crowd. Although it's still early, there are at least a hundred people here.

"This isn't funny, Calvin!" comes a sharp reprimand. "I'm your girlfriend, not some one-night stand!"

I turn toward the sound and see a stunning blonde with flowing hair and a gorgeous bee-stung mouth. She's wearing an ocean-blue bikini, and her body is flawless, not an ounce of excess fat anywhere, even though her breasts are full. She's talking on a phone, but her blue eyes connect with mine. A frisson of unease dances up my spine.

I start to look away. But before I can, her eyes fill with tears.

Oh no.

"How could you be so cruel?" Her chin trembles. "I thought you'd be here, by my side."

I feel like the worst human being for turning away, although common sense says I should, since she's obviously having an issue with her boyfriend, and relationships aren't my forte. Hell, I just got divorced.

"Fine. Be that way. By the time you come crawling back, it'll be too late." She lowers the phone, then looks at me tragically. "I'm so sorry you had to witness that."

I look around, wondering if she's talking to somebody else. But nope. I force a smile, hoping it doesn't look as awkward as I feel. "It's not a problem."

"It's so difficult to find the right man these days." A tear slowly rolls down her cheek.

I have to respect how feminine and pretty she is when she's crying. When I cry, my face turns blotchy and my nose runs like a broken faucet.

"Tell me about it," I say, trying to help her calm down. "If it were easy, I wouldn't be alone."

"I knew you'd understand." Despite the tears in her voice, she sounds gorgeous. No stuffy, nasal whining from her.

"Of course."

"The world is full of good people. We just need to be strong for each other."

She takes my hand and pulls me to a bench by the path. She sits down and pats the empty spot next to her. "I didn't catch your name," she says sweetly.

"Sierra Fullilove," I say politely. She's probably just too distraught over her jerk-tastic boyfriend to remember that we haven't introduced ourselves.

"What a lovely name." She smiles. "I'm Rachel Griffin."

13

GRIFFIN

Instead of spending my weekend productively, I'm forced yet again to waste time thanks to my parents. In this case, it's my father.

The hell of it is, there's nothing I can do about it. Sending me a hooker at work is the least of what he's capable of if I don't attend his ridiculous birthday party.

I sit in my Tesla and glare at the road. The only way out would be if my EV malfunctioned in a significant way. I'd be ecstatic if its battery burst into flames.

Unfortunately, my car doesn't cooperate. It drives like a dream.

Fucking modern engineering.

I park the Tesla in front of Dad's mansion and pull my Rams cap low. My wraparound sunglasses cover a large chunk of my features, and I'm sporting two days' worth of stubble to make sure I look nothing like my usual professorial self. Thousands of photos and videos are going to be plastered all over social media before the day is over, and I'll be damned if anybody's going to recognize me.

I climb out and clench my teeth at the sight of the porno statues in the yard. The surrounding shrubs have been trimmed low to ensure everyone has an unobstructed view. Dad calls them "art." But just because something's made of marble and bronze doesn't mean it's art. I could've made a dick going into a vagina with bronze-colored clay in one afternoon and sold it to my father for a million bucks.

The main structure is huge, with ivory walls and turrets the architect added because Dad wanted something "classy." The place is outrageously large—far too big for one person. And the size isn't to accommodate his seven sons and their mothers. We were shipped off to Europe, where boarding schools are plentiful, as soon as we could talk. All Dad had to do was write checks and claim he was giving us the best education available.

He saw us once in a while when he happened to be in Europe on vacation and could spare an hour or two out of his debauched schedule. Every time he visited, he made sure to stage a scene to embarrass and humiliate us in front of everyone. It got so bad that I tried to give myself pneumonia by staying out all night in the cold with wet hair when I knew he was coming.

We were allowed to return to the States when we were old enough. Mainly because it would have looked weird for him to keep us in Europe when the "providing my children with the best education in the world" excuse no longer worked.

I walk up the steps to the main door. It's left open in a gesture of so-called welcome, probably Joey's doing. He likes to be able to see who's coming so he can categorize them by importance and treat them accordingly.

The bastard looks smug and happy in the foyer, tapping away on his tablet. He's in a teal shirt and jeans, his orange hair slicked back from his flour-pasty face. He probably keeps himself pale on purpose. With more of a tan, people might mistake him for one of those Star Trek Ferengi.

Joey looks up. His green eyes meet mine and immediately widen. He flinches, his shoulders rising high enough to touch his ears. He clutches his tablet like a shield in front of him.

That's right, Joey. Who's brave enough to run his mouth now? My eyes on him, I stalk toward him.

"Bathroom break!" he squeaks. He turns around and trots into the house, turning the first corner and then peeking around the wall at me from a position of relative safety.

Coward. On the other hand, he's seen videos of my kickboxing matches. He asked me how long it'd take for me to be able to kick like me, and I told him it might happen when cows start fucking pigs.

Furthermore, my current outfit of a white tank top and black swim trunks probably didn't help alleviate his terror. Joey seems to believe that if I'm in a dress shirt and slacks, I can't get violent with him. But I could kick his ass wearing a straitjacket.

I walk toward where he was standing, noting the artistically arranged pile of wrapped presents. What wouldn't I give to kick the bunch, just to see Joey's reaction?

Actually...I'm going to do just that. Who's going to stop me? Nobody from the college is around to see me vent my ire, and Joey deserves it after pulling that hooker stunt and mouthing off to me afterward.

I casually snap a foot out, aiming for a large box near the bottom. The box goes flying and the colorful tower collapses with a loud crash.

Ah, I sigh inwardly with satisfaction.

"*Oh shit, oh shit!*" Joey scuttles back in, his cheeks bright red. His eyes start to go a little wild. "What the hell, man?"

"Sorry. I slipped."

"*Slipped?*" He glares at me like I just kicked a dying puppy. "You did that on purpose!"

"It's the floor. Too highly waxed." I gesture at the gleaming black and white tiles. "If my reflexes were any poorer, I would've fallen and broken something. Then I would've had to sue Dad for the injury."

"Nobody falls down and breaks something!"

"That isn't true," I say in my most authoritative tone. "More than ninety-five percent of hip fractures are caused by domestic falls."

"How the hell would you know something like that?"

"It's my job to know statistics." I start walking inside, casually kicking aside a few more presents.

"Argh! Asshole!"

"Shouldn't have sent a stripper to my school, Joey." I stride away casually, feeling better. Joey deserves *much* worse, but it's the best I can do without risking an arrest.

I march past four suits of armor and four alabaster horse heads, two on each side and lined up like mortal enemies ready to charge across the chessboard floor. Although I'm moving casually, my senses are on full alert in case Joey's arranged for another, last-ditch-effort hooker. Joey's mission in life is giving my father what he wants, and Dad hasn't given up on grandbabies. Not yet, anyway.

Instead of wasting money on getting him a gift, I should've paid for a human biology lecture. That way he'd learn that nobody can create a newborn baby overnight.

Aside from some odious orgy murals on the ceiling, the inside of the mansion is tasteful enough. But when you have a sensible team of interior decorators and as much money as my father, it isn't that difficult. The real test of Dad's taste is the pool area. He tells Joey what he wants for his birthday bash three months ahead of time every year, and every year the party becomes more ridiculously outrageous.

Finally, I walk through the French doors that lead to the pool area. The mansion wraps around the pool in a U and tall hedges are on the fourth side, providing privacy. That's why Dad feels comfortable letting go here. He's forgotten about smart phones in the clutches of his guests, people desperate to film whatever they think is going to go viral and trying to post a clip before anybody else.

Loud shrieks and laughter pierce the air. I already want to cover my ears and pretend I'm anywhere but here.

Barely dressed people run around with the balloons tied to their bodies; a few have them tied to their heads. I realize that half the balloons are mouths and the other half are vaginas. All of them are covered in a disgusting white goo, which has the visual consistency and scent of...

...*ejaculate?*

Where did *that* come from?

I don't have to wonder long. A guy in red and blue trunks whoops and slams a large, flesh-colored ball to my right. They're connected to a huge shaft shaped like an erect penis that arcs over the partygoers. Syrupy white liquid shoots out of the tip, toward the balloon crowd. They run around, and I realize they're *trying* to catch the goo on the balloons.

"Score one for Team V!" one of the girls on the side yells when a vagina balloon girl catches most of the goo. There are immediate cries of triumph and disappointment.

I sigh. Even though it was something of a gag gift, my brothers and I should've never given Dad a cock cannon for his birthday last year. Because now there are *ten*. And the extras didn't come from us. Dad must have specially commissioned them.

Why me? Why, why, why do I have to have such an embarrassing father?

No sane person would have anything like this at a party. Or in his home. Or anywhere near them. Even the respect-buying Fulliloves probably have more dignity than this.

Not willing to suffer more of the spectacle, I take a pathway to the side. I'm not going to walk under the cocks and risk getting that disgusting, syrupy junk all over me.

"Hey, you're supposed to smack the ball when you enter the party!" one of the girls yells.

"Yeah! That's the rule," a guy calls out.

I turn around slowly. "You gonna enforce it?"

I'm not here to linger and mingle. I'm here to show my face, so Dad will leave me alone for another year. I'm safe for Christmas because he prefers to have orgies in the Caribbean, and he doesn't generally invite me or my brothers to those. Seeing his sons naked would be too much even for him.

"Uh..." The girl shrugs helplessly. "No?"

"Exactly." I walk away, my head throbbing, and scan the crowd, looking for my brothers. I thought I saw Huxley's and Noah's cars outside, but they might not be here yet. I pull out my phone and start texting.

–Me: Hey, you at the party?

–Huxley: Yeah. I just got myself another drink.

–Noah: Can never get enough to get through this fiesta.

–Huxley: I'm going to drink all the good shit first.

–Me: Are we the first to arrive?

–Noah: Unfortunately. Next time, I'm going to sabotage the car the day before.

–Me: I was just thinking how car troubles would be a good excuse for skipping these things.

–Noah: The person who first announces it gets to do it.

–Me: Says who?

There is a pause.

–Noah: Newton. He published calculus first, so he got to claim it was a thing.

–Me: Leibniz published first. The Royal Society said he stole it from Newton, but only because the investigation was directed by Newton.

–Noah: Close enough!

–Huxley: Enough pointless academic argument. Why don't you get over here and see if something can mellow you out? Like this amazing scotch.

Dad is an ass, but he knows his liquor.

–Me: Fine.

I put the phone away and start toward the drink table. The layout for these parties is always the same.

"Can you just imagine?" comes a familiar voice, half cracking with tears, half pleading for sympathy.

Oh crap.

I expected her to be here, but was hoping to avoid her. We've spent enough time together recently.

Retreat quietly before she notices.

"That's awful," comes another voice, egging Mom on.

"I just... It's just so difficult." Mom sniffs delicately.

That's a sign she's about to start another round of drama. I don't know how long she's kept the other woman so she could have an audience for her show. I should escape, but I don't want to, not when she could be saying something that would come back to bite me in the ass in triple humiliation. It's one thing if she exercises her theatrical freedom in another city—or, preferably, another continent —but it's another when she's *right here.*

Damn it. I pull out my phone and text.

–Me: Got something to deal with first. I'll be late.

–Huxley: Fine. Come when you're done.

I put the phone away, arrange my face to show nothing and step forward.

"Mother," I say. She's sitting on a bench with another woman.

Mom is in a blue bikini and posed casually. But I know for a fact that she's rehearsed for hours in front of a mirror to make sure she looks absolutely fantastic from every angle. Mom understands the visual impact her physical presence can have. No sunglasses, either; she knows what she can do with her eyes.

The woman with her is young—maybe in her late twenties. She doesn't have the practiced polish Mom has, but still looks gorgeous in a pink kimono, a pair of huge sunglasses and a giant, droopy hat that hides most of her face. She's crossed her shapely legs, and the way she's angled her body shows she's giving Mom all the sympathy and attention she craves.

When she looks up at me, my skin prickles. If Mom weren't around, I might assume it's from sexual awareness. But it has to be dread: what drama has Mom picked to stage a scene this time? Dad's birthday party doesn't make for the best backdrop, but she has endless varieties in her arsenal and knows how to squeeze whatever effect she wants out of what's available.

"Griff," she says with a wobbly smile, a subtle hint that I'm supposed to give her filial love. "This is my son," she announces to the other woman.

Never waste an opportunity to ensure maximum embarrassment. Now that she's established a connection, she's going to warm up to her act.

"What's the problem this time?" I ask without smiling.

She sighs. "Oh... I had a little spat with Calvin."

"She needed some emotional support," the other woman says. "Some men are awfully exploitative, you know."

Not just men. Women, too, especially when you're talking about one named Rachel Griffin. "Mom, I think you've monopolized enough of her time."

"*Mono*polized? I did no such—"

"Uh-huh. Come on. Let's talk about this elsewhere," I say, not wanting to further impose on a stranger—and not wanting her to know any more about whatever embarrassing man-drama Mom has gotten herself into. This will not end with mere whining. It'll end with her getting drunk and doing something stupid, ostensibly to get over her trauma. I do not need Mom finishing three bottles of vodka and executing a naked cannonball into the pool. The last time she did it, she lost consciousness and sank like a rock, and a guy had to pull her out and perform CPR. She dated the man for rescuing her for a couple of weeks before she got bored and moved on. I saw every excruciating photo and tabloid article about it because she sent them to me with a pride only she could fathom.

"Do you want to sit down, too?" Mom asks, not hearing anything from my mouth she doesn't want to hear.

Oh, for God's sake. "No. I want to take you into the house so we can discuss this in private."

Resentment flashes over Mom's face. She won't go quietly, not when it means losing her audience. Fluid gathers, beading in the corners of her eyes. "I know you're going to side with Calvin."

"I literally have no clue who Calvin is."

"No clue? But I've told you about him many times."

"I'm sure you haven't." I put my hand under her arm and pull her up.

Mom resists, but she's no match for me. I haul her up without much effort.

"Wait a minute." The woman next to Mom looks at me as though I'm a monster.

"What?" It comes out snappier than I want.

"She's your mother. You could be a little nicer."

I give her a thin smile. "Lady, I'm trying to save you here. So why don't you go say hi to all the important movie people so you can get yourself a role and leave us alone?"

She gasps, her cheeks turning pink. Her faux outrage doesn't bother me. Preventing Mom from making a spectacle of herself and embarrassing me does.

Before the woman can complain, I pull Mom away and into the house. Where's a sinkhole when you need one?

14

SIERRA

I wonder if Rachel was okay after that horrible son of hers dragged her away.

It's been a few days since Ted's birthday bash, but that poor woman keeps popping into my head. Maybe because she seemed so fragile...and probably because of the way her son treated her. He sure looked good, with that chiseled jaw he obviously got from his mom and a body he must've spent hours sculpting in the gym. But inside? He's rotten. He could've sat and listened to his mother with me, made her feel understood and appreciated.

Instead, he dragged her away like she was an embarrassment he didn't want anybody to see. Like a huge red zit in the center of his otherwise pristine chin.

But he has no idea how lucky he is. If I still had my mom, I'd spend as much time with her as possible.

I'll bet the Midnight God treats his mother better. A man that protective—and awesome enough to jump to a stranger's defense—is maybe the pinnacle of good behavior. A true gentleman in public, an amazing sex deity in bed—the epitome of chivalry in my book.

I've been thinking about the Midnight God a lot. Actually, it's more like an obsession. I go over what we did together. The crazy orgasms I experienced with him.

I always thought romance novels lied about how great the

orgasms were in the sex scenes, the idea being to talk up the hero's virility and prowess in bed. But maybe romance novelists have their own Midnight Gods in their bedrooms, and they're just writing from life experience.

Because that one-night stand? It's been filling my head with more ideas for our next product line than I know what to do with. I've spent the last two weeks sorting them out so I don't sound like a disorganized babbler when I present them. Now that I'm done categorizing and refining the ideas, I'm finally ready to talk to my new product development team lead.

Carrying a big mug of fresh coffee, I step into the conference room four doors down from my corner office. It's large enough to accommodate twenty attendees. Grandma, who founded the company, liked functional, contemporary comfort, and the interior is mostly natural wood, with colorful ergonomic Embody chairs around a rectangular oak table. There's also a huge window that overlooks the verdant woods that surround the headquarters.

Ellie is waiting inside, her long fingernails tapping on her tablet. Since Silicone Dream doesn't have a dress code, she opts for the comfiest outfits in her closet. Today she's in a teal shirt, black Nike tights and a pair of purple Converse. She has, of course, also thrown on a white lab coat that she loves to wear just for the hell of it. But then, everyone in new product development and R&D has their own quirks, and Ellie's is pretty benign, considering. A guy who quit last month to move to Seattle with his wife when she got a job with Amazon preferred to walk around topless—or at least expose his chest, which had more hair than a mink dipped in Rogaine. He said covering it made it too itchy.

"You look good," Ellie says with a grin.

"Thanks." I take a seat opposite hers. "I wanted to...you know. Try something fun." Like wearing a pastel-pink sleeveless dress and matching pumps to work. While I was married, I refrained from putting on the clothes that I preferred. I went for more of a conservative banker look—lots of navy and black, business suits with actual jackets. Todd was already unhappy about what Silicone Dream does, and my dressing like the CEO of a financial institution lessened his embarrassment about my job.

But hopefully all of his complaints are in the past. He pestered me incessantly during the entire divorce proceeding—and after—

about getting back together, but since he got his face kicked in New Orleans, I haven't heard from him.

"Did you throw out *all* your boring outfits?" Ellie asks. Her eyes are narrowed and gleaming with petty hatred for my ex. She called him "that dickhead" while we were married. She calls him "that fucker" now.

"Basically. Took a while, though. It's amazing how much crap you end up accumulating."

Ellie snorts. "Especially when somebody's forcing you to buy shit you don't need." She leans forward. "Anyway, let's talk work. You have some ideas for the new line?"

"Yes!" That one syllable bubbles with more enthusiasm than I've felt in months. "I want to call it 'Midnight God.'"

Her well-shaped eyebrows rise, twinkles in her wide eyes. "So he was really that good, huh?"

Thinking back on our interaction makes the flesh between my legs tingle. "Yeah. But more to the point, it's a great name."

"Is he going to know it refers to him? He might get weird about it."

"I don't think so. We didn't use nicknames. It was just... We had this zing. A real connection, you know?"

"So when you came, did you scream out 'Oh, yes! Yes, hot dude!'?"

I laugh. "I don't usually say much when I come."

"But you said he gave you the best orgasms of your life."

"He did, but..." I shrug. "It was just a hot, anonymous sexy time." A memory I cherish. I force myself to switch gears. "Okay, we're here to work, not have *another* postmortem about my one-night stand." I tap my legal pad. "This line needs to be premium. Every product should look and feel top-of-the-line luxurious."

Ellie's eyes narrow, a sure sign she's lost in thought—and designs. "I wish you'd taken a cast of the Midnight God's amazing premium penis," she muses.

I laugh, twirling my pen. "Yeah, I can just picture how that'd go." *Hey, could you just hold still for a moment while this cast fully dries? Oh, and you have to stay super erect while you're at it.*

Of course, I'd have to do something to keep the excitement level up for him. Hmm... Soo many interesting possibilities...

I shake myself mentally. *Back to work, girl, back to work.*

"I mean, you've described it well enough, but...it's like something that seems beyond the realm of reality," Ellie says.

"Believe me, it was *very* real." I sigh like a chocolate addict in front of a Godiva shop, then take a huge sip of coffee.

"You sure you didn't rate his performance higher than it deserves because you've been deprived?" She taps the table. "Unfortunately, Todd's dragged down your bar real low. His dick's too small to be useful."

I almost spit, but manage to close my mouth in time, although my nose stings a little as I contain a hysterical giggle. Ellie says she can tell everything there is to know about a guy's penis by just looking at him head to toe. I don't know how accurate her statement is, since I haven't seen the penises of the men she's analyzed.

"Well, we're selling the fantasy of the perfect orgasm, which our products deliver consistently, thanks to you and the R&D team." I *don't* want to discuss my ex's dick size. Actually, I don't ever want to think about his dick at all. It's like God was feeling rushed when He created Todd.

Ellie takes a little bow. "Thank you, thank you. And keep going."

I laugh. "You know what I think about you."

"Knowing it and hearing it are two different things."

"When we launch the Midnight God line, I'll give you another raise and a fat bonus. How about that?"

"Oooooh, financial reward! So much better than empty words."

"Anyway, we need products that don't just deliver consistent orgasms, but *incredible* orgasms. Ones that leave you shaken to the core."

Ellie gives an evil scientist laugh. "Our vibrators are really good at shaking your core."

"Of course," I say with pride. "But the orgasms could still be...more."

I think back on how it was with the Midnight God. Every muscle in my body tensed and melted into goo. The peak jacked me up with such intense electric bliss that I thought I'd die from sheer ecstasy. But that wasn't where it ended; pleasure zinged through me like aftershocks after an earthquake. Everything about that night left me wrecked—in the most amazing way.

My best friend props her chin in her hand. "So even after two weeks, you really, honest to God, haven't changed your opinion?"

"No." I sigh dreamily. "I'd love to run into him again."

"How would you recognize him?" Practical Ellie. There's a reason she double-majored in mechanical engineering and marketing.

I think back to the encounter, my belly doing a triple twist and my face and neck heating. "By the way he smells. The way he moves. The way he makes my heart flutter... Ellie, the man is perfect. If I see him again, I'll recognize him for sure. Like this"—I snap my fingers—"just from my physical reaction."

"But you might not see him again," she says sorrowfully.

"All the good men aren't just taken. They also aren't local."

The corners of her lips turn downward. "You should've gotten his name. He could've fallen in love and moved out here for you."

"I know." I deflate a little. "Staying anonymous seemed like the smart thing to do at the time. But now that I think about it, I'd been drinking, so my head probably wasn't that clear."

"Most definitely not. I blame the airline for keeping me in St. Louis, because *I* would've made sure to get his name and number." Suddenly Ellie shakes her head. "Actually, never mind. If I'd been there, you might've never run into him because I would've taken care of Todd."

True. Todd has been on Ellie's shit list forever. Probably because he tried his best to see if Ellie would leave Silicone Dream for "a better opportunity in another city." Like New York. Or better yet, Hong Kong. He couldn't stand that I was close to somebody who hated his guts. "Okay, no Todd talk. Midnight God. That's what we're here for."

"Why not hire a private investigator to track him down?"

I wrinkle my nose. "Don't you think that feels a little too...stalk-erish?" After having Todd track me down everywhere, including New Orleans, I'm not too keen on doing the same to the Midnight God, even if it's for a good reason.

"It's not stalking if the other person likes it. He'll probably feel honored if you pursue him." Ellie shrugs, back to her brisk, businesslike self. "Well, anyway. I think we should start with a dildo and vibrator first. They're the classics."

I nod slowly. "But I want them to be unique and interesting in some way, too. They can't be like any dildos and vibrators on the market. The Midnight God isn't like other men."

"Got it. Peterson's out of town until next week, but when he gets back we can start in earnest."

Peterson is Ellie's favorite R&D person to work with. His specialty: the motors and suction units in vibrators. There's no combination of vibration and suction he can't create.

"Perfect."

Loud footsteps come from outside. Shouting between three people penetrates the thick door of the conference room.

I listen, frowning. One voice belongs to Heather and the other to Dan, the head of security—who has to have been called by Heather—because the final voice belongs to Linda. Ugh.

Ellie makes a moue of distaste. "What's your stepmom doing here?"

"I don't know." It isn't like Linda to just show up out of the blue. Or draw attention to herself within the company. She isn't involved in the running of Silicone Dream. To honor my grandmother's deathbed wish and will, I have no intention of letting Linda, Felicia or my father manage the company in any way. None of them care about the company anyway, just the money it generates.

"Does she have an appointment Heather forgot to tell you about?" Ellie asks.

"Heather never forgets anything about Linda." Mainly because she hates my stepmom. Heather calls her a "greedy opportunist" the infrequent times we talk about her. She probably uses more colorful words when I'm not around.

Now there are thumps. Probably Linda pounding the wall with the heel of her hand to show her displeasure. She wouldn't do anything more violent, since she'd rather eat rat poison than break one of her precious nails.

I stand up. "I should probably go see what's going on."

"I'll be your backup," Ellie says, getting up.

I straighten and push my shoulders back, making sure I'm radiating authority. That is the only way to get Linda to absorb even a fraction of what I say, since she has the most extraordinary talent for filtering out what she doesn't want to hear. I open the door and step into the hall, Ellie close behind.

His arms stretched out, Dan is standing in front of Linda, who is doing her best to shove him out of the way. Excessive hair spray has turned her bleached platinum hair into an artistic wire sculpture rather than anything resembling what should naturally grow out of a human skull. Her dress is so tight it looks like Saran wrap. But it's black, so she'll think that makes it "classy." Her diamond earrings and necklaces are huge enough to be blinding, but that's just her wordlessly communicating how well she married. She used to be a bookkeeper for our parents, and the second Mom died, she managed to get Dad to propose. He doesn't like being lonely, and Linda knows how to keep him entertained, which is a valuable life skill for the wanna-marry-up type. Their extravagant wedding took place within three months of Mom's funeral. I didn't have to attend the spectacle because Grandma sent me to Cancun that weekend, but I saw photos.

As the years have passed, Linda's features have grown more sculpted—her pricey plastic surgeon is a man of divine talent—and her face less mobile. I gotta give her credit for her drive, because I can't remember to slather lotion on my face half the time.

"Get your animal off me!" Linda shouts shrilly.

As usual, she expects people to jump to do her bidding.

"Dan is a member of our security team, and he's following my instructions," I say to calm her down. My number one goal is to get her out of the headquarters. "I told him not to let anybody without an appointment come bother me." Mainly to ensure Todd doesn't bug me. But saying so would only upset Linda, so I leave that part out.

"I'm not just *anybody*!"

"Dan, it's fine. Let her pass." She won't quit until she says whatever she's here to say. It must be important for her to make the trip, since she prefers to spend her time in spas and her plastic surgeon's office.

"You have another meeting," Heather says, while giving Linda a look dark with disapproval.

It's a lie, but I play along. "Right. I don't have much time." I turn to Linda with a smile but don't invite her to sit down or come into the conference room, since that would only encourage her to go on and on. "What can I do for you?"

"I want to sit down with a latte," she demands.

"I'm afraid there's no time for that," Heather says. "Sierra's meeting is in five."

Linda shoots Heather a look of sheer hatred. She knows that Heather doesn't care what she thinks because I'm the one who pays the salaries, but I've told my stepmother repeatedly to avoid coming over to the company if interacting with Heather upsets her that much.

Heather checks her watch, then taps the round crystal face with a thin smile.

Linda turns to me and says, "You know Todd still can't talk right?"

"I didn't, but I'm not surprised. That was quite a kick to the head he took." She probably expects me to feel terrible about what happened to him, but it isn't easy to dredge up much sympathy. "Maybe he should see a better doctor?"

"Seeing a better doctor isn't the answer. I thought you'd be..." Linda waves a hand around in the air. "More concerned?"

I raise both eyebrows. "I'm sorry?"

"Why don't you send him flowers? Or visit to see how he's doing?"

"I don't see why I should. It's too bad about his jaw, but..." Honestly, the peace and quiet has been nice since New Orleans. He hasn't been bothering me with annoying calls. Before, I constantly had to block his numbers—he's got a lot of numbers—and now I'm getting more work done.

"Because he got hurt for you!"

Is Todd venturing into creative writing? "That's not the way it happened. Actually, he got hurt trying to hurt me. He also ruined a brand-new dress—"

"Which I can invoice him for," Heather puts in.

"—and I've overlooked the damage. So I think I've done plenty."

Linda's chest puffs as she inhales. It's a sign she's doing her best to control her temper. In a calmer and slightly beseeching tone, she says, "Sierra, he just wants another chance."

This is becoming a waste of time. "He blew his chance, Linda. In fact, he blew several chances, and I can't spend the rest of my life hoping he'll start doing better. I need to move on."

"I see. Well." She sniffs. "I'll let Todd know you need more time to get over your snit."

Divorce isn't a "snit," but if thinking of it that way makes her leave, I'm not going to correct her.

"Anyway, your father and I have decided to do something amazing with Wollstonecraft." Linda gives me a you-didn't-expect-that-did-you look.

Heather clears her throat. "Your meeting..."

I raise a finger—the family's ties to the college are important. It's something that started while Grandma was still alive. She wanted the fortune we were building by giving better orgasms to everyone around the world to have a lasting impact, and decided to focus on funding the local liberal arts college.

Linda shoots Heather a childishly triumphant smile. "One of their classes is going to be doing a case study here."

My mind freezes for a second. "I'm sorry, what?"

"A case study. They're going to learn about what we do and come up with some interesting new ideas help make us grow better."

Uh-oh. Linda never uses "we" to discuss the company unless she has an ulterior motive. Or she needs money.

Heather's rolling her eyes so hard, they look like they belong in a Vegas casino.

"We already have a team in charge of that," I say.

Linda shrugs. "It's a fresh new perspective."

"They're college kids."

"Exactly. Our future customers."

True, but we don't let our customers advise on how to grow our business. Not like this.

"Who's in charge of the program at Wollstonecraft?" I'm going to cancel this "case study" before the college wastes any real time and resources on it.

"Charles Phillips." She pauses like the name should mean something.

When I keep staring, Linda adds, "The head of the English department."

"And why do we need input on our products from English majors?" I ask, bewildered.

Linda isn't listening. "He's sending a class today."

"What?"

Heather starts tapping her tablet furiously.

"Did you just say *today*?" I fight to keep my voice level despite surging irritation. She can't just drop students on Silicone Dream without any warning! The company isn't her plaything.

Linda nods. "Yes. And not just any class, but one that specializes in poetry. Humanities majors have such a fascinating perspective on things. Please don't try to send them back because it would make the company look bad."

"We'll see." I don't want to spend more time arguing. Linda isn't changing her mind and the students are apparently on their way here with their professor. I'm going to have to tell them there's been a mistake and there's no case study, so they'll need to go back to campus and read poems by important but dead people in class.

"Good." She nods.

"When exactly are they coming?" I ask, wondering if I can reach the professor in charge before the class gets here, so we can avoid wasting everyone's time.

Linda checks her watch, then gives me a toothy smile that never fails to send shivers down my back. "They should be in the lobby about now."

15

GRIFFIN

I grind my teeth as I drive to Silicone Dream, the high-tech company whose founder apparently couldn't spell very well. What's worse, the founder's advisors must have also been illiterate.

And yet... The Fullilove family is rich. At least rich enough to have a building on campus named after them.

Another case of money's inability to buy you a brain. *Hmm...* Maybe I should do a research paper on that. There has to be a lot of data on the subject.

Upon reflection, it's become clear that this family is just like my dad. He's an idiot, too. One who believes that money can make up for all sorts of shortcomings. And a lack of class.

This week's lectures are shot, since the instruction time is going to be misspent on this bullshit—something my students can't afford. It's absurd that Charles wants to force this "case" upon them when they would benefit more from learning how to work with data in Excel, get a decent graph and sort out correlations among economic data and indicators. All of those *will* be on the final. This case won't be part of the course grade, as I refuse to redo my syllabus to suit Charles or the Fulliloves.

I park my car and climb out. The company's headquarters screams success. The slick metal and glass tower pierces the sky of

Lovedale. It's one of the tallest buildings in the area, and insists that you know it's important.

A pathetic display.

If the company were truly doing well, it wouldn't be located here. It would be in Silicon Valley. It also wouldn't be turning to undergrads for a case study; it'd be paying for advice from a top management consulting firm.

Look at the bright side, I tell myself, trying to settle a building annoyance. This could be far worse. It could be Dad arranging things to manipulate me into giving him a baby. He'd distract my students with the cock cannons while a platoon of hookers would corner me and try to get me to impregnate them.

I shake off the nightmarish image. No more thinking about giant cocks and hookers. I'm heading to a *respectable* company, even if it is run by moneyed morons.

Besides, even if I wanted to—*which I don't*—giving Dad a baby wouldn't satisfy him. Emmett apparently got his maybe-girlfriend/maybe-not-really-girlfriend-anymore pregnant, which was stunning news. Emmett is positively *anal*. Given his meticulous and excessively orderly personality, I can't imagine him screwing up something as basic as birth control. On top of that, he hates Dad just as much as the rest of us and wouldn't have inseminated some random woman just to make Dad happy.

At exactly ten thirty a.m., I walk into the lobby, where the class has already gathered. My loafers slap the pale blue-gray tiles. I tilt my head and...

What the *fuck?*

I do a double take at the giant clock in front of me. The presence of a clock in a business lobby isn't unusual, of course. But does the clock tower have to be in the shape of a giant penis? And not just any penis, but an anatomically correct, fully erect one done in bright bubblegum purple?

The clock face's design has ornate black Roman numerals, and the hands are artistically done to look like arrows tipped with hearts. Somebody tried really hard to add class to this turgid timepiece. The entire scene reminds me of something my father would pull. I suddenly realize, much to my horror, that the firm isn't a failing high-tech entity like I assumed. It's *a sex toy company*. Thus the name *Silicone* Dream.

My stomach starts to hurt. *Fuck.* And damn Charles to all seven circles of Dante's inferno. I was entirely too close to the mark when I decided the Fulliloves are just like Dad. I would've been happier to be wrong.

My students are staring with their mouths open, but naturally their phones are out and snapping away. *Damn it.* First Sandy the escort and now this monumental embarrassment!

The kids start taking selfies in front of the...thing. *Everything about this God-awful case is going to hit social media.* If it comes back to bite me in the ass during my post-tenure review, I'm going to murder Charles.

Time to get this over with.

I look around. A company that can afford a building like this should have security. And there is a desk...but it's empty. Nobody in the reception area, either.

Some people are chatting and walking briskly on the other side of the turnstiles, which probably won't let me in without a badge.

If I were here alone, I might jump them. But I can't do that when I have the students as potential witnesses.

Where the hell is the company representative we're supposed to meet?

I take out my phone to check the email from Charles's assistant that has the details about today. In the most unlikely case, I mixed up the date or time. But nope. It is supposed to be today. At ten thirty. And now it's ten thirty-six.

If whoever's supposed to meet us in the lobby doesn't show up in the next five minutes, I'm leaving. And my students are getting a lecture on the more advanced topics of regression analysis—

There's a sudden obnoxiously loud voice at the main entrance, and Todd Beaker saunters through the glass doors like he owns Cock Clock, Inc. I look heavenward and give a silent prayer for patience— this idiot can test you worse than a three-year-old having a temper tantrum on a plane. I despise him, and I'm not the only one. At an interdepartmental function three years ago, he publicly declared the economics department a disgrace, a pit of capitalistic greed where overpaid professors produce illiberal number crunchers who sell their souls to the highest bidder. Later, he apologized and said he hadn't realized the economics department was present at the event, but the damage was done. I trust what people say behind my back.

The loathsome Todd is in a crisply ironed pale blue dress shirt, black slacks and Italian loafers, all of which cost more than half the annual salary of your typical adjunct professor of English poetry. He supposedly married well and started to spend money like an explorer who'd discovered a pirate's treasure cave. Based on what I've heard, his wife must be socially connected as well, because he began to treat the head of his department with condescension—an act that normally would be professional suicide.

On the other hand, he isn't on the tenure track, so perhaps it doesn't matter if he pisses Chuck off. Todd probably doesn't care if his contract isn't renewed if he has a well-heeled wife, just the way he didn't care that he made enemies out of the entire department of economics.

But if his wealthy spouse is anything like my mother, she might not keep him much longer. His stomach and waist have ballooned since his marriage, a clear sign he let himself go the moment he got his sugar mama. The only part of his anatomy that's remained slim are his shoulders, giving him a decidedly pear-like appearance.

His sandy hair is cut short—the infamous two-thousand-dollar haircut he bragged about during the interdepartmental holiday social—and his face is clean-shaven. White bandages swaddle his head as though he has a dislocated jaw, which is an odd injury for an English professor who spends most of his time sneering at anything that isn't considered the canon of English literature.

Bulges press against the bandages, indicating his joint is swollen as well, except something about them looks off. But the old bluish bruises on his cheek are real, so perhaps he *is* truly hurt.

Although he looks like he lost a fight with a steel door, he holds his head with defiance and pride, his swamp-green gaze superior and determined. Following him is another group of college kids, none of them econ majors. They have the dreamy, unfocused eyes of creative types.

What the hell is he doing here with his poetry class?

Todd notices me and his eyes flash with wary hostility. "What are you doing here?" His words are slightly slurred from the bandages around his head.

"Charles sent me." My answer is cool, clipped. His very presence is suffocating my brain cells. I glance at the giant purple dick-clock. The company representative is late. *Very late.*

"For what?" Todd is staring like he doesn't understand. "Well?" he prods when I don't answer. He places his hands on his hips, his foot tapping the floor as though he's losing patience.

I raise an eyebrow at his attitude. At the same time, my students start raising their phones to record a potential professorial fight. Tanner in particular looks like he's about to pee with excitement. His bright eyes scream, *Fight fight fight fight!*

For God's sake.

Hands still on his hips, Todd squares up to me, slightly invading my personal space. It's a ridiculously stupid move, because if I felt like hitting him, he'd never get a guard up in time.

His face slowly turns red as he realizes I'm not going to react. "Just because—"

A loud clattering of feet on the marble tiles interrupts his posturing. I shift my gaze slightly to see a trio of women and a man marching toward us.

The two women in front are both wearing I'm-the-boss expressions. The older one is walking with unnaturally fast steps, like she's trying to get to us first without looking like she's running. Her bottle-pale hair is piled high and is apparently held together by too much spray from the way it unnaturally reflects the light. Overly rouged lips are set in an unattractive semi-sneer.

In addition, her dress isn't doing much for her. It's skintight on an average body that's seen better days. She should've worn something that would hide her "liabilities," as my mother would put it.

She seems like one of those women who wants to be like Mom, but doesn't have the taste or beauty to pull it off. Instead of accepting that and making the best of what she has, this one is clinging to a futile effort. An unmistakable sign of poor judgment, since she's clearly old enough to know better.

The other I'm-in-charge woman, however, is younger, and something about her feels familiar. Her golden hair flows like a mass of honey down her shoulders and back, framing a small, heart-shaped face with a stubborn chin. For a second, I wonder if she's wearing colored contacts because she has the most unusual shade of purple-blue eyes. Her mouth is lush and generous, coated with a bright red that screams hot nights and tangled sheets.

And her body too. It's slim and beautifully proportioned, with long, straight limbs more fitting for a ballerina at the Royal Ballet than somebody who works at Cock Clock, Inc. Her posture is also like a ballerina's—erect with her head held high. Her breasts are full and look soft, pressed against the fabric of her sleeveless pink dress, and a silver metal belt cinches her small waist just so. She's wearing a pair of stilettos that look very much like the ones Purple Girl was wearing in New Orleans.

Don't be stupid, I warn myself. Purple Girl was actually sweet. With class. *Without* drama. The female duo—and this whole place—reeks of drama. Like bad-telenovela-level drama.

And yet...I can't seem to tear my gaze from the younger one. It's like she's a magnet that's pulling me in.

I suddenly realize where I've seen her before—she's the enabler from Dad's birthday party! The one who encouraged Mom to go on and on. I had to exhaust what was left of my patience to calm her down after I dragged her away, because she *really* wanted to go back to the pool area and find her appreciative audience of one again.

Why didn't I recognize the drama encourager instantly?

Probably because she's actually wearing clothes. And she isn't wearing huge sunglasses or a huge hat.

Does she recognize me? I look for signs, but she's entirely too calm as she looks at me. So. She has no clue that we've met. Which is fine.

Todd turns from me and says, "Linda!" in the perkiest voice I've ever heard from him.

I force my eyes away from the vision in pink.

"Todd!" the weird-hair woman calls back, her eyes going wide with recognition and affection.

She runs past the turnstiles, dashing toward him with her arms spread, as though they're filming a tender loving reunion scene. All you'd need is Tchaikovsky's *Romeo and Juliet* overture to complete the effect.

Is *that* his wife? If so, he has my condolences.

Suddenly, Todd blinks and grimaces, very much like a student who's turned in his midterm a second ago only to realize he made a stupid math mistake on one of the questions. He then pastes on a smile and turns to the other woman. "Sierra!"

Sierra's mouth flattens until you can hardly see her lips.

"I came out *especially* to see you," Todd says, beaming at her.

What about Linda, who has an arm wrapped around his shoulders? I doubt she's old enough to be his mother.

The third woman, who's been walking behind Linda and Sierra and *is* old enough to be Todd's mother, ignores the commotion and studies me. Unlike the others, she seems sensible, with a neat bob and no-nonsense shoes.

I pray she's the one I need to deal with, because it's obvious this unfortunate group is the people from Silicone Dream I'm supposed to meet with my class.

"Are you from Wollstonecraft?" she asks.

"Yes."

Linda swivels her head in my direction. "What?" she screeches, her voice echoing through the lobby. She lets go of Todd and comes closer until she's only a couple of steps away. "Charles Phillips sent you?" she demands rudely. It's clear she's expecting a *no* for an answer.

Drama Queen, you guessed wrong.

I stare back at her. "That's right." She can't seem to tear her gaze from my face, which isn't unusual. A lot of women stare at my face. But most don't do it this overtly or obnoxiously.

I resist an impulse to make a V with my fingers and poke her eyes.

"You're a professor?" she demands again.

"Yes." *Don't let her do anything crazy. Don't let her do anything crazy.*

I don't tell her my name. Given my luck this week, she might just decide to peel that dress off and flash me in front of my class, with the bubblegum-purple cock clock in the background.

"But Charles sent *him!*" she yells, pointing at Todd.

My gaze slides to Todd, and then to Sierra, who's standing to the side observing the scene. She seems to be perfectly placid and at ease, which is irritating. She isn't the one being inconvenienced by this farce or who's been kept waiting.

"No, he didn't," I say, hoping Linda makes enough fuss so Todd and his class can do this "case" and I can return to campus with what's left of my sanity. My patience for drama this month has hit bottom and is pulling out a shovel.

"But of course he did! I was hoping for a professor who specialized in poetry from the romantic era."

The woman's lost her damned mind. "Nobody in the department specializes in poetry."

"Yes, they do!"

"No, they do not," I say in my most authoritative voice. In my peripheral vision, Todd licks his mouth nervously, then nibbles on his lower lip. How is he doing that with his jaw injury?

Sierra's speculative gaze slices from me to Linda, then to Todd, and back to me. For some odd reason, my mouth dries.

Must be the heat. My blood is boiling because my time's being wasted by these jokers.

"Are you telling me Wollstonecraft has no poetry class in its English department?" Linda shouts like a loon.

"Not at all. But you asked *Charles* Phillips," I point out. No number of buildings with their name can be worth this bullshit. I should fund the research center that Charles is panting after. Have it built anonymously on the condition that he never bothers me again.

Her face is bright red now. "*And?*"

"*And* Charles is the head of the economics department."

"Incorrect. He is the head of the *English* department," she says triumphantly.

God save me from people who have half the info. "Chuck Phillips is the head of the English department. Two *very* different individuals."

Linda's jaw slackens, while Sierra's eyes quicken with interest. Neither bodes well.

Sierra steps up, making placating hand gestures. "Okay, why don't we all just take a step back and see if we can't figure this out? Now, Todd, who sent you?"

Todd blinks. Potential responses are flashing through his eyes furiously, but none of them sticks. He ends up staring blankly like a student who's been caught daydreaming in class.

"Well?" Sierra asks with a smile. "Come on now."

"Um..."

Since even Todd can't be idiotic enough to have forgotten who sent him, there's only one answer: he came here on his own. If he wants to be part of this Cock Clock, Inc. study that badly, he's welcome to it. As a matter of fact, he should've told me the moment he walked in. I could've left before I had to deal with the drama of all these...*people*.

"Well! I guess this means I need to make a decision," Sierra says before I can announce I'm leaving. Her disposition is entirely too sunny, which is outright terrifying. Nobody should be this happy.

"About what?" Todd suddenly sounds like a panicked hyena.

"About who should be doing the case." She turns to me. "So. Uh. You are...?"

The impact of being the sudden focus of those purple-blue eyes strikes my chest. My heart stills as I note that her hair looks more golden than honey in the light, which is a nonsensical observation... but still makes me want to smell her shampoo.

Jesus, Griffin. What the hell? Are you trying to make an idiot of yourself?

"Griffin Lasker. Professor of economics." It comes out brusque, and does nothing to hide my distaste for everything about this place and the people and my reaction to Sierra. "I specialize in econometrics."

"Which means what, precisely?" she asks, still sunny.

"Statistical analysis of economic data. Nothing that can help with *that*." I point at the giant purple cock.

"I doubt poetry would help, either," she counters with a saucy wink.

Does she think I'm joking? I need to get out of here before I do something I'll regret. "Your being sixteen minutes late most certainly didn't help," I add coolly.

She frowns, as though I'm being unfair in my criticism.

There's nothing unfair about the situation if she'd just think it through. "Time is money."

"Oh." She reaches into her purse and takes out her wallet. Opening it, she pulls out a few bills and moves closer to me. "Here." She places the folded twenties in my palm, curls my fingers over them and pats the loose fist twice.

I can just hear, *There, there*, over the blood raging in my head.

She smiles winsomely. "Will that cover your time? If not, just let me know."

Her shampoo has an apple scent. I decide then and there that I hate apples.

16

SIERRA

Griffin Lasker, professor of economics, specialist in econometrics, who happens to have the most gorgeous face I've ever seen grace a man, glares at the money I put in his hand like it's a bag of anthrax. Then he glowers like he wants to strangle me.

He said time is money, so I was accommodating him, but maybe I should've given him more. I don't want him to feel like I took advantage of my relationship with the college to waste his precious time.

I still can't believe a man who looks like that is a professor of economics. He belongs in an Armani photoshoot. Or modeling Calvin Klein underwear. Those sharp, deep-set gray eyes, sculpted cheekbones and full, firm lips are wasted on a college campus. He wouldn't have to smile to shill products. He could just brood with disapproval—like he's doing right now—and women would throw money to buy whatever he was selling.

And just check out how broad his shoulders are. He's tall, too, easily six-three or six-four. The impeccable suit he's wearing can't hide the power of his body. I bet you could grate cheese on his abs.

Or run your tongue along the ridges, feel his muscles flex and breath shudder...

Wait, wait. Hold on a second. I can't indulge in X-rated fantasies about him right now, no matter how much libido is churning in my veins. Or how my mind is trying to figure out if we've met before, because something about him feels vaguely familiar. He reminds me of the rude man I met at Ted's party, but there's no way an econ prof would have been invited to that bash.

Focus, Sierra!

Right. Can't afford to be distracted when Todd and Linda are hovering around like vultures waiting to rip some flesh from a corpse.

It doesn't take a genius to know what Linda's up to. She's been trying hard to get me to reconcile with her precious nephew Todd. According to her, I will never know true happiness or the "meaning of womanhood" without him by my side. It hasn't occurred to her that I wouldn't have divorced him if I had found either of those while we were married.

This case study is a clumsy attempt to force us into close proximity. And maybe she really believes it'll work, because that's how she snagged my dad. They spent an awful lot of time together, a lot more than her job as the family's bookkeeper strictly required. I didn't understand back then because I was too young, but now I can see it quite clearly. No wonder Grandma disapproved of Linda. Grandma hated people who wanted what didn't belong to them, and as far as she was concerned, a person already in a relationship was off-limits.

Thank God for Linda's sloppiness. She generally finds the ties the family has with Wollstonecraft College boring and pointless, except when she thinks the connection can be used to benefit Todd. I'm not surprised she didn't know there are two professors named Charles Phillips, and one of them goes by Chuck.

Dr. Economics looks like he's the type who chews glass for a hobby, but I don't need a friend. Just a pretext.

And it's great that he's a sexy pretext. Todd's sense of competition won't be able to tolerate it.

"We have finance people who can do numbers," Linda interjects suddenly, obviously antsy that things aren't progressing the way she envisioned. "We need somebody who can add humanity to our products."

I turn to her. "I'm not sure what you mean by 'we' and 'our products.' But if you're ever elected to one of our boards, I'll be sure to give your opinions proper consideration."

Angry resentment flushes her face. She's always found it insufferable that Grandma didn't leave *her* Silicone Dream. "I'm your mother!"

"*Step*mother," I correct her firmly. She likes to talk about what a big, happy family we are when it suits her purpose, but basically ignores me when it doesn't.

"You are always so awful, never accepting that I'm family now. I'm your mother in every way that counts."

If she thinks I'm going to back down, she needs to think again. "When is my birthday?" I smile sunnily, so she knows I'm not bothered. Not anymore. Not really.

"What?" She lets out an I-can't-believe-you're-asking laugh. "Is this a test?"

"You can just say you don't know."

She looks around for help, but there isn't any. Todd has no clue. Finally, she says, "It's a lot—"

"When is Felicia's birthday?"

"January tenth, but—"

"Exactly."

"Just because I can't quite recall your birthday doesn't mean I'm not your mother," she insists. "I'm very busy. Things slip through the cracks all the time." She looks around to see if anybody's judging her.

Todd is giving her a sort of fake sympathetic understanding, while Griffin's eyes are narrowed and trained on her like artillery pieces.

Be still my heart. It's nice to have a man who doesn't buy her excuses. More than nice, from the way my pulse is fluttering.

"You know how much of my attention goes toward taking care of your father," Linda says, like that makes everything better.

Todd gives her shoulder a supportive pat. Griffin's expression doesn't just say she's an idiot, but a *despicable* idiot.

Okay. So he's an equal-opportunity grouch who thinks badly of everyone.

"If you're that upset, I'll throw you a birthday party this year," Linda says.

That would be something to see. She's done all sorts of petty things to make sure I feel excluded and unwanted, and forgetting my birthdays is the least of it. She wouldn't have come to my graduation—and made sure Dad wouldn't have either—if it weren't for Grandma. But then, Linda always sucked up to Grandma, since she controlled the purse strings.

"You know, I think I've made up my mind. We could use some more guidance with the new product launch, and I need somebody to help crunch our data." I flutter my lashes at Griffin Lasker like he's my hero. "I think I'll go with Charles's pick."

"But!" Todd exclaims, then stops. He gestures wildly with his arms. "Don't you want your...things to be classy?"

"There are different types of classy. In this case, I don't think iambic pentameter is going to be a good fit for our marketing campaign."

In my peripheral vision, I note Griffin looking at me and Todd like we need to return to our asylum. I want to tell him it's my ex-husband who's crazy, but I rein in the impulse. No need to get into a mutual-blame shouting match with Todd.

"I doubt econometrics can help with what you're doing here," Griffin says, every syllable dripping with disapproval. From the cold expression on his face, he probably thinks he's hiding his disgust well—but he isn't.

For some reason, it makes me want to push all his buttons. Just to see if any of them lead to an "angry professor."

"I disagree." Giving Griffin an extra-sunny smile, I move toward the students that have been milling around this whole time. "I think these econometrics students will do an amazing job sorting our data and giving us some ideas for product development." I put a hand on the shoulder of the student standing closest to me, a sign to Todd that I've made up my mind, and it isn't changing.

My ex clenches his hands and glares at the student like he wants to leap across the distance and backhand the poor kid. Meanwhile, Linda is texting and Griffin's face is scrunched, his lips tight.

He's furious he's stuck. He's made it clear he doesn't want to be here, but we all have to do things we don't like. Best just to put a good face on it, I always say.

"Dan, why don't you help Linda, Todd and his English class go where they need to go"—I gesture toward the main door—"and then process the econometrics students and give them visitor's passes? And Heather, once that's done, please show the students around." I turn to Griffin with my most charming smile. "I'd like to have a conversation with Professor Lasker about the direction of this... er...case."

17

GRIFFIN

"This way," Sierra says as she takes me through a turnstile and to the left.

I expect her to take me to a meeting room, a large space that exudes wealth and power and is filled with outrageously expensive furniture that would make anybody feel unworthy of parking their ass on it unless their ass is appropriately covered in expensive bespoke clothes. Original art by masters whose works are generally seen in the Louvre. Air luxuriously perfumed with flowers so finicky and difficult to grow that only those who can afford a dedicated team of gardeners can enjoy them.

On the other hand, she thinks a giant purple cock is suitable for her lobby, so for all I know, she could be guiding me to a kink dungeon proudly festooned with huge pink butt plugs.

Nothing this woman does is going to shock me.

She leads me into a long hall. Once we finally reach the door at the end, she pushes it open and we spill out into a lush garden. My step falters for half a second.

The garden doesn't have any orgy topiaries. It's actually a normal garden with some shrubs, trees, roses and daisies. Nothing weird. Nothing outrageous. Nothing that smells like semen or flavored lube.

A few benches sit under the trees. The benches aren't shaped like genitalia or outfitted with restraint cuffs, either. They're ordinary, like the type you'd find in any public park.

It's *too normal*.

Still, I conceal my unease. Hiding how I feel is what I do best, having been surrounded by drama kings and queens who love to feed off my reaction. I'm not giving Sierra anything to turn this into a *spectacle*. After having observed my parents for decades, I know how easy it is to turn a private moment into a scene.

"Would you like to sit down?" She gestures at one of the benches under a giant gingko tree with green fan-shaped leaves.

"No, thank you." I'm not in the mood to sit down for a chat. Damn it, I shouldn't be here. Period!

She shrugs and takes a seat, lifts her feet off the ground, then lets out a soft sigh of relief that her stilettos aren't bearing her weight. "Can I be frank?"

Shit. When a woman says, "Can I be frank?" nothing good follows. It's equivalent to a starting pistol going off at a race. No-holds-barred drama is going to pour out of her mouth. Tears will ensue if words alone aren't sufficient to elicit a proper response. If Sierra's an expert, she'll have a handkerchief or Kleenex. Or perhaps she expects me to hand her one. Mom used to, until she realized I'd never carry a hanky or Kleenex for her to sob into.

"Sure." I brace myself. Wollstonecraft owes me more than keeping me tenured for putting up with this.

"If you haven't already gathered, I didn't want any case study," she says. "I didn't even know you were coming until Linda showed up this morning."

No semi-trembling words. No tears. She's entirely too calm. My mouth dries. What the hell is in her Act Two?

"As you saw, there's an issue between me and Todd." Sierra's mouth twists into a self-deprecating line. "He's my ex-husband."

I give myself a moment to process, studying her for a sign that she's fucking with me to get a reaction. But no. She's dead serious.

"*You married him?*" Why? She could do nine million times better than that...that unfortunate accident of procreation. Then I realize something else. "He was a member of the Fullilove family?" The all-important family that even pompous Charles Phillips is obsequious to.

She nods, rocking her body back and forth a little on the bench.

Damn. That explains so much about his attitude over the last two years. The heights of obnoxiousness he imposed upon everyone, including the head of his own department. He knew his marriage to a Fullilove would keep him safe from the administration's wrath.

People don't change, so he had to have been insufferable at home, too. I caught that comment about iambic pentameter. The asshole must've talked to her like she was an idiot student in his class.

Drama queen or not, I feel sympathy for Sierra despite my best efforts not to. Nobody deserves the punishment that is Todd Beaker. But I don't say it—that might encourage an overwrought sob-fest about her awful ex-husband.

Not that Todd Beaker isn't worthy of one. I'm just not interested in somebody's past marital dramas. Not even a little.

"Linda wants us to reconcile," Sierra says.

"Isn't it a little late if the divorce is final?" The question slips out before I can catch myself. This is all because Sierra's acting like a normal human being at the moment.

"She doesn't want to accept that. This case is one of her attempts to force us to spend time together." Sierra shrugs and smiles. "Probably not going to happen."

Good for you, I think with reluctant admiration. When relationships go sour, the best ending is a clean and swift one. No room for going back. No false expectations or hopes.

"I know it's a waste of your time, but I need to ask you to do the case until the end of the semester. You don't have to bring your students around all the time. Maybe once a month, just to satisfy whatever guidelines your department has set out."

She's being far too reasonable. What's the catch?

"I promise I'll make it worth your while." She smiles again, and my heart suddenly launches a thousand ships.

No, no, no! What am I thinking? This sex toy executive is not Helen of Troy.

I force myself to focus on what she said. *Worth my while.* What does that mean?

Her family purchased respectability by donating a huge sum of money to Wollstonecraft. When people hear the name Fullilove, they don't think about a giant clock dildo, but a family whose name you can see on a building at one of the most selective liberal arts colleges in the state.

"What are you offering precisely?" I ask in my most suspicious tone, the kind I use when Mom calls in the middle of the night sobbing, saying she wants to die *because*.

"Anything you think you need. Maybe something that could help with your tenure...?"

Thunderclouds gather in my head. How dare she offer to tamper with the tenure process! Not that I need help. It's simply an offensive quid pro quo. But before I can voice my distaste, a piercing scream cuts into our conversation.

"Are you fucking offering him *tenure*?" Todd comes crashing through some knee-high shrubs like an outraged rhino. Veins pulse visibly on his forehead and throat. They're somehow off-sync, which gives a bizarre effect. Forehead pulse, throat pulse, back and forth, like flickering light bulbs.

Which fits, given the intellectual wattage of the man involved.

"Are you?" His chest heaves rapidly and he seems to be having trouble remaining upright. He covers his side with a hand. Probably has a stitch.

"What are you doing here? Where's your class?" Sierra stands up. Smart of her. With the heels she's almost as tall as he is, which helps tip the power dynamics a little bit in her favor.

"I dismissed them."

Guess it isn't a big deal for his students to miss a lecture on anapestic tetrameter.

"I saw you take him outside and I wanted to talk," he says to Sierra.

"She brought me out here to talk to *me*, not to you," I inform him.

"I'm her husband."

"Her *ex*-husband. An object in the rearview mirror of her life."

Todd manages to straighten up. "Look, Lasker, this isn't about you." Condescension drips from his tone.

I can't believe nobody beat the attitude out of this pathetic dweeb in school. Most guys learn very fast they can't behave like this unless they want to get punched, or unless they're strong enough to be the bully.

Sierra puts a serene look on her face and raises a hand. "It *is* about Griffin because we're discussing the case study for *his* class."

There's nothing special about the way she says my name, but for some reason, it catches my attention. I roll it around in my head.

"Sierra, you aren't going to find another man like me."

I snort inwardly. *That's for sure.*

"I know you and understand you and forgive you for all your flaws," Todd adds.

I squint, running my eyes up and down his rather lacking frame. Does he not have functioning eyes? Even a cursory glance would show *he's* the flawed one. Begging on his knees wouldn't be sufficient to earn him "forgiveness."

"This isn't the time," Sierra says. "And I don't believe it ever will be."

"I forgave you for being frigid—"

She gasps.

I stiffen at his triumphant tone. His gaze slides, meets mine and asks, *You still wanna be here?*

Something inside me snaps.

"If she was frigid with you, it was probably your fault," I say. "When a woman doesn't respond in bed, it generally means the man doesn't know what he's doing."

What the hell are you doing? my mind screams.

That's a great question, but...no fucking clue. I should just walk away and leave them to what will undoubtedly devolve into a shouting match. Instead, I seem rooted to the spot and am saying things I shouldn't.

But leaving isn't an option. Not when toady Todd is smirking with the satisfaction of a man who knows he's hit the mark, and Sierra is staring at him speechless, her face a shade of embarrassed red.

"What do you know?" Todd says, practically spitting the words. "It's not like you ever slept with her!"

I let a smile take over my face. "Don't be so sure."

18

SIERRA

Todd inhales sharply. I hold my breath, more shocked by what Griffin's implying than Todd's claim about my being frigid because he's always complained about that. In his world, me not climaxing just for being in the same room as him is a problem —*with me*.

But I didn't expect Griffin to come up with that response. And he delivers the line with such steady calmness that even *I* wonder for a moment if he and I had sex at some point.

Todd swivels his entire body in my direction. An apoplectic shade of purple is stark against the white bandage. "You've been *cheating* on me?"

"Um, we *are* divorced."

He looks lost. "But we're in the process of reconciliation!"

"No, we're not." As I say it, I'm torn between relief and sadness. Relief that I left him, but sadness to see that he's changed so much— that he isn't the man I thought he was when we first met.

Back then, he was more attuned to my moods, more considerate of my needs. If this scene were taking place three years ago, he would've known Griffin was lying just by my reaction. But now Todd is so lost in his own thoughts and feelings that he isn't picking up on anything.

Ellie says that people don't change, and that I just failed to notice Todd's selfishness at first. But my failure doesn't make me feel any better. Not when he's embarrassing me.

Todd's eyes narrow, getting that weird, determined gleam.

Oh dear, I know that look. He's going to have a tantrum about how we're meant to be and my evil divorce lawyer broke us apart.

I'm not letting him indulge that delusion. It's time he *sees* the reality of his situation.

I loop my arm around Griffin's and tilt my head so it's resting on his shoulder. The muscles underneath stiffen, but I pretend I don't notice. My fingers flex on his biceps, which are *thick*. He must work out. You don't get arms like these from grading papers.

Up this close, he smells *good*. Like soap and male and wood and...

Oh no, no, no. Getting turned on and distracted in front of my ex wouldn't be good, even if the cause is the hottie professor in my clutches.

"Now listen, Todd. It really is time for you to go," I say with a you're-not-part-of-this smile.

Todd opens and closes his mouth a few times. *Doesn't that hurt with his messed-up jaw?* Or maybe the Midnight God didn't kick him that hard. He should've.

Wait... There's something wrong with the bruises on his face, which are more blue than purple now. I look closely. They're sort of sliding down his slightly sweaty skin...

"Did you *fake* those bruises?" I ask, more out of shock than the need to confirm. I know more about makeup than he ever will.

"What?" He covers both sides of his face with his palms, rather than just the left.

"Your bruises are melting."

"No, they're not," he says, but he sounds uncertain.

Griffin leans forward.

Todd turns his head away. "Stop! *Stop it!*"

"Oh my God," I say. "They *are* fake." I wondered how they could last so long. It's been two weeks since the Midnight God kicked his head.

"That's low." Griffin straightens. "His jaw injury might be fake, too."

"What?" Todd screeches like an opera singer who just sat on a thumbtack.

I frown at Griffin. The Midnight God kicked Todd hard enough to make him pass out. "What do you mean?"

"Nobody talks that much with a dislocated jaw," Griffin explains.

"Maybe they don't have as much at stake!" Todd says.

"No. It—hurts—too—much." Griffin's tone says, *I can't believe I need to explain something this simple.* "You're lucky to be able to suck down liquid meals."

Now that Griffin mentions it, I can see Todd hasn't lost any weight, either. "You faked how bad you were hurt for sympathy points? Seriously?" I shake my head.

Todd looks like he's about to burst into flame. His gaze darts between me and Griffin a few times as he weighs his chances.

Finally, his eyes quit moving back and forth and his eyebrows start twitching—a sign he's attempting to think of something clever to say and failing. Every time this happens, he says something clichéd and then becomes furious that that was the best he could do. And sure enough...

"This isn't over!" He takes a step back, his eyes on the point where Griffin's and my arms are looped together, then he turns and stalks away.

When he's out of sight, I let go of Griffin. "Thank you."

He says nothing, although I think I can hear a low vibration in his chest that sounds awfully like a growl. I glance up at his face to see his eyebrows pinched, his eyes narrowed and his mouth tight.

"Is this confrontation going to cause problems for you at Wollstonecraft?" I ask.

"Doubt it. He's in a different department." His lips purse briefly in distaste. "He does strut around insufferably, but that's more of a nuisance than a professional challenge."

"As long as your job is safe."

"Perfectly. His king of the campus act is irritating, but that's all."

It's weird that Griffin is focusing on this. I don't understand how Todd's behavior on campus is relevant to what we're discussing.

Griffin sees my confusion. "He's been abusing his marital connection to you to be as obnoxious as possible," he says. "It doesn't affect me, but it might affect the other professors in his department."

I gasp. "How come nobody said anything to me?"

"Perhaps nobody wanted to talk poorly about him to you. How

am I supposed to know?" Griffin's gravelly tone says, *He's your ex, not Wollstonecraft College's.*

Well, this is less than great. I make a mental note to speak to the head of the English department. The family didn't endow the college so that Todd could act like an ass.

But—stick a pin in that one for later. Right now, Griffin and I have another matter to finish discussing. "So, back to what we were talking about before—"

"I'm already tenured. I don't need your help."

Wow. He must be very good at what he does, because he seems too young to be tenured already. "Okay. Just wanted to make sure interdepartmental politics didn't end up hurting you, since Linda's gotten Chuck Phillips involved." Quite a few college professors have jumbo-sized egos, and are apt to get offended at the most innocuous comments. Chuck looks like he's a nice, laid-back guy, but he can be incredibly petty. He hinted strongly I should consider endowing the English department, since I married Todd, and didn't do much of a job hiding his disappointment when no extra money appeared.

"What does she have to do with anything?" Griffin asks, looking like he wants to murder somebody—hopefully not me.

"She's my stepmother, and she tries to wield her influence when she shouldn't. She doesn't control how the family endows the college, but she's been trying to make it seem like she does, despite the fact that I'm the CEO. Anyway, I didn't want anything to hurt your career at Wollstonecraft. That's all."

He nods. "I see. Thanks."

"You're welcome." I tilt my head in the direction of the headquarters. "Should we go back inside?"

19

GRIFFIN

The sensible security guy—Dan?—and Heather must've finished processing my class, because my students are waiting on the top floor with visitor's passes on their chests. Unlike the lobby, the vestibule is a respectable space with carpet like you'd find in any normal corporate office, and the décor is simple and inviting.

My students are looking around avidly, ready to absorb whatever information—or sex toy lore—they can. Their attitude chafes. They spend most of my class acting as though they're going to burn in hell if they pay attention for even ten minutes.

I decide then and there to make the final impossible to pass without listening to my lectures. The class has two textbooks, but I can use them as supplementary material and do my own spin on every concept.

Heather starts the tour, showing what goes into researching and manufacturing adult products. I'm a little surprised that there's more than just making a mold off an erect penis in the process. But then, this isn't my area.

Some of the girls look shocked as Heather displays earlier prototypes, while the boys giggle like idiots.

"Is it okay if we take pictures?" one of the frat boys asks with a suspiciously innocent look.

"Actually, no. Everything's proprietary here. Don't forget you all signed NDAs to keep our products in development secret when you received your visitor's pass." Heather speaks calmly, like a professional.

That piece of paper won't mean anything to these kids. Most of them have probably never even read a contract before scrawling their names.

"They'll sue you for millions if you break it," I say. "You'll spend the next half a decade in court, and then another few years in jail. *And I'll make sure to fail you as well.*" That should put the fear of God into them.

The tour doesn't take that long, probably because Heather can't show us everything. Even if she wanted to, we can't stay here for long, since the students have other classes to get to.

As Heather takes us to the elevator bank, Sierra comes out. "I hope you found the tour interesting. We'll send you some data sets to analyze later in the week." She smiles.

"Speaking of *anal*-yzing data, how often does your average college girl use one of the things we saw here?" Porter says. He elbows the guy next to him, and there are some snickers. Tanner, of course, laughs uproariously like the embarrassment that he is.

Sierra looks at them in slight confusion, then her expression turns here-we-go-again. It's irritating, as though she's judging *me*.

"Show some respect, or you'll fail the class," I say coldly.

The boys flinch, but Tanner's eyes grow hard and rebellious. "You can't fail me because I laughed at a joke," he says.

"No. But there will be a dozen other opportunities before the end of the term." I stare him down.

Within seconds, he breaks eye contact. He knows he can't afford to piss me off any more than he already has.

The two elevators arrive, and the college kids pile inside. As I walk past Sierra, I murmur, "Sorry about the inappropriate comment."

She smiles and shrugs. "I've heard worse. But thanks for coming to our defense."

Her simple thanks makes my heart skitter.

"Your students are waiting." She tilts her head at the elevators.

I nod curtly and step inside one of the cars. The descent is deafeningly silent, but of course every juvenile thought going through the kids' heads is going to be plastered all over social media in the next hour.

When we reach the lobby, they spill out, rushing to the parking lot and shouting at each other. I follow more slowly, then stop to consider the giant purple cock. *Just whose idea was it to put that there?* It's such a Ted Lasker move.

My phone pings, and I pull it out.

–Charles: How did it go?

If he's that curious, why didn't he do the case himself? Or was it because he knows what the company really does?

Still, he's the big cheese... So...

–Me: No problems.

At least I don't have to fake-smile when I text.

–Charles: Splendid! I knew you'd be perfect for this. It's always good to make an impression with youthful academic brilliance.

Ponderous, pompous... Should've sent Benson if he wanted to impress Sierra Fullilove with *youthful* academic brilliance. He's two years younger than me.

–Charles: I'm counting on you to bring good news.

I shake my head. *Asshole.* He didn't say anything about "good news." What does he think the Fulliloves are going to do? Build him a new research lab because I stopped by for a case that even the CEO knows is utter drivel?

–Charles: It is part of our job, after all.

He adds a smiley emoji. I bite back a snarl. Punching the head of my department would be one sure way to get my tenure revoked.

20

GRIFFIN

I'm ten minutes early for dinner at my favorite steakhouse in downtown L.A. with my brothers Grant, Huxley and Sebastian. Noah said he might join us, but he's as unreliable as his muse, whom he blames for an inability to finish his first novel. I told him if I were that undisciplined I'd have published zero papers, but he said rather haughtily that creativity is different from "rearranging numbers" and can't be rushed.

It's tempting to do a research paper on prolific authors. Isaac Asimov put out over five hundred books during his seventy-two-year life. Alexandre Dumas's published works add up to about a hundred thousand pages...all in longhand.

Shoving it in Noah's face and watching him struggle to come up with an excuse would be quite the entertainment.

The hostess, in a neatly pressed white shirt and black slacks, smiles, lines crinkling in the corners of her eyes. My brothers and I are regulars, and she makes sure to let us know she appreciates our patronage.

"You're the first to arrive tonight," she says, and then she takes me to our favorite table in the back. It has enough privacy to carry on a conversation about pretty much anything, including our mothers' sperm donor. There's no other way to describe Ted Lasker, especially given that he fathered all seven of us in a span of four months when his vasectomy failed. He was apparently incredulous such a thing could happen—*to him*. In his mind, things like that happen to *other people*, "other" meaning those who are unfortunate enough not to be rich or famous.

I'm sure it was a seismic shock to find out that biology is an impartial bitch who doesn't care about his tax bracket. Or how many hit movies he's produced. Or how many young, nubile things want to screw him for a chance to break out.

The hostess places five dinner menus and two drink menus on the table. I ask for two fingers of scotch, straight, and it appears almost immediately.

Nursing it, I sit back and relax. The place smells of aged meat, grilled to perfection, and freshly baked bread and butter. For a restaurant that's supposed to specialize in steak, they have bread that puts most bakeries in the city to shame, always served warm with a salted butter that makes a gluten overdose irresistible.

Tonight there's also live music—a pianist playing jazz on a white baby grand. It reminds me of New Orleans. Not the migraine-inducing part with my mom, but the hot-as-hell part later on.

I wonder what Purple Girl is doing. Is she thinking about me? And I wonder why thinking about her is also making me think of Sierra. They're nothing alike. Purple Girl was non-drama and normal. Sierra is all about drama. And most definitely abnormal.

Perhaps it's because my libido overheated with both women. But that isn't enough of a commonality.

My phone pings, and I pull it out.

–Dad: Did you see my last text?

Joey, I saw.

–Dad: Because it shows you read them, but you aren't responding. I'm wondering if the app is broken.

The app is working fine. I'm not responding because I don't want to waste my time. Time is money—

The memory of Sierra handing me a few bills interrupts my thoughts—the feel of her soft skin against mine as she placed the money in my palm. A combination of annoyance and discomfiture stirs. It isn't so irritating that I want to go to the gym and work out, but it is making itself known, an emotional splinter working its way deep into my mind.

I still can't figure out what possessed me to involve myself in her post-divorce spat with Todd. Granted, he's as gross as a piece of gum stuck to the bottom of your shoe. But as a rule, I remove drama from my life as much as possible.

For whatever reason, I just didn't want that asshole saying terrible things about her, including how she is in bed. *Frigid, my ass.* A woman who works at a company with a cock clock as though there's nothing wrong with the scenery isn't frigid. It's more likely Todd has a tiny dick or doesn't know what to do with what God gave him. Or both.

I pull up the browser on my phone and look up Silicone Dream. I should've done this before going to the company, but I went on what Charles said about it being a high-tech firm. *That lying prude.* The only thing "high tech" about the company is the Bluetooth remotes on their more advanced vibrators.

I thumb through the company's mission statement.

To provide products that make intimate moments between consenting adults more intense and pleasurable.

Well, well, well. Talk about a highfalutin mission. But then, Dad says a lot of bullshit about how he creates his movies to bring joy to people, when he's really doing it for money and ego.

The section on the history of the company shows all the products it's launched. Strap-ons seem to be their top—

"Well, well, well. Learn something new about your brothers every day." Huxley leans over me and points to the screen. "Is 'passion mauve' your favorite color?"

I sigh. I should've known he was looking at my screen from the cologne he likes so much, but it's hard to smell him over the food in the restaurant. Also, he has eagle eyes and doesn't need to be right behind me to see. He should've been an air force pilot rather than an ad executive, assuming he could fold that tall body into a fighter jet cockpit.

Dark-haired and squared-jawed, like all of us, Huxley likes to wear expensive bespoke suits. He says they project power and authority, which help him guide confused and uncertain clients. I say he likes them because they make him look like a boss, nothing else.

"No wonder he's so uptight," Grant adds with a laugh, coming up from behind Huxley. Grant works in venture capital with Emmett, and they've made a fortune off GrantEm Capital. My investments with some of the companies they funded are what added all those liberating zeros to my portfolio. Actually, all of us have made fortunes investing with Grant and Emmett.

"Very funny. Uptight describes Huxley, not me." He's the second oldest but acts like he's the oldest, always bossy.

Huxley considers for a moment. "Have to agree. 'Tight' doesn't really describe someone with an anal dildo fetish."

"Speaking of anal," I say, "how's business?"

Grant raises both his hands, palms up, all good humor and harmlessness. He's the smartest of us, but underneath the sweet-guy façade lies a nuclear asshole. People who screw with him don't end well.

"Just making an observation," Grant says. "Both of you often act like you have a stick up your ass." He takes the seat opposite mine and leans back as far as he can. He knows better than to sit next to me after that observation.

Huxley positions himself to Grant's left. "Hey, I'm not the one looking at things to shove into my ass."

"What was who looking at?" Noah says, strolling in, all loose-hipped and happy as usual. Either his book is going well or he's decided to give himself a break. My money is on the latter.

Then Sebastian arrives. He's in a suit, probably from a business meeting or something. He's the heir apparent to Sebastian Jewelry. The reason his name is the same as the company on his mother's side isn't because his mom has some weird identity issue. It's due to the fact that our dad decided remembering seven boys' names was too much work and named us after our mothers.

We should all thank our lucky stars none of our moms have names like Iphigenia Twocock.

"Nothing," I reply.

At the same time, Grant says, "A strap-on."

Noah quirks an eyebrow. "Do you know if you read strap-on backward, it spells 'no parts'?"

I look up at the ceiling. "Now I can die happy."

"Just sayin'." Noah laughs and sits next to me.

Our regular waitress appears with her typical perky smile and light brown hair neatly pulled into a ponytail. Mina is from Iowa, a senior at UCLA, studying history, and works two part-time jobs. We always tip her generously, partially to help fund her education and

My Grumpy Billionaire

partially because she's a damn good waitress, and good work deserves to be rewarded.

She exemplifies typical American apple-pie wholesomeness, and it annoys me that my hormones don't react to someone like her. Instead, they went wild around Sierra. And now I'm doubly annoyed that I'm thinking about a dildo CEO. *Again.*

Mina has a magical ability to sense what's needed. When Noah's with us, she always brings out the restaurant's killer bread and salted butter before taking our order because he's constantly starved for carbs. Tonight isn't any different. He's ripping into the bread like he hasn't eaten in centuries. I don't know where the calories go, because his abs are as tight as an anaconda's embrace.

"Everyone getting your usual?" Mina asks with a smile.

There's a general murmur of assent around the table. I lift my glass. "And another scotch, straight."

"Got it."

When she's gone, Grant turns to me, his eyes bright. "Maybe you should forward pictures of the strap-ons you like to Joey. He might get the hint and quit sending you women."

Thinking about what Joey did makes my blood boil. He's lucky he isn't here.

"Uh-oh. You look mad," Noah says between bites. "Don't kick Grant in the face. The only blood I want to see is from the steak."

"I'm not going to kick him in the face. I'm just furious I had to go to that damned company because of what Joey pulled."

My brothers don't ask for details. They already heard when I ranted and vented to them after my blood-pressure-raising call with Joey.

"Couldn't have been *that* bad," Sebastian says. Soothing tempers and egos is what he's good at. He has to be in order to survive the weird family dynamics and tension on his mom's side.

"Terrible. Fucking awful." I shove my fingers into my hair and clench. My scalp hurts, but I don't care. I need an outlet for my frustration.

"Don't do that. It causes premature hair loss," Noah says.

"Do I look like I care?"

"Griff'll look like a model even if half his scalp is bare," Huxley jokes. He can tell I'm about to erupt.

"It's just a case study. How hard could it be?" Grant says.

"Remember how I was supposed to restore 'dignity' to the department after that hooker incident?" I ask.

My brothers give me a look full of sympathy. Their hookers invaded their homes, a less intrusive ordeal than what I had to suffer. "Yeah..." they drag the answer out in uncertain unison.

"How am I going to do that with college kids doing a case on a sex toy company?"

My brothers stare. Even Noah quits stuffing his face with bread.

Finally, Grant breaks the silence. "I thought you said it was a high-tech firm."

"That's what Charles told me."

"Ooh..." Noah gives a slow I-see-how-he-fucked-you-over nod.

Hux bristles as though he's the one being treated unfairly. It makes me feel marginally better. Then our food and drinks come and we dig in.

"How's Emmett doing, by the way?" I glance at Grant. He sees Emmett in the office.

"The miasma of doom and damnation around him is becoming darker each day," Grant says. "He's trying hard to act normal, but I can tell he's failing. I wouldn't want to be the one giving him a deliverable, because he's looking for reasons to nitpick, right down to the font type."

"I thought you used a standard font," Huxley says.

"Yeah, but he's going to say the font is too generic or it's too small, too big, too"—Grant makes a vague gesture, waving his fork around—"something. You can't argue with him when he's in this kind of mood."

Noah pulls out his phone. "This is why I'd never work for him," he says absently, scrolling through something, probably social media feeds. He checks every hour, a waste of time in my opinion. Nothing useful is on them, and spending more than a minute rots your brain.

"Huh," Noah grunts. "When did you start dating a dildo heiress?"

We all look at each other. Grant says, "Who are you talking to?"

"Griff," Noah responds, looking up from the screen.

"What?" Did Mina sprinkle psychedelic mushrooms into my brother's food?

He angles his phone so I can see the video. Some asshole filmed the interaction between me, Sierra and Todd in the garden and posted it online.

Damn it.

"Damn," Grant says with a whistle.

Sebastian nods sagely. "No wonder you didn't want to do the case. Nothing good comes of mixing business with girlfriends."

God save me from people leaping to conclusions. "No, it's just a misunderstanding."

"I don't know." Noah studies the phone screen. "She's wrapped around your arm like a little blonde octopus. It's cute."

Cute? Is he kidding? I only put up with it because she needed to convince Todd.

Grant looks at the screen. "Must've been nice having a pretty girl on your arm like that."

"It was *not* 'nice.'" Not even a little. Nope.

Huxley snorts. "He must've pushed her away and the video just didn't catch it," he says with a broad wink.

"I didn't push the lady away because that would have made me an asshole." I'm not an asshole by nature. I'm only an asshole when I'm *driven* to be an asshole.

"What are the chances the people in your school won't notice?" Noah says, his eyes glinting with amusement.

Just like that, my mood plunges. The steak in front of me turns as appetizing as a grilled eggplant, which is outright gross. Charles. Damn Charles and his salivating over any possible funding for the research lab he so desperately wants. He's going to be on me like a tick until I get Sierra to commit to having the damned lab built.

Fuck. Me.

21

SIERRA

I open my eyes at exactly six, as usual. Normally, I linger in bed for a couple of minutes in total silence, but today my phone starts ringing at six-oh-one.

Must be something important. I pick it up off the nightstand and frown when I see it's Dad calling. What does he want?

Our conversations don't generally go well. Before Mom passed away, we exchanged what was necessary. Things like greetings or asking for schedules to plan for stuff like Father's Day brunches or birthdays.

But since Linda came into the picture, we haven't even done that. I have a recurring contract with a local florist to send Dad bouquets on Father's Day and his birthday. On Christmas, I send him a box of the specialty chocolate treats he likes. He doesn't reciprocate—not even a quick text wishing me happy birthday or merry Christmas—but I'm used to that now. Expectations bring nothing but heartache.

The phone quits ringing. I shrug. *Guess we won't be talking.*

Then a text arrives with a ping.

–Dad: I know you're up. Can we talk? It won't take long.

I stare at the text, wondering what could be so urgent. The phone rings again, and I hit the green button.

"Hey, Dad," I say.

"Sierra." His tone is a mixture of impatient annoyance—probably over the fact that I didn't pick up earlier—and relief that he's getting to talk to me. "Why didn't you answer earlier?"

"I just got up," I lie, since I don't want to get into this. "What is it?"

A beat of silence. "I thought we taught you better than that."

"Better than what?"

"You could've said, 'How are you?' first."

Is it me or does he sound peeved?

"I am your father."

Old resentment stirs up like sand brushed up by sudden currents. My hand tightens around the phone. We no longer have the kind of relationship where we check on each other, and it wasn't me who wanted that. I was actually shocked he came to my wedding two years ago, although in retrospect, it was probably Linda's doing, since she so adores her nephew. "I have to get ready for work. You said this wouldn't take long."

He makes a vaguely flustered sound. "Yes. Well. It's about what happened yesterday."

"What in particular?"

"Are you really going to be that cruel to Todd?"

"To—" This can't be happening. "Are you honestly calling me at the crack of dawn to talk about my ex-husband?"

"He's still family."

Dad might as well have reached through the screen and backhanded me. I just stare at my phone, speechless. Where was he when I needed him? Did he feel this way when he begrudgingly forced himself to show up for my graduation because of Grandma? Or decided to forget my birthdays and Christmas and...

I shake my head, *hard*. I promised myself I wouldn't dwell on any of that, so I'm not going to start now.

"Maybe your family. Not mine." Despite my best effort, my voice quavers.

"Don't be absurd—"

"If you don't have anything else to discuss, I'm hanging up. I have to get ready for work."

Without waiting for a response, I hang up. I don't want to waste any more mental energy. Closing my eyes, I concentrate on my breathing for a few moments.

Calm. Chill. Zen. Todd isn't worth it, and Dad isn't either.

I have a petty urge to tell the florist not to bother sending flowers to Dad anymore, but I control the impulse, which will pass. Mom asked me to be nice to Dad because he doesn't mean to be neglectful, and I'm going to honor her wish.

Plus, it makes me a better person. There's no reason to stoop to his level.

I breathe deeply some more, until all the tension from the call from Dad dissipates. I don't want to take negative energy with me to work.

I open my eyes and glance at my phone.

6:45

Oh shit!

I hop off the bed. Crap, crap, crap! It took longer than I expected to shake off the bad mojo from Dad. Argh! I rush through a shower. No time to dry my hair all the way, so when it's dry enough, I just rub some hair gel through it and twist it up. Skewer the topknot with a black chopstick and I'm good to go.

Then I throw on the first dress I happen to grab—bright lavender with mustard accents—and slip on the nude sandals from yesterday.

"Good enough," I say, then run downstairs and jump into my Ferrari.

Driving to work, I put on my makeup piecemeal at the red lights. A little bit of concealer. Mascara. Finishing powder. Lipstick. Presentable enough.

The dash on my Ferrari says I'm on time. Grandma always told me being punctual is paramount in setting a good example and achieving success in life, and I don't want to be the kind of boss who comes in late for no good reason.

Plus, I have a morning meeting.

I park and trot across to the lobby, my huge purse slung over a shoulder. Thankfully, Todd isn't here to scream my name. He probably has a lecture or something today.

It is lovely to enter the building without some horrific spectacle. Wouldn't it be great if Chuck put Todd on some committee that meets in the morning every day? I swore to myself I wouldn't interfere with Todd's career, but the temptation is so, so strong.

Dan waves. "Good morning." His smile is extra broad. He

must've gotten lucky this morning. Not that I monitor my employees' sex lives, but his wife told me he gets that special, sappy smile when she lets him have her in the shower. Yes, it is TMI, but she was drunk when she told me at our New Year's Eve party two years ago.

"Good morning," I say, smiling back and acting like I don't know why he's so mellow and happy.

"Go you." He gives me a thumbs-up.

"Um, go me...? Thanks?" *What's that about?*

I ride the elevator with two other people—Spence and Jack from marketing, who are holding hands. They announced their engagement three months ago, and I'm happy for them, since they make a handsome couple. They grin at me, their eyes eager.

It's a little freaky. The last time they looked at me like this, I had to mediate an argument between the marketing team and the product development team. I *really* don't want to get stuck between them again.

On the other hand, they keep giving me that expectant look. Fine. I might as well get this over with.

"Is there something you'd like to tell me?" *Tell me you're getting along great with the product development team. Tell me you're—*

"I like how you trade up," Spence says with a wink.

"Me?" I haven't bought a new car or home. Heather hasn't bought me new office furniture.

"Don't act coy. We all know." Jack pats my shoulder. If gestures came with vocal cords, this one would be saying, *You go, girl!* "We're one hundred percent behind you."

"Woohoo!" Spence pumps his fist.

"I see. Thanks." I smile back, hiding my unease. Dan and now Spence and Jack. What's going on? What did I trade up while I was sleeping?

They step out of the elevator on the fifteenth floor. When I reach my floor, Barbara is at her desk, reading something. Then she pulls back and punches the air with her fists. "Yes!"

"Good morning, Barbara." I smile. "Did Michelle nail her audition?"

"She did, thank you, but it's not about that." She looks up at me, her eyes shining. "Oh, I'm so *happy* for you!"

"Okay, did something happen yesterday after I left the office?"

"You don't have to pretend." She props her elbows on the desk, linking her fingers together, then rests her chin on the hands. "We're all just thrilled you've moved on. The chapter with that jerk is finally finished, and the page has been *turned*!"

"Chapter? Jerk?"

"Todd."

"The divorce was finalized a few weeks ago." And everyone at Silicone Dream knows about that. I made sure of it.

"Yeah, but we're doubly thrilled that now you're dating a man you *deserve*." She winks. "An ex doesn't really feel like an ex until you replace him with something better, you know?"

"Uh... Who exactly are you talking about?"

"The hottie! I don't know why you didn't tell us sooner. Those shoulders... That ass...! Mmm-mmm."

The Midnight God has some of the best shoulders I've ever clutched. I can confidently say the same about his ass as well. But how could my employees know about him? Actually, they couldn't be talking about him because I'm not dating him.

When I continue to stare blanky, she sighs. "You're worse than Michelle trying to play dumb."

"Barbara, I'm not playing dumb. I am lost."

"Please. Everyone's seen the video."

"*What video?*"

She frowns and shows me her phone. I lean forward, then put my hand over my mouth as the scene in the garden plays out, starring me, Griffin and Todd.

"Who posted that?" I ask.

"Some kid from Wollstonecraft. He tagged Todd, but not Griffin Lasker. Probably too hot to be tagged. Just look at that man."

Well. Yes. Barbara is correct. Griffin is scorching, and he made me think of similarly hot sexual acrobatics when I met him, but *we're not dating...*

I should probably correct everyone. On the other hand, would that complicate things? Make Griffin look like a liar for implying that we're dating? He did it to save me from Todd's ridiculous antics, and I don't want to repay him by backstabbing him without saying something to him first. Plus, I don't want Todd to learn Griffin and I lied yesterday and charge back here to discuss a future reconciliation only he wants.

"Sierra! There you are." Heather waves. "I was wondering when you were coming in. You have a meeting at nine and have a couple of things to review beforehand."

"Sorry," I say, turning to my assistant. She was probably a little antsy, since I like to review the agenda for each meeting five minutes before it starts.

We start walking toward my office.

"You should've told me about him," she chides me softly. "You know I'm discreet."

I just give her a neutral smile.

"That econ professor is so much better than the horrible thing you divorced. And good for you. The only real mistakes in life are the ones you don't learn from, and that goes for relationships as well. I'm so relieved you're being *extra* selective now."

"So am I." If we only look at the exterior, Griffin is pretty much perfect. It's just that there are other considerations.

Such as how he finds this company embarrassing. I didn't miss the disapproval in his gaze when he looked at the monument to our first major product in the lobby. When I was taking him outside to talk, he was looking around, searching for something to criticize, verbally or otherwise.

The only difference between Griffin and Todd's disapproval of Silicone Dream is that Griffin likes to communicate with his eyes, while Todd likes to vocalize. Oh, and Griffin doesn't tolerate people bad-mouthing the company.

I reach my office and place my purse on the desk. Heather hands me some coffee just as my phone pings. I check the screen, praying it isn't Dad or Linda.

–Ellie: You sly girl you!

I close my eyes briefly before reading the rest of the message.

–Ellie: You didn't tell me you found yourself a new lover. And all this time I thought you were still pining over that Midnight God. What kind of BFF are you?

I should've known she'd text me as soon as she saw the video. She's probably unhappy she found out the same way everyone else did.

–Me: It's just a big misunderstanding!

–Ellie: What do you mean?

–Me: You saw in the video how Todd was saying that crap about me being frigid, right?

–Ellie: Yes! You should've said that nobody can get excited over a jalapeño!

I laugh.

–Ellie: Not just any jalapeño, but a pickled jalapeño! Limp, small and not so spicy!

I laugh harder.

–Me: I love you girl. Anyway, before I could bring up any limp veggies, Griffin defended me, that's all. Note that we never said we were dating.

I give her a moment to process that.

–Ellie: Ohhh... Okay. In that case, I guess you can still be my BFF.

–Me: Haha, thanks. Anyway, don't tell everyone yet because I should probably talk to Griffin about how to clear things up first.

–Ellie: Got it. We don't want to put our knights in shining armor in bad positions.

–Me: Exactly.

I tap the edge of the phone and wonder if Griffin is okay, or if people are treating him oddly at work.

Nah. The reason my employees are so excited about this is because they hate Todd. The faculty and staff at Wollstonecraft have no strong feelings about me one way or the other, so Griffin's day is probably going along as usual.

22

GRIFFIN

"Good morning," Benson says as I walk into the econ department. He's a nice guy, if a little awkward at times, still slightly unsure of his place in academia. He might be able to disguise it better if he presented himself with a little more care. His white cotton dress shirt hangs off rounded shoulders like an uninspired rag, and his slacks are missing creases and slightly frayed at the bottom. The short brown hair on his head sticks out in all different directions like a poorly constructed bird's nest—and unlike with some of my students, the effect is wholly unintentional.

Currently, his owlish brown eyes are extra wide in awe.

He's only given me that look once before, when he learned that I won the John Bates Clark Medal. Why is he showering me with unspoken admiration *today*?

But he isn't the only one looking at me with awe, speculation or petty vindication that silently screams, *I knew it!* Everyone is. And all the while, they murmur that polite "Good morning" as I walk down the hall.

It might be morning, but there's nothing good about it!

Then it hits me. According to the gleeful text Noah sent this morning, the video from yesterday has gotten hundreds more likes and shares. He's certain everyone on campus knows. No shit, Sherlock. If I'd known it'd come to this, I might've let Todd mouth off instead of getting involved.

I shake myself mentally. *Be honest. You would've still said something.*

But I might not have implied that Sierra and I were dating. There were other ways to shut Todd up.

A couple of women laugh. I turn a corner and see Professors Julia Manchester and Lori Johnson, who are ambling in the same direction I am. I want to snarl, *What's so damn funny,* until I catch a bit of their conversation.

"...apparently got the reaming from Chuck he deserves," Julia is saying loudly with excitement.

"He didn't think Chuck would know by now?"

"Guess not. I wish I'd been there. I heard it was epic. Like *Beowulf.*" Julia sighs. "If English professors are saying that, you know it's *good.*"

They're gossiping about the English department. What's so exciting about somebody in another discipline getting reamed?

"Ask around for the video," Lori says. "Somebody's bound to have recorded it. Everyone hates him."

"Except his mother."

Julia looks skeptical. "If I had a son like that, I would've disowned him a long time ago. Cut my losses and had myself a new one who could do better."

"A high-strung poodle could do better than Todd."

Guess Chuck finally grew a pair after two years of disrespect from Todd.

If Chuck's been being obsequious due to Todd's marriage to Sierra... Well, that makes him even more spineless than the average administrator. It isn't as though the Fullilloves are going to take their endowment back.

"Any functional mammal could do better." Julia stops in front of her office. "And speaking of mammals, did you know he has a Hello Kitty tattoo on his butt?" She smothers a giggle.

"Seriously?" Lori laughs. "How do you know?"

No, hell no! I stalk past them, my strides longer than usual. I don't need to know how Julia knows, just like I didn't need to know about Todd's butt tattoo. Neither do the other econ professors, but I don't feel like warning them—not that it would do any good. There's no secret Lori can keep, and everyone in the department is going to know about the Hello Kitty tattoo on Todd's ass before lunch.

Just as I reach my office, Charles glides up. It's as though somebody texted him that I was coming. He's in his best shirt—so impeccably starched and pressed that the cotton has acquired a satiny sheen. His black slacks are sharply creased and similarly pristine. There's even a maroon tie around his neck with a shiny platinum pin with a winking diamond on the tip. He only wears it when he has an important meeting.

"Good morning!" For once, his tone isn't ponderous. It's bright and eager, like he's a college boy ready for a dream date with the hottest sorority girl on campus.

From the intensity of his gaze, I gather that the important meeting is *me*.

My internal alarm goes on full alert. "Good morning." I unlock my office. "Would you like to come in?"

Whatever Charles has to say probably isn't something I want to discuss in the hall. More than one curious professor is loitering.

"If I may," Charles says with a broad smile.

It's the same damn smile he gave me when he told me Silicone Dream was a "high-tech" company. He must've found a new way to screw me over, thanks to that stupid video. Granted, I was lying in it, but no one other than Sierra knows that.

I shut the door behind us and gesture at the visitor's seat. "How can I help you?" My tone is brisk as I sit down at my desk. Time to get this visit over with. And figure out who I need to sue to take the damned video down.

He lowers his body onto the chair and groans, like it's a torture to press his ass on the hard, molded plastic. "You know, I never realized your office was so small." He says it like it's a huge problem he'd like to rectify immediately.

"I like it small." It discourages people from visiting or lingering. The space is already full with him inside.

"Ah." He smacks his palms on his thighs, then runs his hands along the slacks—a delay tactic. He looks around, his lips pressed together. "Cozy and intimate, then."

I shoot him a bland smile. If he's trying to bring up the inappropriate behavior of coeds in my office, I *will* dislocate his jaw. If anybody has a complaint about inappropriate behavior, it's me.

He clears his throat. "You should've informed me of your relationship with Sierra Fullilove. I realize it can be uncomfortable to give advice to one's girlfriend."

I just give him a hard look. I want to correct him, but don't want that disgusting Todd hearing the truth and telling everyone he's in the process of reconciling with Sierra. He doesn't deserve her, and she doesn't deserve him. Perhaps we'll wait a couple of weeks and then quietly feign a breakup.

"My wife loathes getting advice from me, even when she's asked for it." Charles chuckles urbanely. "But...perhaps your relationship means it would be easier to, ah, arrive at a good conclusion if you told her what she wants to hear." He gives me a hopeful look.

"Can you define 'a good conclusion'? I'd hate to misinterpret."

"Good. Satisfactory. Whatever the family thinks is appropriate, of course, but it would be nice if they could... Well." He huffs, his cheeks turning red with the embarrassment of having to spell out an indelicate matter.

"The research center," I say, amused that he's so predictable, and disgusted that he's this shameless. Bisons will propel themselves to Mars with their farts before I lift a finger to help fund the research center.

Fundraisers mean peopling. Or at least pretending I'm happy to be wasting my time with people—the sum of whose collective brain cells don't reach double digits. I'd rather have my legs broken by my sparring partner.

"Yes!" Charles's eyes brighten with relief. "Just so."

"You should call Sierra's assistant and set up an appointment to discuss it."

He blinks at me. "Ah..."

"Please don't misunderstand. I *would* do it, of course. Anything to help the college out. But unfortunately, Silicone Dream's corporate governance doesn't allow for interference or undue influence. And I do rather fit the definition." I give him a blank smile. "I'm sure you understand the ethical issue. We wouldn't want a scandal attached to the center."

"No, of course not." Disappointment dims the bright greed in his eyes.

"I knew you'd understand. Now, if that's all... I have a call scheduled with Keith Lenin to discuss our research."

"Of course." Charles stands up and starts to leave. It takes a while because he drags his feet, probably hoping and praying that I'll change my mind and agree to put some subtle pressure on Sierra after all. I maintain my bland smile of vague neutrality, and let it drop the second he's out the door. Smiling takes entirely too much effort.

My office phone rings. I consider letting it go to voice mail, then decide maybe I should pick it up in case it's something important.

"Griffin Lasker."

"Good morning!" comes a chirpy female voice. "This is Sierra."

Yes, I know. Every cell in my body just sprang to life like a puppy jumping to its feet at the sound of its owner coming home.

No, not like a puppy, I decide. I just don't like it that her voice is so chirpy. It's unnatural for people to be this happy in the morning, especially when the day started out less than stellar.

"Is this a bad time?"

Lady, this entire day is bad. "I can spare a few minutes."

"Oh good. I just wanted to see if you were okay. I mean, you probably are, but I didn't want to assume. Just in case."

"Things are going as expected." *A total shitshow.*

"Awesome." She sounds relieved. And happy. *Why is she so happy?* "People are being a bit weird here, you know?"

"They don't think you date?" I say, suddenly irritated that people are reacting weirdly around her, too.

"I guess it was just unexpected. Kind of a shock, maybe?"

What could be so shocking about her behavior? Is there a morality clause for her conduct? But what kind of morality clause could be applied to a sex toy company CEO?

"Everyone at the company is super excited about me moving on. I guess they don't like Todd much."

I grunt my approval. At least they have good taste in *some* areas, I decide, recalling the purple dick in the lobby.

"So, it didn't get you into trouble with anybody, right? You don't have a girlfriend or anything?"

Her concern is cute, but a bit late. "I wouldn't have done it if I were in a relationship."

She sighs. "Oh, good."

For some bizarre reason, it makes me wonder what kind of sigh she'd make in bed. Blood starts to heat and flows in the wrong direction.

I need you up here, in my brain. Not down there.

But, like water, my blood finds its own level and the fabric over my crotch begins to rise. *Great.*

"The only thing that's happened so far is Charles conveying his expectations for the case," I add, irritated at my body's reaction.

"Such as?"

"Just some departmental issues."

"It would help if we told everyone the truth, wouldn't it?" she asks tentatively.

"Probably."

"What do you want to tell people?"

If this were up to me, I'd just announce that the whole thing was a farce. But this affects Sierra too. The video starts with Todd calling her frigid. And the idiot said it loudly enough that the phone caught it.

Asshole.

I should've taunted him until he threw a punch. That way, he could have acquired some bruises that wouldn't melt off his oily face. "Since I started it and one of Todd's students spread it, perhaps you should have a say on how you want to end the rumor."

"Oh." She's quiet for a moment. "Do you want to meet and discuss? I have meetings all day today, but I'll be done by six."

"All right. Where?"

"Not my office. The gossip would *never* die."

And cafés in the area are out of question, since that's where my caffeine-addicted students hang out. "I can be in my office. You can use the faculty parking lot if you come after six."

The kids won't be hanging out that late in Fullilove Hall. They'll be busy thinking about dinner or daydreaming about the upcoming mixer.

"Um. My car's kind of noticeable. I drive a red Ferrari."

At least she's smart enough to bring that up now. Somebody would definitely notice a red Ferrari and want to know whom it belonged to. I don't even drive my Tesla to work.

"How about my place? It isn't that far from campus," she says.

Her place feels a bit too personal. "A woman living alone should take more precautions. I could be a serial killer."

She laughs. "Do serial killers generally announce that they're serial killers before the fact?"

"The smarter ones probably do. Creates a false sense of security."

"Well, I'll take my chances. I have attack hamsters to defend my honor. And I trust you."

Why do I like hearing that so much?

She continues, "Now give me your cell phone number so I can text you the address."

23

SIERRA

After the final meeting of the day, I make the half-hour drive home. I cut the engine and look at the green-shingled, three-story home Grandma left me along with Silicone Dream. Despite all the money she made from the company, she never upgraded her living space. She preferred to stay in the same nice suburban neighborhood where she met and married Grandpa and raised their family.

The white picket fence and spacious yard are the same, along with the crabapple tree with the small cinder block just big enough for a toddler to sit on. I open the door and walk inside. The only things that have changed are here: upgraded appliances, threadbare carpet ripped out to reveal the hardwood floor, and some new furniture that Grandma bought, along with the reupholstered armchair Grandpa loved so much by the fireplace.

After Mom passed away, I spent almost all of my time here.

I flip the light switch in the living room. The mantels and floating shelves are crowded with photos, and for some reason I walk over to see them. Maybe I'm feeling a bit emotional after that call from Dad.

The pictures chronicle the family's history. My grandparents' outdoor wedding in the yard, the crabapple tree smaller. They look so happy together, gazing at each other like they'd found all they could dream of. A few pictures of them and Dad in various stages:

helpless infant, chubby toddler, shyly smiling boy, awkward teenager, quiet young man. Then to my parents' wedding—both looking like the greatest lovers in the world, their eyes on each other longingly. He might not be the best dad, but he's a great husband. To him, children were unfortunate byproducts that divided matrimonial attention.

There are photos of me from infanthood to teenage years. My favorite is the one with me sitting on the cinder block in front of the crabapple tree. There are pictures from my high school and college graduations, taken with Grandma and Ellie. My parents are missing from both. Mom was gone by then, and Dad didn't take any pictures with me because…

Well… He had his new family—Linda and Felicia.

But you would never know from the photos in this room. Despite their grand wedding—with *two* professional photographers—there isn't a single photo from the ceremony on the shelves. Felicia graduated from high school two years after I did, but you wouldn't know that, either. Her pictures aren't part of the collection.

Grandma made it clear Linda and Felicia weren't *her* family when she found out they both treated me like I wasn't there. She was also disappointed that Dad didn't do anything to intervene. But then, he hates conflict or taking an uncomfortable stance, and won't do it unless pushed into it by Linda. That's why Grandma didn't leave the company to him—Linda exerts too much influence.

I've accepted Dad for what he is. It wasn't as hard as people think because I had Grandma…and I have Ellie. He isn't going to change for me, and there's nothing I can do about that. He's happy with Linda now, just like he was with Mom.

I'm not part of his inner circle, just as he isn't in mine. I don't know why that particular knowledge is weighing me down today. It isn't like it's a recent realization.

Shaking off the blue feeling, I walk toward the table on the left of the reupholstered armchair, where the hamster cage is located. Bullet and G-Spot quit running in their wheel and come toward me, their tiny claws wrapping around the thin stainless-steel bars.

"Hey, cutie pies." I can't help smiling. Their mere presence perks me up.

Their pink noses flare and quiver, their whiskers vibrating up and down as they sniff me, probably trying to figure out if I've brought them anything to eat. Bullet and G-Spot aren't trainable like dogs, but they're no less affectionate or inquisitive.

When crossed, they're quite vicious, too. Mean enough to draw blood.

"I had a great day. How about you?" I ask.

They emit little squeaks, and Bullet lets go of the bars to trundle around the cage. I give them some sunflower seeds and start toward the kitchen to check the fridge. *Do I have anything decent to serve Griffin when he stops by?* There should be something—I went to the store just a couple of days ago.

I turn on some music, and Killian Axelrod's husky voice fills the house. His band just released a new album, and it's absolutely divine. Some bands get stale after a couple of albums, but so far Axelrod has been amazingly creative. Moving to the drumbeat, I sing along with the song.

Inside the fridge are two different kinds of juice and a few bottles of lemonade. They should do. *Starting to get hungry, though.* I pick up my phone to order a pizza. As I enter the topping options—extra cheese and pepperoni—the doorbell rings.

Must be Griffin. *And just in time for pizza if he wants some.* I'll see if he likes something other than cheese and pepperoni, although he doesn't seem fussy. Todd likes grilled artichoke hearts, anchovies and goat cheese on his, which severely limited our pizza options.

I cross the living room, my step brisk, and open the door.

A man I've never seen before is standing on the porch helping to support a lump of what appears to be a human being. Except the supposed human smells like a rat that drowned in a vat of alcohol.

The man shifts so I can see the drunkard's face better.

Oh shoot. It's Todd!

"This your husband?" the man asks.

"No. *Ex*-husband."

He shrugs. "Close enough." He pushes Todd in my direction. "He's all yours."

I move back, not wanting to touch Todd. He slumps onto the doorframe like a sack of smelly flour.

The man starts walking away. "Wait!" I call out. I slide around Todd and trot after him.

"Lady, I gotta go." He keeps on walking without sparing a glance in my direction. "Got money to make." He jumps into his black Camry and speeds away.

"Argh! No!" I stamp my foot, then turn around and glare at Todd, who's managed to stand, leaning against the doorway. "What is *wrong* with you? Why didn't you go home?"

He moves his head, his eyes bleary but angry. "Wrong with *me*?" He slurs the words. "The fuck's wrong with *you*? Humiliated me. In fronna everyone..."

"I haven't seen you since you left yesterday." But really, I shouldn't be talking to him. I should be getting Linda to take her precious nephew away. I get my phone out.

—Me: Todd's at my place, drunk as a skunk. Come get him or I'm calling 911 for trespassing.

"Now *everyone* knows 'bout the divorce," he mutters.

I huff an impatient breath. "It wasn't exactly a national secret."

"All my plans. All my dreams. Ru—ru—ruined because of you." He sways, wagging a finger, then pointing it at me accusingly. "People quit respecting me. Now they're laughin' at me..." His already red face is getting redder. Is he going to have a heart attack? Or keel over from alcohol poisoning?

I don't care which, but I hope he does it once he's off my porch. Unlike lawn gnomes, corpses don't enhance the décor.

"It's your fault for being rude to your coworkers," I say, remembering what Griffin said. Although I haven't witnessed it firsthand, knowing how Todd treated people at Silicone Dream, I can picture it.

"They don't deserve my respect!"

"I'm sure they disagree."

"Are you mocking me?" He lurches off the doorframe toward me. I take a step back in the yard, not wanting to let him get close.

"You bitch! I'm supposed to be important. Respected!" he yells as he tacks left and right toward me. *How much did he drink?*

"You have to earn respect!" I say, taking another step back.

"I already earned it! You ruined it!"

"Oh for God's sake, stop blaming other people!" My heel hits the cinder block. I step over it, then position myself so the crabapple tree is between me and Todd.

"Bitch! Come here!" He lunges, swinging his fists wildly.

Is he trying to punch me? He's never hit me before, but then he's never swung his fists either.

On the other hand, he's drunk, so he could just be flailing around for better balance. It's hard to tell which, since he's not the most coordinated guy.

He's coming around the tree when his foot gets caught on the block. He pitches forward. His face smacks into the tree and blood spurts from his nose. "Fuck!"

I watch, speechless, as he slowly folds onto himself, his hands over his face.

"What happened?"

I turn and see Griffin. He looks at me, then Todd, then me again.

"He tried to punch the tree and lost." I take a deep breath and try to settle myself. It isn't every day I'm confronted by a raging drunk on my own property.

"Are you all right?"

"Oh, sure." I give him a smile to alleviate any worries.

Griffin leans over and smells Todd, who has now crumpled over onto his side on the grass. Maybe the combination of pain and alcohol made him pass out. "How did he get here?"

"He must've given this address to Uber or something. A driver dropped him off."

"And you took him in?" *Are you stupid?* I can hear the unspoken question.

"I actually didn't have a chance to do anything. The driver just dropped him off and left before I could ask him to take Todd to his place."

Griffin curses under his breath.

Just then, a blue Mercedes roadster screeches to a stop in front of us. Linda jumps out and rushes up. Her jaw drops as she looks at Todd's unmoving body on the lawn.

"Sierra, how *could* you?" She crouches over him, cooing like he's a poor little kitten. "Oh my God, *look* at him! I think you broke his nose."

"You think *I* did that to him?"

"Just because he showed up distraught didn't mean you had to get violent! You were always such a mean—"

"She didn't hit him. The tree did," Griffin cuts her off flatly.

Linda stares at him. "What?"

"He fought that tree"—Griffin points at the crabapple tree—"and lost."

For a second, she continues to stare. Then she goes back into offensive mode. "He was just trying to communicate better with his wife."

"With alcohol and violence?" Griffin asks.

"He needs his comfort," she says stiffly.

No. *I* need comfort. "Can you just take him away before I have to call the police for trespassing? I will, if I have to," I say, tired of dealing with her and Todd.

Linda looks at me like I'm a monster. "You don't need to do that. I'll talk with him, make sure he doesn't bother you drunk again."

"That would be very helpful," I say, biting back the polite "thank you" Mom and Grandma ingrained in me. This wouldn't have happened if Linda hadn't encouraged him.

She puts her hands under Todd's shoulders, but he doesn't budge. "Can you help?" she demands, looking at me.

"Nope," I say. "You can take your own trash out."

24

GRIFFIN

I almost laugh at Sierra's sassy comeback. Linda's face twists as though she's stepped into a rotting skunk carcass, but she doesn't look to me for support. At least she isn't a complete moron.

"I'm going to throw my back out," she whines.

"Ask Todd to smack your spine back into alignment once he's sober. I'm sure he'll be happy to," Sierra says, then turns to me. "Do you want to come in?"

"Sure."

She starts toward her home. As I follow, I note her hands are clenched so tight, they're trembling.

Well. I'd be shaking mad too if I had to deal with a drunk and inane ex and an annoying step-parent. Thankfully, I have none of those.

Sierra maintains her composure, back straight and step elegant, until she opens the door and walks inside. I follow her into the foyer and shut the door, cutting us off from the outside world.

Sierra leans against the wall and lets out a long, steadying breath.

She's got spunk, I decide with begrudging admiration. I don't want to discover anything to like about her, especially when her shampoo's already distracting enough. And her voice, too—all sassy and buoyant.

"You hanging in there?" I ask, making sure to stay away so I don't do anything I'll regret, such as putting a comforting hand on her shoulder.

"I'm fine. Just need a moment. I didn't expect Todd to show up like that."

"Do you want to sit down? Pace a little?"

She blinks and looks around the foyer. "Geez! Where are my manners? Come on in and let's sit down."

She moves to the kitchen and pulls out a couple of chairs for us. The table is old and covered with nicks and scratches that attest to its age. But no matter how I try, I can't picture her picking it up from a yard sale. The appliances in the kitchen are modern and top of the line, and the furniture is old but made of good wood—oak and cherry, mostly—with excellent craftsmanship. A damaged garage sale table wouldn't fit the décor.

"Something to drink?" Sierra asks, opening the fridge. "I have juice or lemonade."

"Water's fine," I say.

"Of course it's fine. I have lots of it. I should've offered that as an option, too," she babbles as she takes out a pitcher from the fridge and pours two glasses. She brings them over. "Here."

"Thanks."

She sits down. "Thank *you* for coming over."

I look in the direction of her yard. "Does Todd bother you a lot?"

"No. He hasn't really bothered me like this." Suddenly, she frowns. "Actually, he's gotten a bit in my face before, but he was drunk at the time. I thought it was just a one-off thing because he couldn't believe I went through with the divorce."

"People can get a little crazy when they become single against their will. They escalate until they finally accept that it's over or they get thrown in jail." I've seen the drama firsthand. Mom. Dad. Their men and women. It's enough to make anyone cynical about relationships. And jaded enough to want to live alone for the rest of one's life.

Just imagine the blissful peace and silence.

"But today... I mean, it's been *weeks* since the divorce became finalized," Sierra says.

"The news that he's divorced just hit the campus. I understand he had a pretty rough day." Lori got a hold of the *Beowulf*-esque reaming video, courtesy of a professor from the English department, and made sure to share it with everyone in Economics. I watched it on my phone, and was torn between wincing—because it was surgically painful—and laughing—because Todd deserved it.

"I see."

"So he has a new and more immediate motivation to get you back. Your attack hamsters won't help, unless they're the size of Dobermans," I say.

Her gaze slides to a small table by the fireplace. I notice a cage with a couple of the tiny rodents inside.

Cute, but they won't stop Todd.

Damn it. I'm here to discuss how she's going to announce that we aren't dating, but there's more cost than benefit to doing that at the moment. I like to keep things clear, simple and truthful. But Todd's been humiliated on campus, and he's furious. He must think he still has a chance with her, or he wouldn't have tried to do the case yesterday or shown up here today.

When a no-longer-significant other becomes this obsessed, they start doing stupid things. Like stalking. Making threats. Sending roadkill. I've seen how things escalated with Mom and various ex-boyfriends who just couldn't accept that it was really over. There's a reason that when a woman is murdered, police look at her former romantic partners first. Some men just can't deal with getting dumped. The research I did on the economics of domestic violence was harrowing.

Todd might not be one of those extreme cases. But that doesn't mean he's harmless. He might've needed some liquid courage today, but might not the next time. People assume that alcohol changes a person. But it doesn't. It just takes away your inhibitions. Linda's promise to keep him under control doesn't lessen my apprehension. Based on the way she's been fawning over him and making excuses for his behavior, she'd probably call stalking "a friendly attempt to get to know you better" if it was done by her precious Todd.

"Why don't I stay here for a few weeks?" The offer drops from my lips before I can think it through. But once I've said it, I don't want to take it back.

Why can't I just walk away, like I normally do? No idea. But I know in my bones that I'll never forgive myself if anything happens to Sierra.

"What?" she says, startled.

"Just until Todd really does give up."

"Oh, thanks so much for the offer. But I think Linda will keep him under control from now on."

I scoff. "I doubt that. If he were the type to be kept under control, he wouldn't have shown up here drunk."

Sierra frowns, then nibbles her lip. It's distracting.

"Unless you have a friend who looks like a linebacker," I say.

She laughs softly. "I don't think any of my friends fit that description."

"As useful as attack hamsters, then."

"I guess." Sierra laughs harder. It's a lovely sound, and I don't like it. She shouldn't find the situation funny enough to laugh. She should be…

Crying? a sardonic voice in my head suggests.

God no. No crying. I have enough of that with Mom. But Sierra shouldn't be laughing, either. She should stay…thoughtful. Serious.

On cue, she sobers. "I don't know about you staying here. We barely know each other."

"I won't be in your way, if that's what you're concerned about."

"Thanks, but that isn't all. If Todd is having issues at Wollstonecraft, aren't you having some, too? So you moving in with me, even to discourage Todd from showing up, could get awkward… No?"

"There isn't anything I can't handle. I'm not like him." It's the truth. I don't like drama or having Charles annoy me by gazing at me with those beady, greed-filled eyes. But those are inconveniences I can bear. Sierra getting harassed or hurt by Todd? That I can't tolerate.

"Well, I'm not really sure it's necessary. I think I'll be fine—"

"Do you know anything about crime statistics? Do you know how many women are harassed—or worse—by their ex-husbands?"

She considers that for a moment. "No, but I can imagine." She clears her throat. "So…what? We pretend like we're dating for a bit, then just quietly pretend we broke up?"

"Yes. And we won't have to explain the video from yesterday. Just shrug it off. The less we talk, the less material people have to speculate about. There'll be something more exciting for people to talk about tomorrow or the day after. Econ professors don't make the most interesting subjects."

"That's true. Although I do run a sex toy company," she says wryly.

"Next time, that tree might not be able to keep you safe. If Todd had shown up sober, or at least sober enough to move well, things might have ended very differently." I don't want to scare her, but she needs to see the reality of what could happen.

She worries her lip for a moment.

"If he gives up after a few weeks, great," I add. "If he escalates, at least you won't be alone and you can get a restraining order or a guard dog or something. I'll be out of your hair either way."

Finally, she nods. "Makes sense. And I have a guest bedroom. Okay, just for a few weeks, then."

"I wouldn't want to stay any longer. I'm not signing on to be a permanent fix."

"I would never want to impose on you that way," she says with a polite smile. "Thanks, Griffin."

I stand up. "I should probably get some of my things."

"Okay."

"Call 911 if anything is wrong," I say. "You can never be too careful."

I leave. Linda is still struggling with her trash, but at least Todd isn't on the lawn. He's halfway to her car.

"Hey, could you give me a hand here?" Sweat is pouring down her face and neck. "I know the only reason you didn't offer is because of Sierra." Her tone says, *Sierra's such a bitch, but you aren't like her, are you? You're a gentleman.*

I shoot her a cool glance and even cooler smile. "I didn't offer because I didn't want to."

25

GRIFFIN

I pack my things into a suitcase and bring it in my Prius. An hour later I park in front of Sierra's home and stare at the light coming from the living room windows.

Now that I'm here, I feel like I'm trapped in a *Twilight Zone* episode.

This must be how some people feel after leaving a dealership with more car than they initially expected. I was planning on "breaking up," not moving in. But the urgent need to protect Sierra overrode everything.

It's an unfamiliar feeling. The only other time I made an exception not to get involved in someone else's drama was that time in New Orleans, but I was in a mask, so no one was going to figure out who I was. In addition, the woman was in trouble, and that guy was just begging to have his ass kicked.

But I wasn't anonymous yesterday or today, and this drama involves people I know. One of them works at the same college I do.

It's only for a few weeks.

Nobody twisted my arm. I've made sure I can't be manipulated. I can suck it up for the good cause of keeping Sierra safe.

I get out of the car and grab my small suitcase. There's no response when I knock on the door—which is strange, because music is coming from the inside, and the lights are on. I knock again, louder this time, but still nothing. Maybe she's changed her mind about the whole pretend-dating thing.

Stepping back, I glare at the door. My first reaction should be relief that I don't have to do it. But instead, I'm irritated enough to want to kick the damned door in.

Which should make for a great headline: *Enraged Professor Breaks Down Girlfriend's Door in Domestic Dispute.*

It wouldn't be true, but that's news for you. Nobody clicks on an article with a truthful headline.

A cool evening breeze brushes over me. I pull out my phone to call, then see a text.

–Sierra: Have to do some chores. I left the door unlocked. Come in when you get here.

Why the hell did she leave the door unlocked? No chore is that urgent!

Shaking my head, I walk inside and make sure to lock the door behind me.

"Sierra?" No answer. The only sound I can hear is the husky vocal from Axelrod's new album. At least she has good taste in music. It would be a pain to live with somebody who liked musicians I didn't. I once had the misfortune of going on a date with a woman who absolutely adored Yoko Ono. I had to ditch her within an hour.

"Sierra?" I call out again. No response.

Maybe she's in the bathroom. Who the hell knows?

I leave the suitcase in the foyer and step inside to have a better look at the house I'm going to be in for the next few weeks. The place is cozy. She's a CEO, so I assumed she'd have a large, fancy home, if not a mansion. The décor is surprisingly normal—no purple cock clocks or anal plug thermometers. You could actually take pictures of this home and put them up on a real estate site without any issue. Hell, you could host a Bible study here, and nobody would know that Sierra runs a sex toy company.

The furniture is homey, selected for comfort and a welcoming feel. The living room and dining room have lots of wood—hardwood floors and wooden furniture. But instead of wood, all I can smell is a trace of mouth-watering apples.

There aren't any apples in the living room or dining room. It has to be Sierra—it's the same scent I smelled on her hair yesterday.

What does she do that her entire home smells like her? It reminds me vaguely of animals marking their territory.

Framed photos on the living room shelves catch my eye. Dad once observed that the photos people choose to display in their homes reveal a lot about them. It wasn't life advice, more like something I overheard him telling his people while setting up a scene.

He's probably right, though. He might be a complete asshole, but he's good at tugging heartstrings, which is what makes his movies do so well.

So I look the photos over, hoping to find something that will alert me to her flaws. They don't have to be terrible ones. Just bad enough that I won't feel any weird sexual awareness around her.

People I don't recognize. Another couple looking happy. Must be Sierra's parents. The woman and Sierra share a striking resemblance.

Sierra's dad doesn't look much like her. Murky brown eyes and a weak chin make him look unfocused and indecisive.

There's a high school graduation photo with Sierra and somebody who's probably her grandmother. A college graduation shot that's the same.

I step back from the photos. There's nothing with Linda. No recent shots of Sierra's dad, either. I can understand why she wouldn't have any pictures of Linda. But her father?

Well. The man was dumb enough to marry Linda, so maybe he deserves to be cut out of Sierra's life.

I go back to her college graduation photo. She's smiling, her eyes twinkling. But something about her expression bothers me. It looks almost as if she's faking her happiness in the picture.

She's just too damn happy. It's weird and unnatural. Like she has something to hide underneath that brilliant smile.

I turn and bump into a small table. I right it, grabbing the hamster cage before it can fall. The hamsters inside squeak and scurry around in the sawdust.

"I see you've met Bullet and G-Spot."

Sierra walks up in a loose cotton T-shirt with *Silicone Dream* written across the chest and boxer shorts that come to her mid-thigh, revealing long, shapely legs. The sight of them puts an X-rated image in my head.

Jesus. Cut that out. Getting a hard-on after telling her I'm going to feign being her boyfriend for a while to keep her safe from her ex-husband isn't going to inspire much confidence.

I look away from her legs. My gaze drops to her bare feet. They're narrow, nails painted pink. Her toes are small and cute.

What the hell...? Now I think her toes are cute.

Think of something other than her legs wrapped around my waist or how cute her toes are!

My mind searches for something to grab on to distract itself. "You named them Bullet and G-Spot?" *Not the best topic to switch to, genius.*

"Yup. Unlike Bullet, G-Spot likes to escape from the cage." She pauses for a moment. "And, of course, when that happened, Todd could never find her." Sierra winks.

I snort. Given how self-absorbed he is, he wouldn't be able to find something as obvious as two breasts with a map.

She comes closer. Her face is scrubbed clean, her cheeks naturally rosy. Without any makeup, she looks younger and more vulnerable.

Infinitely more kissable.

Don't go there.

I yank my mind back. I don't do relationships. Not the way Huxley or Grant do. I have sex. Uncomplicated, no-strings sex. I don't have to like the person I'm sleeping with, as long as she's hot and keeps things simple.

Sierra doesn't seem like the type for uncomplicated sex. She has photos of her family. She was married for two years to that horrible waste called Todd, probably because she liked relationships and all the attendant messy complications. It seems pretty obvious that she didn't marry him for the sex.

She opens the cage. The hamsters trundle forward. She picks them up, placing them on her palm. "This is Bullet, and this is G-Spot. Both girls."

I look them over. G-Spot is a bit larger, with a white spot between the eyebrows—assuming hamsters have eyebrows. Bullet has a pale sandy streak down her back. Their pink noses vibrate, their whiskers quivering.

"Let them smell you. They like to meet new people."

I put my hand out. Bullet hops on first, then G-Spot. The

whiskers tickle as they sniff me. "So these are the vicious attack hamsters."

"Yup. When they bite, it's hard, enough to draw blood," Sierra says with a fond look.

"Have they done that before?"

"To Todd, when he grabbed Bullet too roughly. He let go immediately."

Hmm. Manhandling small animals is a terrible trait. Even if Todd isn't a serial killer, there's clearly something wrong with him.

She leans toward my hand and smiles at the hamsters. This close, the apple scent is strong. Plus, I can feel her body heat.

If this keeps up, I'm going to start getting hard-ons in apple orchards.

"I brought my stuff." Anything to disrupt this train of thought.

"Great. I can show you your room now, or we can have dinner. Unless you already ate?"

"No, not yet."

"I was going to order pizza, but then Todd showed up. I have some really good sliced roast beef, though, if you want a sandwich."

"That's fine."

She takes out a loaf of crusty bread and a bag of roast beef, some horseradish mayo and a packet of salad and lays everything out on the dining room table with two plates. We sit down and make a quick and easy dinner.

"By the way, I forgot to ask earlier," she says, "do you have any pets you want to bring over?"

"No." I don't bother with the salad and take a bite of the huge sandwich I made with nothing but meat and the mayo.

"Oh." She completes her sandwich with a slice of bread and a small frown.

"What?"

"I just thought... You seem like a dog person." She takes a small bite.

Perceptive. "I do like dogs."

"So why don't you get one?"

I shrug.

"Is your place too small?"

"No." My home is a three-story single unit with a sizable yard. I hire a high school kid on the block to mow it for me.

She gives me an inquiring look.

"I've never had one, so I don't really want to start now." I know the answer is weird, but I don't want to elaborate. Ever since I lost Churchill when I was seven, I've never wanted another dog. I'm never going to forget how frantically upset he looked as he was dragged away. Or how he barked for me.

My chest hurts just from remembering the incident. I begged as he fought to stay with me, but Mom didn't want me to have him. He was taking all my attention. It didn't matter that my grades didn't suffer. Or that my behavior didn't deteriorate. I loved that dog too much, and that was a problem.

Emmett, Huxley and Grant came up with a plan to get my bulldog back, and all of us executed it. It failed miserably. In retrospect, a bunch of seven-year-olds weren't going to outsmart a very determined adult drama queen.

"Well, there's always a first time," Sierra says. "I wanted to get a dog, but Todd didn't want one."

"Is that how you ended up with hamsters?" *He* couldn't have wanted hamsters, especially when one of them is named to mock him. Or maybe he just didn't get the joke.

"No." She laughs. "He didn't want them, either, but we bet on a game of poker, and I won. So..." She smiles, reliving the triumph. "But maybe I'll get myself a dog, too."

"That would be wise. A big, mean one that will deter Todd or anybody else and is only nice to you."

She gives me a long, curious look. I can't decide what she's thinking. Probably something more complicated than *I want to get laid*.

Finally, she says, "I'll keep that in mind."

For some reason, my blood heats at the benign response. I bite into the sandwich. It must be that apple scent driving me insane.

26

GRIFFIN

The guest room Sierra takes me to after dinner faces the master bedroom. The only thing separating us is the hall. And the doors, of course.

It makes sense. If Todd decides to break into the place, I'll be right here. I don't think he's quite that deranged, but then, I didn't think he had it in him to show up at Sierra's place drunk, so anything's possible.

"This is the biggest room, other than mine," she says, gesturing me in. "You have your own bathroom. It has a tub and a separate shower stall. Fully stocked with body wash and shampoo. I can give you conditioner if you need it. Towels are in there, too. If you need anything else, let me know. You can explore the rest of the house later. There isn't much except for three rooms on this floor, downstairs, which you already saw, and the basement which you can look at tomorrow. Mi casa es su casa and all that."

"Okay." I stop at the sight of the bed. It's king-size, which is fine, but... "Pink sheets?"

She looks at them. "Fuchsia."

"Pink."

"No. They're fuchsia. Very different. And brand new. Nobody's ever slept on the bed or the sheets," she adds, like somehow that makes it better.

It doesn't. And for some reason, this room, too, smells like apple.

"Did you spray the place with air freshener?" I ask, breathing shallowly. I'm going to become positively Pavlovian over this damn scent.

She frowns. "I don't use air freshener. Why? Are you allergic to something in the room? Are you having a reaction?"

She sounds almost too eager as she asks. Does she want me to keel over?

It is possible, I decide. A woman this chirpy and happy must have a dark side nobody knows about to counterbalance all that brightness.

"I have some antihistamine," she offers, looking up at me helpfully.

Like a puppy waiting to be praised. And loved.

My heart feels weird. *Fuck. Me.* I better not be having a heart attack in a house that smells like apple and a woman who's driving me crazy with her smile.

"I'm not allergic," I say, before she decides to order an EpiPen over the Internet. "I just thought the place smells…" *Like you. Hot. Sexy. Fresh. Makes me horny.* "Funky," I say, blurting out the first antonym that snaps into my head for what I've been thinking.

She looks horrified. "*Funky?*" She walks around, sniffing. Finally, she stops at the foot of the bed. "I don't smell anything except fabric softener."

"You've been here for too long. Your nose becomes numb to the scent." I'd rather drink bleach than tell her I'm feeling horny over the infernal apple scent.

"You've been here for a while too. So how come you can smell it?"

"An exceptional nose," I tell her. "If I were a dog, I would've been a bloodhound."

"Hmm." She looks skeptical. "Well, if the smell bothers you that much, you can open the windows. Actually, let's just do that right now. Air the room out a little." She pushes the curtains—which are in a shade in between purple and pink—aside and opens the windows. "There. That should do it. Now, do you need anything else? Other than an air freshener?"

"No."

"At least it's just funky, not skunky," she jokes.

Is that supposed to make me feel better?

"Good night. And thanks for staying here." She flashes a sweet smile, then leaves.

The second she closes the door behind her, the room feels empty. I exhale, trying to gain a logical perspective on the situation. My own bedroom is twice as large as this one. There's no reason to feel so...alone.

I brush my teeth, change into a pair of boxers and slide under the sheets, clicking the bedside lamp off. I put my nose in the sheets and inhale. She must use apple-scented fabric softener, because I can still smell that damned fruit. Just like her shampoo.

At least nothing here smells like silicone dicks.

My mind doesn't do pep talks very well.

Right now, I'd rather smell rubbery silicone. The smell of the apple is driving me crazy. I keep thinking about how Sierra looked yesterday in that dress that showed off the sensual lines of her arms and legs.

And was she wearing a bra when we were having dinner downstairs?

Cut that out, I order my unruly mind. *There was nothing to see.*

Only because the shirt was big. She probably wasn't wearing a bra. If it were tighter, her nipples would've shown through the fabric.

Argh. I turn over and force myself to count sheep.

By the time I reach two hundred and thirty-seven, I give up. It's no use. Every time I shift and my bare skin touches the sheets, my nerve endings prickle, and my blood heats. My dick is painfully hard.

No number of sheep is going to help that.

There's supposedly this powdered aphrodisiac that's absorbed through the skin. When you want to seduce somebody, you just find some way to get it on the other person's body.

Noah told me that after spending some time in a Southeast Asian jungle. He likes to talk about all sorts of asinine things he's seen and heard after trips he takes to photograph wildlife. There's no way there's powdered aphrodisiac sprinkled on the sheets.

Then why are you hard for no reason?

I sigh and run a hand over the sheets. Nothing.

Could be super-fine powder...

I bury my face in the sheets and inhale. If there's powder, I'll cough.

But nope. Nothing. I can breathe fine.

However, powdered aphrodisiac or no, the fact that I have a throbbing erection doesn't change. I know I'm not getting any sleep until I do something about it.

The solution is simple. Jerk off real fast, then roll over and go to sleep. I've done it many times before. Just not in a girl's room that smells like apple porn.

I push a hand under the sheets, fist my shaft and move up and down mechanically, the way I always do when I need a quick release.

The expected pleasure builds, but it's flat. There's no buildup, no swelling that's going to push me over the edge. Now it's worse because my dick's harder, pulsing rapidly, but it isn't going to let me come.

I raise my head off the pillow and glare at my dick in the dark. *Just how picky are you?*

My penis stays silent, but it twitches once. It feels like, *Fuck you.* Bastard.

I drop my head back on the pillow and close my eyes, hand still around my cock. It shows no sign of settling down. The scent of apple is stronger, and my crotch is throbbing so badly, it's painful.

Although I've been resisting the idea, I know exactly what I need. It requires more than just a mechanical pump.

I let my mind wander into fantasyland. I envision Sierra. *Not* wearing a bra underneath her shirt. She's lying on a bed that smells like her, her golden hair spread like filaments of sunlight. Her gorgeous eyes gaze up at me like I'm her dirty dream come true. She's lost her shorts, and isn't wearing anything except the shirt. For some reason, the shirt on her makes the scene sexier. Perhaps because she's pushed the fabric up so her breasts are bare, all pretty and soft. She cups them in her small hands, offering them up.

I flick my tongue over the rosy tips, and she sighs softly. I gently pull one into my mouth, using my tongue to make her feel good. She's sensitive, her nipple growing harder and pointed. I suck, then lightly nip the tip.

A groan vibrates through her. Her knees bend; her thighs spread wide. I let go of her nipple and shift, raising my torso. Her feet are pointed, like a ballerina's—shockingly elegant and sensual. She runs the tips of her toes against my thighs, the motion restless. She is a goddess—my sex goddess.

The flesh between her legs is as pink as the sheets on my bed. It glistens, and I want to lap her up, hear sweet moans of pleasure from her lips.

So I do—I devour her, savor her sweet taste, her heady scent. Apples and summer and dreams and heat. My senses soak them in, reveling in them. She whimpers, rocking herself against my face, chasing her pleasure mindlessly.

The blood in my veins roars. My skin stretches taut, and I feel like a beast starved for her. So close, but not enough... Not yet...

Air saws in and out of my burning lungs. My grip on my pulsing dick tightens, my fist moving faster.

"Griffin..." Her sobbing moan penetrates the thick haze of lust.

Oh, yes, baby.

That's all it takes to push me over the edge.

I throw the sheet off and come so hard the hot white liquid almost hits my chin. *Jesus.* I lie there panting in the darkness.

This is going to be longest few weeks of my life.

27

SIERRA

I let out a soft breath once I'm in my room. It was awkward to pretend that nothing was wrong the entire time Griffin and I were eating dinner. I should've remembered to save a bra, but I spaced out and put all my bras through the hand-wash cycle while he went home to grab his things. He didn't come back until I left them almost all hanging in the laundry room to dry. One I took to dry in my bedroom so I wouldn't have to go downstairs to grab a bra in the morning.

I was careful, so I don't think he noticed I was braless. But that didn't help the way the cotton brushed against my bare nipples, which were very...interested. I'm divorced, not dead, and Griffin is divine. I checked him out during the evening—subtly, of course—hoping to find something I wouldn't like.

What a spectacular failure that was.

His eyes are gorgeous, his nose is perfect and his mouth is yummy. Even his eyelashes are stunning. Eyelashes!

Maybe I've discovered a new fetish.

I'm certain when he was in high school, he was one of those boys who still looked hot even when he had acne, assuming acne would have dared to show its ugly self on his pristine skin.

It's unfair how he looks so effortlessly amazing. If I want to look that good, I have to calm my curls—thank God for the dry climate in SoCal—and spend time and energy on makeup and so on.

But now that I'm in bed alone, in the dark, my nipples are like stone. And I'm slick between my legs.

My God. I'm turned on after that dinner...and taking Griffin to his room. It's that scent of his—some kind of hot, sexy male pheromone that makes my whole being clench with need.

My body refused to calm down even when he told me his room smelled bad—although why he said that is beyond me. That room smells fine. I know because I put the sheets on the bed while he was gone. I would've noticed if anything was off.

I toss and turn for a few minutes, unable to settle down. The ache between my legs is growing unbearable, throbbing and sucking up all my attention. I'm not going to be able to sleep unless I do something about it.

A quick O or two will scratch the itch. I reach into the drawer next to my bed and pull out a vibrator. It's small, but packs a powerful action. One of my favorites from Silicone Dream's Love Yourself line.

I slip a hand underneath the shirt to touch my breast, then slide the other one into my underwear so the bullet can go between my legs. Closing my eyes, I picture the Midnight God. My mind says I can do Griffin, but I refuse. That's going to be too weird with my having to face him every day for the next several weeks.

I imagine how lush and hot the kiss with the Midnight God was in New Orleans, his mouth commanding and controlled.

Yes.

The pleasure unwinds, spreading through me like luxurious silk. I fall into a blissful sensation as I tug at my nipple like he did that night, a soft sigh escaping my lips.

The bullet vibrates against me, sending a hot, pulsing delight that starts in my clit and travels throughout, until my fingers and toes tingle.

I cup my breast, imaging it's the Midnight God's large hand on me. His hot breath on my neck where I'm sensitive. His lips trailing endless kisses that drive me wild.

Oh my *God.*

I move, rocking against the vibrator. Fantasize it's his finger there, touching me, toying with me, tormenting my senses until I'm begging for more.

I imagine him whispering, *Good girl.* The pleasure swells and swells...about to reach the breaking point. My breath skitters, air shuddering in my chest.

He notices I'm about to come. His dark, gratified laughter brushes over me. He lifts his head. The mask is gone from his face, and I see...

Griffin...?

My heart doesn't stutter with shock. It races faster, full of exhilaration, and the orgasm I've been reaching for crashes through—

"Griffin," I sob, my back arching and my pelvis tilting like I can somehow get more of him by doing so.

The vibrator slips from my folds. I turn it off and, still breathing hard, stare into the dark. *Wow.* I just came—*hard*—while just picturing Griffin. That's a first—I generally never come from fantasizing about a guy's face.

I think I said his name out loud, too.

I turn to look at the door. It's closed. I closed his door, too, and I didn't speak that loudly—I'm sure of it—so Griffin probably didn't hear me moan his name like a porn star.

Or maybe he did. Should I go check? I could tiptoe over to his door and stick my ear up against it to see if I can hear anything. If he heard, he might...

What? Say, "Hey, I heard that!"?

No, no. That isn't like me. Besides, he doesn't know I was having an orgasm while I said his name. And if he did hear me, he would've come over to see if I needed something.

So I toss and turn instead, wondering. If it was any other guy, I'd just laugh it off, but not with Griffin. I'm not sure why. Maybe I'm just too emotionally drained after dealing with Todd's drunken tantrum.

Despite all the twisting and turning, I do eventually fall asleep.

I wake up at six o'clock, as usual. Instead of immediately grabbing a shower and going downstairs for a cup of coffee, I lie in bed and stare at the ceiling for a moment, listening for noise in the hall.

But there's nothing. Guess Griffin's still asleep.

I pick up my phone to check the day's weather and if there are any messages from Heather. It's Saturday, with no need to rush through my morning routine. And it's been a while since I lazed around. So I'm going to indulge myself today.

I am *not* avoiding Griffin.

Several texts from Dad have landed on my phone since I last checked. Since I don't want to ruin my morning, I ignore them. Knowing how he is, they're about—and *for*—Todd. Dad wouldn't bother to text to see if I'm okay after what happened yesterday. It's almost like Todd is his child, and I'm just some orphan he found under a bridge and decided to take in out of the goodness of his heart.

But it's a nice day and I'm not going to be bitter! I check my emails and respond to a couple from Heather that require my attention. After dismissing the notification banner about the texts from Dad, I force myself out of bed and take a long shower. The hot water sluices down, the white suds swirling down the drain, washing away the old resentment Dad's texts stirred.

Once I'm done showering, I dry my hair and make sure to put on my newly clean and dry bra. I slip on a floral sundress and walk out into the hall.

The door to Griffin's room is ajar.

So he is up. I wait a little, but there's no sound of showering. Or anything else.

I go downstairs. There's no smell of coffee in the kitchen. I peek out the window to see if he went to Starbucks to grab his morning java, but his Prius is still in the driveway.

"Griffin?" I call out.

Silence.

Weird. Where did he go?

Since I need my morning caffeine before I can interact with people, I start the coffee machine and put a sliced bagel into the toaster.

I'm just about to text him when the door to the basement opens and Griffin comes up.

"What were you doing down there?" I say, putting down my phone. Then I glance at him and all the gears in my brain sputter as my hormones cartwheel like unruly, happy children.

Griffin is holding a scrunched T-shirt in one hand. He's in nothing but black Nike shorts and running shoes.

His chest is carved and thick, his shoulders muscled and more gorgeous than I imagined. It's gotta be illegal for a man to have a body this scrumptious.

You just want to cuff him to your bed, my dirty mind whispers.

The temperature in the house jumps twenty degrees.

"I found a treadmill in the basement," he says, barely out of breath.

That's the treadmill I bought last year on New Year's Day with every intention of exercising. But that didn't spare the poor machine the fate most home exercise equipment suffers—it ended up as a clothes rack.

Griffin adds, "So I ran there instead of outside, just in case Beaker decided to make a nuisance of himself early in the morning."

I vaguely register what he's saying. My eyes are riveted to the sweat dripping down his bare torso. The clear droplets roll down the powerful neck, the collarbones, the broad pectorals. They pause for a second over his nipples—my fingers itch to flick them off—then resume their downward journey and glide over the deep ridges of his abs. There must be something wrong with me that I want to lick them off his body, starting from the six-pack and sliding up, up, up, running my tongue all over his chest and nipples and collarbones and neck. If any other guy asked me to do that, I'd probably throw up.

Think of something other than his sweaty body and sex. Not that there's anything wrong with sex, but he's here to help me out, and I don't think *he's* thinking sex. He's made it pretty clear I'm not his type with his judgmental gaze.

"Did you, uh, sleep well?"

"Not too bad." He drags out the words like he wants to find some fault with the quality of his sleep but can't.

I smile with relief. Guess he slept like a baby, oblivious to the world.

For a moment, he gives me a stare so hard and piercing that the hair on the back of my neck starts to bristle. "Heard some noise, though," he says finally.

"Noise?"

"I thought I heard somebody call my name."

I knew I was too loud! I give him my most virginal smile. "Who was it?"

He arches an eyebrow, his knowing eyes on me.

Think of something. "Oh, that. No, I, uh, I saw a spider last night." I generally fib better, but it's cruel to expect someone to lie effectively when they haven't had their first cup of coffee.

"Do you normally cry 'Griffin' when you see a spider?"

"'Griffin'? Oh, no, haha, I said, '*Snuff 'im.*' You know, to psych myself up."

He's not buying it. "Uh-huh."

"It was a very *impressive* spider."

"Of course. Did you take care of it?"

"Yes. It won't be coming back."

Hahahahaha. If my inner voice had a finger, it'd be pointing at me.

"Anyway, you want to grab breakfast? Or maybe shower first?" I add the second option fast, trying to get him out of sight, so I can quit ogling his bare chest and spouting nonsense.

"Shower. By the way, do you have somebody you can hang out with this morning? Between ten and one?"

"Uh. I guess...? Why?"

"I have a brunch I can't cancel." He shakes his head. "Never mind. I'll cancel."

"No, no." I put my hands out. "Don't do that. You should totally go. Do your thing. Have fun. I'll go out with Ellie."

"Ellie?"

"My best friend. She and I are going out," I say, although that isn't entirely true. Ellie and I haven't made any plans. But I don't want Griffin to cancel or feel forced into taking me to the brunch. It's obvious he doesn't want to do either. "We're going to the mall, so we should be okay. Todd's not going to show up drunk and confront me where there are lots of people around, even if he stalks us to the mall." And unlike at the masquerade, my ex's face would be fully visible. He would loathe to attract negative attention to himself so openly.

Griffin studies me to see if I'm really okay with it. I show him my most confident façade, the mask I use every time I need to look like I'm in charge when I'm really improvising.

"If you're sure," he says finally. "But if you need anything—"

"Don't worry. I have your number."

28

SIERRA

"What's up with me coming over and taking you to the mall?" Ellie says as she minces her way into my home. Her hair is in a messy bun, and she's wearing a tight T-shirt and denim shorts. Her feet are in flip-flops, and she's walking gingerly. She does it every time she has a pedi, trying not to damage the work done on her toes.

"Cute daisies! Love 'em," I say, looking at her toenails.

"Thanks." She points at the driveway, where Griffin's car was parked just moments ago. I told him she was coming and shoved him out of the house so he wouldn't be late to his brunch, lest he have to hear some lecture about time and money. She just missed him. "And what was that hottie professor doing here? Did he stay the night with you?"

"He did," I say, since she has the tenacity of a starved bear on the hunt when she's onto something.

Her eyes light up, and she leans forward. But before she can start her interrogation, I say, "Thanks for coming over."

"No problem. You said it was a major crisis." She sits down in Grandpa's armchair. It's become Ellie's favorite seat in the living room. "So what's the crisis? Does it have anything to do with the hottie who just spent the night? Was it good? Was *he* good? And I guess this means you've found a new guy to fantasize about, now that the Midnight God is out of reach?"

"No." I sit down. "It's gotten super complicated since yesterday."

I tell her what happened with Todd and Linda and Griffin. Ellie listens with her eyes wide. Then, when the story reaches the part about how Todd conked his head against the tree, she pumps a fist.

"*Yes! I knew* I liked that tree."

"Anyway, Griffin decided to continue the dating rumor and move in here for a few weeks until Todd gives up. He's worried about Todd's behavior, although I doubt Todd's really going to get super dangerous or anything."

"What if he never gives up?" My best friend's eyes are too sparkly. "Does that mean Griffin will never move out?"

I shake my head. "No. I'll get a restraining order and a mean dog or something. Griffin wants to be gone as soon as he can."

"How come?"

"He knows I have feelings."

Ellie's eyes go wide.

Before she jumps to conclusions, I add, "*For his body.*"

"Tell me more about these feelings," she says, then moves next to me on the sofa. Giving up her favorite seat means she's really into the story now.

"Well... He's gorgeous. And I'm not dead, and..." I lower my voice, like I'm telling her my biggest secret. Well, it is my biggest secret since the Midnight God. "I used the bullet last night."

"So? You're an adult."

"Yes, but I kind of moaned out his name when I came. *And he heard.*"

Ellie's jaw drops. "Oh my God. Did he come over to give you a real O from his real body?"

My cheeks heat. That would've been amazing, but... "No. But it was a little awkward this morning."

She gives me a long, hard stare. "It wasn't just *awkward*. Come on. What else happened?"

"He was really hot."

"You said that."

"No, I mean because he was all sweaty from exercising. And topless."

"Aaaand...?"

"And the feelings I had for his body last night came back."

"Uh-huh. And...?"

"Aren't I supposed to have issues? Maybe start being premenopausal? Hormones drying up, vagina having the moisture level of a desert? Me *not* getting horny at a sight of a sweaty hunk after a run?" I start to get flustered and mildly confused. After my divorce, I swore I wouldn't be attracted to another haughty, judging type. Griffin isn't exactly haughty...but he definitely judges. I shouldn't be attracted to him.

But I'm crazy about him—or his body. What's up with that?

"A *desert?*" Ellie rolls her eyes. "Sierra the Sahara? Please. You're *twenty-nine*. Nobody goes premenopausal that early."

"But I have blocked fallopian tubes," I argue, more out of the desire to avoid admitting she's right, and I'm going back on my vow already.

"Which doesn't prevent your ovaries from working. It only takes away a place for your egg and some marauding sperm to tango." Ellie gives me an evaluating look.

"What?"

"Just what's going on here? You'd normally laugh off a situation like this. I mean, so what if some guy knows you masturbate? Hell, *not* masturbating would be weird, given your job—and the fact that a lot of perfectly healthy and sane women enjoy making themselves feel good."

"Yeah, but..."

"I think you're just nervous because you care."

"What?"

"If Todd heard you masturbate, you'd laugh in his face because you don't care. And the same with most any man—but not Griffin."

A dawning horror begins to break over me. "No, I—"

"You care about what he thinks."

"I don't! He's...he's really judgmental. Not my type at all."

"Girl, your brain can say whatever, but your body doesn't lie. If you get all hot and bothered just thinking about him?" She gives me a couple of slow, exaggerated nods. "Oh yeah. It's on."

"Are you saying I have feelings for more than his body?"

"Maybe, maybe not. But he's more important to you than you're willing to admit." She pats my shoulder. "Listen to your fun box. It's doing better than your brain, which picked Todd. I *know* your vag didn't pick him."

She's right. But that doesn't mean my hormones are going to make the right decision.

29

GRIFFIN

Technically, I should be driving to Emmett's place for a brunch my brothers and I have from time to time, but he's in no condition to host anything after an ugly breakup.

So Sebastian's holding it at the Aylster Residence. There are three Residence units at the Aylster Hotel, and Sebastian has one that he uses when he's in town. He splits his time between L.A., where Sebastian Jewelry's West Coast headquarters is, and Northern Virginia, where the company's main headquarters and his grandmother are.

I give my Prius to the valet at the separate private entrance to the Residence. The elevator is waiting in the opulent lobby. On a table near the elevator is a vase full of tulips, some purple and some pink. The former reminds me of Purple Girl's hair, and the latter reminds me of Sierra—and those damn sheets and the pink between her legs in my fantasy.

Good thing *I* was quiet. It's hot as hell that she felt something for me—enough that she touched herself thinking about me.

An impressive spider, indeed.

My blood starts to heat, but I dismiss the whole line of thought. Brunch with my brothers isn't the place to mull that over.

The elevator dumps me at the entrance to Sebastian's unit. I open another door and step inside a huge living room. The furnishings are modern minimalist, ivory accented with dark teak. Lot of buttery leather, and several watercolor paintings of green mountains on the walls. The floor is pale champagne marble, buffed to a glossy sheen. A few geometric-patterned rugs add to the ambiance. But they can call it a "residence" all they like. No matter how carefully decorated and appointed, it's obvious the place isn't a real home.

The huge dining room is already set up with catered food from the Aylster's kitchen. Although the Residence comes with a full kitchen, nobody wants to be poisoned by Sebastian's cooking.

Everyone except Emmett is already seated with his food and drinks. Nicholas notices me and lifts a flute with a smile.

"Hey, there, professor!" he calls out cheerily.

I nod in greeting. "Hey back."

"Want some?" He gestures at an open bottle of Dom chilling in an ice bucket.

"Yes."

He pours me some and hands me a glass. The youngest of us, he invests and owns a lot of businesses and keeps himself busy. Everyone calls him Nicholas because his mother goes by Nick or Nikki.

I take the empty chair next to him. "Thanks." I have a sip and soak in the buttery aftertaste of the cool, bubbly wine. It's hard for a brunch to go wrong when it's served with Dom.

"So, how's your love life?" he asks.

My brothers' gazes swing in my direction. Other than Emmett, I'm the only one supposedly in a relationship.

"There is no love life. It's just a misunderstanding."

"Well, that sucks," Noah says.

"She's really pretty," Nicholas says.

"You saw the video?" He's generally too busy to look at social media junk.

"Noah forwarded it," Grant says with an easy grin. "He's our own private NSA."

I grunt, then grab some eggs and pancakes. As I pour syrup over them, I wonder what Sierra's doing with her best friend.

The door opens again. I tilt my head and blink in surprise as Emmett walks in.

Outwardly, he's fine. He's lost a bit of weight, but when he's busy, he tends to skip meals, so that isn't unusual. His hair is neatly styled so it lies perfectly on his skull. The pale blue T-shirt and shorts appear casual, but they're from a boutique in Milan, and look pricey. As he walks past me, I can smell the soap from a fresh shower. He doesn't smell like alcohol. Or any other vice.

But then, overindulging in substances isn't how he copes.

And I know he's coping after that breakup with one of his associates. His eyes are slightly bloodshot—a sign he isn't sleeping well—but he has the grim look of a man determined to live well, no matter what.

"I wasn't sure if you'd drop by," Sebastian says.

"How could I miss our brunch?" Emmett's smile doesn't reach his eyes. He parks himself next to Huxley, who's doing his best to pretend he isn't worried because he knows Emmett would hate that, especially coming from him. Emmett gets annoyed when he thinks Huxley's trying to manage him.

"Here." Nicholas pours him a glass of champagne.

Instead of taking it, Emmett just looks at it morosely. Is he reliving some memory where he and his girl celebrated something together?

The moment stretches awkwardly. We all wait to see what he does. He lets out a sigh and takes the flute. "Thanks." He forces more wattage into his smile, which only serves to turn it into a grimace.

"I have something stronger," Seb offers.

"Thanks, but this is fine," Emmett says in a tone that says *he's* not fine.

"Do you know that there are seven-point-eight billion people in the world, and about half are women?" Noah says. "Three-point-four billion chances is a lot."

If Noah's trying to be positive, he's doing a terrible job. And his math is off—half of seven-point-eight is three-point-nine.

Emmett's narrowed eyes agree with my assessment. He doesn't correct Noah's math, though, which means he's in worse condition than I expected. Emmett loves to correct math.

Grant clears his throat, then subtly shakes his head.

Noah is undeterred. "Your odds of winning the Mega Million is, like, one in one hundred and seventy-six million. Getting a new hot chick can't be harder than winning the lottery."

If Emmett didn't look so miserable, I'd do a slow clap. To

Emmett, women aren't fungible. The girl he lost is "special." To him, she's undoubtedly The One out of the three-point-nine billion, and there isn't going to be another like her.

It's an effort not to roll my eyes. Because when you love something, everything goes sideways. Inevitably, it gets taken away and your entire world falls apart until you can get your head screwed on right again.

If you can get your head screwed on right again.

It's stunning that Emmett hasn't learned this lesson, but then, his mother is one of the nicer ones. I learned it when I was seven. For that—and that alone—I suppose I can be grateful to Mom.

Instead of responding to Noah, Emmett says, "What are you getting for your grandmother's birthday, Seb?"

Noah looks a little annoyed, but Sebastian smiles, like there's nothing wrong with the abrupt change in topic. "I don't know yet. She wants a great-grandbaby, but..." He shrugs.

"Her too?" Huxley sighs. "What's up with this baby fetish all of a sudden? She's in Virginia, so we can't blame the water."

"She's getting old. Probably wants to hold a great-grandbaby before it's too late," Nicholas says.

"That woman's going to outlive all of us." Sebastian shudders. "She has more energy than anybody I know. More than a teenager." He sighs. "And I can't think of anything to give her. She has everything."

This is a shock. Seb's never met a person he couldn't come up with a present for.

"If her having everything is the problem, make it personal. Make a video of you singing 'Happy Birthday' for her and be done with it," Huxley suggests.

I cringe internally. That is such a showy thing to do. On the other hand, some people would like it. My mother, for example, would show it to everyone and make an embarrassing scene out of it to garner as much attention as possible. This is the biggest reason I don't sing. I'd rather eat glass. Or lick the lavatory after a meal service.

Seb snorts. "No. I don't need Warner Chappell Music coming after me for illegal use." He's still pissed that the campaign his company wanted to launch had to be redone because of the music.

Huxley grins smugly. "Nope. The song's in public domain now. The court ruled in 2015, in case you weren't following."

"Why were *you* following?" Grant asks. Hux is in advertising, not music.

"One of our clients wanted to use it for their TV ads around that time."

Sebastian shakes his head. "Regardless of the song's copyright status, I'm not going to traumatize my grandmother. I actually like the woman." He pauses. "Most of the time."

"True. You sing like a dying wildebeest," Noah says.

As my brothers laugh—except for Emmett, who's doing a terrible job of faking it—I'm reminded of how Linda couldn't remember Sierra's birthday. I presume this means Sierra's dad doesn't do anything either. If he'd made it clear it was important, somebody like Linda would remember, too.

Although Sierra acted like she didn't care, she must have some resentment or disappointment about it. It's just that those feelings are likely old and resigned, very much like my feelings toward my mother's drama and needs.

I make a mental note to find out when Sierra's birthday is. If it's during the time we're pretending to be dating, I'll do something for her. I'm not going to be a fake boyfriend who forgets her birthday, even though my experience celebrating birthdays probably isn't typical: wild parties like my dad's, drama-filled scenes like my mom's or just a huge dinner together with my brothers, since all of us were born four months apart.

30

GRIFFIN

On Tuesday afternoon, I lean back in my office and tap my fingers on the desk.

Sierra's avoiding me.

She didn't come home until very late on Saturday. She had another shopping spree with her best friend on Sunday, ostensibly for research. How many sex toy stores do they need to hit to gather sufficient data?

Then on Monday, she left for work before seven and didn't come home until nine. Granted, CEOs tend to put in a lot of hours, but she had no problem leaving the office by six on Friday. Plus, every time she sees me, she has trouble meeting my eyes. Instead, she keeps her gaze focused on my chest.

Why does this bother me? It should make me happy. Bad enough that the apple scent in her house keeps me in a constant state of hyperawareness. My dick snaps to attention every time she's nearby.

It puts me in a crummy mood, especially since I can't quit jerking off at night. It's either that or stay up until morning, and I need my sleep. She hasn't moaned my name since Friday night, so either she's being really quiet or there are no more impressive spiders around.

Annoying. Really annoying. It's like a little tic behind my eyeball. Not the terrible one I get when I'm furious, but a mild one that pulses every so often to make its presence known just for the hell of it.

The worst of it is that I haven't had a chance to ask her when her birthday is. The undone item on my mental to-do list is nagging at me, making it harder to concentrate.

None of my students come by. Just as well. I'm not in the best of moods, and they're probably busy analyzing the data from Silicone Dream. The numbers the company sent are interesting—a bit messy, so they need some cleaning up, but that's a good exercise for my students. Out in the real world, you don't get a textbook set of data, pristine and ready to be plugged into Excel.

I shake off the weirdly annoying feelings about Sierra and read the latest email from Keith. I review the spreadsheets he's attached, then make some comments and send it back to him. Although his analysis is excellent, we overlooked a couple of items. Plus, two of the exhibits were misnumbered.

Sometimes the most minor, inconsequential things can derail how people receive a paper. Some reviewers, ideologically opposed to a central idea, will try to claim a study is garbage because one exhibit is mislabeled, and then leverage that into a denunciation of the entire body of research. Academia can be as savage as cage fighting.

"There you are!"

I lift my gaze from my laptop at the huffing voice. Todd Beaker is at the door, one hand on the frame, doubled over. Sweat beads around his hairline. He sucks in air like he's been running for hours.

He looks presentable enough in a pale blue dress shirt and slightly wrinkled khakis. His shoes are well-polished Guccis—probably bought with Sierra's money, since there's no way he could afford them on his salary.

His face is swollen and covered with black and blue bruises, like moldy bread dough. Sadly, his nose is unbroken. That tree could've done a better job of kicking his ass.

"I thought you might've left," Todd wheezes.

Don't the English department faculty know how to tell time? Or is it just him? "Why? I still have ten minutes to go before my office hours are over."

"That's exactly why," he says, finally straightening up.

"Just because *you* leave early doesn't mean everyone does." I lean back in my seat, one ankle over the opposite knee. "What do you want?"

"Whatever stunt you're trying to pull, you need to stop."

I raise an eyebrow. "Stunt?"

"I know you aren't dating Sierra." He practically spits the words.

"Why wouldn't I be?"

"You might, but she wouldn't."

"She was married to you," I point out. "Perhaps she's trading up."

His complexion turns into a weird combination of black and red. "She wants to belong—wants a family! We tried so hard to make babies for her!"

She wants a family with children. I ignore the weird twinge in my heart and try to focus on what he's saying. She had to have been desperate to want offspring with Todd. Maybe she was drunk.

"But we failed because she's infertile."

TMI. And what kind of asshole announces fertility issues his ex-wife has to her new boyfriend? Or is this some pathetic attempt to make her seem undesirable, so I'll either admit to not dating her or dump her?

I rake my gaze over his pathetic body. My money is on his being unable to provide viable sperm.

"You can never be the family she wants!" Todd continues.

"Because...?"

"You're the type of guy who treats people like disposable... disposable..." He points at me, finger twitching in the air as his brain works overtime to come up with something cutting.

I get tired of waiting. "Razor?"

He snaps his fingers. "Yes!" Then immediately says, "No! A disposable plate! One of those paper ones, for a picnic."

Perhaps in Todd's world, a disposable plate is worse than a disposable razor. "Do you know when Sierra's birthday is?" If he's going to waste my time, he can make himself useful.

He blinks. "Sierra's birthday?"

"Yes." It shouldn't be this difficult to communicate. He's an English professor, for God's sake.

He gives me a suspicious look, but tells me a date—my dad's birthday.

"Are you sure?"

"Of course I'm sure! I'm her husband."

"*Ex*-husband." It's important to be precise, even if it might not be a trait valued in his department.

Her birthday has already passed for this year. A disquieting mixture of relief and disappointment rushes through me, which is weird. It isn't like I'm happy I don't have to do anything for her birthday. I meant it when I decided to find out and make it more special than it's been for a while.

"What do you have to say to that, Lasker?" Todd asks, pulling me back to the present.

I frown at him. "Are you still here?"

He takes a step into my office, places a hand on his hip and points the finger at me again. "I'm talking to you!"

"I was thinking about something important. My office hours are over now, so you should..." I wave him away.

His chest heaves with fury. That tree should've cracked his ribs as well so he wouldn't be here ranting like a dramatic lunatic. "I'm not finished!"

"In that case, I'll bill you for my time. Ten thousand dollars an hour."

His jaw drops. "Ridiculous! No one charges that much!"

"Your particular rate happens to have an annoyance surcharge."

"Asshole!"

"Who are you calling an asshole in my department?"

My gaze slides to the open door. Charles is standing there, bristling with outrage.

Todd points at me. "He's trying to rip me off!"

"You aren't a student or faculty member of this department. You don't have the right to monopolize Professor Lasker's time."

Wow. Look at Charles defending me. Granted, he hates Todd, so it's likely he'd side with me anyway, but this is going beyond the call of duty.

Charles turns to me. "Griffin, I need to speak to you for a moment if you're free?"

"I am." I smile, mainly to annoy Todd.

Todd glares at me, then at Charles—the venom leaking out, since Charles has a lot of power on campus—then turns and storms off.

Finally, peace. Sort of. I paste on a neutral politeness. "What can I do for you?"

"It's about what you said."

Damn it. He wants to rehash the research center funding. I cling to my polite mask. Barely. "Sure. Go ahead."

"Are you doing anything special for Sierra's birthday?"

"I hadn't really given it much thought. Her birthday isn't until next year."

"What?" He frowns and gives me an odd look. "It's in three weeks."

Fucking Todd. He doesn't even know his ex-wife's birthday. I should've known better than to ask him.

"And luckily, this year it happens to fall on a Saturday." Charles beams. "I presume a party of some sort will be in order and that invitations will be going out soon."

He's actually researched this. "Like I said, we don't know what we're doing yet." There's no way I'm having a party and inviting Charles so he can hassle Sierra to fund the research center.

"Hmm. You'll want to do something special, since it's the first time you'll be celebrating it together," Charles muses.

"Exactly."

"Well, I suppose that's understandable. Then perhaps you can bring her to the faculty cocktail and dinner? All the spouses and girlfriends are invited."

Now it's my turn to frown. "Are you talking about the department social we have at the beginning of the semester? We already had that."

He gives me a fond smile, which creeps me out. My parents gift me with the exact same smile every time they want to spring some bullshit.

"This will be a special event," Charles says. "At my place. To promote tighter cohesion among the faculty. It's a tradition I've always wanted to start."

"I see." *And you waited until this year to start. How convenient.* "I'll ask and see if she'll be free." A lie to get Charles out of my office. I'm not subjecting her to hours of bullshit.

"Excellent. It'll be on Friday four weeks from now," he says. "I'll be sending out formal invitations soon."

"Great."

Charles leaves, satisfied for the moment. I glare at my calendar, irritated that he's roping me into another departmental social event where I have to act like I'm thrilled to be there. Once a semester is plenty.

When I offered to stay with Sierra, I expected things to be simple. Just live there for a few weeks and let my sheer presence be a deterrent to Todd. But now it's becoming complicated. My fault, I suppose, for not realizing that people would have expectations of their own.

Perhaps I should have chosen a different career. Being a kickboxer would have been just as good as being a professor of economics. Better in some ways—nobody mouths off to you or asks you to attend idiotic social events.

I shake my head, take a moment to clear the recent social distractions from it and then turn to the latest set of data from the Bureau of Justice Statistics.

31

GRIFFIN

By the time I get to Sierra's place, it's a little after six. Her red Ferrari is in the driveway, so maybe she's decided to quit ignoring me. Or at least come home at a normal hour.

When I unlock and open the door, I'm hit with the scent of tomato sauce and basil from the kitchen and a fancy riff from Axelrod's new album. Killian Axelrod starts singing, and a wail that sounds like a dying coyote joins him.

I almost drop my laptop bag. I blink, then openly stare as Sierra screeches the lyrics. She's gloriously joyful. Her head is swinging, her body is twisting and moving and she raises her hand and points like she's on the stage and millions of fans are screaming her name.

Unfortunately, she's completely off-key. She can't manage any of the high notes, but apparently can't quite figure out how to substitute lower ones that might be okay instead. Tendons stand out in her neck as she throws her head back and yells out the final lines.

I stand there until the song ends. "Wow."

She turns to me, her face flushed pink with exhilaration. "Welcome home! Is that a great song or *what?*"

"Yes, a great song." I open my mouth again. *Would've been better without you* suddenly gets stuck in my throat.

It's that damn smile of hers, the sparkle in her eyes. If I say what comes naturally, it'll snuff out the joyous light in her gorgeous purple gaze. That certainty makes me choke back my words, which is highly atypical. I generally don't care too much whose feelings I hurt, unless it's going to make it more difficult to get some desired result.

Telling Sierra the truth about how horrific her singing voice is won't cause any personal problems for me. But I still can't do it.

"Who does it hurt but me?" I mutter to myself. I'm the only one listening. Hopefully, Bullet and G-Spot are tone-deaf.

"Axelrod is a*maz*ing. I'm so mad I missed their tour this year. I've never missed one before," Sierra says, checking the oven.

I put my laptop bag on one of the dining room chairs. "So what happened this time?"

"Oh, you know… Got distracted with the divorce, and then by the time I remembered to check, everything around here was sold out." She shrugs. "Now they're off touring Asia or something, so it just isn't going to happen. But I won't miss next time."

Axelrod starts a new song. Before Sierra can join in, I ask, "What's for dinner?"

"Lasagna. I picked some up from the store."

"So you aren't avoiding me today."

She purses her lips, her cheeks growing pinker. "I wasn't *avoiding* you. I was just trying to get used to the idea of having a fake boyfriend. Then I realized I was being rude. You're doing me a favor by keeping Todd away, so the least I can do is be a cooperative fake girlfriend in return." She empties two bags of store-bought salad into a bowl and places it on the table, head bobbing to the beat of the music. "And I can do a lot of my work at home instead of at the office."

"I got the data from Silicone Dream," I say. *Have to keep her talking.* She sounds amazing when she isn't singing.

"Great! I asked Heather to put it together. Your students can come by maybe one more time later in the semester to show us their work if you want."

"I'll make it an extra credit for the final." That'll make my students take the assignment more seriously, especially since so many of them did poorly on the midterm.

The timer on the oven dings. She takes out the lasagna and garlic bread and puts both on the table.

My shoulders sag with relief—you can't eat and sing at the same time. But best to make sure. "What are you working on that you have to bring work home?"

"It's the new line we're designing." She smiles animatedly, her eyes bright.

"You have different lines of toys?"

"Yup. Contrary to what people think, there's more to our products than just dildos."

Someone else might choke at this casual dinnertime admission. But I grew up around wild, out-of-control celebs with zero shame and decorum.

Sierra eyes me, judging my reaction. "We have to do research, product design, features and material selection...lots of stuff."

She's getting the same sparkle she did earlier when she was singing. Hoping that she's better at making sex toys than carrying a tune, I say, "Why can't you continue to sell what you have? Don't you have some core products like Coca-Cola has Coke Classic?"

"Sex isn't like soft drinks. You always have to do more to keep things exciting and new. It's like saying, why not quit doing research because we already know so much? My work has meaning because it helps people feel good about their sexuality and derive more pleasure out of their sex lives. Don't you feel great when your students do well in your class? Or your research unearths something people didn't know before?"

Her question makes me pause. I teach because it's part of being a professor. My students leave me after each semester, when their coursework is over. I try not to make too much of an emotional investment. It isn't healthy.

And it's the same with my research. I'm proud of the work I did on the economics of domestic crime—which won me the prestigious John Bates Clark Medal—but again, I try not to put too much of my heart into it. I care enough to be good at it, but that's all.

"Not really," I say finally. "It's my job. I don't hate it, but I don't love it."

She cocks her head. "Then what do you love?"

"Nothing."

"*Nothing?*" Her eyes grow wide. "No way." She takes her phone and taps a few times. "Not even these little guys?" She flips the screen and shows me a picture of sleepy bulldog puppies lying on top of each other like a layer cake.

My heart does something odd and funky. Something that feels like a smile tugs at my mouth, but I flatten my lips instead. "They're all right."

"Wow." Sierra places the phone, screen down, on the table.

I'm slightly disappointed I can't see the puppies anymore, but I force my attention back to the dinner.

We talk about work for the rest of the meal. And I do my best to pretend I don't notice her studying me.

32

SIERRA

—Griffin: Your passport is still valid, right?

I stare at the text.

"What is it?" Ellie says from the seat opposite mine. We're having lunch at a deli not far from the office. They have the best BLTs in Lovedale.

"Griffin wants to know if my passport is still valid."

"So why are you frowning? You got one for your honeymoon in London. It's still good, right?"

"I know. It's just..." I try to gather my thoughts. "I don't know what to make of him." That bugs me for some reason. Even though he's my "fake" boyfriend, I want to get to know him better. At least become friends. It's hard to become friends with somebody who remains a mystery.

And it bothers me that I keep having feelings and dirty thoughts about a man who is just so...*difficult*. He can't even admit to liking puppies! Does he think I'm going to use it against him somehow? Did I give him the impression that I'm some kind of supervillain?

"What did he do?" Ellie asks.

I shake my head. "He's just confusing me."

"Okay, so talk. Maybe I can help you sort it out."

"All right." I try to gather my thoughts. "So he's all protective and stuff, you know? Otherwise he wouldn't have moved in to keep me safe from Todd."

"Uh-huh."

"And he doesn't look at my work like it's stupid because I'm *just running a sex toy company*. When I told him what we do, he seemed curious. Just asked a few questions without getting all obnoxious and frat boy about it."

Ellie nods. "So far I'm only hearing positives."

"He won't praise or compliment *anything*. Or indicate that he even likes something. We've been living together for almost three weeks, but I don't know what his favorite song is, what kind of food he prefers, what he likes to do to relax. I only know what he *doesn't* like. I think he hates it when I sing because he always interrupts and asks about my day. And you know, if that was all, I'd be annoyed. But then he actually pays attention to what I'm saying!"

Ellie makes a sympathetic noise, although she still looks mystified. "So you're upset that he wants to talk about your day?"

"No! That isn't the point." *Argh*. I'm not sure why I'm having trouble communicating with Ellie. I'm usually better than this. "It's just that I don't know what he likes because he's so closed off about it."

"Maybe he doesn't like anything. He could be one of those people who's always displeased about something. Like my grandma. She hated everything and everyone."

That's true. Ellie's grandma was infamous for that when we were growing up. She didn't even like her own grandchildren.

"I'm sure he loves *something*," I say, refusing to believe I have the hots for a guy who's impossible to please. "He just won't admit it." Which is weird. I can't understand the purpose of bottling up your own bubbly happiness.

"Such as?"

I think for a second. "Puppies. I know he adores them. I showed him a picture, and his eyes went all gooey soft. But then he said they're just *okay*."

"Maybe he's one of those emotionally stoic men. You're lucky he actually speaks rather than grunts."

"Yeah." My eyes stray to my phone still sitting on the table. I haven't responded to Griffin's text yet. I pick it up.

–Me: Yes. What's this about?

–Griffin: Research.

"He doesn't even like his job," I murmur.

"That's not unusual. A lot of people hate their jobs. They work because they need the money."

"I guess..." I sigh. It's hard for me to imagine, since I adore my job at Silicone Dream.

"Okay, what's really up? You weren't this moody even when you decided to divorce Todd."

"I was happy because I was finally getting rid of the deadweight in my life. But this is different."

"How?"

Before I can answer, the door to the deli opens and Todd walks in. He scans the dining area.

"What the heck?" I mutter. It dawns on me that he might actually be stalking me.

The campus is too far away for him to make the trip out here just for lunch. At least he doesn't seem drunk. He's in a pressed white dress shirt and black slacks. The bruises my tree gave him have faded significantly, more yellow now than purple.

Ellie turns around. "What the hell is that asshole doing here?"

He comes over to our table. *Ugh. Just no.*

At least there are too many people around for him to make a scene.

"What do you want, Todd?" I say in my best no-pushover voice.

"I want to apologize."

I blink, then turn to Ellie. "Did you just hear that?" Todd never apologizes for anything, even when it's one hundred percent his fault.

"He wants to apologize," Ellie says, looking as stunned as I feel.

"You don't have to involve her," Todd says. "This is about us. What we've shared." He runs a hand along his belt. "Remember this?"

"Of course. The Prada belt I bought you for your birthday."

"Exactly. Part of our history together." He shoots Ellie a look that says, *You don't have what I have with Sierra.* Which is ridiculous. Ellie's been my best friend since forever. Todd is just one small chapter in my life. Actually, not even a chapter. More like a scene.

"Unfortunately, I don't still have the present you got me that year," I say.

He looks wounded. "Why not? Did you throw it away or something?"

"You bought me a pizza from Costco."

"What?" He sputters. "No. I got you more than that."

"Well, yes. You also bought me a soda."

"But you love pizza," he says.

I nod.

"So what's wrong with me buying you pizza for your birthday?" he demands, his face starting to go red.

Ellie shoots him a what-an-idiot look.

"If you don't know, I can't help you," I say flatly. This is tiring. I hope his next wife is more patient than me. Actually, never mind. I wouldn't wish him on any other woman.

He slaps the table so hard, the furniture shakes. "This is what's wrong with you! You *never* communicate. Just say some cryptic shit and expect me to jump through hoops to get back into your good graces like some pussy-whipped dweeb! Well, guess what? Todd Beaker is not pussy-whipped!"

I freeze. I didn't expect this from a sober Todd. Maybe Griffin's right to be concerned about my ex-husband's behavior.

Ellie shoots him an evil look, her hand clenched around her soda cup. I reach for mine, too. Sadly, those are the only weapons we have. At least I still have lots of ice cubes in mine. Maybe he'll cool down if I toss them at him.

Since he's glaring at me like he's expecting a response, I paste on a smile and reach for a non-confrontational answer. "Good for you...?"

"No. You're going to apologize for treating me like garbage!" His hands rest on his hips, and he's doing his best to tower over me, to physically intimidate me.

Why is he doing this? I wonder, but it doesn't take long to figure out. After all, I was married to the man.

He wants me to admit that I'm partially to blame for our relationship falling apart. He wants to use whatever comes out of my mouth to lever some sort of reconciliation, no matter how hopeless. Since he can't confront me at work or at home, he's trying the deli I like, where I'm not protected by Dan or Griffin.

Emotional exhaustion and annoyance surge first, followed by

shame over my terrible judgment. "I thought *you* were here to apologize."

"No, you have to apologize first. Because this was the overarching issue in our marriage."

"Maybe for *you*. Believe me, there were other issues."

Now people are staring and taking out their phones. *Ugh*. I don't need another embarrassing video shared all over social media.

"I've moved on," I continue. "I have a boyfriend. You should move on, too. Get on a dating app and go find someone who'll apologize for everything you don't like."

He shoots his hand out, trying to grab me. I pull back just in time.

"Touch me and I'm calling the police!" I shout, jumping to my feet. My heart beats in my throat. I hate physical confrontations, and I doubly hate it that Todd continues to force them upon me.

Ellie stands and moves around so she's standing next to me.

"I can't touch my wife?"

"*Ex*-wife! And no, you cannot! I'd rather sleep with a giant spider."

His face is blotchy red and yellow. "I should've known better than to follow Linda's advice."

I shake my head. If this is what Linda meant by keeping Todd under control, Griffin was right to scoff. Todd grinds his teeth, his hands clenched tight. If he weren't sober, or if we didn't have so many witnesses, he might just grab me, like he did in New Orleans.

"We'll chat when you're calmer," Todd says, and stalks out.

"Holy shit. Are you okay?" Ellie says. "What *is* his deal?"

"He thinks he can make me go back to him." I cross my arms and gaze out the window. Todd stomps to his car and drives off.

It's been about three weeks since his defeat against the crabapple tree, and Todd won't accept it's over. Maybe I really should start looking into getting a restraining order. And a dog—a big one with huge teeth that growls menacingly...but only at my ex-husband.

33

SIERRA

When I get home, Griffin's already at the dining table, working on his laptop. He's changed into a white T-shirt that stretches beautifully over his torso and faded jeans that hug his hips just right. Even dressed casually, he looks like a professor. It's the quiet intelligence in his eyes, I decide. It seems to disguise the fact that he's built like a mixed martial arts fighter.

I open my mouth to tell him about Todd stalking me at the deli. But before I can get a word out, Griffin shuts his laptop.

"How fast can you pack?" he asks, in his typical impassive tone.

"Pack? For what?"

"A short trip." His eyebrows snap together briefly. "Only three nights. I wish we could stay longer, but that's the limit of vacation time I could manage for both of us."

"We're going on vacation?" I repeat blankly. "I can't just up and leave. I have meetings tomorrow to wrap up the week." Silicone Dream has Friday reviews.

"They've been taken care of."

"How?"

"Heather."

"You spoke to Heather?"

He looks at me like I'm being obtuse on purpose. "Who else manages your schedule?"

Good point. "So why didn't she say something to me?"

"If she had, this wouldn't be a surprise."

I flip through my mental calendar for what's special about this weekend. Valentine's Day has passed. "What's the occasion?"

"Your birthday."

"Oh." I totally forgot. Ellie would've reminded me on Friday, but I've tried not to think too much about my birthday since Dad remarried. It hurts less that way. *Oh yeah, everybody forgot my birthday—even me! We've been so busy, hahaha.*

Before Grandma passed away, she made sure to take me out to fancy dinners and give me presents. Ellie showed up to celebrate, too. Now that Grandma's gone, Heather puts together an office party for me. But I never expected Griffin to plan a special getaway. We aren't even in a real relationship. As a matter of fact, I'm not sure he likes me much.

"I don't know what to say," I manage finally.

He gives me a small frown, like I'm speaking Latin. "'Thank you' will suffice."

"Thank you." I smile. "So. Where are we going?" Maybe a short jaunt to Napa Valley, or maybe Las Vegas—

"Tokyo."

I go still as I try to process what he told me. "Say that again."

A corner of his mouth twitches in a faint smile. "Tokyo."

"In Japan?" I say, starting to hyperventilate.

"That's the one."

"Oh my God! *Tokyo?*" I squeal, then hug him hard. "Are you *serious?* Tokyo? Thank you!"

He laughs, the sound rusty, like he hasn't done it in a while. Then he stops and awkwardly pats my shoulder before stepping back. "Now go pack."

I nod and leap up the stairs. As I do, the realization that I'm going on a vacation is sinking in. And not just any vacation—*Tokyo!*

I've always wanted to go to Japan, but the timing never worked out. I even wanted to go for our honeymoon, but Todd insisted on London because *he* had always dreamed of going to England.

Buoyant enthusiasm bubbles, and I feel like I can fly. I reach into my closet and pull out a suitcase. I throw in four days' worth of clothes and some toiletries and shoes, then make sure I have some room so I can bring back souvenirs. Even though it's only for three nights, I'm sure to find something supercool I have to have.

I zip up my bag, wanting to get going. I don't know what time our flight's leaving, but the traffic to LAX is atrocious. Not only that, it's going to take hours to check in and clear security. If I forget something, I can just buy it in Tokyo. The city's bound to have everything I could possibly need.

As I start dragging the suitcase out, I stop and run back into my room. My passport! *That* I can't buy in Tokyo.

I snatch it out of the dresser next to my bed, stuff it into my purse and rush out the door. Griffin is waiting at the top of the stairs and takes my suitcase.

When we reach the living room, I start toward the table where I keep Bullet and G-Spot's cage—which isn't there. "Where did you put the hamsters? I can drop them off at Ellie's." She won't mind taking care of them for a few days, for a cause as good as this.

"They're with Heather. I left the cage with Dan, who said he'd give it to her."

I let out a relieved sigh. "Thank you. You've thought of everything."

"I'm efficient like that," he says with a faint smile.

We go outside. I lock the house, then follow him as he puts my suitcase next to his in the trunk.

We settle into his Prius. "So. Do you take fake girlfriends on surprise trips overseas a lot?" As excited as I am, I'm curious about why he's doing this, and what he expects from it. Maybe it's a sign that he doesn't want our relationship to be fake. Maybe he's open to more? The possibility sends a happy zing through me.

"You're my first fake girlfriend, so no," he says.

"So you planned this because…?"

"I felt like it." His gravelly tone says, *What of it?*

But he doesn't fool me. He's slightly uncomfortable talking about doing something nice for somebody, and with that something being acknowledged. It's sort of sweet.

"Nobody else is going to do anything special for you—not your dad or Linda," he adds.

"Well…yeah, that's true. But you don't have to."

"Like I said, I felt like it."

If I look at his expression, he seems mildly annoyed. But his words... Well. Maybe the key to understanding him is looking at his body language, tone and words all separately and figuring out what he truly means, which is the opposite of how you'd normally process communicating with someone. "I see. Well, that's very sweet of you."

"I don't do sweet."

"Doesn't change the fact that it's still sweet."

He shrugs. "I don't mind impromptu trips."

"Do you impromptu travel a lot?" I keep my voice light and teasing so it doesn't feel like I'm probing.

"I used to. Whenever my mother felt restless." His eyebrows pull together, like he's reliving a horrific memory.

Why would traveling with his mom be so awful? "Did she get restless often?" It's a more personal question than the superficial topics we've discussed since he moved in, but I feel more confident about broaching it, knowing he has some feelings for me.

"Often enough. It wasn't as bad when school was in session."

"She volunteered at school?" I smile. "My mom did too. Said it made her feel useful and happy." She was one of the most involved parents in the area, and got antsy when she wasn't doing something for the school.

"No. She couldn't pull me out of school because she could never hire acceptable tutors in time. It was best for everyone that she never volunteered. It wasn't expected, either." He sounds annoyed and scandalized, like I suggested his mom dance naked at his high school reunion.

I just nod. For a guy who planned a special trip, he seems grouchy all of a sudden. I think back on what I said, but can't figure out what could've triggered the gloomy mood. "This trip isn't getting you in trouble or anything, right? You didn't have to take off too many days or...?"

He shakes his head. "I don't have any classes on Friday or Monday. The tricky schedule belonged to you."

"Okay, well, thanks for going to the trouble." I make a mental note to do something special for him after the trip.

"It wasn't a big deal," he says with a deep scowl.

"Then why are you in a bad mood?"

He glances over. "I'm not in a bad mood. This is how I am. And I'm trying to concentrate on driving."

"Most people can drive without staring at the road like it's their mortal enemy."

"Good for them," he mutters.

The skin under his eye is twitching. Maybe he's just feeling worried about flying, which might explain why he hates the memory of traveling with his mother. "You know, if you smile you'll feel better."

"Is that a scientific observation?"

"Nope. Life experience. It works! Try it."

He sighs, then pulls his lips back, baring his teeth. After relaxing again, he says, "I don't feel any different."

I can't stop laughter from bubbling up. I let it go, my hand on my belly. "Of course not, silly! That's the weirdest attempt at a smile I've ever seen. No, you have to *really* smile. Like this." I smile at him.

"Very nice. Maybe you'll win the Nobel Smile Prize."

"If I do, I'll give you half the prize money so you can do more research."

He snorts, then lets out a soft, reluctant chuckle. The tightness in his shoulders eases as he loosens his grip on the steering wheel.

"The traffic sucks right now, but we should be able to make our flight, right? I packed fast." I grin, hoping to further lighten his mood. "Wanna listen to some music? It always cheers me up."

His gaze slides toward me. "Are you going to sing?"

"Sure, why not? I love singing along."

He winces slightly.

Aha! Okay, he doesn't really care for my singing, even though he won't say it. "If you want—"

He interrupts me. "The only thing I listen to before flying is Maria Callas's arias."

"Maria who?"

"Callas. One of the best sopranos of the twentieth century."

I'm not a huge opera fan, but this is Griffin's car, and he's taking me to Tokyo. "Okay."

An orchestra starts, then the soprano's voice fills the car. It's a tune I recognize from commercials and TV shows, although I don't know the name. "What's this song called?" I ask.

"Puccini's *Madama Butterfly*."

"Mada*ma*?"

"The original Italian title."

I pay attention to the music. The soprano sings beautifully, her voice mellow and sweet. I glance at Griffin to see if he's feeling less hostile. He still has a small frown, but he's no longer looking out the windshield like we're in the middle of a zombie apocalypse.

Maybe this is the kind of music that relaxes him. I pull out my phone and Google Maria Callas, so I can make sure to have some of her songs in the house for him. I might even buy him tickets to an opera for his birthday.

I imagine how happy he'd be to be able to go to a gorgeous opera house and listen to his favorite arias. The more I think about it, the more excited I become. I'll go ahead and do just that, even if his birthday is after our fake breakup. I have a feeling Griffin will prove to be a civilized "ex-boyfriend," even though the idea of us not being together sends an achy pang through my heart.

34

SIERRA

Even though it's late, LAX is packed. But then, the airport is always congested. Lines snake down the departure lobby. I sigh, wondering if we have enough time to check in and clear security.

"What time is our flight?" I ask.

"Eleven fifty-five."

"We have three hours." I glance at the lines for the security. They're even longer than those at the airline counters. "Which airline?"

He points at a dark blue and white logo three yards ahead. I trot to the line and stand at the end. There are at least a hundred people ahead of us.

"Wrong line," he says. "We're not flying economy."

I follow him past the shorter lines for business-class passengers and straight to the counter for first class. I've never flown first class, not even for my honeymoon. Todd wanted to, saying that it was the least he deserved—and with every expectation that I pay for the entire honeymoon—but Heather booked us into business. Given how much she hates him, she probably wanted to buy economy tickets, except in that case I would've suffered too.

So first class is a shock. I know how much professors make, and these seats cost a lung. Economy would have been fine, actually, especially since he must've bought the tickets in the last week or two. I hope he hasn't overstretched himself.

He strides toward the uniformed ground crew like he owns the airline.

"Did you get an upgrade?" I ask, walking quickly to keep up.

"No," he says. "Why?"

"It's just so...extravagant."

He shrugs. "It's no big deal."

Maybe he has lots of frequent flier miles he can redeem for free tickets.

The superbly efficient ground crew checks us in. Another crew member—a willowy Japanese lady with a polite but warm smile—comes out and escorts us, holding our passports and tickets.

Griffin follows her like this is normal. I bring up the rear, marveling at what first class can get us. I've never had anybody escort me through an airport. I feel like royalty, and I'm excited and grateful that Griffin's giving me this experience.

She takes us through a special lane, bypassing the lengthy, serpentine lines that everyone else is standing in. Even the TSA agents are nicer, like they know we're important.

Then she escorts us to a gorgeous lounge across from a huge window facing the runway. Polished pale gold and cream marble and tiles spread out. The walls are covered in faux dark wood, and the air smells like sandalwood and lemongrass. One of the three uniformed women seated at the counter stands at our approach. "Welcome," she says.

Our guide hands her our passports and boarding passes to scan them into the system. She turns to us. "This is the first-class lounge. You can relax here until it's time to board at eleven thirty."

"I'm sorry, when, exactly?" Griffin said the plane was taking off at eleven fifty-five.

"Eleven thirty. The doors will close at eleven fifty. If that is all...?"

"Yes, thank you," Griffin says.

She smiles, then leaves.

"We aren't flying on a prop plane, are we?" I ask, watching her walking away.

"Across the Pacific?" Griffin seems to find the idea amusing. "No. It's a Dreamliner. And yes, they can board in twenty minutes."

"Wow."

"Don't worry. We'll make it to Tokyo safe and sound."

The lady at the counter gives our boarding passes and passports back to us. Another staff member comes out and leads us to an empty table that overlooks the tarmac. We can see a huge Boeing jet out the window.

"Is there any food?" I ask the lady. We left without dinner, so I'm feeling peckish and not seeing any buffet. I really hope they have food here.

"You can order whatever you like from the menus," she says, gesturing at two white leather-bound menus on the table. "Take your time and I'll come by later."

As she walks away, I look at the menus. "Wow. Fancy."

"It isn't bad. There's going to be a meal service once we're in the air, so you might want to leave some room," Griffin says.

"Got it." Normally in-flight meals aren't that appetizing, but seeing all the effort the airline put into this lounge, I have a feeling the first-class ones are going to be amazing.

The menu lists all sorts of premium alcohols, cocktails and hot food. I ask for an omelet and some OJ, since it's morning in Tokyo. Griffin gets a hot turkey and cheese sandwich and two fingers of scotch.

I look around the sparkling lounge and the well-heeled passengers sipping drinks or munching on snacks. I thought I was used to nice trips. Grandma didn't believe in suffering when she traveled, but she preferred domestic destinations. Which meant none of the incredible experience I'm getting at the moment.

Since Griffin's reading something on his tablet, I put on my best I-travel-like-this-all-the-time face and text Ellie to let her know I'll be out of the country. Her reply comes immediately.

–Ellie: WHAT!!!! No way! How come you didn't tell me????!!!!!

–Me: Griffin planned a surprise trip. I just found out when I got home.

–Ellie: Did you tell him Tokyo was on your bucket list?

–Me: No, but he just knew.

–Ellie: Damn. I know he's your fake boyfriend, but make him your REAL boyfriend, girl. A guy who flies you to Tokyo for your birthday is a keeper!

–Me: And not in economy, either. We're flying first class!

–Ellie: Holy shit! I want pictures!

I surreptitiously snap some photos of the lounge and send them to her.

–Ellie: Wow. He sure knows how to treat a girl. I totally approve of this upgrade. That fucker would've never remembered your birthday.

I almost shake my head. Todd always handed me something extra on our anniversary, ostensibly to celebrate my birthday. My telling him it wasn't my birthday never really penetrated. I considered writing a Shakespearean sonnet to tell him, thinking maybe that'd make it easier for him to remember, since he has no problem memorizing famous English poems. But that would have been way too much work.

–Ellie: I want pictures of the plane too! I want to live vicariously through you.

–Me: Okay!

–Ellie: We'll do something for your birthday when you're back.

–Me: Works for me!

35

GRIFFIN

Since we're in first class, we board through a separate jet bridge connected to the front of the plane.

"Oh my God. Our seats have *doors*," Sierra whispers as we step into the first-class cabin.

"They're called suites."

"I can see why. 'Cause these seats are suh-weet!" She looks around, eyes wide.

Her excitement is cute. What's even cuter is how she's trying to act cool, even though her eyes and ear-to-ear smile are giving her away.

"I guess all the romance novels where the heroine gets upgraded to first class and starts flirting with the hottie next to her can't really happen, huh?"

"Not unless you want to scream-flirt over the engine noise through two doors and an aisle."

She laughs softly. "That *would* kind of ruin the effect."

Her suite is on the other side of the aisle from mine. I slide my laptop bag into the storage space underneath the ottoman, go over to her suite and stand by the giant TV. Normally, I'd be pulling out my tablet to review government stats or some paper published by another economist, but I don't want to miss her reaction. If she's happy flying this way, it's money well spent.

The thought makes me pause. I've never spent money and thought about how I felt about it. I use money out of obligation. Mortgage, utilities, clothes, cars and food. Gifts for Mom and Dad for whatever occasions they deem special enough—as a bribe, praying they'll be placated with a present and leave me alone as long as possible.

Since I want to hide who my parents are and how much I'm worth, I generally avoid ostentatious spending, even though my bank account can easily support whatever luxury I could wish for.

This trip was an impulse. I splurged because I didn't want Sierra folded uncomfortably all the way across the Pacific, especially since I made plans for her in Tokyo. She won't be able to enjoy herself if she's jet-lagged and exhausted. There aren't any other reasons for my uncharacteristic desire to treat her to a first-class experience.

Besides, it's her birthday. She deserves some special attention and treatment.

A cabin attendant comes over with a tray of champagnes and various juices. "Would you like something to drink?"

Sierra eyes the champagne flutes. I take two glasses and hand her one.

"To Tokyo," she says.

"To your birthday."

Her cheeks turn a gorgeous shade of pink. "Thank you."

As we sip our drinks, the purser stops by and introduces herself with a warm smile, encouraging us to contact her if we need anything. Another smiling cabin attendant places thick menus into the pockets on the wall by the doors.

Sierra glances at the menus. "I guess we're eating separately?"

"If you want, we can ask them to set both dinners in one suite."

"Really?" She perks up. "That's okay?"

"This is first class, and it's your birthday. You can have whatever you want."

36

SIERRA

I never knew I could feel so rested and refreshed after a long flight. I suppose that's why people fly first class. The turndown service transformed my seat into an actual *bed*, and I napped—but not too much because I didn't want to stay up and be too tired to enjoy my day in Tokyo.

But as I press myself against the floor-to-ceiling window of the two-bedroom suite and look down at the glowing vista of nighttime Tokyo, I'm too excited to sleep.

Griffin says something to the uniformed front desk clerk who escorted us to our suite. She says something back, bows and leaves.

"Want something to eat?" he says.

"No thanks. Look at this *city*! It's *gorgeous*." I rest my forehead against the cool glass.

"What's so wonderful about it? It's just a city."

"Noooo!" I give him a horrified look. "It isn't like some other city. Look at all those people. The energy. Even air feels different in Tokyo!" The vitality of this city can't be beat. It isn't just the modern sleekness, it's the *history*. It's impossible to forget how old the city is when you pass by old-style buildings with chrysanthemum emblems that must've been standing there for ages. In this suite alone, there are well-polished antique cabinets and tables that must've survived centuries of history since the era of the samurais.

Griffin stands next to me and places his forehead against the glass too. "I don't feel anything different."

"Don't even try to make it sound unexciting. You're failing."

He doesn't respond, but continues to look down at the view. The reflection of his face shows a small frown, like he's really unhappy about something. Is he not enjoying the trip?

Maybe he's just tired. I don't know if he got any sleep during the flight. I didn't want to be weird and check up on him.

On impulse, I turn and place a kiss on his cheek. He goes still, then looks at me, the entire force of his presence focused on me. My heart starts racing, and my mouth grows weirdly dry.

Our eyes meet and his frown deepens. Something that looks like an internal debate crosses his stunning features, but I can't imagine what he could be debating, especially when his eyes are burning and I'd like to kiss him, this time on his mouth.

I inhale his mesmerizing scent and start to lean forward—

He takes an abrupt half step back and points to a door to his left. "You can take that room. Good night." He starts walking away.

"Good night," I say automatically to his retreating back, befuddled.

I sniff my shirt, just in case. It smells okay.

As I walk slowly to the room filled with antiques from some ancient period in Japan, I'm left with the question—what happened?

37

SIERRA

"So what are we doing today?" I ask over a late brunch. I was hoping to get up early, but I guess waking up at six doesn't transfer when there are sixteen time zones to overcome.

Griffin suggested room service, but I insisted on using one of the restaurants. As luxurious as our suite is, I want to soak up as much of the city as possible. That means getting out of our room, even if we're staying inside the hotel for our meal.

Also, staying in the suite makes me feel slightly ambivalent. Everything that happened in the last twenty-four hours or so is amazing. I really wanted to follow Ellie's advice and seduce Griffin, make him as happy as he's made me—but then he just abandoned me!

Am I *that* un-sexy? That undesirable?

Maybe it's the jet lag. He could've been tired. Just because my shirt smelled okay yesterday doesn't mean I was seductive, especially after a full day and a long flight. My makeup was two days old and my face was overly shiny. I could've looked like a trout that started to go bad.

A trout. My God. Think of something sexier than that to refer to yourself. How can I have depressing thoughts when I should be having some of the best moments of my life? Negativity doesn't help anybody, and I plan to enjoy my time here, no matter what.

We're seated in a huge restaurant overlooking a serene Japanese garden complete with green bamboo and little streams. I'm eating steamed white rice, miso soup, seaweed, simmered fish and some other Japanese food that I don't recognize. It's all stunningly presented in gorgeous blue and white porcelain bowls and plates that are smaller than my palm. Griffin's enjoying French toast. His food is on a standard white plate with a golden rim in fan and mountain patterns.

"We have a massage session scheduled with the spa here to help us shake off the jet lag," he says.

I knew it! "Ooh, that sounds amazing!"

"Afterwards we'll have an hour to relax before the evening."

"Are we free to do whatever we want then?" I ask, eager and excited about the possibilities. "I'd love to go to Tokyo Skytree. It's the tallest observation deck in the world, and I've wanted to go ever since I saw it on TV. It's going to be amazing to look at the city at night from that high up." I smile dreamily. It's going to be awesome to celebrate my birthday there. Who cares about becoming a year older when you're up there with one of the largest and most vibrant cities in the world at your feet?

"Not today," he says. "We have different plans. But we can go tomorrow."

"Okay." Maybe Griffin has something he wants to do. Although today's my birthday, we can do what he wants first. After all, he planned and paid for this amazing trip. I can be flexible.

Actually, I'm just happy to be here. Nothing can change the fact that I'm in Tokyo for my birthday.

After brunch, we head to the spa. When he said it was a massage, I expected something like what I had back in Lovedale. But no. The bilingual menu states that this is a full "detox and rejuvenation program." After we fill out forms about our health conditions, the spa staff take me and Griffin to separate treatment rooms.

I change into a robe, and the treatment starts off with a soak in some kind of fragrant herbal hot spring water. My spa lady places an hourglass filled with sparkling green and blue sand on the foot of the tub, letting the grains slip slowly down. The warm water feels so good that I sigh and sink deeper into the tub. I could get used to this. Maybe I should see if I can buy the salt they tossed into the water, so I can re-create the experience at home.

When the green and blue sand has all fallen to the bottom, she helps me out of the tub. "Please be careful, as the floor can be very slippery." Her voice is soft and pleasant. "Your massage is over there."

She takes me to an airy room set up with a bed. I lie down and she starts to massage me…

When I open my eyes, I'm momentarily disoriented. My masseuse has brought me a cup of warm ginger tea. "Did I fall asleep for long?"

She checks the time. "A little over ninety minutes."

"Wow." I must've been more tired than I thought. Or the masseuse is just that good.

I sit up and realize I feel fantastic—my head clear, my body full of energy. I could run a marathon now! Yes! Just perfect before Griffin and I tour the city.

She hands me the tea. "It's hot, so please be careful."

"Thanks." I sip the tea. Sweet with a tang of ginger and lemon grass. Yummy. "Is Griffin done too?"

"Please allow me to check." She pulls out a phone and taps the screen. The device pings. "Mr. Lasker finished ten minutes ago and is at the concierge now."

"Thanks." He must've gone there to arrange what he wants to do later today. It'll be cool if he wants to see the city. I'd love to walk around and just drink in this giant metropolis.

I go back to the suite and change into jeans and a cute pink top with fake gemstones in front that spell *I Heart Japan*. I slip on my teal ballet flats, which have been broken in already, and make sure my phone's fully charged so I can take lots of pictures. If Griffin needs me in something else, I have a cute dress I can throw on quickly.

Griffin comes up soon after. He's in the same casual blue T-shirt and shorts. Whatever magic the spa people performed relaxed him so much that he actually looks vaguely pleased. He seems more approachable and sweeter like this, rather than his usual impassivity or outright annoyance.

Wonder if he's going to be more amenable to kissing now? Because on the rare occasion his mouth curves like that, I want to kiss him.

As soon as the thought pops into my head, I shake myself

mentally. I don't want a repeat of yesterday until I can figure out what went wrong last night. Based on the fact that he isn't avoiding me or treating me weirdly, it doesn't seem like he was upset by the kiss itself.

"How was the massage?" he asks.

"Amazing," I say with a smile. "Thank you."

"It was nothing. You look more energized now."

"I was so relaxed, I ended up napping. So! All set up for our day?"

"Yup. The concierge took care of everything."

"Great! What's the plan?"

"An early dinner first. We won't be able to eat later. Or at least I don't think you will."

That's an odd thing to say. "How come?"

"Probably be too overwrought."

I laugh. "What are you planning that you think I'm going to be too overwrought to eat?"

"It's a secret."

"Not even a small hint?" I give him my best pleading face.

"Nope." He considers. "We can do room service or hit one of the restaurants here. The traffic's pretty bad, so that might be the best." He checks his watch.

"Okay. Let's do that. As long as we're doing Japanese food."

"What are you in the mood for?"

Excited, I start rattling off all the stuff on my "must-try when in Japan" list. "I want to try sushi and ramen. I read that ramen is famous in Tokyo. Oh and the Japanese-style curry and rice! I saw on YouTube that it's the most popular food among the children. I absolutely *have* to taste it."

He lets out a laugh. Everything inside me does happy shivers at the unexpected and rare sound.

He sobers quickly, like he's shocked he laughed at all. *Why doesn't he want to laugh and be happy?*

"I don't think we can have all of them," he says, "but the hotel has an excellent sushi restaurant."

"Perfect!"

38

SIERRA

The dinner is fancy, served by a lady in a kimono. The wooden platform-looking serving plate has only ten nigiri pieces, but that's perfect. I'm not overly hungry because of our late brunch.

Griffin checks the time as we finish up. "Excellent. Our driver should be waiting for us."

"We have a driver? I thought we were taking taxis. I read they're pretty fancy."

"The concierge arranged it for us. If you want to try a Japanese taxi, we can do that too. But not today."

Okay, my curiosity is definitely piqued. We're both dressed fairly casually, but our ride is anything but. Where are we going? I can't get any clues from Griffin's impassive face, and I have a feeling he isn't going to tell.

In the lobby, a uniformed doorman bows as the huge glass doors slide open automatically. A gorgeous white limo is idling outside, along with a few other gleaming cars. Bellhops take suitcases as several sharply dressed Japanese men enter the hotel, their temples gray, their faces set in odd expressions somewhere between stoic and grim.

Man. They don't know how good they have it. If I got to live in Tokyo, I'd tap-dance to work every day.

Griffin leads me to the ivory limo.

"Oh my God, that's our ride?" I say, trying to sound cool and failing. It isn't my first time riding a limo, but it feels so extravagant, especially after the first-class flight, the stunning suite and the lavish soak and massage. I've never splurged like this, not even on my honeymoon.

"Yup. Told you the concierge arranged for everything."

"But a *limo*?"

"Why not?" He shrugs like it's nothing.

A driver in a black suit and hat opens the door, his hands in snow-white gloves.

It's so formal. I feel like I should do whatever the Japanese version of a curtsy is. Then the driver adds to the formality by bowing.

Griffin says something to the man in Japanese and they have a short exchange.

I stare. *Griffin speaks Japanese*, well enough to communicate with our driver. That's so hot. My libido is surging, and I have a crazy impulse to kiss him again.

Come on, Sierra. Control yourself. He isn't interested in you that way.

I wince inwardly at the brutal voice in my head, which somehow sounds like Todd, then slap it down. The old negativity from my ex-husband isn't going to mess things up. Plenty of men find me interesting.

Besides, I noticed Griffin checking out my ass as we left the sushi restaurant. He's probably just being a gentleman.

The limo moves in a stately way through the traffic. There are tons of cars and buses crawling along incredibly narrow lanes on busy streets. All the vehicles gleam like they've just been washed. But what's most fascinating is the massive number of pedestrians on the sidewalks.

There are cyclists too, but not like the ones you see in L.A. They aren't wearing helmets or fancy cycling outfits. They're in regular street clothes and riding bikes with baskets in front for their bags or other belongings. A few are on basket-less bikes, but they either have back packs, or their bags are dangling from the handlebars.

"Don't your eyes get dry when you keep them wide open like that for so long?" Griffin says.

"Nope. I'm not going to miss a thing. I've never been this fascinated." I turn to him with a huge smile. "Thank you."

"Don't thank me yet."

I let out a disbelieving laugh. "What? You have something even more amazing scheduled than the trip and the massage and this limo ride through the city?"

A corner of his gorgeous mouth tilts upward. "Yup."

"Like?"

"Oh, you'll see."

Now I'm really curious, but Griffin refuses to say more.

The limo continues through the city and eventually a huge structure comes into view. Architecturally, it looks like a gigantic version of one of my breakfast bowl lids. Thousands of people are milling around it, but they seem orderly, with a few uniformed personnel directing them.

"What's that?" I ask.

"Tokyo Dome," Griffin says.

"Isn't that a baseball stadium?"

"Among other things."

As the limo approaches, the driver and Griffin have another exchange in Japanese. The car stops a few blocks from the Tokyo Dome, and the driver hurries out to open the door for us.

"Are we going to see a game?" I ask. Some of the YouTubers I follow said going to a Japanese baseball game is a treat because the fans are hilariously fanatical and oddly polite at the same time.

"You'll see," Griffin says again, taking my hand.

A hot zing races from the bare skin of his palm all the way to my heart, making it boom loudly in my ears. Delicious shivers skid along my spine, and I realize his reaction last night definitely wasn't about the kiss or me. It was something else.

He tugs gently, and I climb out of the limo. We walk through the crowd toward the stadium, our fingers linked. It feels like we're a couple on a date one lovely summer night.

Then as I absorb what's going on around us, I realize we aren't here for a baseball game.

Holy...

A familiar melody starts blasting, and half the crowd seems to be in T-shirts with a single word: *Axelrod*.

"No way..." My whole body starts shaking with surging excitement and shock. "We're going to the Axelrod concert?"

Griffin nods with the faintest hint of a smile. "Yup. You said you never missed a tour. No reason to start now."

"Oh my *God*!" This time I squeal and throw myself at him to hug him hard. "Thank you, thank you, thank you! You are the absolute *best*!"

He lets out a stunned laugh, then hugs me back, giving me a squeeze that turns my insides gooey with joy. "Like I said, don't thank me yet."

"How come? You can't possibly top this," I say, looking up at him while my heart is doing every flip known to man. Actually, I think it just invented a few.

He shrugs, then plucks two T-shirts that read *Axelrod Tokyo* from the merchandise booth and buys them. "Here. Happy birthday." He hands me one of the shirts like *that*'s the present, not the trip, not this concert.

Laughing, I take it. "Thank you."

We find the gate on our tickets and go inside the dome, already full of concertgoers milling around. My ears pop as we enter. "Whoa, what was that?" I rub my ears and swallow to clear the weird stuffy feeling.

"The interior is pressurized to support"—he points at the rounded ceiling, looming over us high above—"that."

I notice there are no support beams. "Oh."

"Be careful when we leave because it can feel like you're being pushed out."

It takes me a moment to work it out. "Because of the air pressure?"

"Right. The pressure difference between here and outside. I read that the air expulsion can be as strong as forty-four-point-seven miles per hour."

"*Really?*"

"But that's if only a handful of people are leaving. It shouldn't be that bad when everyone's exiting after the concert."

"I'll keep that in mind." I don't want to fall like a klutz and embarrass myself.

Griffin and I walk with our hands linked. I have no expectations about where we're going to be. He only learned that I like Axelrod a few weeks ago, so I doubt we'll be in front. But at the moment, I don't care if we're all the way up in the nosebleed section.

Thousands of folding chairs are set neatly in front of the stage. So many people are already here, swarming like ants. Griffin leads me through the crowd, stopping when we reach the front row, just left of center stage.

I raise my voice so he can hear me over the noise. "This is where we're sitting?"

"Yup."

"How did you do that?" An unlikely idea pops into my head.

"Magic," he says, like it's nothing.

"Did you buy our tickets from a scalper?" Seats this good for a band this popular cost thousands of dollars, assuming you can even find them in the first place. I know Griffin has to have some money, but usually I'm the one expected to fund this sort of lavish excursion. Not that what he's doing for me feels bad. It's just…I'm touched he went through so much trouble, because it isn't just about money, but his remembering that Axelrod is my favorite band and making this trip and the concert happen for me.

He cares. *Really cares.* And that means more than anything in the world.

"A scalper?" Griffin gives me a look that says, *Do you think I'm stupid?* "No. I just…know somebody who had to cancel at the last minute."

"So you didn't have to trade your liver or anything?"

"No."

I smile, relieved. "Okay. Great."

Since it's going to be a while before the concert starts, we sit down. The Japanese fans are civilized and polite, keeping to themselves and chatting with their friends without smoking or starting to drink heavily. Some of the girls behind us giggle.

"Do you think they're going to stay seated and all that once the concert starts?" I ask, unsure what the etiquette in Japan is. People here seem much more formal than in the U.S. They might pull out opera glasses.

"I don't know. I've never been to a rock concert in Japan before. I've only been here once to watch a baseball game."

"You like Japanese baseball?"

"I don't follow Japanese sports, but I was invited, so…" His tone says it was anything but pleasurable.

I look around, hoping I won't have to keep my butt glued to my chair. What's the fun in that?

The lights come up, then dim again. Fireworks go off on stage, bright yellow and red sparkles shooting up. The crowd buzzes in excitement, jumping to their feet.

Griffin are I are on our feet too. I look at the stage, mesmerized.

When the lights come back, Axelrod is on stage! People start screaming, and excitement sweeps through the giant stadium in an electric surge.

All four members wave to the crowd. Killian Axelrod yells, "Hello, *Tokyo!*" and the crowd goes insane. A drumbeat starts and then the rest of the band jump into their first number.

The band sounds *so* good live. The music pulses like a living thing, making me feel like I'm on some heightened plane of reality. Killian's stage presence is mesmerizing, and my heart thuds loudly in my ears as feverish excitement shivers through me.

Giddy, I take Griffin's hand. He glances at me, and I smile. My smile broadens when he gives me a lopsided grin that makes my heart soar.

You. Are. The. Best, I mouth at him.

He raises his eyebrows and tilts his head in helpless agreement. The gesture makes me laugh again.

My pulse throbs to more than Axelrod's music. It throbs to the pulse I'm feeling through Griffin's warm, dry palm. I wish I could freeze this moment and preserve it forever.

The band plays for the best part of an hour, hitting all my favorite songs. Then they take a quiet moment.

"I don't normally do special requests, but this one I couldn't ignore," says Killian Axelrod. "It's from a man who wants to do something very special for the most special woman in his life. He asked us for help, and I thought...why not?"

I look around, but there are probably fifty thousand people packed into the dome. *Who is this lucky woman?* I'd die of a happy heart attack if anybody did anything like this for me.

Killian looks out at the crowd. "Sierra Fullilove, *raise your hand!*" He raises an arm in the air.

I stare at him on the stage, dumbfounded. Did he just say *my* name?

"Come on." He puts a hand over his eyes and squints. "I know you're here, Sierra."

The people start to buzz, looking around for somebody with her hand raised.

I stay frozen, my heart still. I can't decide if I'm feeling cold or hot, but my head is spinning, and I can't process anything.

Griffin taps my shoulder. "That would be you."

"He really said my name?" I feel like I'm dreaming.

He nods, then takes my hand and raises it. "Here!" he yells, cupping a hand around his mouth.

"There you are. Shy, huh? But right in front. Perfect!" Killian grins, and a dimple flashes in his cheek.

My face is hot with shock, anticipation and nerves. I've never been the focus of somebody this famous, somebody I've been fangirling over for years. I can feel the weight of other people's gazes, and squeeze Griffin's hand.

Killian starts to sing, strolling over until he's standing directly in front of me. "Happy birthday to you..." His voice is mellow and sweet.

Oh my God. My heart melts, especially when he croons, "Happy *birth*day, dear Sierraaa..."

He turns the mic to the audience, and they raggedly sing the last "happy birthday to you" then holler and clap. The girls around us loudly proclaim something in an envious tone and yell out, "Happy birthday!"

I'm still shaking with disbelief that Killian Axelrod sang just for me. And I know exactly who gave me this amazing, once-in-a-lifetime experience.

I turn toward Griffin. He's looking at me with a small smile, his eyes bright and satisfied. I lift my trembling hands and cup his warm cheeks.

I kiss him; his mouth parts. Cheers erupt around us, and I pull back in mild shock, remembering we're surrounded by tens of thousands of people.

I hug Griffin hard. My heart gallops against my chest, and I can feel his thumping too. I bury my face in his shoulder as my eyes heat with tears. All the loneliness I've felt since Mom and Grandma died starts to shrivel and die. In its place is a sense of belonging and love.

Griffin might be my fake boyfriend, but what I feel for him is real.

39

SIERRA

My head is buzzing. The rest of the concert feels louder, brighter and more wonderful. But what I really want to do is kiss the stuffing out of Griffin in private.

Leaving Tokyo Dome and climbing into the limo doesn't register. All I can sense is the hyperawareness prickling at my nerve endings. I want Griffin more than my next breath.

In the back of the limo, I thread my fingers through his and squeeze. His pulse throbs against my palm. When we finally stop in front of the hotel, we climb out with hands still linked. We don't let go as we cross the vast lobby toward the elevator bank. My feet slap against the endless marble of the hotel lobby. *Why did they make this lobby so huge?*

A uniformed clerk holds the door to one of the elevators. We slip right in. Griffin punches the close button endlessly.

The second the doors close, I'm on him, looping my arms around his strong neck. I resume the kiss the crowd interrupted at the dome, devouring him like a dying woman, my mouth wild and desperate. Our tongues tangle, and my God, he tastes so good, all lusty, delicious male.

I wrap my legs around him and vaguely note the elevator stopping, the doors opening. *Are there other people around?* I don't care.

Griffin strides out, carrying me with about as much effort as he would carry a pillow. Every step rocks me against him, sending one delicious wave of friction after another. I'm already wet, and I want to feel him hot and hard against my bare flesh.

He maneuvers the room key, pulling away from me to see what he's doing. I bury my face in the crook of his neck, lick the taut skin and hum with satisfaction when his breathing hitches.

The door opens, and then we're inside. Dim lights come on in every corner as he drops the key card into its slot.

He kicks the door shut with his heel and then his mouth is devouring mine again—sultry, seductive. His tongue strokes me, aggressive, then sweet and teasing. I kiss him back, my body winding up at the wild taste of him. He's like the best brandy—heady and intoxicating.

I lower my feet to the floor and slip my hands under his shirt, spreading my fingers over his hard chest, greedy for more of him. I want to feel all of him, taste all of him, have him inside me so deep that we're united.

Tonight, he's mine, and I'm his. Everything else can wait until tomorrow.

"You drive me crazy," I manage between pants, ripping the shirt over his head and throwing it somewhere in the suite. I finally undo his pants button. The zipper lowers with a soft hiss. I push his pants down—somehow he's lost his shoes already—then his black underwear until everything pools at his feet. He kicks the garments away as though they're trash.

His erection springs forward, the cock head almost touching his flat belly. I wrap my hand around the thick shaft, feel the rapid pulsing against my palm and fingers. He's long and huge—big enough that I can't fully circle him with my fingers.

Driven with need, I drop to my knees and wrap my lips around him. A low groan tears from his throat, the muscles in his belly tightening.

He's hard, yet the skin is velvety against my tongue. I pull him in deeper and moan as the intense taste of him fills my mouth. It intensifies my hunger for him, making my whole body throb.

His breathing grows rougher. I glance up. His eyes are two gorgeous pools glazed over with mounting need, his sharply defined cheeks flushed.

At the sight of him losing himself, I grow wetter, my flesh

aching. I tilt my head back, wanting to see his face break into an orgasm I'm responsible for.

He tunnels his large hand into my hair and holds my head firmly. He thrusts to the tempo I set. I wish I could tell him how amazing sucking him is. How his excitement is driving me wild.

Suddenly, he pulls out of my mouth with a soft pop. Chest heaving, he lifts me up and kisses me with all the desperation of a starving man.

Yes, yes. I kiss him back, a moan caught in my throat. He cups my ass, lifting me as he carries me to the bedroom—his. Through my thin shirt, I can feel his erection pulsing against my belly, and I'm dying with unfulfilled need.

The second we're in his room, I yank my shirt off, dropping it over my shoulder. He unhooks my bra and pushes it away, his long, strong fingers hurried. I let out a soft sigh at how cool the air feels against my bare breasts. He takes a nipple into his mouth, sucking hard. My knees buckle as hot streaks of pleasure race through my veins. His arm wraps around my waist to keep me upright as he continues to suck and lick. Every flick of his tongue over the tip of my breast sends an electric shock of pleasure along my spine.

Desperate to be closer, I unbutton and unzip my jeans. He rains searing kisses along my shoulders as I bend to shove my jeans and underwear down my legs. When they get stuck on my shoes, I kick them off and strip the rest of the way until I'm fully nude.

I straighten up. He looks at my naked body, his gaze burning with a desire that makes me even hotter.

"You're perfect. So pretty, so pink"—his eyes fall to my breasts and the neatly trimmed juncture between my thighs—"and all mine."

I shiver as he lifts me and takes the other nipple into his mouth. I moan mindlessly, my back arching. His thick, muscled arm supports me, and I grip his broad shoulders, clinging and begging.

I sense him carrying me toward the bed. The backs of my knees hit the mattress. I slowly topple, held in his arms while he covers me with thousands of wet kisses, his tongue flicking out to taste every inch of me, like I'm the most delectable treat in the world.

An orgasm's building. It's so close, I can feel the vibrating energy of it.

"Inside me," I beg, moving my legs restlessly against him. "*Now*. I want to climax with you."

He inhales sharply, his eyes glittering. He reaches for a small black bag on the nightstand and pulls out a packet of condoms. Delicious anticipation shivers through me as his straight white teeth bite into the foil, and he yanks it until it tears and then rolls the thin rubber down his gorgeous cock, ready to drive into me.

He runs his index finger down the slit between my legs. I moan at how good it feels, but want more than this, more than an orgasm. I want *belonging*.

He thrusts into me, his cock huge and invading, and I cry out. The fantasy I had thinking about him doesn't even compare. His fingers link with mine, our palms pressed tight like we're fused and he'll never let go. He drops his head, claims my mouth as he moves in and out, his thrusts growing deeper and more powerful.

Bliss winds around me, sharp and intense. I fight to breathe, and then the orgasm that's been so close shatters me. It's so strong that I can't even scream; my vision goes gray and then white.

Griffin groans my name as he stiffens and empties himself.

We stay wrapped around each other, sharing the same air, our hearts racing. He places tender kisses on my mouth, neck and shoulders. I caress his thick hair, loving the sweet moment he's taking to show this wasn't just about orgasms or sex. I feel like we're intimately connected, not just in body but in our hearts as well.

40

GRIFFIN

I reach out, then open my eyes when my hands touch cool sheets. Slightly disoriented, I stare at the spot where Sierra should be.

I didn't dream the night. Or going to sleep with her nestled against me, my arms wrapped around her like a shield against the world.

Did she go to the bathroom? I don't hear anything.

"Sierra?"

No response.

I get up and look around. Her clothes and shoes aren't strewn on the floor anymore.

Did she go back to her room? For some reason, the thought annoys me, and then the annoyance annoys me more. I don't generally like getting up with a woman I've spent the night with. They tend to cling or start thinking they can make demands on my time or connections—if they know about my parents, especially my dad.

I booked a double-bedroom suite out of habit, and perhaps I shouldn't have. But I didn't want Sierra to feel like she had to sleep with me in exchange for the trip. When she kissed me that first night here, I wasn't sure if she really wanted me or if she was just doing it because she thought it was what *I* wanted. I wouldn't have given in last night, either, until I was certain she wanted it for herself.

And it would have been fine if she didn't want to sleep with me throughout the trip. This is all for her. Despite what she thinks, it wasn't as perfectly planned as I would've liked. Until yesterday afternoon, I wasn't sure if we were going to the concert. One of the most unreliable people I know promised to have the tickets for me at the hotel, and I only accepted the offer because it was that or go through Dad or Joey, and I'd rather choke on cat vomit than ask anything from either of them.

I use the bathroom, brush my teeth and throw on a robe, then pad out of the room. My clothes turn out not to be strewn all over the floor, either. They're draped over an armchair facing the TV.

The memory of her kneeling and giving me head sends a hot rush of desire along my spine, making my cock stir.

Down, boy. I'm not on the prowl right now. If Sierra wants another go, I won't turn her down, but this isn't just about sex.

The door to her room is ajar. I knock gently a couple of times and stick my head in.

"Sierra?"

The room is quiet, and the bed hasn't been slept in. But she's been in here. Her purse is lying on the sheet, and her flats are set neatly by the foot of the bed.

So where did she go?

I step inside. The layout of this room is an exact duplicate of mine. The king-sized bed, a gorgeously lacquered cabinet that is an interesting fusion of Japan and West. A minibar and a couple of plush armchairs.

The faint sound of water running comes from the bathroom. That door has also been left open.

I find my mouth curving into a relieved and anticipatory smile. "Sierra?"

"In here," she says, sounding happy.

I walk inside and see her in the huge shower stall, her body wet and covered in thick foam.

"Good morning," Sierra says with a smile through the glass door.

"Good morning. Why are you up so early?" Her glistening nude body looks even better in the morning.

"I always get up at six a.m.," she informs me primly.

"We're sixteen times zones away, and you got up late yesterday."

"It's a habit. That massage reset my internal clock, and no

number of time zones is going to stop me from getting up at six." She shrugs a shoulder. It makes her breast jiggle.

Blood heats, pooling in my highly eager dick. "So you have no interest in going back to sleep?"

"Nope. Wide awake." She opens her eyes exaggeratedly.

I chuckle. "Well... We have a lot of time on our hands, then."

"How would you like to spend it?" She gives me a saucy smile.

"Hmm... I can think of one very satisfying way."

She laughs as I drop the robe, open the stall door and enter. The sound turns to a soft sigh when I kiss her. She tastes faintly like toothpaste and a sweetness that is all her. The hotel's body wash smells like lemon and mint, but I still get that whiff of apple. It's like the scent is an ingrained part of her, and my cock grows harder. I love how delicious she smells.

My hands glide smoothly along the taut skin of her leanly muscled back. Although the water is warm, she shivers. Her beautiful purple eyes grow languid. The sound that she makes in her throat is full of anticipation.

"Griffin," she sighs.

"Tell me what you want," I say against her lips.

"Just you," she says. "Just you."

I pull her closer and kiss her again. Strangely, it doesn't feel like a simple prelude to sex. There's something more, like a "welcome home" greeting. It's slightly unsettling, but...

I caress her shoulders and slide my hands down until I can touch her breasts. I cup them, reveling in the slick sensation, so different from the way she felt last night. Her body is warm and slippery all over. I want to stroke her until she purrs like a satisfied kitten.

I trap her nipples between my fingers, and Sierra lets out a soft moan against my lips, her tongue stroking mine desperately. She pulls me closer until we're flush against each other. Now my throbbing erection is trapped against her stomach. She rocks against me, stimulating my cock, and blood rushes downward until I feel like I can break bricks with it.

I pinch her nipples, hard. She stiffens, her fingers digging into my shoulders.

"You like that?" I say. She opens her mouth; no words come out, but she nods very decisively.

There are so many things I want to do to her right now. So many ways I want to take her. But I don't have a condom.

I pull my mouth away from her. A question flickers in her eyes. I turn her around.

"Brace yourself against the wall, and stick your ass out like you want me to fuck you," I command.

Trembling, she places her palms again the tiles, then tilts her hips until her gorgeous ass is pushed back, offered just for me. Her eager obedience is hot as hell.

"Good girl." I run my hands along her gorgeous curves. Her taut butt fits them perfectly.

She whimpers with need, squirming. To reward her, I move my fingers along her folds. I feel a slickness down there that's not from the water. It's hotter and thicker, full of pure greed. She moans loudly, moving against my fingers.

"Griffin, please."

I push two fingers into her and feel her inner muscles tighten, gripping them like they're my cock. Need prickles all over my skin. I want her more than anything. If I don't have her now, I'm going to die.

Since I can't drive my cock inside her without protection, I use three of my fingers to ravish her, fucking her and making her feel good. Meanwhile, I fit my cock in the groove between her ass cheeks and move against her.

"Oh my God, oh my God." Her breathless sobs echo against the walls.

My blood boils at the shivers running through her and the needy sound she makes. I move faster and harder. Then I reach around and grab a breast, pinch her nipple again. Her entire body tightens, and her pussy spasms around my fingers as she shudders. The sight of her orgasm makes everything inside me freeze too, and I bury my face in the curve between her neck and shoulder and groan my pleasure as I cover her back with my cum. The water continues to spray over us and slowly rinses away the thick white liquid.

For a moment, she feels like mine. My girl.

41

SIERRA

After our amazing shower sex, I dry off and get dressed in a casual pink and purple dress that stops a couple of inches above my knees and some comfy sandals. I can hear the sound of the TV in the living room. A male British anchor is talking about the financial outlook in Europe, and I marvel at Griffin's interest in such topics.

I guess that's why he's an economics professor.

A super-hot, super-sexy economics professor, I think with a grin. He knows how to make a girl's body sing.

I pick up my phone to check for messages. I haven't glanced at it since the start of the concert.

Tons of texts from people at Silicone Dream wishing me happy birthday. Several texts from my stepsister, too.

–Felicia: You should've invited me to your birthday celebration!

–Felicia: I would've been happy to go to Tokyo with you!

–Felicia: I could've been there!

–Felicia: Well, anyway, happy birthday.

Well, you know what they say. It's the afterthought that counts.

Since she's never shown any interest in me, it's painfully obvious what she's really upset about. I kind of want to block her, but that would be a bit too mean. It isn't like she called me names. Best just to ignore her.

I read the final set—the ones from Ellie.

–Ellie: Happy birthday, girl!!!!!!

–Ellie: I just realize I'm late to this because you're in Tokyo, which means you're 16 hours into the future! But my math says it's still your birthday in Tokyo, so yay me for being on time!

–Ellie: OMFG!!! The video! This video!

She's attached a YouTube link. I click on it to see what's so exciting. It's a video of Killian Axelrod looking for me, then singing "Happy Birthday." Somebody at the concert recorded it on their phone and posted it last night. It has almost a million views so far.

I grin. Now everyone's going to know what an amazing man Griffin is. *And he's all mine.*

–Ellie: You've gone viral all over the world! Everyone wants to be you. Hell, I wanna be you! I wanna have Killian Axelrod sing me Happy Birthday. I'll die a happy woman.

I laugh.

–Ellie: Griffin is amazing, girl. He's a keeper! When a man treats you like this, you have to hold on to him with all you've got!

–Me: I know, I know.

–Ellie: I wonder how he managed to get in touch with the band? I didn't know econ professors were so well connected! I should start trolling campuses to get me a hot sexy econ prof!

Hmm. *That's a good point.* The band must get thousands of emails and letters from fans. What are the odds that the one Griffin sent just happened to catch their attention, just in time for my birthday, and at this particular concert?

On the other hand, it could be serendipity. Sometimes things just magically happen to bring a smile and some joy. Like how I met the Midnight God and then met Griffin. It's like the universe just knew what I needed.

Questioning my good fortune would be ungrateful. Like Griffin said, when something amazing happens, I should just say, "Thank you."

–Me: I'll be cheering for you. Now I gotta go get something to eat and see this city.

I drop the phone into my purse and head out into the living room. Griffin's in a pale azure button-down shirt and dark slacks, looking absolutely stunning. He's rolled up his sleeves, and I finally understand why so many women drool over arm porn. There's something raw and sexy about a fully dressed man displaying well-muscled arms.

Power. Strength. Competence.

That's what those lean arms represent. My mouth tingles with the need to lick his bare skin, and I mentally shake myself. *We just had sex!* If I don't come to my senses soon, I'm going to be spending the rest of my time in Tokyo rolling around in bed with Griffin instead of seeing the city. And as tempting as more orgasms are, we can always have sex after our tour today. And when we're back in the States.

He turns off the TV and holds out a hand. "Ready?"

"Yep." I thread my fingers through his and squeeze with all the affection I'm feeling for him. "So where are we going?"

"Whatever we feel like. But we need to be at the Skytree by seven."

Excitement blasts through me. "We're going there today?"

"You said you wanted to go, so I made a dinner reservation. Thought you'd enjoy the view and the food."

"Yes!" I say, flushed with joyful anticipation. I'm touched and amazed he's remembered everything I said I wanted and liked *and then made it happen.* I've never been in a relationship like this. Even though we started as a kind of sham, it's turned into something else. Especially when I can imagine myself with him years and years from now, still having fun and being happy.

We grab a couple of muffins and some coffee from the hotel café and leave. The blueberry muffin I picked isn't even half the size of what I would normally get in Lovedale, but it's soft and tasty, full of sweet fruit.

"The portions are so tiny," I say, finishing the last bite. "No wonder everyone here is skinny."

"Japan competes with the French to see who can serve the least amount of food and get away with it," Griffin remarks. He demolished his muffin in four civilized bites.

"Seems to be working, though."

"It does work. The Japanese and the French have some of the longest life spans on Earth."

"No, I mean look how busy this place is." Every table is taken, and people are waiting patiently in a long line for their coffee and pastries.

Griffin surveys the place and nods. "Anything you want to do in particular before our dinner reservation?"

"Yes. First, I want to buy some souvenirs for people I know, so I don't forget before we leave."

"What kind of souvenirs?"

"Not sure yet. It depends on what I can find." I think about what Ellie, Heather and others like. "Maybe stationery? Hello Kitty pens or something?"

He considers for a second, then leads me out. We walk a few blocks to a huge department store called Mitsukoshi. "This place should have everything you want."

The department store has the most adorable stationery and pens, along with an "Amazing Must-Have Items from Tokyo" section on the second floor. I buy cute washi tape and stickers for several ladies at Silicone Dream who like to decorate their planners. And a gorgeous pink and purple glass pen and ink set for Heather because she collects glass figurines and objects. A huge display full of intricately carved, flat wood squares and circles catches my eye, and I study them.

"What are they?" I ask. They're decorative, but I don't think it's something you stick to your windows or fridge doors. The display is in Japanese only.

"Coasters," Griffin says.

"Coasters? Like you put drinks on them?"

He nods.

"Aren't they too pretty to be used as coasters?" They are artsy. Many of them have themes from nature. Some feature animals, including cats. Unfortunately, I'm not seeing any with dogs. But there is a set of five with peacocks in different poses, and Ellie would absolutely love them.

I reach another aisle full of ribbons and colorful silk flowers and so on with sticky pads on the back. I squint, unsure what they're for —do Japanese people like to stick flowers on their walls?—until I realize they're to be placed on wrapped gifts as decorative elements. A few examples of how gorgeous a present can look if you use those flowers are set up at the end of the aisle.

"They're kidding, right?" The boxes are so beautifully wrapped that it seems like a crime to open them. "I could buy all the stickers in the store, and I still wouldn't be able to create what they did."

A corner of Griffin's mouth quirks up. "Maybe if you sign up for their training, you can."

"Training? There's a class?"

He nods. "Department store employees learn how to gift-wrap everything they sell."

I look through a few more aisles. All sorts of items end up in my arms, including some interesting dog treats that look like traditional Japanese sweets. A bunch of people at Silicone Dream have dogs, and they'll get a huge kick out of them. Once I can't hold any more stuff, I decide I have something for everyone. I pay at the register, then sigh when I realize I haven't planned well in my excitement.

"What's wrong?" Griffin asks.

"I bought too many things," I say. "We should go back to the hotel and drop this stuff off. I don't think I want to carry it everywhere for the rest of the day. I should've stopped here later, at the end of the day." I'm babbling a little, but I feel a bit silly and bad. Griffin didn't complain even once the entire time I was shopping, and I feel slightly guilty. If I were here with most other guys I've dated, I would've heard some complaints—or at least an obvious hint that he was getting bored.

Griffin shrugs. "No reason to go back, unless you want to."

"But all this stuff…"

Griffin gestures at the uniformed clerk who rang me up and starts talking to her in Japanese. She responds, says, *"Hai,"* a few times, then smiles and hands Griffin a piece of paper. He fills it out and signs it.

"What's that?" I ask.

"They'll gift-wrap all your items and deliver them to the hotel by close of business today."

"Oh! Well, that's a nice service. How much do I owe them?"

"It's free."

"Free?" I stare. It isn't like I bought a Rolex or something. "Really?"

"Sure."

"But the gift wrapping too?" I gesture at the lady. "I feel like I should tip her."

"There's no tipping in Japan. And she'll put a Post-it on every item after she wraps it up so you know which present is which."

"Wow." I turn to the clerk. *"Arigato."*

She smiles sweetly and says something, which of course I don't understand. I smile back, and it's like we're speaking some kind of international language that doesn't require words.

"They sure know how to treat a girl like a princess," I whisper as we leave the department store.

"There's a saying here that customers are like gods," he says. "It's part of their training."

Afterward, we hail a cab to head to Shinjuku. A black taxi stops, and before I can reach for the handle, the door somehow opens automatically. "Wow. Did you *see* that?"

"Hard to miss it," Griffin deadpans.

"You know what I mean! That's so cool!"

He laughs. "Get in, Sierra."

I climb inside. The seat is fitted with a pristine white cover. The driver must be confident about keeping his car clean, because stains would show easily on such white fabric. Griffin follows me in and speaks to the taxi driver. The door closes automatically, and we're off.

"How does he do that?" I ask, looking around.

"There's a lever." Griffin points out a contraption that's been added to the bottom of the door. "The driver can open and close the door this way."

"So we're trapped inside and can't leave? That'd make a good horror movie. Or a thriller like *Speed!*"

"You can still open the door the regular way. It's just that passengers don't."

"Do other cars have this feature, too?"

For the first time, Griffin seems a little unsure about something. "Hmm... That's a good question. Maybe some special cars for handicapped people? But other than that, I don't think so."

I hold Griffin's hand and watch the city go by as the taxi moves along the busy streets. Eventually we stop in front of a huge intersection. Griffin pays the driver and asks him about something, and then we're out.

Instantly, we're immersed in brimming energy. Shinjuku is full of people moving briskly. Some are young and in fashionable clothes, their hair dyed brown or dark auburn and styled prettily. A couple of dolled-up girls in pink and white kimonos hail a cab. A few business types in their late forties stop under the shade of a tall building and wipe the sweat off their foreheads with handkerchiefs. Buses stop and doors hiss open as scooters roar by. Catchy tunes blare from a few stores.

"You still want to try ramen?" Griffin asks as I snap photos.

Although I wasn't hungry earlier, once Griffin mentions the food, my stomach decides I need more than a tiny muffin. "Yes!"

"The taxi driver recommended two places." He squints a little as he scans the area. "That way."

We go to a hole in the wall that can only accommodate twenty or so patrons. The ceiling is low, and there are four tiny tables and a counter that can seat twelve. Although it's still early for lunch, the place is already more than half-full, and all the tables are taken. We sit at the counter and have obscenely delicious bowls of ramen. The broth is so thick and rich—without being overly greasy—that it almost seems like a separate entrée unto itself.

After the quick lunch, we head to a gorgeous park with lots of interesting landscaping, including elegant wooden arch bridges I take so many pictures of. I can't believe something like this is in the middle of Tokyo. The park is enormous, and so many different trees line various sections.

"It'll be prettier in spring or fall," Griffin says.

"I can see fall with the autumn foliage, but why spring?"

"Cherry blossom season."

"Oh..." I look up at the gnarled branches, heavy with green leaves, above us and try to imagine them full of small pink flowers. "Maybe we can come back then." I hope he says yes; it'll be a signal that he's open to making our relationship something more concrete than a temporary fake arrangement.

"Perhaps we will."

Good enough, I decide with a small smile. One step at a time.

When it's a little after five twenty p.m., Griffin grabs a taxi to head to the Skytree. Apparently, it's going to take at least an hour to get there with the traffic.

"If the dinner reservation is at seven, do we need to start heading out there so early?" I ask.

"Yes. The Japanese will consider you late if you aren't there at least fifteen minutes early."

"What?" I laugh. "Are you kidding?"

"No. Also we have to factor in the time to enter the tower and take the elevator up to the restaurant deck. It's over eleven hundred feet in the air."

He's right to leave Shinjuku early. The road is pretty congested, which is shocking given it's a Sunday and there shouldn't be a rush hour. Our taxi also has to stop a lot because of heavy pedestrian traffic. I tilt my head so I can look at the Skytree as we approach it. The tower soars into the sky like a blade, sharp and sleek. It's amazing that the Japanese built something so tall, given the frequent earthquakes they get. I read that the tower is quake-proof, but I hope everything's calm when we're up there. I've experienced quakes, having grown up in SoCal, but I don't want to experience one while we're over a thousand feet up in the sky.

The lines are long at the tower. But once we're in the elevator, it ascends smoothly and almost soundlessly.

"This is so futuristic," I say.

"A marvel of Japanese engineering," Griffin says. "They know what they're doing."

By the time we reach the deck where the restaurant is, it's exactly six forty-eight.

"Told you," Griffin says, checking his watch.

"So are we early or late?" I ask.

"We're good. They won't complain."

He's right. A smiling maître d' takes us to a table by the glass wall so we can get the view and the meal. The light is set low, the interior dark and sleek. There's a hint of wine and rich sauces in the air. The center of the restaurant is a gigantic teppan station with a huge metal cooking surface and a counter with seats that wraps around it. A chef in a uniform preps meat, seafood and vegetables at the station.

Our server hands us our menus, but I leave mine on the table without opening it. I can't read it anyway. Instead, I take some pictures of the city below.

Griffin opens his and studies each page, his brow furrowed. I realize he figured out the menu for me at the ramen restaurant, too. "Can you read the language as well?"

"Yes," Griffin says. I stare, wondering what else he can do. He doesn't seem to notice my shock. "Do you already know what you want?"

"I'll order whatever you're getting, since I can't read the menu anyway."

He gives me a look. "It's in English, French and Japanese."

"What?" I open the menu. Sure enough, he's right. There doesn't seem to be a point in studying them, since all the offerings seem to be in "courses," which I understand are set and cannot be changed. "I'll still have whatever you're having. I'm pretty sure everything's good."

He nods and drops his menu on the table. Our server appears immediately. Griffin orders in Japanese, then the server confirms and leaves.

"Okay, so when did you learn Japanese?" I ask.

"When I was younger."

I sigh. "Obviously. But how young?"

"Mm... Eight, maybe?" A casual shrug.

"I don't know how you can be so blasé about something as cool as knowing Japanese. Are there any other surprises? Do you speak Chinese, too?"

His lips twist into a reluctant smile. "No. But I have some other languages."

"Like?"

"French, German, Italian, Spanish and Portuguese."

My jaw slackens. "I thought you were a professor of economics."

"The two aren't mutually exclusive." He shrugs again. "I grew up in Europe, that's why."

"That is so cool. Did you live in Japan, too? Is that why you speak it?"

"No. One of my brothers likes anime, and he insisted on learning it with me."

"You have brothers?" A mixture of envy and longing unfurls.

"Yes. Six of them."

"Wow. Lucky you. I wish I had some siblings, but it's just me."

"Don't you have a stepsister?"

"Yeah, but Felicia and I don't really do anything together. She doesn't consider me her family." After trying for years in the beginning to be close, I had to give up. She resents that I have something her mother wants. She probably hates me more for not bringing her along on this trip. She won't care that it was a surprise getaway completely arranged by Griffin. What matters is that she wasn't invited.

"She isn't in the family photos, is she?" Griffin says.

"You mean the pictures on the mantel in my house? No, she isn't. Grandma refused to add Linda and Felicia to the collection."

"No recent pictures of your father, either." His words are slow and cautious.

"He chose Linda, so..." I shrug.

Our conversation is interrupted by our server bringing a bottle of champagne. He uncorks it expertly and pours it into two tall flutes. Tiny bubbles rise in the golden vintage.

"Cheers." Griffin lifts his glass.

I *clink* with him. The champagne is good—smooth and rich, like liquid cashmere with a mixture of glazed lemon, pastry and candied ginger. It ends on a slightly salty note that is refreshing and lovely.

Or maybe it just tastes so good because of the company. It's impossible to have a bad time when you're with a guy who makes your belly flip and heart flutter, sending languid pleasure through you for just being who he is.

The server soon brings our first course. On the huge white plate in front of me, there are exactly two bite-sized pieces of fish and swirly lines of sauces in green and orange and yellow. Three dollops of green sauce are to my right, each topped with a small pink flower the size of a rice grain.

The plating is maybe the most gorgeous I've ever seen, but the portion size is outrageously small. After snapping a shot of it, I take a bite, then moan at how delicious it is.

"It's criminal that they only give you two bites of such tasty food," I say after swallowing my fish.

"Consider yourself lucky they gave you two. Could've been one." Griffin's tone is serious.

I look at him, then laugh when I note the faint crinkling at the outer corners of his eyes.

After the main course is finished, I get up, ostensibly to use the bathroom. I do need to use the bathroom, but I want to pay for our meal before Griffin can. So far, except for the souvenirs I bought at the department store, he's paid for everything. This is an incredible trip, and I want to do something nice for him.

But when I stop our server and ask about the bill, he smiles. "It has already been paid, madam," he says in accented English.

"Already?"

"Yes. Mr. Lasker prepaid when he booked."

"I see," I say slowly, trying to hide my disappointment. It isn't this man's fault.

"Is there anything else I can help you with?" he asks.

"No, thank you." I flash him a smile, then look back at Griffin at the table. He's sipping his bubbly and looking out over the cityscape as though he hasn't a care in the world.

How can he afford all this? I don't know how much econ professors make, but surely it can't be enough to just casually pay for two first-class tickets to Tokyo…? When I was with Todd, he didn't even pay for beers when we were out because I made so much more money, even though he hated admitting that.

Should I say something to Griffin about splitting the bill? It'd be a nice gesture, but I don't want to offend him or hurt his ego. Men can get really weird about money, especially if the woman has more of it.

He's a big boy. It isn't like he doesn't understand finance, a voice argues in my head. *If he needs help, he'll ask, or you can offer subtly.*

I let out a breath and re-center myself. There's no reason for me to worry about something when Griffin hasn't demonstrated that he can't take care of it. I push aside my unease. *Just enjoy the time and have fun.*

42

GRIFFIN

Sierra takes tons of pictures throughout the dinner. I let her have her fun, and even manage a small smile when she gets the server to take a snapshot of us during the dessert course.

After dinner, we go out to the observation deck for the night view of the city. Sierra radiates a contagious joy as she stares, lips parted, at the glittering metropolis.

"My God," she whispers.

"What's so fascinating? It's just a city. From this far up, basically all you can see is lights."

"Are you kidding?" She looks at me as though I just told her coffee should be declared illegal. "It isn't just a city. It's like the best thing in the world! Look how *beautiful* the lights are! The way the traffic moves. With the sky clear, it's like we have stars above and stars below, some of them moving like streams. Where else am I going to get a view like this?"

I squint at the vista spread out before me. It still looks the same —a city like any other. But Sierra's excitement is worth the long trans-Pacific flight. Would she be shocked or disappointed if I told her I only picked Tokyo because of the Axelrod concert? If they were singing in Rectum, Manitoba, that's where I would've taken her.

"We should come back when we can spend more time. *My*

treat!" she squeals. She probably meant to say it calmly, like an adult, but failed. No emo filter.

It's oddly cute, but I'm not sure why. I don't like people without filters. They're like my parents. Narcissistic, parasitic and over-the-top crazy.

It must be the apple scent. You can't get mad at somebody who smells like the first apple of the season. It's doubly true if the apple also happens to have the power to arouse you.

My blood's been simmering since we left the hotel this morning. I was turned on watching her pick out stationery and pens, for God's sake. But it was impossible not to be when she was enjoying herself so much. The subtle flush of her cheeks reminded me of how she looked in bed last night, and in the shower.

She's been beaming all day, pulling all my attention toward her. I can't look away when she smiles, the purple in her eyes glimmering with pleasure.

It suddenly hits me that the reason I can't take my eyes away is that she's incapable of hiding how she feels. She doesn't look at the world with the cynical indifference common among those trying to appear cool and important. She glows like the sun. Being in her presence makes everything brighter, warmer and more...wonderful.

She leans closer, resting her head against my shoulder, and sighs softly with happiness. I lean down and kiss her, helplessly drawn to her.

Although my head says it's the trip, the jet lag and the champagne, my heart whispers, *It's the girl—Sierra.*

An hour later, our taxi drops us off in front of the hotel. I put a hand at the small of Sierra's back as we move toward the elevator bank when the hair on the back of my neck bristles in warning.

I scan the lobby quickly—

Then I see her.

The perfectly styled golden hair cascading artfully around her slender shoulders. The professionally done makeup and face that used to grace hundreds of thousands of magazine covers.

My mouth dries. *What's Mom doing here?* She's in a cushy chair with some sort of blue cocktail on the table in front of her. She's wearing a bright red dress that flows over her like liquid fire, highlighting the toned body women half her age would trade their ovaries for. I don't believe for a second she's here just for a drink.

Before she can make eye contact, I look away and walk quickly toward the elevators. My phone pings.

I ignore it.

It pings again. Sierra looks at me. "Shouldn't you see what that is? In case it's urgent?"

"It's probably spam."

"Somebody's contacting you at crack of dawn in America."

That doesn't mean it's urgent or important. Not in my world.

"Could be one of your brothers," she adds.

I doubt my brothers would contact me at this hour. They're too capable to need me to handle their problems. The only time they'd contact me is if I went viral—again. Noah was more than excited to group-text this morning about a video from the concert that went viral. He insisted I introduce Sierra to them when we're back in the States. Since he is a persistent texter when he wants something, I had to tell him I'd ask her just to shut him up.

"Or your parents," she says.

Just no, I decide, my whole being rebelling against the idea.

Another ping. The apprehension I've been feeling builds as though there's a tornado creeping closer.

Sierra starts to frown.

Fuck. Me.

Sighing, I pull out my phone. I can pretend to read the texts to make Sierra happy and then put it away.

–Mom: Where are you?

–Mom: I want to talk to you.

–Mom: I'm in the lobby already, so no need to feel guilty about making me wait or anything.

Hah. Guilt is the last thing I'm feeling.

–Mom: By the way, am I going to get to see your girlfriend?

–Mom: I know she's here.

–Mom: I'm not going anywhere until you respond.

There's no way I'm letting her see Sierra. But I can't completely ignore Mom either. She's stubborn enough and dramatic enough to make sure she gets what she wants. If all else fails, she'll make a scene. Then someone will film it and it'll go viral and be talked about for months. She might even let it slip that the drama is about me, and there's no predicting what the ripple effects of that would be. It's entirely possible that she could ruin the respectability I've been able to cultivate for myself in my career.

Damn it. This is what I get for asking Mom to get me tickets to the concert. I should've known she'd demand something in return, and that *something* is going to be my time and attention when I least want to give it to her.

I take Sierra to the elevator and gently place her in the car. When I don't follow her in, she holds her thumb on the open button. "Aren't you coming?"

"I have to make a call," I lie. "A personal matter I have to deal with." True enough, although I omit how unpleasant it's going to be. "I'm sorry. I'll try to make it quick."

Sierra looks vaguely curious, but doesn't probe. "Okay. Take your time."

I wait until the elevator doors close and the car starts ascending. Then I turn around, raise my mental and emotional shields and march toward the table where Mom is sitting.

She looks up, her eyes crinkling with a smile. But the smile vanishes as quickly as it appeared. God forbid she gets a wrinkle.

When the lines form, they never go away. Mom learned that the hard way in her late twenties. I was only four, so I had no idea why she was crying so inconsolably. All I knew was that she was upset, and that upset me, too. She told me she had lines on her face, but I couldn't understand what she was talking about or why she hugged me like I was the anchor in her self-destructing world.

Then one day, when I was older and wiser, I had a eureka moment. A little older still and the emotion became disgust. There's more to life than wrinkles.

She quit crying over every fine line, at least in front of me. These days she does everything in her power to keep her face as smooth as possible. I'm certain the reason the skin around her eyes crinkled at all is because her doctor suffered an accident and she couldn't get her regularly scheduled Botox injection in time for her trip to Tokyo.

"Hello, Griffin." Her voice is pleasant. Calm.

It doesn't reassure me. She can flip to tears and theatrics at will and effortlessly draw everyone's attention.

"Hello, Mother." I remain standing.

She gestures at the armchair opposite her. "Why don't you take a seat?"

"I have plans."

"Again?" She pouts. "You always have plans."

I spread my hands. "It isn't my fault you don't check with me ahead of time."

"I can't talk to you if you aren't going to sit down. I'm not going to give myself a crick in my neck."

Swallowing a sigh, I sit. It's best to humor her for the moment and wrap this visit up. I'd rather be holding Sierra right now. "If you're here to hear my thanks in person, thank you." Hopefully this will satisfy her and we can end this pointless chat.

"You're welcome." She looks slightly happier. "I saw you at the concert and waved and called out, but you totally ignored me."

"I didn't hear you. It was loud." *Thank God.*

She sighs. "That's what I thought, too. So annoying."

Not for me.

"Why didn't you tell me you were trying to impress a girl? I could've arranged for backstage passes. Nothing gets a girl excited like seeing rock stars." She considers for a second then shakes her head. "Never mind. She could've gotten attached to the wrong person. Devlin and Killian are married, but they're still too hot to be taken off the market."

"*Mother.* Don't be a homewrecker."

She rolls her eyes. "I couldn't even if I wanted to. They're newlyweds, so they still care about their wedding vows." Her tone says that'll end soon.

Ideally, they'll stay caring about their vows for the rest of their lives. I don't want to think about Mom having a threesome with some rock stars. Her sex life is something I try to pretend doesn't exist, although it tends to be the reason she contacts me.

"Still, it was fun to hang out with them."

"Glad you had a good time," I say vaguely, while realizing Sierra and I will have to fly back to California tomorrow. I wish we had more time, so I could show her more of Japan.

Perhaps next time.

The thought slides into my head so easily that I stop for a second. It's as though I want our relationship to go on. Nothing in my gut feels bad about it. Actually, it feels right that we stay together.

The sex and everything else say a relationship with Sierra would be nothing like what I've had before.

She's special.

"Your girl would've loved it, too," Mom says, pulling me out of my reverie.

We had plenty of fun doing other things. Like having lots of orgasms.

"Killian could've sung her an encore to celebrate her birthday, since you'll never sing for her."

"I don't sing for anybody." Mom can hint all she likes. I'm not going to be paraded around like some trained bear whenever my parents need an ego stroke.

"Or maybe not," she adds as though I haven't spoken. "Did you know Adriana Mitchell and Don Kasher were there too?"

"And...?" But I don't need to hear her answer. She hates them because they're nothing like her and Dad. A wholesome, respectable couple. Two of the very few normal, nice people left in Hollywood. Fame and fortune haven't made them crazy.

"It was nauseating to see their sanctimonious faces," Mom sneers.

"How insufferable. Can I go now?" I'm half standing up.

"Not yet." She flutters a hand downward. *Sit.* "I want to see Sierra."

"I don't think that's a good idea."

"Why on earth not?"

Is she serious? How can she not know? "I don't want to scare her."

Something that looks oddly like hurt crosses her face. But no. Mom is incapable of genuine feelings. She only shows human emotions when she needs to manipulate someone.

"You're so cruel sometimes." Her voice cracks slightly, and a sheen of tears appears in her eyes.

God give me patience. "I'm trying to spare everyone some unnecessary awkwardness."

"Awkwardness?" She blinks like she doesn't know the word.

I'm not fooled. I've never forgotten how she and Dad embarrassed me in front of my first girlfriend in Geneva.

For some reason—although in retrospect, I suspect they had a spat behind my back—they insisted on meeting her at the same time. I didn't want to introduce Chantel, but she was a nice girl and said she wouldn't mind if my parents really wanted to meet her.

I warned them to behave like *normal* human beings. Chantel didn't grow up like my brothers and I did. She was from a good family, with sane parents. Her father was a highly respected dean at the Sorbonne.

But no. My parents couldn't feign normalcy or decency for even a second. After saying hello to Chantel, they started to insult each other. When that failed to make them appear sufficiently deranged, they started to drag each other's significant others into the mix. And the worst of it was that they both demanded that Chantel pick a side.

It was humiliating. Awful. Chantel dumped me immediately. Said she could never be with somebody she couldn't respect. Guilty by association was the verdict.

Unfair, but I honestly couldn't blame her.

And she wasn't the only girlfriend who left after being treated to the Lasker Parent Shitshow. I've had others.

"Now, Mother. You know you're too beautiful to be sitting here in a hotel lobby by yourself." Anything to steer Mom's attention away from this terrifying desire to see Sierra. "Where's your boyfriend?"

43

SIERRA

While Griffin is dealing with his personal emergency, I take a quick shower to sluice off the day's sweat. Once freshened up, I put on a T-shirt and shorts and settle into an armchair in the living room, my feet propped on the matching ottoman. I check emails, respond to a few and mark several sales notices from my favorite online stores.

Ellie's probably still asleep. But I send her the best shots from today anyway so she can look at them when she wakes up.

–Me: The Skytree is amazing. We should visit it together one of these days.

That done, I surf around on a bunch of social media apps to keep myself occupied until Griffin comes up. But after almost an hour of scrolling through feeds, I start to get worried. Griffin said it wouldn't take long, and he's usually precise about time.

I shoot him a text.

–Me: Everything okay?

A couple of minutes pass with no response.

What did he say when he put me in the elevator...?

Nothing that raised a red flag, but he seemed a little grim, like his best friend's dog died.

I should probably go down and see if he's okay.

I put on a bra, grab my phone and room key and head out. Luckily, there's an elevator waiting.

My Grumpy Billionaire

Once I'm down in the huge lobby, it takes a moment of scanning before I locate Griffin. He's sitting at a table with his back toward me, talking with a woman in a bright red dress.

Who is she? He said he needed to make a phone call, not talk to somebody.

I take in her delicate features and shiny golden hair, feeling like I've seen her before. Is that...Rachel? The woman at Ted Lasker's birthday party?

She notices me and waves. "Sierra!" she calls out across the lobby.

Griffin turns around. His eyes collide with mine, his mouth flattening into a hyphen. And if hyphens had feelings, this one would be angry.

Maybe I should leave. I must've interrupted something *very* important and *very* private.

But before I can make my escape, Rachel stands and gestures for me to join them.

I shake my head with a polite smile. But she strides toward me, her stilettos clacking against the floor as she struts like she's on a runway, showing off her red dress. Her sudden hug makes me yelp.

"Oh my goodness, it's so *good* to see you. How long has it been?"

"Um. A few weeks?" I squeak.

"Too long," Rachel says. "Come, come join us." She smiles, putting an arm around my shoulders and pulling me to the table where Griffin's watching us as if we're stars in a B-movie not even our moms could like.

"Isn't it amazing to reunite in *Tokyo*?" she says.

"Totally. I, um, didn't know you were going to be here." I'm not exactly sure how I'm supposed to react, especially when Rachel seems happy and Griffin is growing increasingly grim. If this were a cartoon, a thundercloud would be gathering over his head, shooting lightning and rumbling.

"Oh, I'm *everywhere*. That's just how I am. I was doing a photoshoot." Rachel is breathless with enthusiasm. She pulls me down until I'm seated in an armchair next to Griffin.

"A photoshoot?"

Rachel seems surprised. "Yes, dear. I'm a model."

"Oh. So *that's* why you looked so familiar!"

"It's okay. Not everyone knows models," she says, her mouth slightly tight.

"No, no. It's just...I just never thought I'd meet anybody famous, so I assumed you were somebody who looks a lot like a model I've seen. You know what I'm saying?" I pat her hand, looking at her with all the *trust-me* I can muster.

"Well." Rachel smiles, mollified. "Now you have. This is your lucky day!"

Griffin lets out a soft growl that says I'm anything but lucky.

I ignore his grumpy mood for the moment. I'll deal with it later in private, in case he says something to upset Rachel about her fame and recognizability.

"So." Rachel settles back in her seat. "What are you doing—"

"You were telling me about how sorry Fabio was," Griffin cuts her off. "He groveled and asked you to take him back. I want to know if he was on his knees when he did that."

"Fabio can wait." Rachel takes a sip of her cocktail. "Sierra is such a delightful young woman."

Griffin's hands clench and unclench on the table. Who is he strangling in his mind? Hopefully, the answer is this Fabio person.

"So tell me what you've been doing in Tokyo," Rachel says.

"Griffin brought me here to celebrate my birthday."

"The concert."

"You saw the video?"

She laughs. "My dear, I was *there*. I was just telling Griffin that if he told me that he wanted to impress a girl and celebrate her birthday, I would've gotten him backstage passes."

I gasp. "Backstage passes?"

"Mm-hmm. It would've been no trouble at all. Next time, just come directly to me." She winks, then pulls out a card. "Here's my number."

"Is it okay?" It's such a generous offer.

Griffin starts to reach for the card, but stops when I look at him curiously. He leans back in his seat and closes his eyes, letting out a long-suffering sigh.

"Of *course*." Rachel's words drag me back to the conversation. "Especially for a girl my son went to all this trouble for."

Shock smacks me. "Your *son*?" She can't be older than thirty-five. Her skin's absolutely flawless, not a wrinkle or pore in sight. "You don't look old enough to be his mother."

She laughs, her finely carved cheeks flushed. "You're so sweet! I know, but I most definitely am his mother. Where do you think he got his looks?"

My gaze swings back and forth between her and Griffin, who's clenching his jaw. Now that she mentions it, I can see the resemblance. Griffin has his mother's face, only bolder and more masculine. Those cheekbones are identical. So are the eyes and the sensual slant of their eyebrows.

"Anyway, he's never done anything like ask me to get sold-out concert tickets for any of his girlfriends before. You must be special."

My face warms with pleasure. It stokes my feminine ego to hear that, especially since I have feelings for him—I want him to be in my life as a real boyfriend, rather than just a placeholder to repel my leechlike ex-husband.

I shift my gaze toward Griffin. His face is impassive, but the skin around his eyes is tight with tension. Is he embarrassed that his mom's gushing over me? Bet he's awkward about expressing his feelings. It's kinda cute.

Rachel continues, "And I like you, too, of course. You were so nice to me at Ted's party."

"I'm sorry that we didn't get to talk more. Were you okay after your other son pulled you away?"

"Other son?" She blinks.

I nod.

"I only have one son."

I tilt my head in confusion. "Griffin said he has brothers," I point out.

"Oh, they aren't mine," Rachel informs me in a casual tone. "Griffin's the only one that's mine."

I glance at Griffin.

He nods. "We're technically all half-brothers, but we call each other brothers."

"You confused her," Rachel says. "It's important to be correct."

"Which is why I call them brothers." His voice is pained.

"I'm sorry about his tone," Rachel says to me. "He gets grumpy for no reason. He was having one of his temperamental moments at the party."

I stare at her, then Griffin as the implication of what she just revealed rolls through my mind. The rude guy at the party was *Griffin?*

"Did you realize we'd met before when you came to the company?" I ask him.

He props his elbow on the table and covers his face with a hand. His eyebrows are pinched tight, and his eyes are closed, like he's dying of a migraine. "Yes."

"So why didn't you say something?"

The muscles in his jaw bunch and flex. "Because I don't want people to know that I was at that birthday party."

"Griffin is still a teenager in some ways," Rachel says. "He's continually embarrassed about his—"

"*Mother.*" Griffin opens his eyes, pinning her with a piercing look. He presses his lips together, like he's trying to contain cutting remarks.

Rachel clears her throat. "But he's not *all* bad," she says with a slightly awkward laugh. "He's so good about answering my calls and coming to my rescue and making sure I'm all right. As a matter of fact, several weeks ago, he flew out to New Orleans so he could escort me to a party."

"*Mother,*" Griffin says again, his tone glacial.

If he used that voice with me, I'd probably pause. But Rachel's immune. Must be the Mom Shield™.

"There's no need to be shy. Women like it when men are nice to their mothers." She turns to me. "Don't you agree?"

"Yes," I say. "A guy who disrespects his mother will treat his significant other the same way."

Rachel beams at Griffin. "See?" She looks at me. "Anyway, if it hadn't been for Griffin, I would have been devastated. I couldn't imagine going to a party without a date. It would be *so* gauche. Especially a masquerade party in New Orleans."

I nod, although I don't understand why she would have to have a partner for a masquerade event. It isn't like anybody was going to recognize her, provided she had the right mask and covered her hair with a wig.

"But he was such a good sport about it. I was so distraught over my date standing me up that I totally forgot to tell Griffin to bring something a little bit more casual for the party. So he ended up wearing a suit and a black mask. Thank God his suit was black so everything matched. I can't be seen with a man who can't dress himself."

A black suit and mask? Shock cascades over me. What she's saying describes the Midnight God.

"Anyway, he stayed until I could find myself some suitable company to hang out with. As nice as it is to be escorted by my son, I needed a *date*. And, of course, I'm sure he wanted to hang out with someone else, too."

"When was this party?" I ask, my gut tight.

"I can't remember the exact date. My assistant would have it. But it was quite the memorable night. They had these alligator hors d'oeuvres, the most amazing selection of men, and they had these sex-lube samples. They tasted like *actual chocolate*. I didn't know lube could taste like that. I wish you'd been there. You would've loved them."

Oh my God! I cover my mouth. That was the masquerade party that I went to! "Those samples came from Silicone Dream. My company. And I *was* at the party."

"Really? What a small world!" Rachel laughs.

"I know." I look at Griffin, who is studying me closely. Excitement bubbles like the finest champagne, effervescent and shivery. "I was wearing a purple wig that night."

"You must've looked adorable!" Rachel says. "Do you have pictures?"

"Yes." Smiling, I tap my phone and pull up some photos from the night. I find the selfie of me posing next to the suit of armor. "Here."

Rachel leans forward, then smiles broadly. "I was right! You look so cute!"

I tilt my phone so that Griffin can see the photo. "Look!" I grin.

His eyes narrow. "You're Purple Girl?"

"Purple Girl?" I repeat.

"That's what I called you inside my head."

"So you two met in New Orleans, too?" Rachel asks, nearly breathless with enthusiasm.

I nod, my eyes on Griffin. The Midnight God. Oh my God! *The Midnight God is Griffin!*

Something about the situation leaves me shaken to the core. I thought I'd never run into him again. I told myself I'd consider it a sign—fate—if we did.

But we *did*—we have—and I didn't even realize it! We crossed paths at Ted's birthday party. Then again when he came to Silicone Dream to do the case. Again, when he came over to my place and saw what Todd did and decided to move in with me for a few weeks to keep me safe until my ex-husband gave up.

It's like fate has decided to beat me in the face with Griffin until I figure out he's not a fluke.

He's a keeper. You don't keep orbiting each other like this and not have it be destiny.

"Wow," I manage finally.

The tip of Griffin's right eyebrow twitches. He looks at me thoughtfully, then turns to his mother.

"We have to go," he says, rising to his feet and towering over us.

"But Sierra hasn't had a drink yet," she says. "Neither have you."

He makes an exaggerated show of checking his watch. "It's late."

"It's not even midnight!" Rachel protests.

His jaw flexes. He clearly doesn't want to talk with his mom around. But with just two of us, he might want to talk about the fact that we've been in each other's lives, knowingly and otherwise. And I *definitely* want to marvel with him about how we've been in each other's orbits for so many months.

"It *is* getting late," I say. "I've been up since six, so I should get some beauty sleep."

The tension in his jaw eases as he extends a hand. I take it and stand. His bare skin feels hot and dry. Sexual awareness tingles from my fingertips all the way to my face and chest.

"Beauty sleep is important, but just one drink?" Rachel pleads.

"We had quite enough to drink earlier," Griffin says. "And I'm sure your friends are waiting."

"But—"

"Good night, Mother," he says, leaning across the table and placing a quick peck on her cheek.

Then, before I can say good night to Rachel, he pulls me away, leaving her alone in the lobby bar.

44

GRIFFIN

I pull Sierra away before Mom can tell her any more stories. The only reason I didn't do so sooner is because I don't want Sierra to think I'm trying to hide her from my parents. Been there, done that with an ex-girlfriend who accused me of being ashamed of her. In her mind, the only reason I wouldn't let her meet my parents was that I didn't find her worthy.

Hopefully, Sierra isn't quite that illogical, but she *is* female. Just look at how Emmett got dumped. *He* didn't do anything; it was all Dad. But Emmett paid the price.

Anyway, Mom talked for a bit and Sierra got enough social time. No reason to torture myself further by sitting there, dreading the situation and wondering when Mom will start acting out or do something that will humiliate me. And hopefully Sierra didn't figure out from the conversation that the ever-embarrassing Ted Lasker is my father.

When we're in the suite, Sierra turns to me. "Isn't that amazing?"

"What is?" I ask, going over what Mom said that could be considered "amazing," even by Sierra's standards.

"How we've known each other since New Orleans! It's like fate!" She looks at me like I'm a delinquent student who doesn't pay attention. "Do you think maybe we knew each other even before New Orleans? Like we met at another party or event?"

"I doubt it." Yes, it's interesting that we ran into each other in New Orleans. The statistical probability of that, plus us meeting each other at Dad's party, then again at her company, is very, very small. A true outlier event. But it's a series of coincidences, not something to drop one's jaw over. And it most certainly is not *fate*. More like a human tendency to retroactively assign meaning and connection to unrelated events.

Still, I'm not going to ruin her good mood by pointing out the absurdity of getting excited over freak coincidences. Her reaction is too cute and sweet. I can let her be happy and enjoy her exuberance.

I'm an economist, not a monster.

"I'm really glad I got to talk to your mom again. Otherwise we would've never known we met at the masquerade party. I wish we could've talked more." She shakes her head. "Actually, I wish the three of us had had a chance to talk at the party."

"Party?"

"You know. Ted Lasker's birthday party. Then you and I might've found out that we'd already met in New Orleans. And we would've had more opportunities to get to know each other, don't you think?"

I stare at her. Nobody in my social circle wants to spend much time with my overly dramatic mother, unless they want to break into modeling or acting using her connections. Since Sierra isn't interested in either, she must really like Mother for some reason.

I don't get it. But when she's looking up at me, eyes glinting with happiness, the reason doesn't seem to matter.

"You're right." A vague response is better than voicing what I really think and snuffing out that light in her eyes.

"I'm curious why you pulled us apart there. Did you think I'd embarrass you or something?"

Not you, but Mom. But I don't want to get into the humiliating family history. Some people love oversharing for sympathy and attention. Not me.

"No. You could never embarrass me." I claim Sierra's mouth in a hot kiss, directing her focus to something more productive and fun.

It's our last night in Tokyo, and we should make it memorable.

45

SIERRA

The morning Griffin and I return to the States is hectic. Our flight lands late, and we only have time to grab a quick shower before rushing out to resume our normal lives.

No more walking around the busy streets full of signs I can't read or seeing gorgeously wrapped gifts and snacks.

That's okay, though—it gives me another reason to go back to Tokyo. Next time, I'm going to do all the planning and make it my treat to Griffin. And budget more time, so we can see Osaka and Kyoto, too. Actually, I want to see the aquarium in Okinawa as well. Apparently, it's the third biggest in the world and has whale sharks! And the pictures of the beaches in Okinawa look amazing.

I walk into the lobby of Silicone Dream, feeling good in one of my cutest purple dresses and nude heels. Dan greets me, waving a beefy arm and smiling broadly. "Good morning. Happy belated birthday, Sierra."

"Thank you!" I reach into my bag and pull out a wrapped box. "Here's a small gift for you and Sally from Tokyo."

He takes the present. In his hands, it looks even smaller. "Wow. Thanks. What is it?" he asks, placing the box near his ear and shaking it a little.

"It's a box of red bean paste in mini-cakes shaped like bells. I think you'll enjoy it. It's sweet and delightful."

He lowers his arm, placing the box on the security desk. "I shoulda got something for you. I mean, it's *your* birthday."

"Oh, no need. I got the best present I could have ever wanted." The amazing trip and the romantic, sexy time with Griffin. I'm still swooning. There *was* a little bit of an awkward bump with that whole mom thing, but it's no big deal. Nothing can possibly ruin our magical four days in the Land of the Rising Sun.

"Oh, I'm sure. Don't know what could beat getting a song from Killian Axelrod."

"You saw the video?"

Dan laughs. "Everyone's seen it."

I flush with pleasure at the memory. "Griffin made a dream I didn't know I had come true."

Dan nods. "Seems like a good sort. Nothing like that ex-husband of yours."

"Comparing anybody to Todd is setting the bar low."

He snorts. "True enough. Well, I'm just happy you have somebody treating you the way you deserve."

He isn't quite old enough to be my dad, but I don't mind. It's sweet of him to care.

"I'll be up later for the party."

Heather and Ellie must've arranged to have the birthday party today. As usual, they'll probably do it during lunch, so everyone can come over and have some cake. Except Barbara, who has a special fresh fruit cup just for her.

"Awesome," I say. "I'll see you later, then."

I rush to the elevator, which is just closing its doors. I can see somebody through the gap and call out, "Wait!"

The doors reopen. Ellie's the only one inside. She gives me a once-over and says, "You look good."

"Hard to look bad after so much fun in Tokyo."

"And not just *any* fun, but X-rated fun." Ellie waggles her eyebrows.

"That was amazing, too." My mouth curves into a smile. Then I remember something. "Oh my God, by the way, I have to tell you something. It's about my destiny."

"Yeah, Griffin. Any guy who treats you like that is definitely destiny."

"No, no. I mean, yes, but there's more. *He's the Midnight God.*" My voice rises almost to a squeal.

She gasps. "No. Way. *Seriously?*"

"Cross my heart and hope to die."

She leans closer. "How did you figure that out?"

"His mother also happened to be in Tokyo and saw Axelrod perform. We ran into her the next day and started talking. And that's when it came out that he was in New Orleans attending the same masquerade party that I did."

Ellie pulls back, her arms folded. "But that doesn't mean he's the Midnight God. There were lots of other men at the party."

"The details matched. Besides, when I showed him a selfie from New Orleans, me in costume, he recognized me."

"Oh. My. God."

"Exactly." I point at her stunned face. "That's *exactly* what I thought."

"He's our sex toy inspiration."

"I know. The first."

"Seriously. I feel like we should make him a special penis plaque or something."

I laugh. *He'll probably appreciate being the first person to get to use the products on me more than getting a plaque.* The thought crosses my mind fast…and then something about the way it sprang into my head makes me stop laughing.

It's just the memory of his glamorous mom and his rather tight reaction about her and…

Ellie's looking at me. "What?"

"What what?"

"Come on. Something's bothering you. We've been friends for too long for me not to know. So what is it?"

The elevator stops, and we get off. Ellie pulls me to the side, obviously determined to hear everything.

"Come on. We have some time to spare"—she swivels her head left and right—"and nobody's around."

"Okay. It's…" I breathe out softly. "According to his mom, he was really sweet to her in New Orleans, right? But when we met again, later, he was totally weird with her and me."

"What do you mean?"

"You remember how I went to Ted Lasker's birthday party this year?"

"Yeah."

"That's where I actually met his mom for the first time. We were talking, and Griffin showed up and just, like, almost literally dragged her away. Like he was afraid we were going to do something inappropriate."

Ellie thinks for a second. "Wasn't that before he came to the company along with Todd for that case study thing?"

"Yup."

"So he couldn't have known who you were, like what kind of person you were, at the party."

"Right. Not even a little. So am I weird for thinking it's kind of odd?" When Rachel first mentioned it, I was too tired and excited from seeing Tokyo to really think about it. But now...

"Maybe he was worried about what his mom might say to you."

"But why? She's really nice."

Ellie shrugs. "Beats me. Have you talked to him about it?"

"Not yet. He was busy with some research he had to look over, and I didn't want to bother him." He spent most of the time in Tokyo doing things to make me happy, so I'm sure he was behind. "Plus I'm just trying to figure out what I think about it first."

"He didn't drag you away or anything strange like that when you were talking to his mom in Tokyo, did he?"

"Well...he kind of did. He was *dying* to end the conversation. But then, he'd been talking to his mom for over an hour by that point. And we'd been up since six."

Ellie smirks. "*And* he wanted to take you away and have his way with you."

"That too." I flush, recalling the hot sex that ensued.

"Maybe you're overthinking it. Some men just don't want to talk about their families. My last boyfriend was so secretive about his that I thought they worked for the CIA."

"Didn't Brian hate his parents?"

"Yeah."

"I don't think Griffin hates his," I venture cautiously. "Not based on what Rachel told me."

Ellie taps her chin and is about to say something, but then my phone pings.

–Heather: Are you in yet?

Crap. It's five past my regular time.

–Me: Yes. Just catching up with Ellie. I'll be right over.

"Gotta go. That was Heather."

"She sure keeps you on your toes." Ellie makes a whip-cracking noise.

I laugh, then reach into my bag and pull out a small wrapped box. "For you."

"Hey, thanks!"

Feeling good about putting a smile on Ellie's face, I walk toward my office. Heather falls in next to me, her trusty tablet in hand.

"Morning!" She smiles. "Must have been an amazing concert."

"Thanks. It was."

"We have cake and we're going to sing for you, but it's not going to be as good as Killian Axelrod."

I grin. "It's the thought that counts, Heather. Killian Axelrod I admire from afar, but you and people at the company are my family. People I can hug and share my life with."

"You're the sweetest." She taps her tablet. "Anyway, here's your schedule for today. There's a production team meeting in the morning at nine thirty. And you have an appointment with Dr. White at eleven sharp."

Oh, that's right. I asked Heather to schedule an annual pap smear after my birthday. It's not something I look forward to, and if it were left up to me, I'd probably forget. But Ellie's mom had cervical cancer that was discovered during a routine pap smear ten years ago. Since then, Ellie made it her mission to make sure that every woman in her life goes in for their checkup. She didn't have to try that hard to convince me. I was there when her mom had surgery to remove the cancerous cells. Thankfully, it was a success and the cancer hasn't come back. But I'll never forget the doctor saying that if it had been discovered later, the prognosis wouldn't have been so positive.

Then it hits me: *I had sex with Griffin on our last night in Tokyo.* I count the hours. With flight time and everything, I will just make the twenty-four-hour abstinence requirement before the pap.

"Got it," I say. "So nothing scheduled after ten thirty, right?"

"Nope."

"Excellent. How about this afternoon?"

"You have a quarterly financial review so you can be ready for the meeting with the bankers tomorrow morning."

When we reach my office, I put my purse down and take out the gift I bought for Heather. "Here you go. Something for you from Tokyo."

"Thank you." She studies the package. "It's wrapped so beautifully. I feel guilty about opening it."

"I know, right?"

"Did you wrap this?"

"Ha!" I shake my head. "I could never wrap anything that nicely."

Heather laughs. "Should I open it now?"

"Go for it."

She unwraps the package with care—you just can't rip into it when it's covered in textured gold paper and topped with an elegant mauve peony—then opens the box, revealing a glass pen and inkpot set. Her eyes widen, and a broad smile breaks over her face. "These are *gorgeous*."

"I thought of you the moment I saw them."

"Thank you so much. You're such a sweet girl."

"My pleasure."

Heather is worth thousands of those gorgeous pens. She's loyal and does more work than I ever thought possible.

At the production team meeting, I hand out some snacks I brought from Tokyo. I give dog treats to the team members with dogs. "Make sure you don't confuse the human treats with the canine ones."

"Oh my goodness," Jerry says, looking at both. He has a couple of basset hounds he adores. "They look exactly the same, except there's an anime dog sticker on the dog treats."

Everyone laughs, and I feel my mood rise in response. I'm so blessed I can bring joy into their lives—and share in the happiness.

We have a good meeting, discussing plans for Silicone Dream's existing products and what we're going to do to fit the Midnight God line in as well. Under Jerry and Georgia's competent care, we won't have to make a huge investment or any major adjustments. After the meeting, I grab my purse and let Heather know I'm heading to Dr. White's office.

A short drive later, I park my Ferrari and walk into a gorgeous white building that houses the gynecologist's office. The inside is mainly soft green and cheery yellow. Several comfortable couches with good back support for pregnant women line the waiting room. Against the wall are two bookcases, one with children's books and the other full of reference books on pregnancy and women's health concerns.

I walk to the reception desk and say hello to Cassie, whose short red hair clouds around her generously freckled face like a lion's mane.

"Good morning." She smiles, all friendly. "On time as usual. And all the way from Tokyo!"

I laugh. "I guess you saw the video."

"Oh my God, your boyfriend is awesome. He *is* your new boyfriend, right?"

She knows about Todd's and my attempts to have a baby and our separation and subsequent divorce. "Yeah. I'm dating someone new."

"Good for you."

Cassie told me that she always knew I'd ditch him when I told her we'd filed for divorce. She said she could always tell how long couples are going to last by observing the husband's behavior. Her opinion of Todd couldn't be lower after seeing him act like he was doing me a huge favor by begrudgingly accompanying me a couple of times for the fertility issues we were having. As far as he was concerned, they were mine and mine alone to resolve. His penis shot only the highest-quality sperm, thankyouverymuch.

"Tell me how you felt when that gorgeous man sang for you on stage," Cassie says in a squealy voice.

I let out a breath, shaking with remembered excitement, and start fanning my face. "Honestly? I thought my heart would burst. I still get shivers thinking about it."

"Lucky you. I was so jealous!" Grinning, she slides a clipboard with the standard patient questionnaire across the counter. "Anyway, fill this out, and Dr. White will see you soon."

I take the clipboard, which has a pen attached by a shiny metal chain, and take a seat. I've answered the questionnaire many times over the years. Now it's just a formality to make sure my address is the same, my insurance is the same and I haven't developed any new health conditions. Everything gets filled out on autopilot until: *When was your last period?*

Good question. I pull out my phone and open the app that I use to record my period. My cycle is highly irregular, so I try to track it just in case it's important for my doctor to know to make a diagnosis.

But there aren't any dates from the last two months. I sit and stare at the phone for a moment. I know I didn't forget to enter the data because I always tap the app to let it know my period has started as soon as it does. It's a habit as ingrained as taking a shower in the morning.

I go back further until I hit the month when my divorce with Todd was finalized.

Three months ago.

If I didn't have a fertility issue, this might be a *holy crap* moment. But I can't get pregnant. Todd and I tried—even sought help from Dr. White—but it never happened, for which I'm eternally grateful. We even tried to time it so that we had sex during my ovulation using the cycle-tracking app, until Dr. White told me about my blocked tubes.

I jot down the date on the paper, hoping it's nothing serious. It's nice to skip a period or two, but it isn't exactly normal... Is it? Even though I'm irregular, I always have one at least every six weeks.

I get up and give the questionnaire back to Cassie, who unpinches it from the clipboard and slips it into my patient folder. I return to my seat and try to stay calm, but find myself tapping the floor with my heel. I think about what happened to Ellie's mom. She had some irregular bleeding, but I don't remember her saying that she didn't have her period at all.

It's probably not cancer.

Even if it is, we're catching it so early that I should recover without any problem. There's no way I'm losing to a tiny cluster of misbehaving cells. It hasn't had enough time to advance to stage one. Probably still stuck at stage zero-point-five at the most. I'll be fine.

Cassie smiles at me from her station. "Sierra, Dr. White will see you now."

Less than fifteen minutes later, I know that my world will never be the same again.

I'm most definitely pregnant.

With triplets.

46

GRIFFIN

At nine a.m. sharp, I park my car and walk into Fullilove Hall. A couple of lecturers on contract with the college loiter near the entrance, sipping coffee from the café run by the school. They nod in greeting, and I nod back as I make my way to my office. I have research notes from Keith to review before my class at ten thirty.

When I reach the top of the stairs, I run into Julia and Lori. Julia's holding a thick manila folder full of Scantrons, while Lori's clutching her phone.

"Excuse me," I say, hoping one of them will get of the way so I can walk past.

Julia is the first to react. "Sorry." She takes half a step back.

Lori cocks her head. "You seem to be in a good mood."

"Same mood as always." But that isn't technically correct. It's hard to be in the same mood I'm always in when I had such great sex last night. But I know better than to say anything, especially when Lori's around.

She raises an eyebrow. "I have a question for you."

"Go ahead." She probably has some issues with her research. She's a good professor, but data analysis is not her forte. Right now, she's doing some research on social media's influence on human behavior, and that's a lot of data to sort through.

"The guy who asked Axelrod to sing 'Happy Birthday' to his girlfriend was you, wasn't it?" Her eyes glint.

I should've known. Nothing excites this woman like fresh gossip. If she'd show half this much excitement for economics, she could be head of the department.

"Yes." There's no denying what happened in Tokyo. The videos have been posted and viewed by everyone already. On top of that, the professors here know that I'm dating Sierra.

"I knew it," Lori says. "Must be nice to have a girlfriend who can take you to Tokyo to celebrate a birthday and go to a concert." Her smile reminds me of a well-baited hook.

"I'm sure it must."

"Yeah, it just seems— Wait, what?"

"Sierra didn't foot the bill for our trip." I could let everyone think I leeched off her, but if the truth comes out later—especially since Charles is dying to have a chance to talk with her—it'll be awkward.

"Oh, so you went Dutch."

"No. I paid for it."

Lori is looking like she can't figure out what to make of me. "You flew her out to Tokyo?"

"I have a lot of credit card points from all the traveling I've done for conferences." It's a complete lie, but I'm not telling anyone I used actual money. If the faculty knew how much I spent on the trip, they'd wonder how I got the money in the first place. And if someone starts digging, they might find a connection between me and my dad. A horrific outcome. I don't want my good reputation and name tied to that subhuman scandal-monger.

I try to keep all my interviews and conversations away from my family. I don't even tell people who my brothers are. Not because I'm ashamed of them, but because some of them don't hide the fact that they're related to the ever-embarrassing Ted Lasker.

People say they don't care who you're related to. That's a lie. Ask any family member of a serial killer.

Plus, Charles would be insufferable trying to get me to bring a large donation to the college from Dad. I'd rather brush my teeth with arsenic.

Lori gives me a probing look, but I just shrug.

By the end of the morning, everybody in the department is going to know that I paid for the trip with credit card points. Hopefully, none of them approaches me for tips on how to accumulate said points, because I have no idea. I have a black AmEx, mainly for its excellent concierge service, and a cashback credit card to use when people I know in real life are watching.

While Lori and Julia exchange looks, I slip past and go to my office. Those two can talk until their tongues cramp, but I have work to do.

I go over Keith's notes, draft an email and hit send. Then I notice an extra copy of the class syllabus on the desk, and I realize I need to set up a time to wrap up the case at Sierra's company. Although it's complete BS, I need to go through the motions to make Charles happy.

Since my students should be almost done analyzing the data, I should have them form groups of four and do short presentations. If I limit each presentation to ten minutes, it shouldn't be too painful.

Satisfied, I send a quick email to Heather to see when a good time would be for my class to be on site for the presentations.

My phone pings with new texts.

–Sebastian: Hey, you're back in town?

–Me: Yes.

–Noah: Awesome! How about dinner? We have a reservation at Manny's Tacos in downtown L.A. I got us a private room.

I look at the invitation with suspicion. They're never this eager to see me.

–Nicholas: They just want to meet the woman who inspired you to go that far.

They? I snort at Nicholas's choice of pronoun. He means "we."

It wouldn't be a bad idea to introduce Sierra to everyone. I've never done that before, but it feels natural in this case.

–Grant: Don't worry, we didn't invite Emmett. He's still having issues with Amy.

That's smart. Seeing me with Sierra would be like a punch to the stomach. Emmett deserves better.

Perhaps I should kick Dad in the face for Emmett's birthday. That'd cheer him up for sure.

–Me: Dinner's tonight? What time?

–Sebastian: Yes, at 7. But come earlier if you want.

—Me: I'll be there. No guarantee about the lady, though. She's a CEO, and usually very busy.

I have just enough time to grab a coffee before the class starts. Just as I'm getting up, Charles sticks his head into my office.

"How did it go?" he asks.

I sit back down with a frown. Could he be any vaguer? "What do you mean?"

"The fundraise that you did." His gaze says, *Tell me everything.*

"Charles, what are you talking about? What fundraise?"

"With Sierra Fullilove! You took her to Tokyo."

"For her birthday," I say, enunciating slowly.

"Oh, no need to demur. I simply want to know if you made any progress. You paid for the trip, correct?"

"Yes." It's an effort not to grind out the single syllable.

Charles starts washing his hands in the air. "Excellent! Submit the receipts, and I'll see how much we can reimburse you. But next time, do talk to me first. Makes it *so* much easier to allocate budget."

"The receipts. Yes, I'll do that." *This ought to be fun.* "We flew first class to Japan. Stayed in a two-bedroom suite in downtown Tokyo. And had two of the very best seats at the concert."

Charles's complexion turns progressively paler.

"And the champagne we had at one of our dinners cost over a thousand dollars."

"Over a *thousand* dollars?" His eyes are about to pop out of their sockets in shock. "Was it made of gold?"

"No. But that's what she deserves." She had a glass. I had the rest. I debate if I should give him that piece of information, then decide not to. I don't want Charles passing out in my office. I have a class to teach.

He wipes his hands on his shirt, clearly calculating feverishly. He wants to object to splurging, but he doesn't want to say out loud that Sierra doesn't deserve nice things. "This is why you should have told me ahead of time," he says finally. "Then you would have known how much you were authorized to spend."

I cling to my patience. Ripping into Charles's annoying tendency to insist he's right at all costs isn't going to help my career at the college. "Charles, listen to me. I treated Sierra to a trip to Tokyo because I wanted to. It had nothing to do with the research center."

"I don't understand. How could you afford to pay for all that?"

Guess Lori hasn't been able to unload on Charles yet. "The credit card points I've saved. How else?"

"But they only cover air and hotel!"

"Yes, but I also have some money saved. My field *is* economics, after all."

He's looking at me like I'm the most irresponsible financial derelict he's ever met. Probably assuming that I've been scrimping and saving all my life and blew everything on this trip.

"So there are no funds coming in for the research center?" he asks.

"No. But if you like, you can ask Sierra directly when you see her next time."

He brightens. "That's right. She'll be coming to the faculty social dinner."

Damn it, I forgot about that dumb dinner. "I suppose so." I tap my fingers against the desk.

Charles gives me a look. "She *is* coming...?"

"Unless there's something else she has to take care of. After all, she's a CEO, and emergencies do occasionally crop up."

That should ensure Sierra and I have a good reason to *not* attend the dinner. Having to endure Charles's begging is a form of torture. I wouldn't wish that on anybody, except for Dad and Joey. It's one of life's unfortunate little ironies that I can't sic Charles on them, because then he'd figure out who my father is. And I'd rather lick a feral cat's anus than have that happen.

47

SIERRA

Oh my God. I am pregnant. With not one baby, not two babies, but *three* babies!

Talk about going from zero to sixty in one second. It feels surreal, especially after having tried to have just one baby for so many months, to be told I'm with triplets.

Once I'm fully dressed again and sitting opposite Dr. White, I ask, "There's no way you could be mistaken?"

"The sonogram doesn't lie." Dr. White looks at me with motherly concern. "The babies are your boyfriend's, correct? The one who took you to Tokyo?"

"Yes." *Thank God for that.* I do not want anything to do with Todd. And if they were his babies, it would tie us together, giving him another way to try to worm his way back into my life.

"So. I suggest that you start taking prenatal vitamins."

"Right," I say numbly.

"Don't stress, take it easy, get plenty of rest. And do some light exercise like walking for half an hour a day. Your health is critical."

"I understand what I do directly impacts the babies." As I say it, I remember what I did in Tokyo. Cold fear slides up my spine, leaving my palms clammy. "I had a few drinks during my time in Tokyo. Some champagne and mimosas. Are they going to be a problem? Are my babies going to be okay?"

"That shouldn't be a problem. You aren't the only woman who didn't know she was pregnant and had a little alcohol," she assures me warmly, patting my hand. "I think it's more important to focus on what you can do going forward. Getting worried and stressed about what's already done isn't going to help."

I let out a sigh of relief. "Okay. And thank you. I needed to make sure."

"Sierra, you are a good, responsible girl. You always do the right thing, and your babies will be fine. Triplets are unusual, so they require extra monitoring. Why don't you come see me again next week?"

"Sure," I say. Dr. White specializes in fertility and high-risk pregnancies. "This caught me by surprise. I honestly thought I couldn't get pregnant."

"These babies beat the odds." She smiles. "They really want to be there"—she tilts her chin at my belly—"with you."

I process her words through the numbness that's been spreading through my mind since she told me I was pregnant. And gradually, optimism starts to bubble up, pushing away the anxiety.

These triplets aren't just any triplets. They're miracles. *My* miracles. My family. We belong to each other, and I already love them to pieces. Unlike a lot of women in my situation, I am lucky enough to be financially secure.

I should discuss the babies with Griffin later today. I don't know how he'll react, especially since I told him I couldn't get pregnant. Will he be happy about the new lives we've created? Upset? Maybe a combination of both. But no matter what, he's going to be shocked.

I exhale, then put a hand over my fluttering belly. If he wants to be part of their lives, fantastic. If he doesn't...

Well, I'll be disappointed because I want them to know their father's love, especially since I never experienced it myself. But I can raise them on my own—I can get help, hire full-time nannies, maybe—and I'll make sure these babies know they are loved. I'll be giving them double and triple the love.

Dr. White hands me a small black-and-white photo, the image she showed me on the screen earlier during the sonogram. There are some white dots I can't make sense of, but they are supposedly what the babies look like right now inside my womb.

"Again, congratulations. If you need anything or have any questions, just reach out anytime. I'm here for you."

"Thank you."

After my time with the doctor is over, I leave the office and climb into my Ferrari. I take a moment and look out the windshield at the bright, sunny sky. I wish my mom and grandma were still here so I could tell them the good news. That I'm going to be a mom, and they are going to be a grandma and a great-grandma. And share laughter and tears of joy as we celebrate the precious new lives growing inside me.

My phone pings.

Griffin.

–Griffin: Are you free for dinner in downtown L.A. today?

Why downtown L.A.? It'll take at least an hour to get there. I want to see him at home tonight, so I can give him the news in person.

–Me: Can't we do it somewhere in Lovedale?

As I sent off my reply, my belly starts to feel funky. Must be the nerves.

–Griffin: My brothers want to meet you. Not all of them can come, but at least four will be there.

I stare at the text, trying to figure out priorities. I want to talk to Griffin about the babies, but meeting his brothers is important, too. They're going to be the triplets' uncles.

It probably wasn't easy to have four of his brothers to meet. Given how Griffin is, his brothers are probably busy men.

–Me: Okay. Where exactly are we meeting?

–Griffin: Manny's Tacos. The original one.

–Me: I have a late afternoon meeting, but I'll drive to the restaurant straight from work. Should be there between 7 and 7:30.

–Griffin: That's fine. The reservation's under my brother's name. Noah Lasker.

I send him a smiling emoji.

The dinner invitation ups my optimism. If he weren't thinking about a future together, he wouldn't invite me to meet his brothers.

Being with Griffin isn't just about giving me these babies, I realize with a wave of happiness. He's giving me a big family I can belong to, with his amazing brothers and his amazing mom and undoubtedly amazing dad.

48

GRIFFIN

Manny's Tacos is a local chain restaurant owned by a family that's been in Los Angeles for at least a couple of generations. My brothers and I love the place because the food is amazing, the price is right and the portions are generous. None of that French two-bites-at-best stuff here.

The one in downtown is the original, and the largest. I park my car in a garage attached to an office building two blocks from the restaurant and walk over. As I open the door and step inside, the mouth-watering aroma of sizzling meat, onions, bell peppers and spices hit me hard. My stomach growls.

A smiling hostess comes over. "Hi and good evening. How can I help you?"

"There should be a reservation under Noah Lasker."

She looks at a small tablet, then lifts her head with another smile. "Your party is already here. This way, please."

She takes me to the back where the private room is. It's large enough to host a dinner for twenty people, and I don't know what magic Noah pulled to grab it for us. Not that I'm complaining. After Sierra and I went viral with that concert video, it's best we aren't where people will notice and try to talk to us. Some local social columnist figured out that I was the man who requested the song and sent emails and left voice mails on the phone in my office, requesting an interview.

I'd rather skydive with a defective parachute.

In the room are Huxley, Sebastian, Grant, Noah and Nicholas. As expected, Emmett is absent. Sierra hasn't arrived, but it's barely seven.

A pitcher of margaritas sits on the table. Manny's has the best—strong with a clean finish. There are seven coupe glasses as well, two still unused, while my brothers took the others to start drinking.

Noah is hogging a basket of chips and salsa, but that's to be expected.

I take an empty seat next to Sebastian and pour myself a margarita. "We didn't invite Emmett, right?" I don't want him to get morose when I'm introducing Sierra. I want her to like everyone.

"No. Even if we had, he wouldn't have been in the mood. He's working late. I don't know why. Nothing's urgent enough to work at the pace he set, but everybody is pulling all-nighters to please him," Grant says with a small, resigned sigh.

"Is he still pining over Amy?" Noah looks utterly confused. "He should just get himself a new girlfriend." Noah's never been in a relationship for long. He claims he "just knows" when it's time to move on. And he moves on quite frequently. His sneakers have been with him longer than any girlfriend.

"Emmett isn't like you," I say.

"I'm tempted to get him a hot hooker to help him get over her," Sebastian says.

"He'll murder you." I try not to grind my teeth at the memory of the damn escort and the public embarrassment it caused me in front of my students and Charles.

"Not me. *Joey*," Sebastian says. "He'd be the most likely suspect in Emmett's mind."

Nicholas looks at the ceiling contemplatively. "I like it. A horrible death at Emmett's hand would be well deserved."

"I think it's the baby that Emmett can't give up. You know he has a thing about his responsibilities. He probably wants to be the best dad possible, if for no other reason than to prove that he's nothing like *our* dad," Grant says. "Somebody should tell him that babies create an enormous carbon footprint or something. He's into the environment."

"I saw a paper about that last week," I say vaguely, recalling some preliminary research.

"Seriously?" Huxley raises both eyebrows. "That's harsh."

"Well, yeah, if you view babies as an opportunity to shill your clients' products." Nicholas's tone drips with cynicism.

I just shrug. Economists look into all sorts of topics. There are papers on abortions and their impact on violent crime—

"Did you agree with the premise?" Sebastian asks.

"I never prejudice myself that way. My job is to rip apart their assumptions and methodology, look for holes in their analysis."

"Tell me more about this paper," Grant says.

"It was an early draft, but it basically calculated all the waste that gets created because of a baby. Babies need new things all the time, every few weeks at least," I say, trying to recall exactly what it said. The data used should be refined somewhat, and the statistical analysis could be more rigorous. But it was an early draft, so I don't bring up those shortcomings. "The conclusion, which is preliminary, was that if we care about the environment, we should have fewer babies."

Huxley scoffs. "Right, save the planet and face extinction."

"Fewer, not none." Personally, I think the paper's conclusion is ludicrous. There are things you can't measure via statistics and data. Fear. Loss. Joy. Advertisers select images of sheer happiness when they showcase new parents in their campaigns because they resonate, because they touch something fundamental in all of us.

The door to the private room opens, and Sierra walks in.

Everything in my body prickles and comes alive. Her purple dress reminds me of our night in New Orleans, where we had our first scorching encounter. Actually, everything about her reminds me of tangled sheets—even if her smile also reminds me of a sunbeam breaking through a cloudy sky. No matter my mood, it's hard to be glum when she smiles.

"Sorry I'm late." She waves. "Hi, everyone. I'm Sierra."

Everyone turns to look at her. From the expressions on my brothers' faces, I'm not the only one who thinks she's amazing.

Huxley looks at her up and down, assessing her like he would a potential spokesperson for one of his clients' brands. Noah starts to let out a whistle but catches himself. Sebastian takes one look at her, then raises an approving eyebrow in my direction.

I stand and go over and kiss her, wrapping my arm around her waist possessively. "I'm glad you made it."

She smiles, her shining eyes on me. Only me.

I like that more than I care to admit.

I indicate my brothers in turn. "Grant, Sebastian, Noah, Nicholas and Huxley."

"Nice to meet you all," she says with a huge smile.

Nicholas beams, which makes him appear utterly harmless and sweet, which is a lie because he can be a complete asshole. Grant smiles the warm, polite smile he always puts on when he sees somebody he decides to like.

I take her to the empty seat next to mine and start to pour her a margarita, but she shakes her head.

"Oh, no thanks," she says. "I, uh, have a small headache."

"Did you take something for it?"

She nods.

"If you want, we can cut the dinner short," I whisper.

"I'll be fine. Besides, I love Manny's." She smiles, patting my hand reassuringly.

"You look better in person than in the video," Noah says, snagging Sierra's attention away from me.

"It was taken too far away," Huxley says. "Too grainy."

"I guess everybody saw the video, huh?" Sierra smiles. "Some of the local reporters want to interview me about the trip."

Should've expected them to go after her, too. Killian Axelrod didn't say my name, but he sure said hers. "Do you want to talk to them?" I ask.

"No. Somebody from marketing said it might be a good way to mention our products, but I don't want to turn the trip into a marketing opportunity."

I squeeze her hand. So many people I know do everything in their power to turn even the most miniscule thing into an attention-whore moment. Then everything turns into a competition to see who can one-up the other, cheapening the experience without realizing what they're doing. Fame is one of the most sought-after currencies, and many people don't care what they have to sacrifice or whom they have to trample to get it.

"Good for you. They won't bug you for long. The moment some

juicier bit of gossip pops up, they'll vanish like roaches when you turn on a light." Grant's tone is cynical, but oddly reassuring.

"If you wanted to avoid the so-called reporters nipping at you for a story, you shouldn't have outsourced the singing to Axelrod. You should've done it yourself," Huxley says, giving me a meaningful look.

Asshole. Bringing it up in front of Sierra, trying to make it appear I don't care about her enough to bother. "I don't sing."

"No, you *choose* not to sing." Hux wags a finger.

Sierra looks at us curiously.

He leans closer and lowers his voice as though he's about to reveal a military secret. "He sings like a dream, but won't."

I roll my eyes. "I'm not a dog doing some trick."

Nicholas snickers. "No dog sounds like you." He turns to Sierra. "If he ever sings for you, you'll know he loves you."

I grit my teeth at how annoying my brothers are being about this. I don't want Sierra to assume I don't have feelings for her just because I won't sing. I can express my feelings in other ways. This is real life, not a damned musical!

"I'd love to hear you sing," Sierra says, her eyes sparkling with good humor. "But not if you're uncomfortable."

"See? She's sweetly reasonable, unlike you assholes." They don't bother to hide their disappointment over another failure to corner me into singing. Huxley thinks it's a waste of talent. What he really believes is he could use my voice to sell something.

"Forget singing. Let's order some food," Noah declares as he swallows the last of the chips. "I'm starving."

49

SIERRA

Griffin's brothers are nice and interesting. Grant is laid-back, but his eyes are sharp and just a tad sardonic. Grandma told me everything about a man can lie except the eyes and penis.

Noah seemingly blurts out whatever comes to his mind, but I doubt that's all there is. He manages to avoid any inappropriate or uncomfortable topics. He might give his brothers a hard time, but not me. Also, he can't seem to stay away from social media. I counted at least three times he pulled out his phone to check the feed.

Nicholas is calmer, but there's a competitive streak in him that comes out from time to time, particularly when they talk about sports. Sebastian seems polite and friendly, and very knowledgeable about gemstones. Griffin tells me that Sebastian is the heir to the Sebastian Jewelry fortune.

Huxley assesses everything like an auditor looking for discrepancies. He reminds me a little of Ellie's disapproving grandma.

Throughout dinner, I get to hear about how they grew up in Europe. They regale me with stories that make their childhoods seem exotic and fun. I wonder if our triplets will have that sort of life or if they're going to be closer to home. I don't think living in Europe is going to be an option while I'm the CEO of Silicone Dream, even though I think it would be really cool.

Noah interrupts my thoughts by mentioning that Griffin is an excellent rider and kickboxer. That explains the incredible kick he gave Todd in New Orleans.

"Do you still do both?" I ask.

"Sometimes," Griffin says nonchalantly.

"He's good at polo, too," Nicholas says. "Although I'm better." He winks. "Actually the best out of all of us."

"Who's the guy who fell off his horse in the middle of our last game?" Huxley says. "Oh yeah… You!" He jerks his thumb in Nicholas's direction.

"The horse got spooked," Nicholas says.

"Were you hurt?" I ask.

"Just his pride," Griffin remarks dryly. "He's got a thick hide and an even thicker skull."

I laugh.

But one thing seems strange: throughout the conversation, they never bring up their father, even when they mention their mothers. Wonder why.

"Did your father ever come to visit you in Europe?" I ask conversationally after our dessert arrives.

A noticeable pall comes over the table. It's almost comical. Everyone freezes. Unblinking, Griffin peers at me over his ice cream sundae. Sebastian holds a margarita to his lips without drinking it. Grant's fork stops midair, a chunk of cheesecake suspended at the tip, and Noah almost drops his phone.

"You guys okay?" I ask, slightly amused.

"We didn't expect you would want to know about our father," Griffin says slowly.

"He's a boring old geezer." Noah waves his free hand, like he's swatting at an annoying fly.

"We don't know him that well." Sebastian's tone is oddly wistful. "He's busy." Huxley nods in agreement.

"I see." Obviously, they don't have a good relationship with their father either. Now that I think about it, Griffin hasn't ever brought up his dad. Weirdly enough, it makes me feel closer to all these men.

"How about you? Grant asks.

Griffin cuts his eyes sharply at Grant, but I place a calming hand on his forearm. "I don't get along with my father. He's moved on. He doesn't want me." I thought saying that out loud would always burn.

But it doesn't. Not now. All I feel is a dull ache, like an old wound that's almost healed. I don't know when that started—maybe when I started to spend more time with Griffin. It's difficult to hang on to old pain when you have somebody who makes sure you know you're important.

Huxley winces. "I'm sorry."

"At least we have that in common," Sebastian says.

"Yeah. But you have each other." I leaven it with a smile to let them know I'm fine.

"Thank God," Nicholas says earnestly.

Griffin takes my hand and squeezes. He leans over and whispers into my ear, his warm breath tickling my sensitive skin, "And you have me."

50

GRIFFIN

By the time we return to Lovedale, it's a little past nine. We park our cars and walk along the path that cuts through the front yard. Sierra unlocks the door, and we enter the house together. An entirely ordinary ritual, but oddly right.

"This makes us feel like a real couple, coming home after a long day at work," Sierra says, a smile in her voice.

"It does," I agree, then wonder if it's the couple-ness of the moment that's making me feel like I can lower my guard and relax.

Our suitcases lie in the living room. We left them there this morning, not bothering to drag them upstairs in our rush to get to work on time.

"We should take them up to the master bedroom," she says.

It's a casual way to bring up the topic of my sharing her bed. "I'll do it," I say just as casually. There's no way I can stay away from her after what happened in Tokyo. She's got me addicted, and the apple scent from her skin has been driving me crazy all evening. "I know your suitcase is heavy."

"Not anymore. Half of it was the souvenirs, which I took to work."

She goes to the kitchen and pours a glass of cold water.

"How's your headache?" I ask.

"Much better."

"Need an Advil or anything?"

"No thanks. It isn't that bad," she says hurriedly as she opens the fridge to put away the pitcher of water. "Want something to drink?"

"I'm fine."

She downs the water in a few big gulps. Perhaps she's been dehydrated. Flying can do that to you, and if you aren't careful, you can get a mild, hangover-like headache afterward. That's why I always make sure to drink a glass of water per hour of flying. I should've advised her to do the same. But she seemed fine after our flight to Tokyo.

She puts the glass in the sink, washes her hands and then dries them thoroughly with a paper towel. Her fingers are restless, and she continues to shift and move around without purpose.

"Are you okay?" I ask, watching her from the kitchen counter.

"Yeah." She flashes a smile, but it can't hide the nerves.

I pat the stool next to me. She stays standing by the sink.

"Everything fine at work?" I ask.

"Oh yeah. Silicone Dream is doing great."

I narrow my eyes. "Did Todd stop by?" Per Lori's endless gossip, which I've been forced to endure, he's probably going to be dropped by Wollstonecraft. Deservedly so, but he might try to beg Sierra to exert her influence at the college to renew his contract.

She starts. "Todd? Ugh, no. No. Not at all."

"Then what's wrong?"

"Oh." She goes unnaturally still. After a long moment she clears her throat, then gestures at the dining table. "I have to tell you something. We should sit down."

The dinner I had churns uncomfortably in my belly. When a woman says, "I have to tell you something," it's never anything good. It's either a true Class One catastrophe, or it's something really stupid she's going to have a major drama over.

Since Sierra isn't a drama queen, it's gotta be the former—a consequential disaster.

But if it's not about Silicone Dream or Todd, what could it be?

I sit down, folding my hands on the table to calm myself. Sierra takes her seat and runs her hands down her thighs.

"I heard what you and your brothers were talking about at dinner. About how babies create a carbon footprint," she says gingerly, as though she's taking her time to pick the right words.

Is that all? The topic isn't worth this much anxiety on her part. "That was just a research paper." I don't want her operating under the misconception that my brothers or I have anything to do with the paper. "It's not even published." Why is she so nervous about wanting to discuss the paper? The topic's a bit obscure, and probably only an economist would think it's interesting. But, of course, there's nothing wrong with laypeople wanting to know more.

"Do you believe the findings?" Sierra watches me intently.

I don't understand why she's so edgy, but I'm getting a feeling that I should answer her as thoroughly as possible.

"The data they used is okay," I say finally. "There are some parts where I thought their math could be better. They also overlooked a few possible causations and other explanations, but they're hard to explain without the paper in front of us so you can see exactly what I'm talking about."

"I don't care about the math. I want to know if you agree with the conclusion that the babies are nothing but a carbon footprint."

She misinterpreted what we said. But then, it's difficult to understand research from mere eavesdropping, and I don't mind taking the time to explain the nuance if the topic is of such interest to her. "The paper didn't say that. It states that they generate—"

"Are you trying to be technical?" Her voice is loud and slightly shrill.

I pull back. "I'm trying to be thorough, since you seem interested in the paper."

Sierra takes a deep breath. "Sorry. I shouldn't have raised my voice. I don't care about the paper. I want to know if you think that children are bad for the environment."

"No," I answer.

She lets out a long sigh.

"But if you're not interested in the paper and the details of the research, why are you asking about it?" Most people aren't interested in economics research. I wouldn't have brought it up if it weren't for Grant.

"Because..." She inhales slowly, then exhales in a whoosh. "I'm pregnant."

I sit, feeling like somebody just swing a hammer into the base of my skull. All thought vanishes from my head, and I blink a couple of times, trying to force the gears to start turning again.

Statistically speaking, condoms aren't perfect, but we only had sex recently. Doesn't it take longer for an egg to get fertilized and settle in the womb? Perhaps there are new ways to determine pregnancy faster. That area isn't my expertise. But...

I finally croak, "When? How?" I wince inwardly at the second question. *How* is obvious. I must be more shocked than I thought.

"It must've happened when we were in New Orleans. I just found out today when I went in for my regular checkup with my gynecologist."

"Didn't you say you couldn't get pregnant?" I keep my voice matter-of-fact so she doesn't think it's an accusation. It won't do to upset her right now. Even a numbers geek like me knows this is a critical juncture in our relationship.

She winces. "Yes. I did. Because I thought that was the case. But my fallopian tubes are only *partially* blocked. Apparently, *some* swimmers can still get through."

Wow. That wasn't what I thought she was going to say. So my guys are that persistent and strong, huh? It gives me an absurd sense of pride.

I can't decide if I want to categorize this as a Class One catastrophe or not. My stomach isn't twisting with a sickening feeling. But it isn't happy and relaxed, either.

"What do you want to do?"

The question slips from my lips. I don't know what answer I want to hear. Even if having the baby is going to forever change our lives irrevocably, if the little life we just created is anything like Sierra, it's going to be adorable—and totally worth everything that's going to come. But it's Sierra who's going to be most impacted by the pregnancy, and I want to be ready to support her no matter what she decides.

"I want to keep them." She places a protective hand over her belly. "They're my babies. *My family.*"

I wait for her to add to that, but she doesn't. I'm vaguely disappointed, although I can't put my finger on—

"Wait. *Them? Babies?*"

Biting her lip, she nods. "Triplets."

"*Triplets?*"

"Yes."

I run a hand across my mouth. "Wow. Triplets."

"Yes." She waits a beat. "That means three."

"Yeah." I feel like I've been ax-kicked. Triplets are incredibly rare. Even the most generous studies only put the number at one in every nine thousand pregnancies.

Condom failure, partially blocked tubes...and now *triplets*. What are the odds? My brain's too sluggish to do the math, but it has to be on the order of getting struck by lightning.

Except this doesn't feel like a disaster. I can't put my finger on what I'm feeling precisely, but it isn't...bad.

She gives me an uncertain smile. "Griffin, I know this is shocking. Take some time to think before you decide what you want to do."

"What do you mean?"

"I don't want to force you to be a father to these babies if that's not what you want."

I stiffen. Is this why she was so tense and nervous?

Just what kind of asshole does she think I am? Even Dad did the bare minimum of financially providing for us, although anything else seemed too much bother.

"I'll do the right thing." The words shoot out.

She flinches. "Meaning...?"

"Sorry, didn't mean to snap. I'll be a good dad. I want to be involved in their lives. I am not going to shirk my duties and be absent or uncaring." And I realize this is exactly what I want to do for our babies. I want them to have a life that's better than my own.

"Okay." She smiles.

It isn't as bright as her regular smile. I don't know what's bothering her. Didn't I just solve all her worries about the triplets?

When she gets up and kisses me, I decide perhaps she's still suffering the aftereffects of having to announce an unplanned pregnancy and cradle her gently in my arms.

She shouldn't be anxious. I didn't just say those things. I mean to execute them all like a responsible, respectable adult.

51

SIERRA

Griffin holds me all night, caressing my still-flat belly. I lay my hand over his, needing the physical connection and comfort of touch.

He said all the right words, the kind any woman in my situation would be happy to hear. But something still bothers me all night. It's nothing overt—more like that unease you get when you can't remember if you turned off the stove before leaving home.

But even as the mild apprehension lingers, I can't put my finger on why. Nothing's unusual in the morning. We go through our routine of showers, breakfast—no coffee for me—and getting ready for work. Griffin tells me to eat for four, and I laugh.

It's probably just nerves. Being pregnant is a huge shock. I still can't believe I'm carrying three babies! Once I get used to the idea, I'll go back to my normal self, no problem.

At work, Heather forwards me an email from Charles Phillips from Wollstonecraft College. The name is vaguely familiar. I look at his signature, and realize that he is Griffin's boss in the economics department.

Dear Sierra,

Griffin has undoubtedly mentioned our upcoming faculty social by now, but I wanted to check in with you, to let you know how important it is and how much we would appreciate your joining us. Spouses and significant others (forgive me for the horrible circumlocution) will attend, and the event will be low-key and "chill," as the students like to say.

There will be plenty of food and drink, and if you would be so kind as to inform me of any allergies or preferences, I shall, of course, be happy to accommodate them.

The email ends with the date, time and location of the event and a firm but polite request for an RSVP. I pull back, considering my schedule. Griffin *hasn't* said anything about any college social. If it were Todd, I'd assume he didn't tell me because he was too ashamed to be seen with me—a sex toy CEO and somebody who doesn't know anything about English poetry. But this is Griffin. He was probably distracted and busy with the trip to Tokyo. And yesterday we had dinner with his brothers, then I dropped the bombshell on him.

I shoot him a text.

–Me: I got an email from Charles Phillips about a faculty social. What's the dress code, etc.? The English department was much more formal than I expected.

Then I head for a meeting with Ellie's team. Everything goes smoothly, although the room feels a bit stuffy. Maybe it's premature to worry about it already, but ever since hearing that I'm pregnant, I keep wondering when I'm going to be struck by nausea or a sensitivity to smell.

After the meeting, I invite Ellie to lunch. "Are you free?" I want to tell her about my pregnancy and what happened last night.

"I'm always open for lunch. Let's go." She grabs her purse. "I pick the place?"

"Please." I don't have the mental energy to decide what I want, and I trust Ellie's judgment. Right now, my brain's devoted to processing my to-do list at work and the fact that I'm pregnant.

She drives us to Milano, an upscale Italian bistro. Their menu is excellent, but a bit pricey.

"What's the occasion?" I ask as we walk in.

"Your birthday," Ellie says. "I know we did the cake yesterday in the office, but I'm your best friend. It's in my contract to do something extra special for you."

We get seated at a table by the window, and I order their pasta lunch special. Ellie gets the specialty three-cheese pizza—her favorite. As soon as our waitress is gone, I lean across the table. I should probably ease her into the idea, all smooth and cool-like.

I take a sip of water. "I'm pregnant."

She chokes, then starts laughing. "Okay, that's a bad joke."

"I'm not joking."

"Come on. How can you be pregnant? Didn't your doctor say you were, you know..." She doesn't want to say the word.

"Infertile? Apparently no, not really." I tell her what happened.

"Incredible. So Griffin's alpha sperm overcame the obstacles and did the horizontal tango with your egg?"

"Yes," I say, laughing a little. "If eggs and sperm can even be horizontal. Oh, and I'm having triplets."

"*Oh my God!*" Her jaw actually drops. "*Triple* alpha!"

Our waiter brings our food. As I smell the delicious pasta in front of me, I say, "I'm going to be a mom."

"And I'm going to be an auntie! Woohoo!" She pumps her fist with a huge smile. "I'm so excited for you. Did you tell Griffin?"

The weird nagging feeling suddenly resurfaces. "Of course."

"What did he say?" She leans forward, all too eager.

"He just said he'd do the right thing." I stab my fork into the spaghetti.

"Meaning?"

"He plans to be a good dad."

"Okay, but how, exactly?" Ellie scowls. "*Your* dad thinks he's a great dad."

"I know. Dad acts like he's fulfilling his duty for a responsibility he can't shake off, while claiming he's doing the right thing for me."

Saying it out loud, I realize what's been bugging me. It's the fact that Griffin also said he'd do the right thing for the babies.

"I don't want Griffin to be in their lives out of obligation." I feel uncharacteristically glum.

"A man won't stick around out of obligation," Ellie says, all brisk and practical. "He will for other reasons. I'm surprised he didn't propose something a bit more romantic, especially after what he did for your birthday."

I pause as sudden hot shivers run down my spine and pool in my gut. It's *longing*. I sip my drink to cover my reaction and re-center myself. "We've only known each other for a few weeks."

"But he's the Midnight God!"

"Well, yeah," I say. "But we only found that out last weekend."

"Still."

"I don't want him to propose because of the babies. I want him to propose because he sees a future with me. Growing old together."

I wanted that with Todd and failed because I married him for all the wrong reasons. He was there when I was lonely, and he seemed sweet. I didn't think it would be a problem.

"I hope Griffin is the one I can still hold hands and dance under the stars with when both of us have gone gray," I say quietly. My heart flutters at the image.

Ellie's expression softens.

I continue, "But I need to be sure that we're making the right decision at the right time. And for the right *reasons*. I want Griffin to want to be with me—to be my family because he loves me the way I am and because being with me makes him as happy as I am with him."

"Men can be oblivious about their feelings," Ellie says, shrugging. "Give him some time and space to work out what he's feeling for you. He's a smart guy. He'll figure it out soon enough."

52

GRIFFIN

"So next Wednesday, we'll be visiting Silicone Dream and you'll do your presentations in front of the executives. I expect you to exceed my expectations."

Some of the kids groan, while some look determined. The ones that didn't do well on the midterm, which is about eighty percent of the class, know that this is their chance at redemption. That's why I made it extra credit rather than part of the final. If we're going to waste Sierra's time, I want these kids to put in the effort.

"Any questions?"

No hands go up. I dismiss the class and walk to my office. As I unlock the door and step inside, my phone on the desk pings.

–Noah: Did you see this?

A link to a Hollywood gossip site is attached.

–Me: You know I don't read that trash.

–Noah: It's trash about your mother. They have your picture, too. Just wanted to mention it so you'd be prepared.

My picture? Panic clenches my heart, *hard*. What the hell? I do everything to avoid being attached to her and Dad—and whatever crap they get themselves into. I have a reputation to protect. How am I going to get any respect if people find out I attend birthday parties with dick cannons?

I click the link and read the so-called "article." Apparently,

Mom had a huge public scene with Fabio in Milan yesterday. He screamed at her at a restaurant, accusing her of using him. Which is rich, coming from him, considering he was hoping to utilize her connection to Dad to break into the movie business.

Apparently, he became so angry he threw wine on her. Which, unfortunately, turned her dress translucent, and she wasn't wearing a bra. Of course, the article has a picture of her nipples showing through. I really *didn't* need to see that.

Scrolling to move the picture out of view, I keep reading and note with approval that Mom slapped him in return.

Fabio accused her of cheating on him with other men. The article has two pictures: one with her leaving with another man—which explains why she hasn't called—and another of me and Mom in the hotel lobby in Tokyo. No picture of me sitting there with Sierra, naturally. That would change the narrative.

The only good thing is that the angle of the shot makes it hard to see my face. But the photo gives credence to Fabio's claim, and makes people speculate about who Mom's "mystery lover" is in the comment section.

A sickening feeling congeals in my gut. I should've known better than to talk to Mom in a well-trafficked public space like in the lobby. I've always managed to avoid getting photographed by paparazzi—especially with my parents—because I've been extremely careful.

–Noah: That's you in the pic, right?

–Me: Yes.

–Noah: How can they link you to your mom romantically? That's sick.

–Me: No shit. Thanks for the heads-up. Hopefully this blows over and nobody figures out it's me in the photo.

–Noah: Yeah. Luckily, you're pretty incognito. Not even people at your college are going to think that's you.

True enough. I lean back in my seat, embarrassed about the situation. Hopefully, Sierra will be too busy with her new sex toy production schedule to notice the "article," and this journalistic offal will die a quiet death, unnoticed and without trending.

–Me: This isn't trending, is it?

–Noah: Enough that I noticed. Why?

Dammit.

–Me: Sierra knows who my mother is.
–Noah: Ouch.
–Me: Exactly.

Sierra does not need to see what Mom does on a regular basis. Nor does she need to see pictures of my mother in a translucent dress with her nipples sticking out.

I start to put the phone down, then note another text that arrived while I was in class. It's from Sierra asking about the faculty social.

Charles contacted her directly, curse the man. Smart of him, but highly irritating, because I was going to wait until the absolute last minute to make sure she couldn't go. She shouldn't have to waste a precious Friday evening dealing with that parasite.

–Me: Business casual should be fine. But you don't have to go if you don't want to. Just so you know, Charles intends to pressure you to donate money for a research center he wants built. It won't be pleasant.

–Sierra: Isn't this important for your career at the college?

I pause, surprised at the question. None of my ex-girlfriends ever cared about my career. I feel a corner of my mouth quirking.

–Me: Not to the point of being worth your discomfort.

–Sierra: It's okay. Your boss won't be the first to ask for money. Chuck did it too when I was married to Todd. I can handle it.

–Sierra: By the way, I'll be home late tonight. Don't wait up. *wink*

53

GRIFFIN

I have a call with Keith to discuss our research. After we're done with the meat of the conversation, we talk a bit about social stuff. He has a wife and three kids in elementary school, and he's dying to tell me about what they're up to, his voice soft with love—a normal person being a good dad. He grew up in a small farming community in Ohio, and I wonder if that's what it takes to learn by example. Most people in Mom's circle wouldn't recognize good parenting if it fell on them like a meteor.

"Vivi does ballet, and it's just adorable," Keith says.

"How long's she been doing that?"

"About two years? Although Sandra says she's getting tired of rehearsals."

"You going to push her to continue?" I ask. My parents would, regardless of the child's feelings, if they thought ballet would reflect well on them.

"I don't think so. She can explore other things." Keith chuckles. "She's still so young."

After a few more minutes of chatting about his family, we end the call and I head to Sierra's place. By the time I park my Prius and get out, it's a little after seven. Lights are on in the living room. I cock my head. I swear I turned off everything before I left this morning.

My confusion vanishes when I spot Sierra's Ferrari in the driveway—but didn't she say she was going to be home late?

I walk inside and call out, "I'm home!"

"Hey," Sierra answers from the living room. She's pacing in a loose pink nightshirt, her bare feet padding quietly on the wooden floor. Her cheeks are flushed, and her eyes seem slightly glazed.

If I didn't know better, I'd think she'd had a little too much to drink. But when I get close, she doesn't smell like alcohol, and I've seen how protectively she puts her hand over her womb, as though she'd die to protect the lives growing there.

Then I notice she's wearing a bra under the nightshirt, which is odd. I don't know any woman who likes wearing a bra, and Sierra's no exception. She takes hers off as soon as she can, and she's been getting rid of them as soon as she walks in since the Tokyo trip.

"Are you okay?" I ask.

"Yeah. I'm fine. All good." She sounds like she's trying to convince herself.

"I thought you were working late today," I say, giving her an opening to talk about issues at work if they're what's bothering her.

"I had a meeting scheduled with a couple of team leads, but their kids came down with chickenpox, so they had to leave this afternoon. Apparently it's going around in the daycare center." She stops, her throat working as she swallows. "And so I came home."

"Okay."

She seems nervous. And restless. "Did you have dinner?" she asks abruptly.

"Not yet."

"You want some pizza?"

A box of pepperoni pizza sits on the edge of the coffee table. She's eaten only a slice.

That isn't the only one on the table. Some of the items aren't something I've ever seen before, but I'm sure they're sex toys of some kind. Maybe the production team isn't doing a good job or something.

Unfortunately, my dick doesn't care much about issues she could be having at the company. It wants to know if it's okay to play with the toys.

Look how soft and pretty she is. Just kiss her and push that nightshirt up...

I smack down my cock's brain and ignore my heating blood. I want to figure out what's going on first. Perhaps she isn't feeling that great. One of the professors in my department whined endlessly about his wife's weird cravings and mood swings during their pregnancy.

Except...Sierra doesn't seem moody. Her chest rises and falls rapidly, and the flush spreads to her neck and chest, too.

It's almost as though she's turned on.

Perhaps she got turned on looking at the toys.

Except none of them look used. Plus, nobody reacts this intensely to just looking at sex toys. Otherwise, adult stores would turn into orgies.

"We have some frozen lasagna if you want," she says.

"Pizza's fine."

I put down my laptop and a bunch of papers under the table and sit in an oversized recliner. I take a slice and bite into it.

Sierra takes the loveseat. "It's amazing how easy you are with food. After the trip to Tokyo, it wouldn't have shocked me at all if you only wanted caviar and sushi pizza," she says, tapping her hands on her knees.

"Ugh. That sounds disgusting."

"Unagi might not be so bad on a pizza," she jokes, running her fingers through her unbound hair and tossing it over a shoulder.

"That is the most disgusting thing I have ever heard in my life." In addition, I'm not a huge unagi fan. I like maguro, but tuna pizza is gag-inducing. "Stick to sex toys. Restaurants aren't your thing."

"Don't worry. A woman's gotta know her limitations."

"So what are you working on?" Hopefully, talking about her work will settle her down. I gesture at a smooth stick about a foot long, made with white plastic. "Is that from your company?"

"No. It's actually a device I bought from one of our competitors overseas."

I wipe my hands with a napkin thoroughly before I pick it up. I hit a button, expecting it to vibrate, but instead, a blue light comes on at the tip of the device and starts blinking.

"What does this light do? It better not be a signal to let the user know that the device is on. I'll know it's on when it starts vibrating."

And we can use it on her, my dick suggests.

I ignore it. She wouldn't have bought a mere vibrator from a competitor. There has to be more.

Sierra smiles. "It's a signal that it's ready to pair with your phone through Bluetooth."

"So you use your phone as a remote?" It's a little clunky if your phone's large like mine, but I suppose it could work.

She laughs. "No. It connects to the camera and viewing app you need to install."

"How unexpected." I scrutinize the stick. "Are you supposed to make a sex tape with it?"

"No." She nearly chokes with laughter. "This is basically a vibrator/dildo. When you use it while paired to your phone, it's going to show you what it looks like inside."

"As in, inside the woman's vagina." I turn the stick in my hand, wondering what kind of research was done before deciding that viewing the interior of a vagina is a popular kink.

"Yes."

I frown. "Can't you do that at your gynecologist's office?"

"Trust me, the sonogram they use does *not* vibrate."

"I learn something new every day."

She laughs again. "You're welcome."

I stare at the blue light, then turn it off. "Does watching your vagina turn you on?"

"No. But maybe for some people?" She shrugs, her cheeks pinker than before. "Men are very visual."

"I doubt men get turned on by looking at the inside of a vagina. Or at least it can't be a common kink. Otherwise every porn site would have it."

"You never know…"

"Well, it's certainly not one of mine."

She laughs, the sound breathless with arousal. "So what is?"

I look at her, my gaze connecting with her dark, glittering eyes. "Feeling your pussy and tasting it."

She makes a soft purring sound in her throat. "Traditional."

"I'm a traditionally fun guy."

Smiling, she stands and moves over, until she's standing over me with her hands on the armrests. Her eyes on mine, she leans forward until our faces almost touch. Her fresh apple scent is distracting. For some reason, it seems warmer and tastier, making my mouth water. I drop the white stick on the table and cradle her soft cheeks. Her mouth curves invitingly. I straighten and lean forward, and her lips part.

She tastes luxurious and lush, full of heat and open carnality. I've had women who weren't shy about what they wanted in bed. But Sierra goes beyond that. There is an inherent sweetness to her that can't be faked or manufactured. And that's what's driving me crazy, making me hunger for her endlessly.

Her delicate hands unbutton my shirt and slide across my bare chest, leaving hot trails of sensation. I tunnel my fingers into her warm, silky hair, holding her as I devour her mouth.

Her lips fused to mine, she shifts, straddling me. Through the layers of our clothes, I can feel her heat. Her eagerness stokes my desire until my skin feels tight and searing.

"God, you taste so good," she whispers against my mouth, then smiles dreamily like she's about to share a secret. "I was waiting for you to come home."

"Should've texted me."

"I didn't want to bother you when you were working. Also, I didn't expect to be this excited. It was all I could do to not jump your bones the second you walked in."

"Are you guys making aphrodisiacs now? Is this a test run?"

She laughs breathlessly. "No. We don't make things like that. But we *do* have to test our new products before we can market them." She licks her lips. "We usually hire a team of testers and send them products to try out and give us feedback. Couple of them couldn't do it this time, so I volunteered. We need at least fifteen evals."

My whole body heats until I feel like I'm about to combust. "What toys are we going to test?"

"The test is already in progress."

"It is?"

"I've had them on since three this afternoon. I didn't think they'd be this maddening. I tried to act cool and in control, but I don't know how well it worked."

That explains the state she was in when I arrived. The unusual flush. The bright, slightly glazed eyes. The pacing.

"You did seem a little distracted." I place my hand over the flesh between her thighs. It pulses wetly. "So you've been wearing a vibrator since three?"

"It's not really a vibrator. Well, sort of. It's this new sexy underwear you can wear, and it does this random vibrating. Not hard or frequent enough to make you come, but enough to keep you in a state of readiness the whole time. But that isn't all."

Jesus. "No?" I ask, my mouth dry.

"This bra isn't a regular bra, either. The cups have suction attachments inside. My nipples are hypersensitive right now."

My blood couldn't boil any hotter. "Who were you thinking about when you put them on?" My voice is gravelly, demanding, as I cup her ass and squeeze.

"You." Her answer comes out in a soft gasp.

She grinds her pelvis, rocking against my erection. Her eyes are impossibly dark—more black than purple—as she looks at me, continuing to move restlessly along my cock. "I was thinking about you even before I had these on."

"And you were going to have your meeting like this?" I ask. "Let some asshole see you in this state?" The very idea pisses me off.

She laughs softly. "Don't be jealous. The people I was going to meet with were women."

I push her shirt out of the way. She helps me, raising her arms, then tosses it so it lands over the hamster cage. "Don't need to treat Bullet and G-Spot to a show," she says.

There are two small clips in the corners of her lacy bra. She pinches them, and I undo the clasp in the back and let it drop. Her nipples look bigger and more pointed than normal, having been stimulated off and on all these hours. Now I want to give them the attention they deserve. I take one into my mouth, sucking hard.

She arches her back, screaming her pleasure. "Yes, *yes*! Oh my God. That feels *so* good."

Her hyper-responsiveness is driving me crazy. I pull the nipple deeper, trapping it between the roof of my mouth and tongue and hollowing my cheeks.

She shivers uncontrollably. Her body tightens like a coil under tension. Then abruptly she relaxes, melting against me like heated honey.

"That was fun." I grin, fascinated by how sensitive she is. She came the same way in New Orleans, but it took longer.

"Your sucking doesn't suck." She gives a satisfied sigh.

Amusement rumbles within me. "If you think *that* was good…"

I lift her and carry her to the couch, laying her down. She has on panties that look sort of like a string bikini. Instead of elastic, the "strings" are made with sparkling silver chains that look sexy as hell against her creamy skin. I undo the hooks and pull the bikini off. There are two vibrators inside, one against her clit and the other over the opening of her pussy. No, *three*. A third small bump is designed to stimulate her anally.

"Do you like anal sex?" I ask.

"No. Just light stimulation there," she says, her cheeks glowing. "Are you disappointed?"

I shake my head. "I appreciate your honesty. I don't want to do something you don't like."

Smiling, she takes the bikini, turns the vibrators off and drops it on the table, on top of the white vaginal-cam vibrator.

I touch her gently, running a finger along her cleft and then taking it to my lips. It tastes like her, with a hint of salt and sugar.

She pants, quivering with anticipation. I shower her with hundreds of little kisses along the insides of her thighs. She squirms, but I don't hurry, wanting to squeeze as much enjoyment from the act for her as possible.

When my mouth finally closes over her clit, she jerks like she's being electrocuted. I keep her down and use my lips and tongue to devour her, lapping up her honeyed juices. She comes again, hard, smooth thighs trembling against my face.

She lets out several shuddering breaths, then abruptly sits up, placing her hands on my shoulders and pushing me back until I'm lying on the couch and our positions are reversed.

She undoes my belt, the buttons on my slacks and the zipper and yanks everything down impatiently, still needy after two powerful orgasms. My cock springs out, and she looks at it like she's never seen anything more tempting.

"I'm pregnant, and we said we're clean, so I'm not gonna worry about a condom," she says, slightly breathless. "But if you have any objections, say so now."

I'm so hard it feels like I'm going to explode. "Whatever you want." If she told me to do a cartwheel so we could fuck, I'd do it.

She straddles me, then envelops me. My vision goes hazy as I let her set the pace. Her eyes are narrow and glittering as she looks down on me like some sort of sex deity.

Her breathing grows choppy as she rides me, driving me wild. I brace my feet flat against the cushions and move to give her the deeper, more powerful thrusts I know she loves.

"Oh my God, oh my God." She sobs out her rising pleasure, lets me know how much she loves what I'm doing to her, how I feel inside her.

The familiar tight, prickly sensation gathers at the base of my spine and starts to grow. Doing it without a condom, having direct contact with her bare flesh sliding up and down my shaft, almost makes it feel like a completely different act.

Her movements grow more frenzied, and both of us are panting. "Come for me," I say. I wrap my hand around the back of her neck and pull her down for a hot, unrestrained kiss. I cup her swinging breast with my free hand, brushing my thumb across the tight tip. She grinds against me, my cock buried deep inside her. Her body shakes wildly, and her screams of ecstasy are muffled against my mouth. I groan as a powerful orgasm tears through me, too.

I empty myself inside her and, in this moment, feel completely connected to her. I hold her tight and place tender kisses on her cheeks, forehead, eyes, the tip of her nose and the corners of her mouth. The shiny chains catch my eyes.

"So," I whisper into her ear, "how are you going to rate your new sex toys?"

"Oh my God. A+."

54

SIERRA

"So we finally get to meet the Midnight God, the man who inspired this entire line," Saori from marketing says as she takes a seat in one of our bigger meeting rooms.

Barbara nods. "Isn't it exciting?"

"Seeing His Hotness in the flesh is likely to inspire us to do better," Ellie says.

I laugh softly over their excitement.

Griffin's class is coming soon, and I pulled Ellie, Barbara, Saori and Jennifer from finance. Of course, I'm here too, to see what his students came up with.

Griffin asked me to keep my expectations low, saying that these are just kids who have no life experience. What they're going to say will probably be great on paper, but might not be practical.

But I don't care if the next forty minutes turn out to be a bust. I'll get to see him, which is what matters.

While waiting for them to show up, I finish filling out the report on the products I tested with Griffin. Now that I've recovered from my rosy postcoital haze, I can be more objective. They worked okay, but they could be better. The nipple cups were a bit hard to attach to the bra, and the bottom part didn't stay in place as well as it should have and needed some adjusting.

Our products should not only be easy to use, but comfortable.

It's hard to have fun if you're worried about something sliding the wrong way.

As I submit the eval, Heather brings the students into the room. Everyone is wearing a visitor's pass. Griffin brings up the rear, giving feedback to a girl who's showing him a few sheets of paper. He's easily the tallest in the group, and he draws my eye like the sun draws flowers.

He lifts his head and shoots me a faint smile that warms my heart. Then he goes back to answering the student.

"Ooh, *hot*," Saori says, leaning closer. "No wonder he's your muse."

I make a pleased sound in my throat. He's also the father of my babies, but I haven't made an official announcement about my pregnancy yet. I plan to do that in our company-wide newsletter that goes out bimonthly.

"Told you," Ellie says to Saori.

"I want to touch him. It'll make me work better," Jennifer says teasingly.

I arch an eyebrow in her direction. "No touching, girl. Viewing pleasure only."

"Will was crushed to learn that the Midnight God is a real person. He was telling everyone that the dildo was based on *his* dick," Barbara says, shaking her head. Will is a junior accountant and has more neck than a giraffe.

"I wonder what's in that boy's head," Saori says.

"A flower field," Ellie says. "Full of red poppies."

I laugh softly. That's Ellie-speak for crazy.

Griffin takes the empty seat next to me. I resist the urge to run my hand along his arm underneath the suit and link hands. We're both professionals here.

But wait until I get him home again. With a soft sigh, I turn my attention to the students starting their presentation.

Like he said, these kids don't have any experience, so their insight is limited. However, the mathematical analysis is quite good. Even Jennifer and Barbara don't nitpick, although Griffin presses his mouth together like he wants to say something, but is doing his best to control himself.

Since I'm feeling generous and the students seem to have put in a good deal of effort, I decide to give every group an A. I have no idea what the others are handing out, but I figure a good grade can help make up for the fact that the students had to do a case that wasn't on their syllabus, thanks to my meddling stepmom.

Jennifer and Saori whisper to each other. Some of the kids sitting behind them lean forward, probably hoping to catch a hint about their grades.

When the last presentation is over, the kids get up and murmur to each other, throwing questioning glances at Griffin. Bet they're dying to know how they did. Although our feedback matters, he's the one ultimately deciding what each group gets.

I lean toward Griffin and whisper, "Smile. Make them think that you are going to give them a good grade."

"Why?"

"Look at them. They're nervous and need reassurance that they kicked butt."

"Do *you* think they kicked butt?" Griffin sounds incredulous.

"I'm handing out nothing but A's."

"Hmm. You're overly charitable."

"I always look at the bright side. Your students are smart. Besides, I gave them a little extra because I'm happy to see you." I grin.

"Good point, but I'm a very impartial professor." He speaks seriously, but a corner of his mouth is quirking.

"Then you can give them impartial A's."

"We'll see." He leans closer. "It's been a few days. Do you need to do more beta testing?"

I put a hand over my mouth. "No. But we can have some non-test fun after work." I wink, placing a hand on his chest. "I'll see you soon."

55

SIERRA

On Friday, Griffin and I head to the faculty social at Charles Phillips's home. It's a sprawling three-story Victorian house with a huge yard. White bay windows line up perfectly along pearl-gray walls. The steep roof slopes down sharply, and there's a brick chimney on top.

I stare at it as Griffin looks for place to park. "I didn't know there were still homes with so much yard."

It's a good thing we came together, because the street is strewn with cars. I've been to several faculty socials with Todd. I hope the economics department is more interesting—and sober—than the English department. Most of the English professors at Wollstonecraft loosen up after about five to six drinks. But by then, they've imbibed enough to behave obnoxiously.

After circling around a bit, we find a spot one street over. As we climb out, Griffin's phone pings.

"Is that Charles, wondering where we are?" We're a little late.

"No. It's from Grant. Apparently, Emmett made up with his girlfriend. Huxley's sure they're going to get married, and Seb says he better buy the rings from him or else." Griffin's mouth curves into a faint smile as we start to walk toward Charles's home.

"Was Emmett at the dinner?" I think I heard somebody mention the name at Manny's Tacos, but I'm not sure if he was there or not.

"No. He's the only one you haven't met yet. He wasn't in a good place mentally after he broke up with his girlfriend."

"It must've been terrible for him to not want to hang out with any of you."

"She didn't just break up with him, but she quit working for him and was moving to Virginia to work for a direct competitor who's been poaching his staff."

"That's a betrayal," I say, feeling sympathy for Emmett. I'm sure his girlfriend has her side of the story, too, but that doesn't mean things were easy for him.

"You can't backstab someone and expect forgiveness. She probably groveled. Emmett's too proud to grovel for anybody."

"Am I going to meet him?" I ask, excited about another uncle for our babies.

"Eventually, yes. He's a workaholic. But you'll love him. He's loyal. Always has your back."

We walk up the stone-lined path and into the brightly lit home. The soft strains of a piano float in the air, elegant and classy. The interior is mostly natural wood and high-end wallpaper with abstract patterns that make the home appear more contemporary. A huge glass vase stuffed with long-stemmed red roses sits on a stand in the center of the foyer.

The place is fairly packed with professors and their significant others. Given my experience with Todd's socials, I figured I'd be able to tell which was the faculty member and which was the spouse/partner, based on the level of arrogance and how well they could deploy famous quotes as they talked with each other. But that's not the case at all. I'm pleasantly shocked to realize that the economics faculty seem a lot more human than the professors of English at Wollstonecraft.

In the dining room is a huge spread of garlic bread, potato salad, pasta, pizza, cheese and crackers. Several bottles of wine and hard liquor sit next to the food. I bypass the alcohol and grab a cup of orange juice.

Griffin takes a small glass of white wine and starts introducing me to his colleagues. I shake their hands, memorizing names and specialties. It's the easiest way to make people feel heard and appreciated.

When I meet Lori, I'm fascinated. She researches social media and how it influences people's economic behavior.

"It's a form of behavioral economics," she says. "Are you familiar with it?"

"I've read a bit about it in some business articles. So how do you measure the impact social media has?" I ask.

"Honestly, it isn't easy. But right now, my partner and I are looking at what's trended in the last five years and how that impacted people's behavioral patterns by looking at those who most likely saw the trending topics. Thank God for hashtags!" She sighs exaggeratedly.

I laugh.

"And to see if we can catch more recent examples, I have several social media apps on my phone and have notifications set up so that I get an alert if anything's getting lots of views and shares."

It's a good explanation. Simple without getting too technical like some of the other professors.

When somebody else snags Lori's attention, Griffin whispers into my ear, "She lives for gossip, so this is exactly her kind of research."

I laugh. "Somebody's got to do it. Social media is becoming an important part of everyone's life. You can sell anything there, including yourself."

"Do you use it to promote your products?"

"Yes, but...it's complicated. A lot of platforms don't like to see adult products."

"Prudes," he mutters.

"Oh my God. So unfair. But we have other ways."

A man who looks like he has a bowling ball for a head walks over. He has a deliberate, trundling way of walking that reminds me of my hamsters.

"Hello, Griffin," he says, placing a fat-fingered hand on Griffin's shoulder. "So happy to see you here. And I presume this vision of beauty is Sierra Fullilove?"

I smile warmly. "Yes, I am."

"*Enchanté.* I'm Charles Phillips. Head of the economics department."

He extends a hand. I take it and give it a couple of good pumps. His palm is surprisingly dry and cool.

"I'm so glad we finally get to meet. Your grandmother and I were fairly close."

"Yes, she said nice things about the department." It's more to be polite than anything. Grandma rarely spoke about any of the departments at the college.

Somebody comes over and taps Griffin on the shoulder. They whisper something, and Griffin looks at me. "Mind if I speak to him for a second?" His eyes say I can always refuse.

"Go ahead." He doesn't have to stick by my side the entire time we're here. I want him to be able to socialize with his colleagues. And it isn't like I don't know how to handle somebody who wants money.

"Griffin's a remarkable talent. Brilliant mind," Charles says.

"He really is," I say, pleased that the head of his department recognizes that.

"Did you know that he won the John Bates Clark Medal?"

"No. What's that?"

"It's an annual award given to a particularly bright young American economist. Many of the recipients have gone on to win the Nobel Prize."

I grin, happy for Griffin. He made it sound like he wasn't too crazy about his work, but he has to love it if he's that good at it. How else would he muster the enthusiasm and perseverance to do the work necessary to win an award as prestigious as the one Charles mentioned? Give Griffin a few decades, and he'll win a Nobel, too. I just know it.

It's sort of cute how he won't admit how he feels out loud, especially when it's something positive or affectionate. I make a mental note to tease him later.

"I'm thrilled to hear that," I say.

Charles looks at me, his chest puffed out like a seal who's done a particularly difficult trick. "Yes, and his research could use—"

"Oh my *God*!" Lori's voice cuts through the crowd. She looks at her phone and then at Griffin. "You're the secret love child between Ted Lasker and Rachel Griffin?"

What?

Stunned, I stare at Griffin wordlessly. Ted Lasker, the movie producer? Is *that* why Griffin was at that party? He's standing completely still. His face is bloodless, his eyes unnaturally dark as he stares at Lori. Everyone else is gaping like he's a Martian who just landed in the middle of the party.

"What are you talking about?" Griffin finally says, his voice terrible.

Lori pulls her shoulders together like a kid who's unsure if she's in trouble. "There's this article that just went viral. It says that you're the secret love child of Ted Lasker and Rachel Griffin." She holds her phone up in defense. *Don't get mad at me, it wasn't me.*

"Rachel Griffin? That name sounds familiar," one of the younger professors says.

"She's a supermodel from, like, twenty, twenty-five years ago? She was the hottest thing on the market back then. And she's *still* hot. She does photoshoots and stuff like that these days," a middle-aged female professor answers, staring at Griffin like he's a stranger.

"Hey, so you're named after your mom," somebody to my left exclaims. "Did not know that."

"And you inspire *sex toys*?" Lori says.

I flinch at how loud she is, but the stronger feeling is shock. *How did she find out?* I never made that public, and the people at Silicone Dream wouldn't have spread it around. We like to have fun, but part of fun is being discreet.

"*What?*" Griffin says.

"There's a comment in the article that your girlfriend is creating an entire line of sex toys in your name. Well, the nickname that she gave you."

Griffin looks at me, but I shake my head. *I didn't...*

"Who gave them the quote?" Griffin demands.

"I think it was a student in your class."

Oh my God. I cover my cheeks with my hands, which are now clammy with horror. One of the kids must've heard whispers about the Midnight God when they came to Silicone Dream for their case presentation. I remember how they were trying to eavesdrop on what Saori and the others were saying.

"What nickname?" Griffin demands. But he still isn't looking at Lori. He's staring at me. If looks could kill, I'd be burning in hell already.

"The Midnight God," Lori says at the same time I whisper it to myself.

What little light remains in his eyes dims. From the awful expression on his face, I might as well have disemboweled him.

56

GRIFFIN

The whispers and judgmental stares from everyone burn like acid. Furious humiliation makes my neck tighten.

What the fuck is this thing about my parents? And the sex toys? Sierra never said anything about making sex toys about me.

But I know she did exactly that. I saw her mouth move, her face white.

Everyone at Silicone Dream knew. So did my students. The only person who didn't know was me. The fact feels like a blade between my ribs.

"It appears Griffin's talents aren't limited to economics," Charles jokes lamely.

A few people laugh, but it's anything but funny. It's my fucking *career*, the respect I've labored so hard to earn. All the work I've done to stay anonymous and distance myself from everything my parents have done is gone. Lurid speculation burns bright in so many of my colleagues' gazes. Whereas before there was nothing but polite respect.

Sierra gives me a nervous smile. It feels like a slap.

A scream burns in my throat. *How could she do this to me?*

My phone pings. I take it out with shaking hands to check the message, praying that the site has retracted the article.

–Dad: Sex toys, eh? I'm so proud of you!

Fury explodes. My vision goes red and the top of my skull aches, as though it's about to blow into the sky.

Dad—either directly or through Joey—has never told me he was proud of me. Never. Not over my academic accomplishments. Not over the polo matches I've won. Not over the amateur kickboxing championship belts I've collected.

But I should've known. Inspiring a line of sex toys is exactly the sort of crass undertaking he'd admire. He's never seen anything disreputable he didn't love.

More texts arrive in rapid sequence.

–Dad: That's MY penis you've inherited, son.

–Dad: Can't wait to rub it in Josh Singer and Salazar Pryce's faces that my son inspired a line of sex toys!

–Dad: Now go use that inspirational penis I gave you and make me a grandbaby. I've got some great lines I'm gonna use when I see Josh Singer with your kid.

I put the phone away. Maybe more texts come, or maybe not. I have more important things to worry about.

Perhaps leaving right now isn't the best move, but if I stay here, there's really no guarantee that I won't say or do something that I'll permanently regret.

"Thank you for the party, Charles. I'm afraid I'll have to leave now. Not feeling well all of a sudden." The social proprieties must be observed.

I walk toward the door. Sierra's shoes clack rapidly against the tiles behind me.

Normally I'd slow down or wait for her. I do neither. I can't decide if I'm relieved or annoyed that she's following me. I can't just ditch her here at Charles's home, but I definitely do *not* want to see her right now.

I march to the street where I left my Prius and get behind the wheel. She hurries into the passenger seat.

I start the car and drive. Silence sits over us like a smothering blanket. I clench and unclench my hands around the steering wheel. It feels difficult to breathe through the crackling tension.

"It'll blow over by tomorrow," Sierra says tentatively. "Monday at the latest."

"Is that what you think?" I snap.

"Well... I hope so." Her voice is small.

"It's easy for you to say because it isn't about you. You aren't the one people are whispering about. You aren't the one whose career and respectability just got wiped out."

She bites her lip.

Her reaction only makes me madder. "Or maybe you think this is just amazing. I saw you smiling. You should've just gone ahead and laughed with them too." Just like my dad, who's so fucking *happy* right now. *Proud,* he said. I want to kick something. Hard.

"I wasn't doing it because I wanted to mock you. It was either smile or cry, and I thought you'd hate it if I cried."

She's right. I would've been even madder if she cried like this entire clusterfuck was about her.

"Why didn't you tell me about the sex toys?"

"Because it never came up...? I didn't know you were the guy from New Orleans until, like, two weeks ago, and I just didn't think about it. I'm sorry. I didn't think you'd find out like this or that it would be such an issue."

Fuck. I grit my teeth so I don't start screaming. That'd make her burst into tears for sure. "I have to face those people on Monday. And every day after until Friday. And then the next week, and the week after that. And when they see me, all they'll be thinking about is the fact that *I'm a sex toy.*"

"You are not a sex toy. You just inspire some of the products that we're making. Two *totally* different things! If they treat you differently because of this, you can find a position elsewhere. You are a phenomenal economist. You won that special John Bates Clark Medal. You're going to be in high demand."

Is she listening to herself? Can't she hear how selfish and ridiculous her suggestion is? "I don't want to go elsewhere. I like being here, near my brothers. Why should I have to give up something I like? Damn it, every time I want something and think I have it, it just gets ripped away."

"If you want something, fight for it. If people treat you badly because of this, you have to fight that to hold on to what you have. Don't let anything or anyone take away what you want. If you do, you aren't fighting hard enough."

It's all I can do to hold on to the steering wheel so I don't strangle her. So easy for her to say the words. But she doesn't understand what it's like. I've spent so much of my life avoiding the spotlight—in spite of what my parents are, in spite of my environment.

"Like how you fought for the family of two you created by marrying that loser Todd?" I say, wanting to hurt her as much as she's hurt me. "You wanted it one day, and then poof, you just gave up on it the next?"

She looks at me like I backhanded her. And I hate it that the pain on her face is making me feel like a villain.

I haven't done anything wrong.

"I let him go because I decided I didn't want him anymore," she says, her voice cracking a little. "Just because I wanted him once doesn't mean I want him forever, not when I realized he wasn't the man I thought he was. If I still wanted him, I *wouldn't* have given up. Because if I want something, I go for it. Nothing's going to stop me, and I cut out people who get in the way."

"Good for you. But I'm not you." I stop the car in front of her house. "Get out."

Her purple eyes are dark, wounded and pleading. "Don't do anything rash while you're angry."

"I'm *not* angry." A word as pedestrian as "angry" isn't enough to describe what I'm feeling. "What I am is serious. Get out, Sierra, before I say something I shouldn't."

She climbs out and shuts the door. I speed away. But in the rearview mirror I can see her standing there, watching.

57

SIERRA

I stand in the driveway until Griffin's car is completely out of view. How can this happen? And why did he act like I'm the enemy?

Okay, I screwed up by not telling him about the Midnight God thing. And I probably should've asked my employees to watch it around the students. But is it such a terrible crime? Are his coworkers going to look down on him for it for the rest of his life?

I drag my feet inside my home. Loneliness weighs my shoulders down. As I trudge up the stairs and walk into my bedroom, the sight of his pillow on my bed is like a knife in the heart. The skin around my eyes heats with tears, and I quickly look away and go to the bathroom to wash my face. But on the vanity sit his razor and aftershave.

Letting out a shaky breath, I brace my hands against the cool edge of the vanity. The mirror shows me a reflection of his body wash in the shower stall. Everywhere I turn, something of his pops up, reminding me of him.

Maybe I should've been more supportive or apologetic, although I don't know what I could've done when he was so angry with me. And what he said about me and Todd was hitting below the belt. I didn't expect that, and it hurts.

After splashing my face with cold water, I dry myself off and slowly walk back to the bed. The mattress dips under my weight as I sit on the edge. Time passes, and after while I realize Todd hasn't come by to bother me here, not since he lost that fight with the tree and Griffin moved in. If there hadn't been that emotional opening during the trip to Tokyo—and the triplets—Griffin would've "broken up" with me by now and gone back to his place. It was supposed to be a temporary arrangement, after all.

So it's okay that we've broken up, even if it's a lot more emotional and painful than just saying *thanks and goodbye*. Being alone always sucks.

Something flutters in my belly, and I place a hand over it. I'm not really alone. I have three small lives. But I've deprived them of their father...haven't I? I'm not sure if Griffin will want anything to do with me or the triplets now.

Feeling like an old dishrag, tired and wrung out, I slowly sink back on the bed and cover my eyes. Then I tell myself that the hot liquid making my fingers wet isn't tears, even though my heart says I'm a terrible liar.

58

GRIFFIN

–Noah: You okay?
 –Emmett: We need proof of life or we're calling 911.
 –Sebastian: I'm worried about you.
 –Huxley: It's going to blow over. Trust me on this.
 –Nicholas: Tell me you're okay.
 –Grant: Don't make me go over there.

When I open my eyes the next morning, I see hundreds of texts from my brothers. I only read the last six or seven and snort at Grant's threat.

 –Me: I'm not dead. I was sleeping.

There. That should shut them up.

 –Emmett: Do you need anything?
 –Grant: Are you hung over?
 –Me: No. I didn't drink.

The devastation I felt last night wasn't something alcohol could soothe. The problem is that I don't know what could.

 –Nicholas: Good for you. Excessive drinking solves nothing.
 –Me: I'm fine. Don't worry about it.

It's a lie. I feel anything but fine. As a matter of fact, I feel worse than I did yesterday. My career is fucked, all the respect I worked for lost. And the girl I thought was special couldn't keep her mouth shut. The fact that I'm her sex toy muse is the final nail in the coffin.

Charles sent a couple of texts, but I don't look at them. They aren't going to be anything positive, and my mood is gloomy enough.

My phone rings. I stare at the ceiling. If it's a gossip-seeking reporter, I'm going to pitch the phone against the wall.

The screen reads *Mom*. What does *she* want?

The phone quits ringing. Maybe she butt-dialed.

The phone starts ringing again. I pick it up.

"Haven't you done enough?" I demand rudely. I'm beyond caring.

"What do you mean?"

"That damn article. All my adult life, I've only asked for one thing: keep me out of your melodrama. I told you I don't want to be mentioned in any of the articles about you. I begged you to make sure our relationship didn't become public. But no, you couldn't do that."

"Griffin, I did my best," she says. "Nobody knew who you were for thirty-four years. It's not my fault the paparazzi are persistent." She pauses for a moment. "You knew you couldn't hide forever. Eventually they were going to find out you're Ted's and my son." Another pause. "Although the love-child angle *is* ridiculous. There was never any love between me and your father."

"Who cares about your relationship with him?"

"I do!"

"Well, I don't!" The ache in my head throbs. "Why are you even calling? To defend yourself?"

"Yes. I don't want you to blame *me*."

"Why don't you think about someone else for once? That might give you some insight into your personality and relationships."

She makes an affronted noise.

"You and Dad always embarrass me, always humiliate me, and always take away what I want the most."

"Don't be so melodramatic! What did this article cost you? Nothing! So what if people know who your parents are? They're probably dying of envy that you have a celebrity mother and father."

"Nobody gives a damn that you're famous!"

"Nonsense! We didn't get famous for being ax murderers!"

I fight desperately for control. She isn't listening to anything I'm saying. "I want a *normal life*. I want people to respect me for my own accomplishments, not thinking about you or Dad when they're dealing with me. I don't want anyone to wonder if there was any sort of special favor bought and sold. I had to work extra hard to have what little satisfaction I can take from my career because of you and Dad."

"We didn't do anything!"

"Are you serious? You always took away what I wanted. Always!"

"Like what?" she says.

"My reputation!" I grind my teeth. "Churchill!"

"Who?"

"My dog!"

"Oh."

"And Taekwondo lessons. Judo lessons. Horseback riding. That cat you took back to the pet store after only two days! Should I go on? There's a *lot* on my list."

"Why are you angry? You got to do a lot of them anyway, including the stupid kickboxing!"

"Because Dad paid for them to spite you!"

"So are you saying you like him better than me?" she demands, as usual making everything about her.

"Oh, for God's sake, *no*! He always took something in return. Respectability and normalcy were his price. He never did anything just because it made me happy. Maybe that's why I'm such a good economist. I learned at a very young age that there's no free lunch!"

"Now who's being dramatic?"

I grind my teeth. Her ability to empathize is nil. I'm wasting my breath by trying to make her see things from my point of view. "If you ever have your peers lose all respect for you, perhaps you'll understand how this feels. Goodbye, Mother."

I hang up and turn off the phone. The vein in my forehead throbs so hard that I feel dizzy. I'm going to have a damn stroke.

Actually, that sounds like a fantastic end to my life.

59

SIERRA

Monday morning, I get up at six, as usual. It is amazing how my body still functions on autopilot, even though my heart has been ripped to shreds.

I have no appetite, but force myself to nibble on half a bagel. I'm eating for four, even if the other three are no bigger than olives.

Griffin hasn't called or texted. Charles hasn't contacted me either. He's probably assumed that his dream of getting me to fund whatever it was that he wanted me to fund is dead and is trying to console himself.

I walk out to the driveway to my Ferrari. It looks forlorn sitting there without Griffin's blue Prius. We were only together for a little over a month, but now it feels like I'm missing a critical part of myself.

As I start the engine, the stereo blasts "Can't Stop Me Now" by Queen. Even this extra-upbeat tune fails to lift my mood. I always assumed people who were blue felt that way because they had a lot of negative thoughts they couldn't block. But I realize you don't need negative thoughts—negative circumstances can be enough to shove you deep into despair. Like finding yourself alone after having known the heaven of being with someone you thought understood and loved you.

After a few deep breaths to re-center myself, I drive to work.

Even if my personal life is falling apart, I still have to do my job. Our customers expect us to deliver, and my employees depend on me.

When I reach the parking lot, I cut the engine and slowly climb out. The SoCal sun feels extra vicious, the air less refreshing.

Somebody scuttles out between two of the cars. My heart jumps with shock and fear until I realize it's Todd.

I should be outraged. Angry enough to start yelling. But right now, I'm just too blue to care. The only reaction I can muster is a vague curiosity about why he's scurrying around like a rat so early in the morning. He hates getting up before seven.

Dan runs out of the lobby toward us. He knows Todd shouldn't be on company grounds. Not that I'll hold this breach against him. Silicone Dream doesn't have a wall around its headquarters, and he can't cover every entry point.

"Get away from her," Dan roars, closing the distance.

"I need to talk to her!" Todd shouts back, enunciating every word properly.

At least he isn't drunk. A huge improvement over the last two times. I try to walk around my ex-husband without making eye contact. "I have nothing to say to you."

"Wait. Please," he says, coming closer. His soap and cologne waft toward me, and my stomach roils.

Covering my nose, I step back.

Todd doesn't seem to notice my reaction. He steps closer. "Look, it's about my job."

I circle him so that I'm upwind. My stomach settles, but only a little. "What job?"

"My *job*. At Wollstonecraft. The college isn't renewing my contract." He speaks as though it's of critical importance.

Dan arrives, putting himself between me and Todd like he's going to physically remove the other man. I put a hand on his shoulder, realizing this contract thing might be a solution to one of my problems. "Let him talk for a moment."

Todd gives Dan a smug look before turning back to me. "You have some pull with the administration. Can you ask them to reconsider? I really don't want to leave Lovedale."

"Why would you have to leave?"

"I can't find another position locally. And I can't work on us if I have to go to Boston."

First good piece of news I've heard since Friday evening. "Boston, Massachusetts?" I say, just to be sure. There could be a less famous Boston somewhere.

"Yes." He frowns for a second. "Or possibly Florida. Those are the only two places where I can find openings."

"I see. Well, good luck." I smile.

"What?"

"I would like nothing more than for you to go someplace as far away from me as possible."

"Sierra!" He puts both his hands over his chest, a picture of beseeching sincerity. "I'm telling you that I am going to work on being the kind of husband you deserve."

"If you'd told me this a year ago, we could've worked something out." I exhale impatiently. "You said you were going to be the husband I deserved when you proposed. You said you would never let me feel lonely or alone, and that you'd always be on my side."

"Yes. I said that. And I know there were missteps, but I've been working on it." His wide eyes say, *Can't you see that?*

"No. You haven't. That's why I divorced you."

"You gotta give me a break! I'm a beginner at this. I need more time to master those skills."

"I don't think so. You were very good at making me feel valued and loved when we were dating. But after we got married, you changed."

"No, I didn't! That damn lawyer is gaslighting you. I love you, Sierra."

"Then what are you willing to do to win me back?"

He stares like I just asked him to recite the entirety of *War and Peace*. "Do you want me to take you to Japan?"

I shake my head. He hasn't changed, not even a little. "That's what I thought. Goodbye, Todd. If you ever show up here—or at my house—again, you'll be arrested for trespassing. I'm also going to have my lawyer get a restraining order. Instead of harassing me, you should focus on getting that job in Boston."

"Linda won't like this," he says.

"Linda can go hang herself for all I care. She's not my mother. And she's not my family."

"But—"

"If she thought she could manipulate me through you, she

should've at least coached you to be nicer." There's no other reason for her to want us to be together. She wouldn't have bothered if Grandma hadn't left me all the money.

He flinches. "I don't know what you mean."

"Then you're an idiot." I turn to Dan. "Let's go."

Dan puts a protective hand at my elbow and we start walking toward the entrance to Silicone Dream. Todd takes a step after us.

"You go on," Dan says to me, then turns to Todd. "Go ahead, asshole. Give me a reason." He flexes his hands and takes a step toward Todd. "Please."

I walk the rest of the way to the building unmolested and enter the lobby. Our huge purple clock is right there in front of me. This is where I met Griffin for the third time. He looked so pissed off and determined never to see me again.

I don't know if that was a sign that we weren't going to work out. Even though the universe kept throwing us together, we ended up not connecting in the end.

I shake off the gloomy thought. So what if it didn't work out perfectly? I'm not going to regret our time together. He made me feel like the center of his world, and I loved everything we did together, including the babies we've created.

It's good that I found out he loves his career and anonymity more than me before I made a bigger emotional investment. But that doesn't lessen the pain from the fact that I'm always going to be number two with the man I love.

60

GRIFFIN

I time my arrival on campus so I have exactly five minutes to reach my morning class from the faculty parking lot. I don't want to run into any other professors or Charles. My phone is still off. I don't want to talk to anybody.

The lot is empty. *So far, so good,* I think as I walk past the threshold and into Fullilove Hall.

The name reminds me of Sierra. How hurt she looked on Friday. And the triplets.

I still can't decide what to think about her. I can't believe she told people that I was the Midnight God. Actually, that part was fine. But telling people her sex toys are based on me was *not* cool. She should've at least asked first.

Of course, my answer would've been an instant no.

I wonder if she's having morning sickness. Or any weird cravings. She didn't indicate anything unusual earlier, but don't hormones take a while to kick in?

Damn it. Stop thinking about her and the babies.

Mulling all this over isn't going to solve any of my problems. Right now, what I should be focusing on is walking four doors down to the right and delivering the best damn lecture possible on econometrics.

Lori appears, coming out of a closer door. I should've known the morning was going too well.

My fingers itch with the desire to strangle her. She might as well have stripped me naked and paraded me around for fun at the party.

I restrain myself. No need to get arrested for assault. *That* would hit the Hollywood gossip sites faster than a finger snap, adding even more fuel to the fire.

"Good morning," she says tentatively.

She isn't blushing, giggling or pointing. Either people find my parents and their scandals disgusting, or they find them ridiculous. In the latter case, they usually giggle and point and whisper—infuriating reactions.

I'm not an extension of my parents. And I'm not some sex toy inspiration for people to speculate over. I've done things that deserve respect. I've worked all my life to be my own person and be judged for what *I* do.

"My class is waiting," I manage between clenched teeth.

She flinches. "Oh. Sorry. Uh, have a good day."

It's all I can do not to demand how I'm supposed to have a "good day." But ignoring her is better than blowing a vein. She's not worth it.

I resume my march to the classroom. Benson comes out of the huge lecture hall where he teaches Introduction to Microeconomics, jerks to a stop and goes back into the hall.

Avoiding me like I'm a plague carrier. The admiration he used to have for my academic achievements is gone. Poof. And all because of a stupid article and a careless comment.

I stride into my class and take my place behind the lectern then scan all twenty-eight of my students seated in the room. Which one of them told the world about the sex toys?

Naturally, whoever it was did it anonymously. People are extra brave when they're hiding behind a fake online identity. I wonder how many of these kids have the guts to tell me to my face what they really think. I might just give them an A for having the balls.

A hand goes up, and I cock an eyebrow. This kid never asks anything in class. "Yes, Mr. Farmer?"

"Sir, is it true that you inspired a line of sex toys?"

There are murmurs around the room. I clench my hands on the lectern. "Do you really want to know the answer?"

He swallows nervously. "I just want confirmation. I heard some people talk about it, but I thought they were making stuff up."

What should I say? And should I give him an A for what little courage he has?

Nah. I don't like his face. Or his attitude. Or his needless curiosity. "You'll have to ask the CEO of the company. I wouldn't presume to know what her company was thinking." I sweep my gaze across the class again. "Any other questions?"

"Have you met a lot of movie stars?" a bubbly blonde says. Joyce McIntyre. One of the first to barge into my office, hoping to sleep with me.

"Yes. I grew up around beautiful people," I say.

"Do you have—"

"Open your textbooks to chapter thirteen."

"Can we talk about the article? I don't think I can concentrate on econometrics until I get my curiosity satisfied," Tanner says with a smarmy grin.

I pin him with my death glare. "If you feel that going over chapter thirteen isn't necessary, you all must already be well prepared. In which case we can have a pop quiz on the topic..."

I let the words hang in the air, and everybody pulls out their textbooks.

"That's what I thought."

Grinding my teeth, I start my lecture, going over the material on autopilot. It isn't anything that requires much focus, and none of my students ask any questions.

As I exit the classroom, I bump into the one person I especially *didn't* want to run into today. "Hello, Charles."

"Griffin." He smiles politely.

"What are you doing down here? You don't have any classes this semester."

He clears his throat. "I tried to reach you, but there seemed to be an issue." He's back to being ponderous. Perhaps he's worried about the chances of getting money for the research center.

"My phone broke," I say.

"I see. You should get that replaced."

I give him an empty smile. When is he going to get to the point?

"I just wanted to make sure if things are okay with you and

Sierra. I apologize for the awkwardness on Friday. Lori and others didn't behave as, ah, maturely as one would hope."

That's rich coming from someone who joked about my talents lying beyond economics. "If you want to know how Sierra's doing, you should contact her yourself." He doesn't have the nerve to bring up the party with her. Otherwise, he wouldn't have been waiting for me outside of class.

"Yes, I would, of course, but she seems to be quite a busy woman."

And I'm not busy? I catch the question just before it rolls off my tongue.

"I was wondering if perhaps—"

"I can't convey any messages to her."

His face scrunches. "Does she want me to come in person to apologize?"

He must be really desperate for funding to go this far. "I really have no idea. We broke up."

"Oh." Charles covers his mouth with one hand, his eyes defocusing as he thinks and readjusts his plan.

"If you don't mind, I have to get going. There is some research I need to wrap up."

"Of course." He waves me away absently.

I go to my office and take out a marker and a sheet of printer paper. I write out the following: NO OFFICE HOURS TODAY. EMAIL IF URGENT.

I tape the notice on my door and leave.

Two professors change direction so that our paths don't intersect. One slips into her office just before I pass by.

Great. Just freakin' great! I've turn into a complete pariah.

If this problem could be fixed by moving to a different institution, I would. But it won't be fixed no matter where I go. The damn article is probably still trending, being seen by everyone.

Even if the hiring committees at other universities missed it now, they wouldn't miss it when they Googled my name before offering a position. *So I'm fucked.*

I go home to my three-level house with its huge yard and tall picket fence for privacy in the back. As I step inside, I don't feel any better.

The house echoes with emptiness and doesn't smell like apple.

61

SIERRA

There are two brisk knocks on my office door. I look up from my laptop.

Ellie comes in. "Hey, got a present for you. From my mom." She hands me a small package.

"Thanks." I manage a smile that I hope looks bright enough and rip it open. It's a gorgeous pink candle, scented like peach. Yummy. I place it on my desk, making a mental note to send Ellie's mom a thank-you email. "How was your trip back to St. Louis?"

"Great." She peers at me. "Is everything okay?"

Guess I suck at fake smiling. I deflate. "Griffin and I broke up. I didn't want to tell you over the weekend when you were spending quality time with your folks."

"What?" Ellie takes the chair in front of my desk and drags it over so she can sit next to me. "What are you talking about? You and Griffin are like soul mates. He makes you feel special and treats you like a princess. You're having babies together!" Something shifts in her expression. "Wait... He isn't getting cold feet over the triplets, is he?"

If I tell her yes, she'll drive over to Wollstonecraft College and run him over. Or at least beat him with one of our failed dildo molds.

I tell her everything that happened at the faculty party, including the article and the comment from one of his students. And how that upset him, making him feel like the respectability and credibility he's worked so hard for have been destroyed. "He was absolutely *furious* on Friday."

"How did his students find out?" Ellie asks, looking gobsmacked. "It isn't something we advertised."

"I think they overheard somebody talking about it when they came over for the case presentation and then couldn't keep their mouths shut."

"Wait, isn't it covered under our NDA?"

I shrug. "It's not a trade secret. It's a fair topic for them to gossip about. Remember how it was when we were in college?" I shake my head, letting out a sigh. "Besides, the damage is done."

"But why is Griffin upset with *you* for that? It's not like you took out a billboard to advertise it."

"Because I didn't tell him about the Midnight God line being named after him. I probably should've said something about it in Tokyo. Then we could've avoided all this." I glance up and see nothing but a normal ceiling, even though it feels like there are storm clouds gathering over me.

Ellie looks skeptical. "What was he going to do if you had told him? Tell you not to make those toys?"

"I don't know. But he felt backstabbed. Some of the other professors there sort of looked at him weird, even got a little bit judgmental, and I think that made things much worse. I'm sure he felt humiliated." I feel awful about that, especially knowing how hard he must've worked for his career. The award Charles mentioned told me everything I needed to know about Griffin's dedication. If somebody did something to damage Silicone Dream, I'd be furious too.

"He's being kind of a prude about the whole thing, don't you think?"

I shrug. "Maybe academia is prudish."

"Yeah, but it isn't like you told people that he went to an orgy or you released sex tapes of the two of you." Ellie bristles. "You know what? Forget him. You don't need a judgmental asshole in your life." Her gaze drops to my belly. "As for your babies, they have you and me! Screw men! I hate seeing you down like this."

I nod slowly. "Yeah. I can raise them on my own." I've already considered the possibility, so it doesn't feel particularly abrupt, although I'm sad that they may not know what it's like to be loved by their father. I sigh. "Every time I go home, I'm reminded of him."

"How so?"

"He didn't take his things with him."

"Then pack them up and set them on fire!" Ellie smiles devilishly. "It's sooooo satisfying."

She'd know. She did that to an ex-boyfriend when we were in college. He deserved it, too. The bastard cheated on her.

"I don't think I can quite do that, especially when I didn't do it to Todd."

"But that fucker took his stuff with him."

"Still." What I feel for Griffin doesn't compare. I still love him.

Ellie sighs. "You're such a good girl. Fine. Pack it all in a box and take it to his place."

I blink slowly as a realization strikes me. "I don't know where he lives."

"You don't— You've never been to his place?"

"He moved in before I had a chance to see his house."

"Fine. Take the box to Wollstonecraft. Throw it in his face and let him know he'll regret this moment for the rest of his life."

I laugh listlessly. It's what she's expecting, and I don't want her to feel like she's failed to cheer me up. But the sense of amusement I got when she told me the same thing about Todd doesn't come. All I'm feeling is glumness—and the fact I miss Griffin so much already. "I don't think it's going to be like that."

"You never know. He might get on his knees and beg you to stay, now that he's had the weekend to think things over. You can superiorly kick his pleading hands aside and strut away, leaving him to grovel in the dust."

This time I smile for real because her suggestion just gave me a *great* idea.

Griffin has probably cooled off by now. I can use the pretext of returning his things to start a conversation, this time calmer and more levelheaded.

Surely he can see that I only want the best for him—and us— and I would never do anything to diminish his genius. Although I love the name the Midnight God for our product line, it'll be easy enough to come up with something else.

Then this whole thing can be chalked up as one of those crises that we'll laugh about five years from now.

Optimism surging, I hug Ellie. "You're the best."

62

GRIFFIN

When I'm home, I set up my laptop on the dining table and check my emails. Keith sent me one with some notes on our research. There are some personal items as well—he's a typical friendly California type—but he doesn't say anything about my parents or sex toys.

Either he hasn't seen the article—knock wood—or he's just too polite and considerate to bring it up.

I open the attachment and try to focus on Keith's points, but it's impossible. Apprehension crawls over me like ants, and I can't shake it off.

Is it the lack of apple scent? Did I get so used to smelling it at Sierra's place that now it feels weird not to?

The living room has nothing but the scent of air freshener used by the weekly housekeeping service. A faint aroma of coffee from earlier lingers in the kitchen. I walk up to my bedroom. *Just my laundry soap.*

My home as it should be.

But something's still off. The prickling sensation strengthens, and I scratch the back of my neck.

Wait a minute...

Where are the reporters crawling outside? A few local ones writing for scandal rags contacted me over the video. There's no way they're lying low after finding out about my parents and the sex toy thing.

A paparazzo could be hiding in the walk-in closet. It happened to Mom once.

Ready to deliver a kick powerful enough to knock out a man with even the hardest skull, I jerk open the door to the closet and am confronted by—!

Nothing. Just clothes, belts and shoes. No paparazzo.

All the bristling energy drains away. I should be thrilled that I'm being left in peace, but instead I feel slightly unnerved. When is the other shoe going to drop?

I pull out my phone and turn it on to see what's going on. A gazillion notifications pop up. Lots and lots of texts, several from Charles—not worth checking, since I already saw him—a few from Lori—not checking those either, since I don't want to talk to her ever again—and four from Dad, probably speaking through Joey's fingers. I read those first, wondering if the lack of reporters has anything to do with him, and if so, which kidney I'm going to end up owing him.

–Dad: In case you're in a snit, I didn't confirm to anyone that you're my son. I'm not that bad of a father.

–Dad: But I also didn't specifically deny it.

–Dad: The exact quote was "The apple doesn't fall far from the tree, boys. Now think sex toys and use your imagination."

I can hear Dad's self-satisfied laugh. I should've broken Joey's fingers when I saw him, so he could never text again.

–Dad: Feel free to thank me at your convenience.

When donkeys start fucking frogs I'll thank him. Until then, he can go piss up a rope.

Then I remember the previous text from him about making him a grandbaby. Fuck. I can't let him know I already did. And not just one, but *three*. I massage my temples in an effort to get more blood flowing around. It doesn't do anything to lessen my headache.

Okay, mental note: Figure out a plan to keep Dad away from the triplets when I can think more clearly.

There are also several texts from my brothers.

–Grant: Fine, you want to ignore us? I got it. But we need to talk about a bachelor party for Emmett. He's going to get married ASAP. We can't let that happen without a proper party.

–Huxley: He just wants to marry her before she changes her mind.

–Sebastian: He better hurry. The supplies for decent diamonds are limited these days. If you want to get at least four carats, that is.

–Noah: He'll aim for at least eight carats. The bigger the rock, the bigger the love.

–Nicholas: Absurd.

–Grant: I say he shoots for ten.

–Sebastian: Or twenty.

–Nicholas: Is this a ring or a club she can swing around?

I scroll down, skimming the banter. It only makes me more morose. I don't resent that Emmett is happy with Amy. He deserves to be happy. All of us do, after the shit we had to put up with as children. But I wish *I* could be happy. Or at least not so pissed off and angry and hollow inside.

Knocks come from downstairs. Must be the damn reporters. *Took them long enough.* Maybe it was hard for them to find my address. This place is owned by an LLC I created, for privacy reasons. But if you're determined, you can trace it back to me.

My phone pings.

–Grant: Open up. We know you're in there. We see your cars.

–Huxley: It's just us. And Nicholas.

Ugh. I don't want to see anyone, even if it's my brothers. But I suck it up, go downstairs and open the door. Sure enough, the three of them are standing there. Grant is carrying a box of pepperoni pizza, and Huxley and Nicholas have six-packs of beer hanging from their fingers.

"What are you doing here?"

"We decide to check up on you. And bring you lunch. You're welcome." Grant walks in, followed by Huxley and Nicholas.

"I figured you'd need some beer. I know you're not teaching in the afternoon," Huxley says.

"Come in, come in, I was just dying for you to visit," I say, closing the door. If I wanted to imbibe, I'd pick something stronger than beer.

Grant places the pizza on the dining table. Huxley puts his six-pack down next to it and Nicholas stows his away in the fridge.

"Your fridge looks like shit, man," he says. "Need to stock up."

Huxley opens the pizza box, takes a fistful of napkins from the napkin holder on the table and passes them around. "Noah wanted to stop by with us, but couldn't because he suddenly had to fly to South Africa for some reason. Emmett's working—he has to work like a fiend to get time off for his wedding and honeymoon. Sebastian had to go to Virginia. Apparently his grandmother is having some health issues."

I hold up a hand. "I am not falling apart," I say, trying and failing to keep exasperation out of my voice. "And I don't need a trio of babysitters. You really don't have to do this."

"People who aren't falling apart don't turn their cell phones off for the entire weekend," Nicholas says.

I glare at him. He's so annoying when he's correct.

"Why don't you have some pizza?" It's phrased like a suggestion, but Huxley means it as an order.

"And beer," Grant says. "Pizza and beer solves everything."

The sight of pepperoni makes me lose my appetite. One, it sounds uncomfortably like paparazzi. And two, the last time I had pepperoni pizza, Sierra and her sex toys and I ended up having mind-blowing sex in her living room.

"Why are you looking at the pizza like it's topped with cockroaches?" Huxley's tone vibrates with irritation.

"It's from your favorite pizzeria," Grant says.

"Thanks. Couldn't tell that from the box. Look, it's not the pizza. I just don't have any appetite right now." I reach for the beer, though. It's cold and I'm thirsty. In addition, one beer never hurt anybody, especially when they're in a mood as foul as mine.

"Why don't you and Sierra open up more fully? Work things out," Nicholas says.

"What makes you think I haven't opened up?" I retort.

My bothers exchange a look. "Because we know you...?" Nicholas says. He swigs his beer. "I've never seen you spend so much effort to try to make a woman happy. She's obviously special."

"And love conquers all," Huxley says, making a heart with his hands.

"If love conquers all, why do I feel so bad? And I definitely *don't* feel victorious."

Grant shrugs. "Because it doesn't really exist."

"What?" I look at Grant.

Huxley reaches over and cuffs Grant on the shoulder. "C'mon, man! You aren't supposed to shock him like that."

"Has to hear it sometime," Grant says. "Look, Griff. The fact that people think love actually exists is what's wrong with the world. They're living their lives on the wrong premise. That's why they have issues." When I give him a flat stare, Grant apparently takes it to mean that I'm confused. "Imagine trying to solve an algebraic equation. Suppose you have the wrong value for the X variable. No matter what you do, you're *not* going to find the right answer for Y because your X is wrong. It's the same thing."

Huxley nods throughout the entire explanation. "Exactly."

I stare at Huxley. "But you say you *love* love."

"Of course! I *adore* love." Huxley spreads his hands. "Without love, how am I going to sell chocolates, dinners, vacations, jewelry and other junk? People will do anything for love. So yeah, for my profession's sake, I don't want anyone to realize that love is a figment of their imagination."

Are they here to tell me this shitty feeling in my gut is nothing but my imagination? I look at Nicholas. "Do you agree with that?"

He shrugs. "I'm okay with people believing in love if it makes them happy. Doesn't hurt anybody."

This is just... "So why did you tell Emmett you were happy for him? Why are we even going to his damn wedding?"

"Because he *is* happy," Grant says, like I'm stupid. "I'm not going to be the bad guy and destroy his illusion. Plus, people always shoot the messenger."

"Exactly." Huxley nods sagely. "Not only am I not going to tell him, I'm not even going to be around him when he figures it out. I don't want to become collateral damage when he explodes."

"Agreed," Nicholas says. "When they can't yell at the messenger, they yell at the people closest to them."

"You guys are no help," I say.

Grant slaps my shoulder. "No, it's just that you won't *accept* the help."

Huxley smiles. "Consider your life a model economists enjoy tinkering with. Just picture deleting love from the model and redoing it. You'll have a clearer and more productive life, and you won't be disappointed or hurt by unreasonable expectations that can never be met."

63

SIERRA

I hurriedly pack all of Griffin's stuff into a box. I wish I had the time to fold his clothes more neatly, but I need to get to the college before his office hours are over. According to the faculty website, there's only half an hour left.

Still, I can work with that. I want us to go back to how we were before that horrible party on Friday. And I'm not going to roll over. I'll work like hell to regain that happiness. For both of us.

I park my Ferrari in the lot, pick up the box and trot toward Fullilove Hall. I've never actually been to the building named for my family. This structure was constructed while Grandma was alive, with money she donated to the college.

It feels oddly satisfying to walk into something my family created to better the world. So many students study here, enriching and bettering themselves.

I reach the second floor, where Griffin's office is located. I look around, wondering which way I should go, since the stairs dumped me in the exact center of the hall.

"Oh! Hi, Sierra."

"Hello," I say to Lori. She isn't exactly my favorite person at the moment. However, I decide that I can't blame her one hundred percent. She was probably too stunned to exercise better judgment.

"Delivering something?" she asks, looking at the box.

"It's for Griffin. Which way is his office?"

She gestures. "That way."

"Thanks."

I march toward his office, taking a deep breath to calm my churning belly. A couple of doors are open, and I see professors at their desks. There is one office with its door closed, and a couple of students are sitting on the floor, their backs against the wall.

I walk past them until I reach the end of the hall. Griffin's office is closed.

Okay, girl. You got this. Tell him you're sorry that the sex toy line thing came out the way it did, and ask him what we can do to overcome that.

All right. I can do that. Stay calm and persuasive.

After taking another deep breath, I knock. There's no response. I check my watch. Five minutes to spare.

Did he go to the bathroom?

I try the knob, but it doesn't budge.

I look around, wondering if there's an announcement about a change in his schedule. Something rustles underneath my shoe. I look down and see a sheet of paper.

I squat down to pick it up. It says his office hours have been canceled for the day. A single piece of curled and dusty tape is attached to the notice.

Nooooo! How can this be? It's like the universe is conspiring against me!

You can't do this after throwing us together! You need to give me a chance!

Lori comes over. "If you want, I can keep the box for you and give it to Griffin when he's here."

"Oh, I don't want to impose." Besides, if I give this to her, how am I going to find a smooth way to approach Griffin?

"Really, I'd be happy to. I feel really terrible about what happened on Friday. I was just shocked and excited. Even though I've lived in SoCal for eight years, I've never met a real celebrity. And Griffin is related to *two*! I just thought it was so glamorous."

"I see." Her explanation helps me understand her better, and I feel a little more forgiving toward her now.

"And the thing about the sex toys was *totally* hot." She leans closer, lowering her voice. "Don't take this the wrong way, but a lot of the female professors here have major crushes on him. But none of us had any luck. He's difficult to get close to." She purses her mouth. "I didn't realize he would be so sensitive about it. But maybe I should've known. He's a very private person. Rarely talks about himself, and never about his family. You know what I mean?"

I *don't* know. In the weeks we were living together, he showed me aspects of himself that made me feel like I was part of his life. He made sure I knew he cared. Introduced me to his brothers.

"I hope he stops being upset soon. I wanted to apologize to him this morning, but I just couldn't get the words out. When I ran into him, he looked like he wanted to kill me."

"Yeah, he isn't too happy right now," I say, trying to inject some sympathy into my voice.

"When you see him, can you tell him I'm sorry? I'm going to apologize to him, too, and explain all this, but maybe if you lay a little groundwork he won't bite my head off."

"Yeah, sure." It's the polite thing to say, but helping Griffin and Lori make up isn't exactly on the top of my priority list. I need to make up with him first!

Lori takes the box off my hands. "In return, I'll give this to Griffin for you."

I open my mouth to tell her that isn't necessary, but change my mind. Maybe giving Lori an innocuous opening to talk to him will be a good thing. That way, he can hear from a third party that nobody thinks he's shameful because of his parents or the fact that he inspired some new sex toys. That'll help him calm down—and then he and I can have a conversation about us.

"Thanks, Lori. I appreciate it."

64

GRIFFIN

Two days later, I go up to my office after class. I can't cancel another office hour, even though I'm pretty sure nobody's going to show. Being available for a couple of extra hours a week outside of class is part of the contract, even if sitting in a room in a building with the same name as my former sort-of-fake-but-maybe-not girlfriend feels as painful as sitting on a bed of hot coals. I still haven't figured out exactly how I'm going to ensure Dad can't get anywhere near the triplets. Maybe I should consult Huxley. He'll know—most of the people on his mother's side of the family are soulless lawyers.

When I get to the door, the note that I wrote cancelling my previous office hour is on the floor. *Guess they don't make tape like they used to.* I make a mental note to bring in some duct tape and pull out my key.

"Griffin."

I tense. *Fucking Lori.* What does she want now? Did she find another lurid article about me, Dad and Mom? One she can trumpet to everybody in the damn building?

I turn around sharply. "What?" I say, not bothering to hide my displeasure.

She takes a half a step back and blinks. She's carrying a large box, which she adjusts, holding it closer to her chest. The defensive gesture annoys the hell out of me. She isn't some poor, helpless victim here.

"Well? You called my name. There must be something you want to say." *Otherwise, get lost!*

"Yeah, I did. There is." She clears her throat. "I, uh, want to give you this box. It came for you while you were out."

I glance at the top of the box. It's taped, but there's no address written. "Who brought it?" Better not have been Joey or one of his hookers.

"Sierra." Lori flashes a shaky smile, which dies as quickly as it appears. "She said it was for you."

The box holds a new, ominous meaning, one I'd rather not dwell on. "Did she say anything else?" I force the words through a tight throat.

"Not that I recall. I mean, she thanked me for holding it for you. If she'd left it by the door, who knows what would've happened?" She lets out an awkward laugh. If it's meant to smooth the tension between us, it fails.

"Thanks," I say. Then I snatch the box from her clutches, turn and go into my office.

Violating my rule, I kick the door shut with the heel of my foot. I dump the box on the desk and rip it open, anticipatory dread twisting inside me.

In it are my clothes, unfolded and hastily thrown together. My body wash. My aftershave. A half-used deodorant stick. Basically, everything I left at Sierra's place.

The weirdly achy throb in my chest I felt when she referred to the triplets as her family but not mine ripples through me again, more intensely this time.

She couldn't make herself clearer. It's a fuck-you-and-goodbye box.

65

SIERRA

–Griffin: Lori gave me the box.

Oh, good. I look at the text as I return to my office after a meeting with accounting. So Griffin and Lori had a chance to talk, like she wanted. Hopefully, she's alleviated his worries about his career.

Smiling, I wait for him to say more.

But nothing else comes. After waiting five minutes—maybe he was interrupted by a student or something—I run out of patience.

–Me: Is that all?

–Griffin: If you find anything else of mine, you can toss it.

My jaw slackens, and all the feeling in my legs vanishes. If I weren't seated, I'd fall on my ass for sure.

How can he not have changed his stance at all? Didn't Lori tell him what she said when I talked with her? Did he listen when she explained that it doesn't matter who his parents are? Or the fact that his inspiring our latest sex toys really doesn't diminish his credentials as an amazing economist?

My phone slips from my numb hand.

Maybe the article and the comment by the student were actually a convenient pretext for him to get rid of me because he's realized I'm not what he wants after all. Just like Mom's death was a convenient reason for Dad to wash his hands of me, treating me as though I had nothing to do with him. Just like exchanging wedding vows made Todd aware that he didn't really want to marry or be a good husband to me.

I blink away sudden tears. *God, I'm so emotional.* It must be the pregnancy.

I put my hand over my belly, needing the contact with the triplets, even though they probably can't feel me. "Little ones, it's just you and me. But it'll be okay. I'm going to make sure that you'll never, ever feel the lack from not having your daddy around. We're going to be great together."

66

SIERRA

The next few weeks are hectic. One of our suppliers says they're having issues procuring enough small motors to meet the demand, and it's putting some pressure on our production schedule.

So instead of going home at a reasonable hour and getting plenty of sleep, too often I find myself driving back at midnight. It's made worse because I'm feeling nauseated but still have weird food cravings that I'm too tired and sleepy to get up and do anything about at three a.m. Every romance novel I've ever read said that it's the hero's duty to bring me pistachio ice cream, canned tuna and steamed asparagus at such times.

But life isn't a romance novel, and I don't have a hero to pamper me.

Today is another day I'm stuck working late. Hopefully, this will be the last time for a while. Ellie stays with me, saying she has some things to review. We commandeer a conference room so we can spread out.

My head hurts from going over so many financial projections, new launch timelines and bids from potential new vendors. To give myself a break, I pull up a browser and screw around on the Internet for a few minutes. I stop when I spot a local news headline about the wedding of Emmett Lasker—the one brother of Griffin's that I didn't meet.

I should just scroll past, but I click on it anyway. I tell myself I'm just curious about how people this rich and famous get married.

The article says that it was a small ceremony with family only. However, the brothers' famous father Ted Lasker did not attend. I scan for more, finally stopping when I realize I'm looking for some mention of Griffin.

"It's so *unfair*," I say, suddenly angry.

"What is?" Ellie says, looking up from the specs on a vibrator.

"The fact that Griffin's brother got married. Everyone knows that his *brothers* are Ted Lasker's children. And you know what? None of them are suffering because of it. And I'm reading this article for some mention of him like, like..." It's hard to think of a good comparison. "Like some loser stalker who doesn't have the guts to stalk in person!"

"He sucks. And not in a sexual way," Ellie says loyally.

"I even tried to give him an opportunity to realize that he overreacted at the social, but he totally blew it! Throw away anything else of his I find in the house, indeed! If I weren't pregnant and busy with work, I'd go over to his house and kick his butt!"

"And I'd hold him for you so you could kick with less effort. And more action-flick coolness."

"You know what? If he's going to blame me for embarrassing him, I'll *give* him something to be embarrassed about!"

"Ooh, *now* you're talking!" Ellie says, her eyes bright. "What's the plan?"

"I'm sending his brother the latest products from our Midnight God line. They'll make the *perfect* wedding present."

"Oooh! Do it, do it!"

"I'm going to. That uptight jerk." A sudden craving for pistachio ice cream only fuels my rage. "Just people knowing that there are sex toys created in his honor brings shame upon him, huh? Well, just imagine his *brother* getting them. Griffin will probably have a stroke." And with that, I get up and go to the Silicone Dream storage room to start rummaging through the boxes.

67

GRIFFIN

Feet propped on the coffee table, I lean back in the plush couch and review the latest draft of the research paper Keith and I have been working on for months. Everything's been labeled correctly, our analysis is perfect so far as I can see and the math is impeccable. Whoever wants to disagree with our conclusions better have some good arguments, because this paper is tight.

Life has returned to normal. I finally stopped making wrong turns toward Sierra's house last week. I deleted all of Axelrod's music from my phone, but only because I decided I don't like the band anymore. The weird burning feeling I get in my gut from time to time is clearly stress over the paper.

And I most certainly do not get an erection while walking by the apples in grocery stores.

Of course, there are the continued stares from the damned faculty. They couldn't gawk more idiotically if I grew a horn in the middle of my forehead. Every time our gazes meet, they flinch and turn away.

Assholes.

My phone rings. My instinct is to ignore it, but it's from Emmett.

"Yeah?"

"Hey, we got a box from you," he says.

I pause for a second. "I didn't send you anything."

"It came through Sierra," Amy explains.

What the...? I told her to throw out my things, not forward them to my brother! Especially to Emmett, who's so happy right now, it has to be morbidly annoying. "Are you fucking kidding me?"

"No," Amy says.

"That should never have gone to you!" It's probably something as stupid and juvenile as a pair of my underwear she found at the bottom of her laundry basket.

"We don't mind." Emmett doesn't sound particularly disgusted. And Amy doesn't sound perturbed. Actually, she seems more excited than anything.

Oh no, damn it! I know *exactly* what Sierra did. An upthrust, straightened middle finger over the breakup. "They're in beta testing!"

"How do you beta-test a dildo?" Emmett asks.

"I don't know. I didn't ask. I don't want to know. She's crazy!" I shout because she's driving *me* crazy. *Again.* After I worked so hard to scrub her out of my life.

"Who?" Amy asks.

"Sierra!" I rapidly go over all the things she's done that I don't like. Her tardiness at the company and the saucy, irreverent sense of humor and... "The woman never follows a schedule. She never plans for anything. She respects nothing! She thinks life is fun and games! Wears really annoying perfume—"

"What's annoying about her perfume?" Emmett says.

Shit, I meant the apple scent, which isn't perfume—I know because I checked her vanity—but I don't feel like correcting myself. "It's distracting!"

Neither Emmett nor Amy says anything.

"She laughs too much," I continue. "Smiles all the time, for no reason. And she's so fucking pink!"

"What's wrong with pink?" Amy asks.

It makes me think of Sierra—her dresses, her sheets, her mouth, her...

Damn it, my cock's getting hard. And I'm talking to my brother!

My dick's obviously broken. And it's Sierra's fault. "Everything! It's so...bright. It's just wrong!"

"So." Emmett clears his throat. "What I hear you saying is she's fun. Spontaneous. Laughs a lot. Smiles a lot, too. And smells good."

Yes. "Distracting."

"Uh-huh. Sounds terrible."

"Like a little sparkly dollop of evil," Amy says.

"She's everything that's wrong with humanity."

"Right. Because humanity needs more grumpiness. Good thing you're around to balance things out," Emmett says.

I grit my teeth. "What I have is discipline, not grumpiness."

"Po-tay-to, po-tah-to. Anyway, the next time you see this pink ray of sunshine, tell her we said thanks for the presents."

"Yes!" Amy says brightly.

"I'm not having this discussion." I hang up.

I breathe out hard and tell myself I'm not upset about the ridiculous call or how happy Emmett and Amy sounded. *I—am—fine.* I just don't like to be reminded of Sierra.

We have babies together.

Fine. I'll set up a trust fund for the triplets. Be involved as much as they like, since I don't know if they'll want to be around a father who has humiliating baggage, a.k.a. their inane grandparents, even if they ideally will never find out that the triplets are mine. And—

My phone rings again. Emmett, undoubtedly. He hates not having the final word. This is what I have to put up with for having overeducated brothers with overinflated egos.

"I told you I am *not having this discussion*," I say.

"Which discussion would that be, dear?" comes Mom's springy voice.

"Mother." *Great.* Another person I don't want to talk to. What drama does she need me to comfort her about now?

"You're welcome."

"Am I? For what?"

"I simply don't understand what it takes to get some credit for the good I've done."

"Try writing a check to charity." *Do you want a gold medal?*

"Hmm... Well, I suppose saving you and Sierra from the media vultures could qualify as charity work."

I put a hand to my head. "What are you talking about?"

"Did you think they just gave up on you out of the goodness of their tiny, shriveled hearts?"

"I thought Dad was keeping them distracted, bragging about his 'inspirational penis.'"

"Your father couldn't care less about you getting harassed by the paparazzi. But you're right about the inspirational dick part. It's incredibly irritating. He was maybe a five in bed. A six if I was drunk. I wish I'd know better back then because I would've never slept with him if I'd had any idea it could've been so much hotter."

God have mercy. "Mother, I do *not* want to know about—"

"In case you didn't notice, Adriana Mitchell and Don Kasher had a scandal break right after yours."

"Mitchell and Kasher had a scandal? Over what? They're the most wholesome couple in Hollywood."

She laughs. "Oh, my dear, sweet boy. There are at least a dozen private videos floating around showing them snorting coke. In half of them, Adriana is at least topless, and three of those were at orgies." She sighs, satisfied. "Not that they're all *that* shocking. I mean, this *is* Hollywood."

"But...Adriana Mitchell and Don Kasher?" They're the couple everyone admired for their charitable work and clean image.

"Yes, the saints. I understand animals may have been involved at some point."

"What? That's just..." I try to process this.

"I know you find your parents embarrassing, but at least we stick to our own species." She tells me this like she should get an award for it.

"Yes, I remember," I say, the old resentment poking through. Normally, I wouldn't bother, but I'm in an extra-crabby mood, and her standard of behavior—which is even lower than I expected—is annoying the hell out of me.

"What are you talking about?" she asks.

"Does the name Churchill ring a bell?"

"Of course. The prime minister from way back when."

I knew it! She still doesn't remember! "No, my *dog*. The puppy I loved. You got rid of him."

There's a pause. "Oh. That nasty little thing?"

"He wasn't nasty!" I shout into the phone. That dog was awesome.

"No, he was a mean little beast. He hated everyone."

"He did not. He was a good, loving dog."

"Maybe to you. But he was a horror to everyone else, always biting and snarling."

"You're lying."

"Why would I lie about a dog that's dead by now? Trust me, he bit me multiple times and I couldn't get him to stop. I thought I would scar! And he was a legal liability. I simply didn't want to put up with him any longer. It was best to get rid of the animal, and I distinctly remember telling you all this when I put him up for adoption. It's not my fault if you weren't listening."

I think back, but don't remember her telling me anything like that. Regardless, it was a crappy thing for her to do. She didn't even get me a new puppy. Never did.

"If you're still that upset about the matter, then by all means go get yourself a new dog. Ideally, a sane one that doesn't try to eviscerate the people around you."

"I'm not getting a dog," I say. "It's too late now."

"Don't be silly. Nothing's ever too late."

Easy for her to say. No new dog is ever going to be Churchill. "Right. I guess that's why you're still clinging to your youth."

"What does that have to do with anything? What would letting myself go accomplish? Nothing. I am beautiful, and I can make an impact. If somebody out there thinks I'm too old, that's their problem, not mine. The hell with them and their approval."

"Are you telling me you honestly don't care? Because it looks to me like you're posting a billion pictures on social media for likes and comments."

"I post them so people know that I exist and I matter. But I don't let them control me. I do what I want. You should learn to do that too. You're far too old now to be caring about what people think." She pauses. "Really. It's no longer cute."

"I won't be lectured by someone who thinks orgy videos are fine as long as there aren't any animals involved."

"It's not a lecture, silly! It's advice from somebody with more experience. How would you put it? I have more data points to draw from."

I don't respond. I'm not going to encourage her by saying she's correct about the data points.

She continues, "Oh, I know. You're probably still upset about what the article said about being Ted's and my love child. And probably still stewing over someone saying that you inspired Sierra to create a new line of sex toys."

I'm definitely not telling her she's correct.

"And all because you want everyone to take you *seriously*."

"I *am* a serious kind of a guy."

"My dear, the word is *uptight*. Do you know what makes your dad impossible to live with?"

"His ego? His ridiculous demands? His I-don't-care-about-anybody-but-me attitude?"

"No. He cares about what everyone else thinks and how he compares to them. Why do you think he has that bizarre competition with Josh Singer, which Josh doesn't even know about? In case you weren't aware, before he started this competition with Josh, he imagined he was in competition with Salazar Pryce. And before that, he was in competition with Jerry Michaels, who produced three blockbuster movies that your father just couldn't beat until three years ago. Your father is a miserable little person, because unless you help him look better than those people, he's going to make your life hell. Who wants to be with a person like that? And you are acting like him. Unless the people around you make you appear to be a respectable *professor of economics*," she intones dramatically, "you don't want them around. Why, I'd bet my villa in Venice that you dumped Sierra over the sex toy thing."

I say nothing. Mom is making me sound like an absolute asshole, and I'm not that bad. I've done everything in my power to be the exact opposite of my parents.

"I knew it," she says.

"I didn't say anything."

"Exactly. If I were wrong, you would have." She snorts. "It's a shame you dumped her. She's a nice girl, and you could do much, *much* worse. Somebody who only wants your money, or the *respectability* of being a professor's wife. Or just falls in love with your face and body. That's also thanks to me, by the way. Again, you're welcome."

"Fine, we broke up. But it isn't because I'm impossible."

"Of course not," she says. "Everyone has a blind spot they can't see. When somebody points out, they deny it. I'll tell you this: you're never going to find a better match than Sierra. I've seen you together, and I can just feel it."

"Right. Like how you felt the same with all my girlfriends before. You know, the ones who decided they didn't want to stick around anymore once they got to meet you or Dad."

"Which shows they weren't right for you after all. If they can't take the bad with the good, what's the point? Not that I'm the bad here, of course. That would be your father. Anyway, don't you guys have this thing in economics about nothing being perfect?"

"No."

"Well, you should. What about sinking cost?"

I roll my eyes. "You mean 'sunk cost'?"

"Pfft. You conjugate it your way, I'll conjugate it mine."

I let out a puff of reluctant laughter at her shamelessness. But that's Mom. She'll never admit that she's wrong about anything.

"I'm saying that what happened before is a sunk cost. So you shouldn't think about it, but only about what you can do from now on. Ask yourself: *Am I happy the way I am?*" She huffs. "I can't believe I have to tell you everything. You're the genius economist. Anyway, I need to go. I have a party."

"Listen, I—"

But there's nothing but silence coming from my phone. Typical. On the rare occasion that she doesn't have some drama to unload on me, she just says whatever she feels like and hangs up.

I stare at the dark screen, my mind whirring. Am I really that uptight and judgmental? I'm willing to see things from other people's point of view. No matter what she says, I'm not closed-minded.

What did Sierra do that was so awful...?

I sit back and stare at the ceiling.

She didn't tell me about the sex toys. There's a weirdly stubborn part of me that insists she should have.

And then...what? Dad made everything about him and his ego. I couldn't have stopped that any more than I could've stopped his sending me a hooker. And his reaction isn't her fault. My students posting about it... Unless I confiscated all their phones, I couldn't have stopped that. So that wasn't her fault either. I was just angry because I feared losing something I'd worked hard for.

Am I happy? Alone in this house, which smells like generic store-bought air freshener, with my non-pink sheets and no red Ferrari in the driveway?

I think back on my time with Sierra. When she told me about the babies.

Sierra wanted somebody to be a good father to her babies—her family...

The air freezes in my lungs. Holy shit. *How could I have been so stupid?*

Her babies are her family. And the father of her babies is also her family. When she told me about the triplets, she was dreaming of having a family *with me*, building a future together.

I misunderstood everything, and I fucked it up in my temper and fear. I've thrown her away, and along with that a chance at happiness because I want my colleagues to respect me.

Grant said that love is fake, that it doesn't exist—a lot of problems are caused by the wrong assumption that love is real.

But I think about Emmett. He was miserable because of love, but he's also very happy because of it. Grant might be right, but who cares about living in a delusion if you're happy? We might all be in a Matrix-style simulation anyway.

I know I can be happy with her. There might be some bad from time to time, but there will be more good.

Fixing it will require an apology. But given how I embarrassed her at the faculty social, a simple "I'm sorry" isn't going to cut it. I'm going to have to make a gesture of commitment so big, she knows I mean it.

68

SIERRA

For three days, I've been craving a peanut butter and jelly sandwich with a jar of relish and a fresh lemon. Unfortunately, I haven't had it. I don't have peanut butter in my house. I'm also missing the relish and lemon.

I should go to the store, but I haven't felt like it since I saw a hugely pregnant woman with her husband lovingly picking out peaches and oranges from the fruit section for her. I felt so alone and sad that I just can't shop anymore. I left the cart right there and trudged back to my car, swallowing tears.

I'm turning into an irrational mess, and I hate it. Even as a child, I didn't react like this when I saw my friends having a good time with their fathers. But now I can't seem to control my emotions. According to Google, this is normal during pregnancy, but God I hope it stops. I don't think I can continue like this until the triplets are out.

I certainly can't afford hormonal irrationality when I have important decisions to make. Like now, in this conference room.

"So we like this new vendor's proposal?" Jennifer asks, gesturing at the one I picked out yesterday.

"Their component meets our spec the best," I say.

"And they have a great reputation for quality," Ellie adds.

"All right then. I'll tell Legal so they can start drafting the contract." Heather taps her tablet a few times.

"Great. Thanks, Heather," I say.

"Do you want anything for lunch?" she asks. She knows I've been nibbling on nothing but crackers over the last several days.

"I'm fine," I say.

"I can get you a BLT from the deli," Eli offers, since that's normally my favorite.

"No," I say. "Thanks, though." I don't want just any sandwich. I want a peanut butter and jelly sandwich, and the deli doesn't have that.

There's a soft buzz, and Heather pulls out her phone. "It's Dan."

He wouldn't be texting unless it was important. "Is it Linda trying to get in again?" My stepmom has been permanently blacklisted. But she isn't the type to accept that. If she doesn't get what she wants, she's going to make a scene, which is the last thing I want to deal with right now.

"No, it's"—Heather looks up at me—"Griffin."

I sit straighter, my head going blank with shock. After a moment, I croak, "He's *here*?"

"Yeah. In the lobby, standing in front of the clock."

By now, his brother must've received the box that I sent. Is this visit about that or something else?

As I ponder, my heart starts pounding. I don't know if it's with apprehension or anticipation.

"You might want to go downstairs," Heather says after checking her phone again. "Just to be sure that there aren't any issues."

Heather knows something is wrong between me and Griffin, although I haven't told her anything. She's my assistant and can pick up on my moods, even when I try to play it off by pasting on a sunny smile.

"Fine. I'll go see what's going on. I probably do need something other than crackers for lunch, anyway." Maybe I can convince myself that the churning emotions in my heart aren't from seeing Griffin again but from hormonal food cravings.

We all get up, grab our purses and go downstairs. The elevator takes forever to come, and the descent seems interminable.

I try not to tap my foot. I'm not anxious about seeing Griffin.

He's probably here to say something mean. I still can't believe he sent that ice-cold text after Lori gave him the box.

Or maybe he's already gone. To him, time is money. Maybe I should get some cash ready, in case he complains.

Wait a minute... He didn't make an appointment. Why is he here? He doesn't seem like the type to drag things out or continue to complain about the same thing over and over again.

And we *are* over. Aren't we?

When the elevator reaches the lobby, I take a deep breath and step forward. *Steady, steady...*

Griffin is standing in front of the purple clock, scanning the crowd that's heading out for lunch. When our eyes meet, he goes still.

I stop as well, letting myself absorb his presence. He's wearing a dark suit. Under his straight, serious eyebrows, his eyes are bright and determined, his mouth set in a grim line.

He's so gorgeous that I can barely breathe. The air in the lobby feels different with him here. I want to hug him and kiss him, but I also want to slap him and call him names, then burst out in tears because I have nobody to make me a peanut butter and jelly sandwich or bring me pistachio ice cream at three in the morning.

I'm going insane. No, he's *making* me insane. I never felt such crazy, conflicting emotions until I met him.

"Sierra! I'm sorry. I screwed up," he says loudly so I can hear him across the distance. "Nothing was your fault. I just reacted badly because I cared too much about what other people think. But that was idiotic of me. What I should've cared about is what *you* think."

I say nothing, trying to process the scene. I have to be imagining this. I've been hoping Griffin and I could make up because it hurt so much to give up what we had. Because I knew we could be even better.

Griffin taps his phone. A familiar melody starts. Is he playing Elvis Presley's "Can't Help Falling in Love" to make his case?

No, he isn't. *Griffin* starts singing over a karaoke version of the song.

All my food cravings go away, and my morose mood vanishes. All I can think is that Griffin is in the lobby, singing me one of the sweetest love songs ever—despite the fact that he hates singing. It was my grandma's favorite. She and Grandpa danced to it at their wedding. She told me every time she heard the song, she felt loved.

His voice caresses my senses like a dream. If I thought my heart was soaring at the concert in Tokyo, it's about to burst now with love and longing.

Griffin keeps singing. I start moving toward him, my arms spread wide.

All that matters is that half of my soul is serenading me in front of everyone, telling me he loves me.

As he hits the last note, I close my arms around him. He hugs me back hard.

"That was beautiful," I whisper, my vision blurring with tears of happiness.

"I love you so much." He pulls back slightly, his expression gorgeously somber. "Forgive me?"

"I love you too. And yes, of course I forgive you. All that matters is that we're going to be happy together." I smile.

He claims my mouth as the lobby bursts into loud cheers and applause.

69

SIERRA

Griffin and I have a quick lunch at the deli. My craving for peanut butter and jelly sandwich and pistachio ice cream has gone away for the moment, and the soup and crackers the deli provides are enough to satisfy me.

He eyes my food. "Is that enough?"

"Yes." I sigh with happiness at the piping-hot clam chowder. It's slightly salty and savory, just the thing my tongue and stomach have decided I need at the moment.

"You're eating for four."

"The other three are the size of a plum. Also, I'm eating more than normal."

He frowns, his math brain probably deciding I need more calories.

"Don't look up statistics and do an analysis to try to figure out if my reaction is normal. Pregnant women are all different."

"I'll keep that in mind."

He's still going to look it up. I know it.

But that's what makes him even more lovable. What he does comes from a place of love—and a need to make sure I'm okay.

"I wish I could leave with you now, but I have a meeting I really can't cancel." I make a face. "Bankers get angry when they think I'm wasting their time."

He nods. "Time is money."

I laugh. He's so serious, but that's what I love about him.

"I don't want to disrupt your work." His tone says my work is important to him, too. And that warms my heart. "Come to my place after you're done." He pulls out his phone and texts me his address.

"Okay. I'll be there as soon as I can."

Just as we get up, the door to the deli bursts open. Todd rushes in, wild-eyed. I start to turn away, but he sees me anyway. No! Talk about rotten luck!

"You have to talk to Chuck!" he screams, trotting toward me. "I can't go to that godforsaken Boston!"

Griffin steps forward, his body a shield. "You couldn't get a job anywhere?"

Todd's arms flail, maybe in appeal. It's hard to tell because he looks more like a drowning man trying to find something to hold on to. "Sierra, don't do anything hasty! This...man...isn't like me!"

For once, I completely agree with Todd. "I know!"

"He treats people like disposable garbage!"

"Isn't garbage supposed to be disposable?" Griffin says.

"His attitude will change when he finds out you're infertile!" Todd yells. Literally everyone in the deli turns to stare.

I gasp. Griffin takes a menacing step forward, but I tug on his sleeve. "Let me," I say. I'm not going to miss this chance.

His jaw tightens, but he nods, putting a protective arm around me.

"For your information, I'm not infertile. It's you who's shooting blanks."

"What?" Todd looks lost.

"I'm *pregnant*," I announce triumphantly.

Todd turns so pale, I wonder if he's going to collapse. I hope he doesn't expect me to catch him. This is what he deserves for the way he's treated me.

"With my triplets," Griffin puts in helpfully.

Todd is now redder than a child left out to play in the beach without sunblock.

"So why don't you think about what that means, while you send out more résumés?" I say sweetly.

Todd looks at me, then at Griffin, then back at me. Then he covers his face and runs. One thing he can't stand is having somebody cut his ego down, and to experience that in public will hopefully keep him away for a long, long time.

"Are you okay?" Griffin asks, his eyes searching my face.

"Oh, I'm fine." I smile. "Better than fine."

"Well, look at that. A barren boaster blaming the woman," the deli owner says loudly with a snort. "Here, honey. Any cookie you want on the house."

Other customers congratulate us, and I beam. "Thank you, thank you!" I say, waving at them. Is this my Oscar moment?

I pick out a chocolate chip cookie from the counter, then kiss Griffin. "See you soon."

After lunch, I work like the devil to wrap up everything as efficiently as possible. Heather teases, "Got a hot date?"

I grin, not bothering to hide my excitement. "Yes."

She shakes her head. "That man sure knows how to get you pumped up."

"He sure does!" I say.

"And hopefully that awful ex of yours will leave you alone now." Of course I told her about the confrontation at the deli.

"Oh, I think he's gone for good." I pat my belly, where the triplets are, with affection.

At five thirty, I'm done. I shut down my laptop and dump everything into my purse. "See you tomorrow, Heather!" I wave as I run out of the office.

"See you tomorrow, Sierra!" She chuckles. "Don't do anything I wouldn't do."

I check the text to see where Griffin lives. He's place is in an upper-middle-class residential area nestled between my neighborhood, Silicone Dream and Wollstonecraft College.

I drive into quiet streets full of nice single units with sizable yards. I turn onto his street and see his blue Prius in the driveway. I park behind it and get out.

My God. I can't believe we're back together again! It's like everything bad is gone. I know we're going to be stronger now. Because now we know how valuable what we have is—and we're committed to fighting for it.

I take a moment to study his house. It's a three-story structure with red brick walls and a gently sloping roof. Lots of bay windows on the first floor, but the second and third levels have shutters, which I'm sure are decorative because they're attached to the walls. The lawn is immaculately cut.

I walk up and into the house, calling out, "Honey, I'm home!" as I open the door. The line is so corny that I have to laugh. But the laughter stops when I see what's before me.

Thousands of flowers of all types and colors line the floor and cover the furniture in gorgeous vases. Their fragrance sweetens the air, and I inhale, mesmerized and impressed by the scene.

But where's Griffin? None of this matters without him.

Then I see him stepping out from a giant arrangement of sunflowers. He's holding a bouquet of daisies.

Tears spring to my eyes, and I blink them away quickly, embarrassed I'm so emotional. I should be smiling, not crying!

"How did you know they're my favorite?" The men I dated before all brought me roses.

"I saw you lingering over that stationery with the daisy print in Japan," Griffin says.

"I did?" I blink.

"You did." He places the bouquet into my arms.

How much does this man love me that he remembers events I don't even recall, and I don't have to say a word for him to know what I like?

"Thank you." I kiss his cheeks, then his mouth.

I push my tongue past his lips, gliding inside and stroking his, teasing and seducing. He wraps his arms around me. I press myself closer, starved for him. His erection presses against my belly, and...

Something else?

I pull back a little, wondering about the hard lump pressing against my thigh.

He looks down, then exhales roughly. "I got the order of events mixed up. Too excited."

"No, no, excitement is good. I'm excited too." I smile, happy anticipation flooding my body like honey.

"Yeah, but mixing this up wouldn't be." He grows serious, even more serious than usual, then pulls out a small velvet box from his pocket and drops to one knee.

"Oh my—"

"Sierra Fullilove, will you marry me?"

He opens the lid, and my hands fly to my mouth. A diamond

larger than my fingernail sits on an elegant platinum band. Light reflects on the emerald-cut stone, sparkling like a brilliant dream.

"—*God*," I breathe out, then blink several times, my face heating with emotion. "Yes. Yes, yes. A bazillion times *yes*."

He pops the ring out of the box and starts to slide it on my finger. I watch, then flinch, pulling my hand back as I remember something.

He looks at me questioningly, a small frown on his face.

"I, uh, haven't disclosed a little condition that comes with being my husband. I don't want it to come back to haunt us later, so I should come clean now."

Griffin's expression goes from serious to grim.

"I'm not changing my mind!" I add hurriedly.

He doesn't seem that reassured. "Then why won't you let me put the ring on?"

Of course he's focused on that. I put my hands on his shoulders and pull at him to get up. It isn't a topic I want to discuss while he's kneeling. I lead him to a couch and we sit down. He remains stiff.

"I just need to tell you this so there's no surprise."

"I'm already surprised," he points out.

I pat his chest, trying to make him feel better. But the longer I stay silent, the more tense he becomes. "There is a prenup you have to sign. It's not me, it's my grandmother's wish. She didn't want the company's control to be diluted, and she insisted that whoever I marry sign a prenup, giving up all claims to Silicone Dream."

"Is that all?" He relaxes. "That's more than fine. Where do I sign?"

"Well, I have to get it from my lawyer first."

He raises an eyebrow. "Guess we'll have to make an appointment, then." He clears his throat. "There is something I have to tell you, too. It'll probably reassure you that I have no interest in Silicone Dream or your money. I've made some decent investments over the years, and they've grown quite a bit."

"Great." I beam, happy to hear about his success. "I guess that's why you're a good economist."

"It's actually Emmett and Grant who did the vetting. Anyway, I'm worth a little over a billion dollars at the moment."

I stare at him for a second, while my mind tries to process that. "A billion dollars?"

"Yes."

"With a B? Billion? I didn't mishear million?"

"Billion with a B."

"That's awesome." I smile hugely, then realize something. "Do you want *me* to sign a prenup, promising not to touch your money?"

He scowls. "No. I didn't bring it up to ask you to sign a prenup. I don't care. Money isn't that important. And what other people think about me isn't important. What's important is you. And our babies."

I loop my arms around his neck and seal the promise of forever with a searing kiss.

70

SIERRA

The second I arrive in the office the next morning, Ellie jumps from her seat and rushes over.

"Show me the ring! I've been dying to see it since you texted me last night!"

I laugh and extend my hand. "Here."

"Oh my God! It's *huge*! How many carats is this?"

I shrug. "I don't know. He didn't say, and I didn't ask." I start walking toward my office.

She follows. "Is it crass to want you to go to a jeweler so we know for sure?"

"Yes."

"Come on!"

I laugh. "How big the rock is isn't important. I already said yes."

"I'm not saying you should take it back if it's smaller than my guess."

I give her a do-share-your-guess look.

"I say it's fifteen."

Looking down at the ring, I suspect it might be that large. Or larger.

"Please. It's for research," Ellie says.

"For what? We aren't adding diamonds to the Midnight God line."

"I've decided to write a romance novel."

"That's great! You should totally let me read it when you're done."

"You'll be the first to get the book. But to write it, I need to know what kind of ring men buy these days, so by the time I get to the proposal scene in my book, I can write one realistically. You know, with authority."

I roll my eyes. "Make your hero a billionaire and he can pop the question in style with a hundred-carat diamond ring."

We burst out laughing.

"So when's the wedding?" she asks.

"As soon as we can arrange it." I try not to swoon with joy as I speak.

"I'm your maid of honor!"

"Of course." I smile.

"Are you inviting your dad and all?" By *all*, she means Linda and Felicia.

I make a face. It's an awkward question. Griffin told me I don't have to invite anybody I don't want, but there's this tiny part of me that wants to see Dad happy for me at the wedding, the way he was at my first one with Todd.

I'm probably being silly and needy, but... Sometimes, no matter how hard you tell yourself you're okay, things linger and fester and...

I sigh. "Dad, probably. The others... I don't know."

"Put a tarantula in your bouquet and throw it at Felicia."

Holding her ever-present tablet, Heather trots over from her work station, her expression serious. *Uh-oh.*

"Sorry to interrupt, but I didn't want to wait any longer." She looks down at my ring and smiles, although it lacks full wattage. "It's stunning. You have to tell me everything about the proposal later. But at the moment, your father, Linda and Felicia are here."

Shoot. Linda's banned from entering, but Dad isn't. I'd bet my Ferrari he got her and Felicia through security.

"They got here fifteen minutes ago," Heather adds.

What could've possibly brought them here? They didn't come to the company even after finding out Grandma left me Silicone Dream, preferring to deal with me through lawyers. "Did you tell them I wasn't here?"

"Yes, but they refused to leave. They're quite determined to see you."

"Where are they?"

"I put them in the junior conference room next to your office."

"Okay. Thanks."

My buoyant mood deflates as I go to the small meeting room. *Come on, girl. You're the CEO, the one in charge. Act like it.*

I inhale in front of the closed door. Focus on the reassuring weight of Griffin's ring on my finger. I'm not just the boss of this company, but of my entire life.

I open the door and stride inside.

Dad's at the head of the table. Linda is on his left and Felicia on his right. They're doing their best to project authority, but failing, since they're nothing at the company.

Dad frowns, while Linda and Felicia's gazes sweep me blatantly.

Dad hasn't changed much from the photos on the mantel, except he's almost a decade older. Felicia's a younger version of Linda with a harder edge. Both are wrapped in designer dresses and high-end shoes.

"Holy...! That's *huge!*" Felicia shouts, her eyes burning with jealousy. "Is that a real diamond?"

I raise my hand and look at the sparkling rock. "I know. It's too pretty to be real." Smiling, I stay standing by the door. "What can I do for you?"

"How about a normal family greeting for once?" Dad's voice is sharply rebuking.

"A normal family wouldn't just barge into my office this early in the morning without asking first."

Dad's eyes narrow. "Your fiancé should've asked for my permission for your hand before proposing behind my back. I don't appreciate finding out about his intentions through a YouTube video."

Wow. Good for Dad for figuring out Griffin proposed based on the video of him singing in the lobby. I can't decide what I'm feeling now. No one wants to say congratulations. Felicia's the only one showing any interest, mainly because she's envious of my ring.

"Dad, it's the twenty-first century. No one asks the father anymore."

"*Todd* asked," Dad says.

I can't believe he's here to compare Griffin to Todd—and finding him lacking. Griffin's the one I chose, the one I know will treat me like his soul mate. He wants to build a life with *me*, not because of my relationship with the college or because I have some money.

But Dad isn't interested in such things. He only cares about what he cares about. From the smug look on Linda's face, he wouldn't have bothered to stop by if it weren't for her nagging him.

And suddenly, I know who doesn't deserve to be in my life anymore.

"Todd did ask. But then, Todd was planning on inviting you to the ceremony," I say.

Dad's complexion slowly turns purple. "Are you telling me we aren't invited to the wedding?"

"That's *exactly* what I'm telling you."

He looks at me like I just kicked him in the crotch. Linda gapes.

"Can you at least help me break into Hollywood?" Felicia says. "Your new father-in-law makes movies, and—"

"I'm afraid that won't be possible. You'll have to audition like everyone else if you want to become an actress."

Felicia opens her mouth. But before she can speak, Dad says, "I'm still your father."

That's the sad part of it all. "Then where were you when I needed you?"

He opens and closes his mouth like he wants to argue, but knows whatever he wants to say isn't going to persuade me.

"I have a meeting soon," I say to get them out of my hair. "If you won't leave, you'll be escorted out. Please don't show up unannounced again. You won't be allowed in."

"You've always been an awful child," Dad says tightly.

I regard him steadily. "Yes, well. I was never going to be the obedient, silent child that you wanted. Turns out parenting actually requires some effort."

I stand to one side as they storm out of the conference room. These people aren't my family. I deserve better.

I run my thumb along my engagement ring, feeling at peace. I belong with Griffin, a man who loves me just the way I am and wants to lay the world at my feet.

71

—Dad: Saw that video of you singing for the girl. I suppose you're going to marry her.

—Me: What if I am?

—Dad: Tell me the date and time for the ceremony. I'll see if I can adjust my schedule for you.

—Me: Well, Joey, that won't be necessary. It's going to be a small ceremony, friends and family only.

—Dad: WTF?

—Dad: I am your family!!!!!!!!!!!!

—Me: Hope you get run over by a semi.

72

SIERRA

–three weeks later

The weather is L.A.-perfect, not a cloud in the sky. A gentle breeze sweeps over us, carrying the heady fragrance of hundreds of flowers in the garden at Huxley's mansion.

Griffin and I invited very few people. Ellie, Heather, Griffin's brothers, Amy and Rachel, and a handful of people from Silicone Dream.

We wouldn't have it any other way.

Huxley has set up a baby grand piano in the garden for the ceremony. His fingers move along the keyboard, playing the music for the ceremony.

My heart flutters, full of bubbling happiness and love, as we exchange our vows and kiss.

From this moment on, we belong to each other in every way. *Family.*

And these people with us today are our extended family.

We march together down the aisle, our first time as a married couple. Our guests cast flower petals in the air from baskets we prepared.

"Time to throw the bouquet," Griffin says.

I smile. The wedding planner we hired said the bouquet toss is generally done toward the end of the reception, but I want to throw mine in the beginning.

Ellie in a pink bridesmaid dress calls out, "Here comes the bouquet!"

I grin at her sparkling eyes. I'm planning to send it in her direction.

I turn around. "Ready?"

The crowd shouts their assent.

Here we go. I toss it over my head, hoping I'm aiming correctly.

As soon as the bouquet leaves my hand, I turn around.

Ellie jumps to catch it, but it bounces off her arms and hits Grant, who grabs it out of reflex.

"Shit." He immediately throws it back in the air like a steaming potato. It flies and lands on Huxley, who acts like he just got hit by a grenade.

He tosses it immediately back in the air. The poor thing finally plops on Noah's shoulder. Thankfully, he holds it in his hand.

"Whew." Huxley stretches his neck. "Good luck, bro," he says to Noah.

I laugh, then go over to Ellie. "Sorry you didn't get it."

"It's okay." She smiles. "Seeing you happy is more important than catching the bouquet."

Noah comes over and hands the bouquet to her. "Here. I don't need it, but you look like you want it."

She takes it primly. "Thank you."

The guests move to the outdoor reception area, lavishly set up with lots of lights and fresh flowers and gorgeous white, pink and gold ribbons.

Griffin and I hold hands and make our way to the reception, looking at each other with huge smiles on our faces. When we reach the area set up for our first dance, he kisses the tips of my fingers, his mouth warm, then lets my hand go and moves toward the microphone near the piano.

He leans over, his face hidden behind the raised lid of the baby grand. What is he doing?

He straightens, and the black Midnight God mask from New Orleans is on his face. I cover my mouth.

"This is for you, Sierra, the love of my life, the light of my soul, the keeper of my heart."

Huxley hits a few familiar notes, and Griffin stars belting out "I Was Born to Love You" by Freddie Mercury. My heart races, and joyous tears spring to my eyes.

Griffin's killing the song, his gaze on mine. But even if he weren't such a good singer, I wouldn't care. Because here's my gorgeous man, singing his love for me in front of everyone who matters.

When the song ends, everyone except me claps. I'm too busy holding my hands over my racing heart.

Ellie taps me on my shoulder. "Here."

I look down at what she's holding—the white mask I had on at the masquerade. Griffin must've kept it, because I left it in his hotel room after our first night together.

Smiling hugely, I put it on.

"Hey, stranger," I whisper as I walk to him.

"Hello, angel. Let's dance."

He pulls me into his arms, and I know that I'm in the paradise I've always dreamed of.

73

GRIFFIN

—fourteen months later

"You're so good at maneuvering this giant stroller," Sierra says as we walk along the winding path at a local park with our little babies. They love to be out and see the world, and we make it a habit to take them out for a long walk every day. Following close behind is our new bulldog puppy Winston, tail wagging hard.

Since our special-order shirts arrived, she's in a pink one that says WORLD'S BEST MOM, and I'm in a blue one that says WORLD'S BEST DAD. Our triplets are all in onesies that read *Number One*. Sierra doesn't believe in making any of our babies number two or three. And I agree. The order in which they came out isn't important. They're always all going to be our number ones.

"I'm a man of many talents," I say with a small smile, then kiss her brow.

The stroller is big enough to carry our triplets—two identical boys and a girl. Dr. White said that we had three boys, so when a girl came out last, it was a huge shock for everyone.

"I think Amy feels a bit jealous that we have so many kids," Sierra says.

"She wants another baby, but Emmett won't give it to her." And for good reason. Amy didn't do well during the pregnancy and labor for their first child.

Sierra makes a noncommittal noise, but I know her well enough to recognize her I'm-plotting-something sound.

"What's going on in your head?" I may need to warn Emmett.

"I'm just thinking that I'm enjoying this lovely stroll at this beautiful park with my awesome family." She smiles.

My heart swells with love, just like every time she does that. It's an automatic response, and I don't think it's ever going to go away.

I kiss her and thank my lucky stars while our babies coo.

TITLES BY NADIA LEE

Standalone Titles

Baby for the Bosshole

Beauty and the Assassin

Oops, I Married a Rock Star

The Billionaire and the Runaway Bride

Flirting with the Rock Star Next Door

Mister Fake Fiancé

Marrying My Billionaire Hookup

Faking It with the Frenemy

Marrying My Billionaire Boss

Stealing the Bride

The Sins Trilogy

Sins

Secrets

Mercy

The Billionaire's Claim Duet

Obsession

Redemption

Sweet Darlings Inc.

That Man Next Door

That Sexy Stranger
That Wild Player

Billionaires' Brides of Convenience

A Hollywood Deal
A Hollywood Bride
An Improper Deal
An Improper Bride
An Improper Ever After
An Unlikely Deal
An Unlikely Bride
A Final Deal

The Pryce Family

The Billionaire's Counterfeit Girlfriend
The Billionaire's Inconvenient Obsession
The Billionaire's Secret Wife
The Billionaire's Forgotten Fiancée
The Billionaire's Forbidden Desire
The Billionaire's Holiday Bride

Seduced by the Billionaire

Taken by Her Unforgiving Billionaire Boss
Pursued by Her Billionaire Hook-Up
Pregnant with Her Billionaire Ex's Baby
Romanced by Her Illicit Millionaire Crush
Wanted by Her Scandalous Billionaire

Loving Her Best Friend's Billionaire Brother

ABOUT NADIA LEE

New York Times and *USA Today* bestselling author Nadia Lee writes sexy contemporary romance. Born with a love for excellent food, travel and adventure, she has lived in four different countries, kissed stingrays, been bitten by a shark, fed an elephant and petted tigers.

Currently, she shares a condo overlooking a small river and sakura trees in Japan with her husband and son. When she's not writing, she can be found reading books by her favorite authors or planning another trip.

To learn more about Nadia and her projects, please visit http://www.nadialee.net. To receive updates about upcoming works, sneak peeks and bonus epilogues featuring some of your favorite couples from Nadia, please visit http://www.nadialee.net/vip to join her VIP List.

Printed in Great Britain
by Amazon